SONG
OF THE
WOLF

Also by Scott C. S. Stone

The Coasts of War
A Share of Honor
The Dragon's Eye
A Study in Counter-Insurgency
Pearl Harbor, the Way It Was
Volcano
Wrapped in the Wind's Shawl
(with John E. McGowan)
Spies
Honolulu
Land of Fire and Snow

Scott C. S. Stone

SONG
OF THE
WOLF

ARBOR HOUSE / NEW YORK

Designed by Richard Oriolo

Manufactured in the United States of America

10   9   8   7   6   5   4   3   2   1

This book is printed on acid free paper. The paper in this book meets
the guidelines for permanence and durability of the Committee on
Production Guidelines for Book Longevity of the Council on Library
Resources.
Library of Congress Cataloging in Publication Data

Stone, Scott C. S.
  Song of the wolf.

  1. Cherokee Indians—Fiction.   I. Title.
PS3569.T642S55   1985   813′.54   84-24168
ISBN: 0-87795-678-2 (alk. paper)

for my son,
Erik,
in love and pride

SONG
OF THE
WOLF

PART
ONE

1932–1940

When he first saw the wolf he looked right through it; a great, gray wolf ghostly in the twilight. It stood on the edge of the tree line, studying him calmly, its enormous paws planted firmly but delicately in the grass of the small rise that led into the trees. Instinctively, the wolf had picked the perfect vantage point to observe the boy, although the boy could not know it. The wolf lowered its head and looked off to one side, avoiding the direct gaze that signaled aggression. While the boy stood there the wolf swung its head from side to side slowly, searching for scents in the still air of early evening.

The wolf was almost exactly the color of the fog that had been forming since the sun had dropped over the dark blue mountains. The boy had been walking toward those mountains much of the day, with no particular goal in mind; he liked the mountains and he liked walking. The wolf may have been heading west as well, but going at a much different pace, pausing to mark his territory, and once stopping to roll happily in the remains of a deer killed earlier by other wolves. He was a big, shaggy wolf with a fractured rib from an old combat, a wound not quite healed properly and leaving a small but noticeable ridge along his right side. The wolf's eyes were wide-set and wise and the boy watched them, spellbound. The wolf was the most beautiful thing he had ever seen, but even as he stared at it, the animal was becoming harder to see. The fog was moving in rapidly and the wolf seemed to go in and out of it, at times becoming disembodied, so that all he could focus on were the calm eyes.

With the fog closing in the boy took a step closer so he could see better. The wolf trembled slightly but held its ground, staring down the rise, looking directly at the boy now, holding his eyes in a sign the boy did not understand. The fog sent tendrils between them, so that for moments at a time they were hidden from each other in the fog and the slow but perceptible fading of light.

Suddenly the boy heard a shout to his left and saw the flickering of a lantern going in and out of shadows, as if held by a man walking. He looked back at the wolf, but it was gone. The rise was as empty as if the wolf had never been there. There was only the fog, drifting closer to the ground now. There were more shouts and the boy sat down, tears in his eyes. They had caught him.

In a moment there were hands lifting him. Someone put a blanket around him, although he wasn't cold. He recognized a neighbor, a man who came to their house sometimes. Rough voices were scolding him, but the man held him close and someone stepped in front of them with a lantern, and then they were moving away from the small glade and heading eastward and down. By the time they were out of the thicker part of the woods he was asleep.

Much later he opened his eyes and looked up at the beams of the cabin. He squinted at them, feeling the warmth of the pot-bellied stove to his right, his eyes also catching the light of the kerosene lamp on the table to his left. He did not open his eyes all the way, but he sensed the people in the room. He lay quietly and listened, as he often did, pretending to be asleep.

"It's the third time he's run away." His mother.

"It's a wonder he didn't get in trouble out there, but then he is Aniyunwiya; he was born to this place." Nathan Bird, the man who ran the store at Postelle Station.

"But he is very sick this time," his mother said. "I wish that doctor would get here."

"Have you sent for Tawodi?"

"No. We don't know where he is. But he will come."

"How do you know?"

"When the boy needs him, he will come."

He kept squinting at the beams, a little frightened now. How sick was he? He felt very light, not sick at all. He was happy that he had gotten a day in the deep woods. But one thing bothered him: was the wolf a dream?

He heard the door open and chairs scraping as his mother and Nathan Bird got to their feet. There was a gust of wind and the kerosene lamp threw quick shadows before steadying again. He felt the new presence in the room. He smelled a hospital smell. Old Doctor Satterfield.

The doctor's hands were cold, but sure. He felt them over his head and neck, felt the doctor opening his shirt. There was something cold and metallic on his chest. He opened his eyes and looked directly into the watery blue eyes of the doctor.

"How do you feel, son?" The doctor's voice was low and gruff, but the boy knew he was a friend. The doctor had helped him once before.

"Hello, doctor."

"You feelin' all right?"

"I feel light."

The doctor buttoned his shirt and pulled the blankets back over his chest. "Get some rest," he said roughly, but he patted the boy on the head.

The boy slept. When he woke again he was drenched in sweat and felt even lighter, but this time he was unable to open his eyes. It didn't matter much. He lay thinking about old Doctor Satterfield, and the time he had gone to the small clinic because of the pitchfork.

Tawodi had told him not to touch the big, metal pitchfork and it was one of the rare times he had disobeyed his grand-father. It had taken all his strength to pick it up, and when he could no longer hold it, the pitchfork plummeted down and drove one of the tines through the center of his left foot, pin-ning him to the ground. He held his breath to keep from screaming, finally managing to call Tawodi without panic. His grandfather had walked over and, without a word, pulled the pitchfork out of the ground and up through his foot. Tawodi then went into the house and came back with the kerosene lamp. He unscrewed the wick, grasped the boy's ankle firmly, and poured the kerosene through the wound. It was then that the boy had moaned. Later, in his cluttered office, old Doctor Satterfield said that Tawodi probably saved the boy's foot, but even as he said that, the foot still burned. He was left with a permanent scar.

Now he lay in the bed and felt himself growing lighter and lighter. He felt detached; he was not hungry, or cold, or any-thing. He felt as if he could simply float from beneath the blankets and right out the door, leaving no trace, just floating out on the fog and back into the woods, where he felt safe.

When he looked up again the beams of the cabin seemed to move, causing him to feel sick. He was aware, all at once, of the blankets over him. They felt heavy. But now he was getting cold. He could hear the thudding of the gusts of wind against the walls of the cabin, and the creaking of the cabin itself. He thought he could hear the fluttering of the fire in the old stove, but now the warmth was gone, and he had never been so cold.

He knew his mother was still in the room. He could sense her there, but faintly. It seemed to be darker now. He heard a strange whisper, his own voice asking for Tawodi. He might have slept again. When he stirred he felt someone near him, but again he could not get his eyes open. He smelled a smell that he knew instantly, a mixture of washed denims, pine; a smell like the deep woods themselves. He tried to smile.

"Tawodi," he whispered.

He felt his grandfather's touch, a light touch for such strong hands. He felt their leathery texture gentle against his cheek.

"Listen to me," his grandfather said. "The doctor says you are going to die. I do not believe it. You must not believe it. You must believe you are going to live, for then you will. Do you understand me?"

"Yes, grandfather," the boy said.

"Good," Tawodi grunted. "I am taking you to the sweathouse. There may be some pain."

But there was no pain. Instead there was a great, floating sensation, a rhythmic movement across the cabin and the opening of the door as his mother stood there, touching him as they passed. Out into the night he squinted upward again, this time trying to get a glimpse of the brilliant scattering of stars through the drifting fog. There was a blast of wind, warmer than the cold he felt inside himself, and then they were in the sweathouse.

Inside the sweathouse he was strangely light and happy. He trusted Tawodi. It would all end happily. There was sudden steam, the hiss of water on heated rock; he was becoming aware of the walls of the small house, built without nails. There was a small hole in the roof and a larger one in the earth floor, and a gathering of pine knots for the fire.

The strong arms put him gently on the low, wooden platform, the only furnishing in the room. He felt his grandfather unwrapping the blankets and he heard a roaring that was himself, gasping at the sudden heat. He felt his grandfather's hands on his hands, the hawk eyes on his eyes. He was naked now, but warmer. He felt Tawodi moving about and there was more steam. The wind seemed to have quieted outside, and the boy suddenly began to know a great sense of peace. He felt the rivulets leaving his body, stream after stream.

He opened his eyes and saw Tawodi's lined face, the eyes borrowed, it was said, from *tawodi*, the hawk, for which the old man was named. His grandfather was naked and squatting near him.

"I am sick?" the boy asked.

"Yes. But you will be well."

"Is she mad at me for running away?"

"She is afraid for you. Later, she will be angry."

19

The boy lay back on the wooden platform, grateful now for the warming steam.

"Tawodi, I saw a wolf."

His grandfather said nothing, but watched the boy's face.

"It was a big, gray wolf, the color of the fog. Sometimes I could see right through it."

Tawodi waited

"He was big, very big. And gray. He was not afraid of me or anything."

"Maybe he was looking through you, too," Tawodi said softly, watching the boy.

"Yeah?" The idea interested him.

The platform was dark with his sweat, and he realized that daylight had come and he could see easily in the small room. His eyes still felt heavy, and he still felt as if he could float. But he was hungry, too. He said so.

Tawodi grinned. "Come," he said. "We will let the fire go now. I will take you back to the house."

Again he felt the wind, but not shocking this time. Now it was gentle, moving over his face. He felt hungry and sleepy both. In a few moments he was in the bed again, feeling fresh sheets beneath him. He wondered whether he was too hungry to sleep, and wondering, slept.

Tawodi was not his real name. It was used because Tawodi never told anyone his real name, a tradition in his own clan. To tell others your true name let them inside of you and put you in danger from them. It could diminish the spirit. His secret name was an ancient one, used long ago by his people to honor warriors, and was a term seldom used anymore. His people were no longer the warriors they once were.

Tawodi, however, had killed a man. Up in the deep coves and hollows, they still told the story.

Tawodi's mother had died young, and he lived with his father in a cabin on a small piece of property deep in the Unicoi Mountains. The property was disputed by a neighbor, a white man who had moved into the area from northern Georgia. Tawodi kept well clear of the man, a large, loud, shifty-eyed farmer whose stubble of a beard was stained permanently with tobacco juice and moonshine. Tawodi would take his collie and circle the man's property to get to a favorite deer trail, and sometimes he could feel the man watching him pass, watching from just inside the screened door of his ramshackle cabin.

The day came when Tawodi, unable to find the dog, went off by himself and circled the neighbor's cabin to the south. It was there, left for him to find, that he saw the body of the dog.

The dog's left foreleg lay broken and crushed in a cruel steel trap, of the kind Tawodi despised. But the other legs had been broken as well. The dog's face had been mutilated. And then the dog had been partially skinned alive. There was enough fur left to enable him to identify his dog, and little else.

He had stared at the remains of his dog, fixing the scene in his mind. Then he opened the trap and slid it to one side. It took him an hour to bury the dog there under an aspen tree. He took the trap home with him. When his father asked about the dog, Tawodi told him, but he did not tell him that he had kept the trap.

It was months before Tawodi, watching the neighbor's house with infinite patience, established a pattern he could trust. When he was able to forecast the days when the large white man went to the market in town, and forecast the route, he began to make his plans. He noted with satisfaction that his act would take place a year to the day since the man had killed his dog.

When they spoke of the incident afterward, the stories differed. Some said that as soon as the man was caught in his own steel trap, Tawodi had shot him. Others said that he broke the man's arms and legs, beat him in the face, and partially skinned him alive. Those who told this story said it took days and days for the man to die, and that Tawodi sat watching him, listening to him plead first for his life, then for a quick death. All the stories agreed on the last thing: Tawodi had taken the trap from the dead man's left foot, cleaned it, and put it back in the dead man's cabin. He would not want to be known as a thief.

The dead man's relatives had come north, talking of revenge, but after a while they left and were never seen again. The Georgian's cabin fell into ruin and the property finally was purchased by a logging company as a barracks site for its workmen. By that time an old Aniyunwiya full blood had begun calling the boy Tawodi, for his eyes, and the boy accepted the name as a convenient way of hiding his own name. And all the rest of his life, working as a hunter and a guide, he never again touched a metal trap.

Tawodi, growing older, thought often about the life he had lived and the life to come. When he died his spirit would wander until it found the form of a child about to be born, and the spirit would enter the child, infusing it with life. Then his spirit would live again in a new body, but, fortunately, he would remember nothing of the previous life except that there had been one. He knew he was an animal and that all animals had spirits, as did the trees, the rocks, the streams. All things. He was not afraid of dying because the Aniyunwiya were not conditioned to fear death. Their myths dealt with life, art, love, pranks, dignity, the deep feeling for wild, high places. In that mystical bond with the earth and sky the Aniyunwiya had found their soul and their legends, and none of their legends dealt in a negative way with death.

One of the most barbaric things about the whites who came to hunt and fish in the mountains was the way they acted in the presence of death. When they shot a deer they walked up to it immediately, perhaps kicking it to see if any life remained. They robbed the deer of its dignity. They would cut into it immediately, dressing it for transport. The Aniyunwiya were shocked by the attitudes brought by the whites. When one of the Aniyunwiya killed a deer, he knelt beside the animal and thanked it for providing food and clothing for his family, addressing the deer as a beloved friend. Then he prayed that the spirit of the deer soon would find another body, and thus be born again in the spring of good leaves and plentiful water. The hunter prayed that the next life of the deer would be long and peaceful. Only then would he take the skinning knife from its sheath.

Tawodi thought often about his people. No one was sure

where they had come from. Some of the whites said they origi-
nated in South America and came north, tying the two loca-
tions to the distinctive basket weaving found in each place.
Others said the Aniyunwiya were part of the Iroquois who
came south after a great battle. He thought that might be true,
knowing that the Aniyunwiya, centuries ago, had been a proud
and warlike people. Now—and Tawodi hated to think of it—
the Aniyunwiya were a people with an assumed religion, a borrowed way of life. Few of them kept the old ways. Most of them
had become farmers. Not Tawodi.

Lately, he had been concerned about the death of the Aniyunwiya as a race.

The full bloods were becoming more and more rare, but he
was not as concerned with the purity of the blood as he was the
attitudes of the people, for his people would live as long as
there were poems about them, and songs and dances. As long as
they were known in the hearts of the people yet to come, they
would have a history. He thought his own spirit would be les-
sened if it could not hear, in subsequent lives, the tales and
songs of his ancestors. If a race disappeared it would be a terrible waste, as if it had not lived at all, as if its accomplishments,
its arts and its beliefs, had not been. He felt that over on the
Qualla Boundary, where many of his people lived, they had
gotten confused about their heritage. There they mixed with
people who sold trinkets from far-off places and wore feather
bonnets of a kind never worn by their ancestors so the tourists
could take pictures. Some people there kept bears in cages, for
amusement. It was contemptible.

Often his people did not think as the Aniyunwiya, and
sometimes when they looked at him, he knew they regarded
him as something out of their misty past. Perhaps. He taught
the youngsters games so old, in phrases so obscure, they had
difficulty with the language. Some of them did not refer to
themselves as Aniyunwiya at all, using the adapted word *Tsa-
lagi*. For the word the whites used, *Cherokee*, he had no feeling at
all.

He heard himself sigh. Many Aniyunwiya now worshipped
the white god and his son, about which there were many

myths. In loud, emotional meetings in churches and tents his people shouted their acceptance of a single god, wailing of salvation and eternal life. They were quick to tell tourists that the Aniyunwiya never worshipped idols, as if they were somehow gaining stature in the sight of the fat, white visitors. They did not tell the tourists that there were a few like Tawodi left in the mountains, who held in reverence the spirits of the intangible world, knowing there were mysteries in the wind, and that thoughts were powerful enough to turn streams around, knowing that the sun was a gift and that the rain, that cool blessing, could come as a favor to those who believed it so. It was said of Tawodi that all in his family held the power, by effort of will, to summon the animals of the forests to them.

He believed also that he was a link to the past.

From the first mornings of their race the Aniyunwiya had devoted themselves to war against enemies, and harmony within the tribe and with their surroundings. Their many wars were conducted against tribes who threatened them, or as a part of the accepted life-styles of all peoples of their time and place. To be a warrior of the Aniyunwiya was to be a warrior of the Real People. It did not mean one could not enjoy songs and dances, poetry, and art. It was not unmanly to be gentle, and a great, enduring characteristic of the Aniyunwiya was the ability to be warlike and gentle and find no contradiction in it. Harmony meant reason and sensitivity, but not always peace. The Aniyunwiya were concerned with concepts of beauty and form, with subtle courtships and respect for children, women, and old people. They also were concerned with the straightness of an arrow, the soundness of a canoe. In their mountain fastness the Aniyunwiya had evolved into a people who were crafty, subtle, war-fierce, tenacious, proud, fun-loving, and compassionate.

Tawodi was related to chiefs but seldom thought about it. Experience had taught him that he was, today, different from many of the other Aniyunwiya, and he thought that in his earlier lives he must have been a great warrior. In this life, he had always known the most important thing he could know—who and what he was. He saw his life as an acceptable extension of what had gone before and what was to come, without illusions and without false modesty. He thought he could see with the vision of an artist or a very good hunter.

He stood outside himself for an appraisal.

He saw a wiry man with a bullet wound on his left forehead and a shock of hair the color of a knife blade. He was of average height and very straight. He had the cheekbones the whites mistakenly thought were common to all native tribes, and his skin was dark and leathery. He wore the white's clothing, faded jeans and a checked shirt and denim jacket. He also wore an old headband, woven in an ancient pattern. Below that headband the eyes were startlingly young and alive.

Now he turned those eyes on the surrounding forest, waiting, scenting, catching the odor of pine and the familiar dusky smell of the deep woods, the burrows of animals, rotting wood, an odor of time. Far off he heard a cowbell echoing in a cove, and the shrill call of some diving, twisting bird. The forest was preparing to drop leaves in the slow passage of another season, but spring was waiting, too, always returning.

The forest spread before him like something he had created in his mind, a pure thought translated into shimmering beauty. The trees were flying banners of red and gold and yellow and the mountains themselves, like old men hunched in a circle, showed their backs to the sky. They were aged mountains, blue, their edges misty in sunlight, wearing white in winter and holding secrets. The mountains had always existed, laced by the rivers and streams of the Aniyunwiya. He let the place-names of the Aniyunwiya tumble in his mind—Hiwassee, Ocoee, Nantahala, Etowah, Oconaluftee, Echota.

Sometimes the winters were harsh, but the land was beautiful, the true homeland of the Real People. Once they had roamed over five hundred thousand square miles, as prone to wander as the buffalo they hunted, and now they were gone as the buffalo were gone, hunted down by soldiers and militiamen who came in hordes to steal gold and ended by stealing land, and then something more precious—the spirit of a race. They had smashed a great deal of it.

But not all.

Tawodi's ancestors were among the ones who had refused to go on that dreadful trek west, called then and now the Trail Where They Cried. Those on the trek had been herded into stockades, then started out in winter on a march of incredible hardships. Thousands had died from cold and exposure. When the whites marched them along the same route in summer, they died from malaria, far from the cool mountains they loved. His ancestors had taken to the hills to fight and had helped win a concession that allowed the remnants of the Aniyunwiya to remain in the mountains, although on greatly shrunken lands. Tawodi's ancestors could not live like a bear in a cage and refused to honor any pledges to stay on the reservation. The ideas of boundaries were foreign concepts and lacked dignity.

He heard himself sigh again. Standing in the dropping sunlight and shadow of a small clearing, he caught a darting shadow in the grass and looked up to see the hawk turning back into the air currents and beginning to lift, its wingtip feathers trailing lazily, like one's hands in the water alongside a canoe, feeling the rushing coolness. He thought suddenly that he could call to the hawk even as it reached for heights he could only imagine, and that it would circle and come to him. Often he had been tempted to try to summon the birds and animals, as he thought he might be able to do. But it was lacking in honor to do so for no reason. Someday he would do it, probably for his grandson, whom he loved. If he could. There was no dishonor in failure, only in a failure to try. When he looked up again the hawk was gone, but he thought he could see the track of the passage of its shadow in the grass.

The ground squirrel raced along a long, fallen branch, trying to reach the security of a dark hole in the dead tree. In his exuberance, in his pride in the new Winchester Tawodi had given him, he slammed a .22 long into the chamber and cocked it in one quick motion, and he shot the ground squirrel as it was inches from safety. By the time he had reached it, Tawodi had crossed the creek and joined him on the other bank.

Why, his grandfather had asked; are you hungry?

No, Tawodi.

But you have killed it.

The boy looked down, suddenly ashamed.

I wanted to try my new gun.

You have dishonored it.

What should I do?

What do you think? What have I taught you?

But you don't eat ground squirrels, grandfather.

Today, now, you do.

Damned gun, he had sniffed. Tawodi had looked at him sternly. The gun is just a tool, his grandfather had said. It is a tool to help you. But you must learn when to use it.

Now, his grandfather had said, I hope you understand what I have been saying to you. You have taken a life needlessly. You must honor this small animal by eating it.

I understand, he had said, and he did. It took him an hour to skin, cook, and eat the ground squirrel, chewing the tough, gamy meat into manageable chunks and washing it down with cool water from the creek. He buried the skin, bones, and organs and smoothed over the cooking site.

Now, Tawodi told him, if you want to practice we will do this: I will tie a piece of wood to the end of some fishing line and swing it from the branch of a tree. That will teach you some things quickly—to point the gun instead of trying to aim; to shoot with both eyes open; to make each shot count, because you are carrying a single-shot rifle and you may not have time to reload.

I like my Winchester, grandfather.

Yes. You may have it a long time. If you are an old man you will re-member how Tawodi gave you a Winchester on your eighth birthday, and how, soon after, he made you eat a ground squirrel.

I will remember, grandfather.

Hey-yeh, Tawodi said, grinning. Not very tasty, was it?

1941–1946

Moving from the friendliness of the small one-room schoolhouse was a shock. Now he had to walk some distance down a dirt road and board a dumpy yellow schoolbus for the ride into the mining town, where there was a high school. Almost everything about it bothered him.

He hated just going into the town; it was barren, dirty, and filled with old people—and very few of the Aniyunwiya. Though not a large town, it still had pretensions, trying through gingerbread additions to the plain stores to recall some mythic past when it was a crossroads. There was a single long main street with a network of roads leading from it, some leading to thrown-together houses rented out by the copper company that controlled the policies and destinies of the people who worked for it. Other roads led to the mines, where tall mine shafts dominated the landscape, and cars of ore were hauled to the surface for smelting.

What he hated most was what that smelting had done. From

decades of such work on the surface, the mistlike residue had blown over mile after mile of forest land, reducing it to dead and dusty remains, which soon were gone. Rains had done the rest, so that now the area was barren and changing with every new season's storms. He did not like streams that were changed because a mud bank had slid into them. Once he had opened a book in the school library and saw a picture of the area. The caption called it "a perfect example of soil erosion in a once-forested section of North America." He had hated that whole idea. What if all the woods had disappeared? Where would they hunt, he and Tawodi? But it was not just the hunting, it was the idea of the deep woods as sanctuary, as a replenishment for the spirit. He had written a poem about it, the first thing he had written that he had ever shown Tawodi. His grandfather had asked if he could keep it and he had said yes, of course. He knew that Tawodi, like all of the Aniyunwiya, had great respect for words, and the idea that he might be a poet had found favor with his grandfather. The possibility had been exciting, because he had blossomed over the past years into an avid reader with an enormous appetite for good writing. He knew he was one of the few in his class who could separate the writing from the plot of a story and deal with a story on more than one level. He quickly caught the fine distinction between theme and plot. His real love, however, was the poets who could fire the blood in a few words. It was an awesome gift, and an awesome power.

The school had presented another problem: what to call him. Deep in the recesses of his heart he knew there was a reason behind the scramble for a name when they had sent him down to register for the school, as the law required. For most of his life there had been no need for names, and then Tawodi had named him in the way of the Aniyunwiya, and so he had his real name. Around the house they had called him Atsutsa, boy, as a symbol that he was not yet named, had not chosen a name he could use. Not all of the Aniyunwiya held the belief that names were to be kept closely guarded, but Tawodi was determined, so he was called Atsutsa by the Aniyunwiya, and boy by the whites. Until now.

When he had prepared to leave for school on the first day, his mother had taken him out under the large oak tree behind the cabin. He could tell she was nervous, but she also seemed determined. He loved his mother; she was beautiful, gentle, and understanding. She no longer worried when he ran off to the woods. She listened with admiration when he read his small verses to her. Yet she had been firm with him, all his life.

"Starlight," he said.

"Yes?"

"You seem worried."

His mother pushed back her thick black hair and he looked at it with a smile. She seemed old to him in some ways, as all adults were, but also young. Tawodi had said she was still a young woman, and he believed it, seeing her this way, with the wind moving her hair softly and rustling the fringes of her long skirt.

"In the new school, they cannot call you Atsutsa; you must have a name."

"I have a name, but I cannot tell them."

"Someday you will tell me, I hope?"

"Perhaps," he smiled.

"I am going to call you after your father. It is a way of keeping his memory alive, as well."

"But I thought you didn't know his name."

"I couldn't pronounce it. But we will call you Dane because he was a Dane, and because it is what I called him."

"Dane what?"

"John Dane. It is a simple but good name. I hope you like it."

He smiled up at her. "I like anything you tell me about my father." He put his hand on her arm. "Don't worry, Starlight," he said. "John Dane is good enough." *But it is not the name I carry in my heart.*

It is here we will name you, Tawodi had said.

They were high in the blue mountains, as deep as the boy had ever been. Tawodi was gesturing toward a small cave, hardly more than an indentation in a hill, but the boy could see it was protected from the wind. He was hungry and it was late afternoon. The boy did not know how far they had walked, but he was tired and cold. Along the way Tawodi had talked to him, very unusual because his grandfather insisted on quiet when moving in the woods. Sensing the boy's fatigue, Tawodi hurried on to the cave. They would rest and build a small fire.

What Tawodi had talked about during their long walk to the cave was the Aniyunwiya and their proud, tragic history. The boy had heard most of it, perhaps all of it, but he did not interrupt. He knew Tawodi was building toward the moment when the old man would give him his name, in the manner of Aniyunwiya warriors.

He would be a living link with his grandfather's history and his own, for in his heart he thought of himself as Aniyunwiya. The white blood meant very little to him.

And his name was everything. It would be his power, his source of strength. As long as he was a young man, and a warrior, he would keep the name to himself, for to tell it meant a loss of spirit, a diminishing of his inner strength. In time, when you were old and no longer a warrior, when the battles were behind you or when death was near, you could tell others your name, in pride, so that it would be remembered. Perhaps old men, old warriors, did not care at some point. Tawodi still cared. For the first time he wondered how long his grandfather had to live.

In the cave they built a small fire. There was very little room, but both the old man and the boy could stretch, and soon they felt the comfort of the small flame. They had no food, for a name day was a fast day, and they could not eat until after sundown. The hunger was making him a little lightheaded, but it was manageable and overshadowed by the excitement of his name. In a few minutes it would be his.

I name you, Tawodi had begun, because you are of the Aniyunwiya. We will thank the spirits and especially the spirits of this place. The old man then went into a long prayer, most of which the boy understood. Afterward his grandfather had looked at him and smiled and said it was good, and it was the time for gifts. He had reached into his jacket and begun pulling things out and placing them before the fire.

First, Tawodi said, the knife of a warrior, and he put down the most beautiful knife the boy had ever seen. It was in a sheath, but he could see the stag handle and the long hand guards. When he slid it from the sheath the knife gleamed in the firelight, the perfect size, the perfect balance. It seemed to dance in his hand.

Next, Tawodi had said, the headband of a warrior, and he handed the boy the headband Starlight had made in secret. It was a deep, dark green, beaded in a traditional pattern. The boy accepted it with a smile, knowing how much Starlight had put of herself into the making of it.

As the old man started to speak again there was a sudden slap of wind and the rustle of branches in the trees behind the small shelter. Tawodi paused and stared out; it was snowing.

Now, said his grandfather, because we were ready to name you the spirits of this place have made a sign. So I will name you as planned, but we will add something. What do you see about you?

The boy looked from the cave. I see woods, he had said, a forest in the late afternoon, dark trees. Clouds are heavy, the beginning of snow. When he looked back because of his grandfather's silence, Tawodi was handing him something in his outstretched hand.

It was an amulet, a circle of silver on a chain, and within the circle there was a stalking animal, caught in a moment, so powerfully and intricately carved that it seemed to flow from the cold metal, the grace and beauty of it springing to life as he stared.

It was a wolf.

And so I name you for it, Tawodi said. Waya, the wolf. But because the spirit of this place spoke to us we will give you the formal name of Waya-unutsi, the wolf of the snows. Snow-wolf.

The boy felt the hairs on the back of his neck rise.

He stared at Tawodi, half in fear, half in exhilaration. The old man was almost a spirit himself. When the boy heard the name he knew at once it was his, had always been, would always be. Snow-wolf. He would move through life as a wolf would move, like the animals who were now his brothers. He would be one with the forest, a part of the wind. He would move as swiftly as sunlight and make no more noise than the moon falling on the river. No more tracks than a summer breeze. When the wolves sang at night he would join them in his heart and when he met them on a trail he would salute them, for they were now and always his brothers.

Tawodi leaned forward and placed the amulet around his neck. He wore it outside his shirt so he could see it, and he sat staring at it. His grandfather began to talk again, telling him that wolves were much misunderstood, except by mountain men and Aniyunwiya who knew them. Wolves had been hunted and persecuted, but they survived and kept their

dignity. The same was true of the American tribes, particularly the An-
iyunwiya. Both the wolves and the Aniyunwiya would survive, Tawodi
said, if you kept them in your heart.

They went home through the thickening snow and the onrushing dark-
ness. The boy hardly felt the trek back. Starlight was waiting with a
hearty stew and did not ask the boy his name. She was pleased that he
wore the headband, and she marveled at his other gifts.

Someday, he told her solemnly, believing it, I will tell you my name,
but for now it is a secret.

That night, when he finally fell asleep, he dreamed he was in a high,
white world but still among green trees. There were soft footfalls beside
him, and through the magic day he was untouched by cold or hunger or
fear.

A morning like a ringing bell, and streaks of silver far off; he
tasted air as clean as a birch twig and felt the fire in his blood,
heard animal noises in the deep woods and his breath in gasps
as he moved up the side of the hill, holding the Winchester,
feeling the pack. He liked the checkered pattern of his mackinaw and the good old feel of his boots.

Up on the crest of the pine-covered hill he stopped to stare
off in the distance, looking at nothing, at everything. The sun
was splintering on the rim of the mountains and far, far away
he could catch the glint of a high-country lake. He cleared his
mind and stood feeling the morning wind and the sun, feeling
the distances, happy to be alone. Deep in the cove below the
crest line he heard the hammering of a woodpecker, so loud it
halted, for a moment, the cries of the other birds. He smiled.
He wondered if he should eat now.

But he turned and moved again, finding his way on and up
to the logging trail that would take him deeper into the world
he loved and respected. He would pass through the pine flats
and camp for the night on the shore of the TVA lake at Hiwassee. He wanted to be hungry. It made him feel leaner, tighter,
and he moved along the loggers' trail, stopping now and then
to listen and sense, sometimes doubling back in a wide circle to
see if anything was on the trail behind him. It took more time,
but his grandfather had insisted he do it, and once he found he

was being trailed by a pack of wild dogs, more dangerous than wolves and with less honor. He had been carrying the Savage then, and he dropped three of them in a great threshing of blood and cries before the others escaped. He had pulled the dead ones off the trail and slit their bellies.

Now he was among the stately, old pines. Underfoot their needles helped him move quietly, but when he looked up he could see their high branches moving in the wind and hear the harmonics of a thousand small currents moving in the green needles, and beyond the tops of the pines he could catch glimpses of a sky startling in its blueness. The trees had a certain dignity. Hungry, now. He felt his stomach growling.

By late afternoon he had passed through the pine flats, and he thought he could smell the lake. He would approach north of the beaver dam. A great flat rock, warmed by the sun—he remembered it well. He would stay there for the night. Tawodi had showed him the rock years before. When he had slept on it that night it had stayed warm until well after midnight, and when he had stirred in the early morning, to pull a blanket over himself, Tawodi had been squatting on the edge of the rock, watching the lake, his eyes glinting in the moonlight.

Now he found the rock and circled it, searching for anything hidden, anything out of the ordinary. When he was convinced he was alone he sat and unbuttoned the mackinaw and ate. He ate very slowly, chewing the jerky thoroughly, finishing with an apple. He lay back on the rock with the Winchester near his hand. He heard a fish jump, shattering the stillness of the lake and sending ripples out to disappear in the flat calm of the blue-green water. Eyes shut, mind far away, remembering.

A fews days ago, when she thought he was sleeping, Starlight came to stand over him. He could see her, blurred, through partially opened eyes. Love and worry in her face. He knew suddenly she was seeing someone else, someone he resembled, and in his heart the old wound opened a little and he turned on his side away from her. He did not want to look at her for a while.

By the time his grandfather arrived he was awake again. The

old man had been up to the small, hidden cabin they had built and had returned as quietly as a shadow, and he came to sit on the edge of the bed.

"It will be a good year for corn and tobacco," Tawodi said in his direct way. "There will be fewer rabbits because there are more foxes. It will be a cold winter. The hill cabin is in good shape, but the trails are not. Perhaps we can work for the government again this summer, if they want the trails cleared again. Or fish a lot." He smiled down at this grandson. "Perhaps this summer we will raid the Shawnee and steal their horses."

"Let's steal their women instead," he said to the old man.

"Hey-yeh! You are growing faster than I thought."

"Fourteen this summer, grandfather."

"You are large for your age. It is the white blood."

"I did not ask for it."

"You are who you are, and I know it. Did I not name you?" The old man stood. "Join me soon, for there is good fishing now, with the new moon."

Tawodi left without saying good-bye, a trait of the older men of the tribe. As he had a thousand times, the boy wished he were a full blood. The thought brought him back to Starlight and he lay thinking about her, and when she came back into the room he turned to stare at her. She was tall and well formed and suddenly seemed exciting, in a way that he had not thought of her before. She had dark bird's wings for eyebrows, and quick, lively eyes, and sadness behind the eyes.

"Starlight?"

She turned to him.

"I was thinking of my father."

"Well," she said. "And what are you thinking?"

"That he must be dead."

"Yes, I believe it is so."

"I wish I could know him."

She looked away, at something beyond him.

"I know he was white," the boy said, "but not much more."

"What difference would it make?"

"None, I suppose, since he isn't here."

She swung her head toward him slowly. "There are lots of mixed bloods here. You are not so unusual."

"Except that they are all legitimate."

Starlight stiffened. It was as far as her son had ever gone.

"And what does that mean to you?" she asked.

"I don't know," he said truthfully. "I just wonder why it happened to me."

Starlight felt the stirrings of both anger and pity. "You are here because we loved each other and wanted a child. And your father would have been proud of his son, the son we made. And I am here, and I love you. I wish you would not hurt for what you are, or what you are not."

"I am a warrior of the Aniyunwiya."

"It is true you are named, but you are not yet a man."

He searched her face. He saw love and concern, but she would never know the depth of his wound, the ache for a father he had never seen.

"Let's forget it," he said.

"You are angry."

"No. Let's forget it."

"You are still hurt. I know you."

"I just don't want to talk about it anymore."

Starlight moved away, troubled. There was little she could say to him. He would have to work it out alone. In pain, too, most likely. As she had done.

"When you are ready we will talk more," she said.

He was silent. She looked back at him. He was sitting up in bed and there were tears in his eyes. His head swung slowly from side to side, fighting it. Her heart softened. It was a difficult time for him. He stood somewhere between youth and manhood, between the promise and the reality, and she wished with all her heart she could protect him from the pain she knew would come, was coming already.

For herself, the loss had become bearable. The years had spread whatever poultice they could on the searing wound of his absence. Lately she had found herself looking back with a remembrance of love and a sense of luck. She had been loved by a man, a good man. He had been gentle and kind, and in her eyes he was both exciting and wonderfully wise. When he was gone the sense of shock was a heart-stopping moment that went on and on. Fourteen years later she remembered the good things and wondered if she could tell those things to the boy. Young enough to know what had happened, he was still too young to understand why.

His voice startled her.

"Yes?" she answered.

"I love you," he said.

She ran back to the bed and put her arms around him. Man or boy, he leaned into her embrace and cried.

"I love you, too," she said. "It's going to be all right."

After a while he lay back, comforted, but with a vague unease. He had been accustomed to working out his problems without Starlight's help, and his need for her words disturbed him.

Finally the days had been too sweet, the mornings too clean, for him to stay at the cabin any longer. He felt the deep woods tugging at him, and he had gotten together his gear and headed toward the lake, eventually to make his way to the hill cabin and meet Tawodi.

But not yet.

Once he had found great pleasure in the swiftness of his thoughts, in his poetry, his speeding ideas becoming more interesting as they flew from their points of origin. But to what end? The quick mind was no special comfort to him now. What was wrong? He rolled over on the rock to look up at the clouds, as if his spirit were drifting up there with the high winds. Silly.

Abruptly he got to his feet and picked up the Winchester. In a few minutes he had the pack tied and swung it up and onto his shoulders. It might help to move.

He looked for the nearest stand of trees and passed through them, selecting the places where the underbrush permitted easy movement. He did not feel like beating a trail. There were deep forest sounds now; the hum of insects. He could taste the stillness and feel the pad of his boots on fresh grass. The dark shadows of the woods were slashed with shafts of sunlight, like some striped animal.

Perhaps Tawodi was at the cabin now. He would be embarrassed to see the old man at this moment; he should be stronger than some child crying on a woman's shoulder. Besides, who needed a father if he had Tawodi? All his life the old man had been there, teaching him to shoot, to track, to trap and fish. Who needed anyone else?

There were voices within him and the sounds of the forest as he moved through it. After an hour he crossed a jeep road and turned toward the sun. He intended to walk, and think, for there was no way he could turn off that functioning mind.

That night, he could not sleep.

He lay on pine boughs. Cold. Still it was comfortable, and he lay listening to the night sounds. The moon was unusually bright. He hoped he would hear his brothers in this frost-colored evening. He closed his eyes against the brilliance of the moon, but sleep would not come. He tried to remember if this was the same area where he had once heard a panther on the hillside across the road. It had been on a clear night like this and when the panther had cried out, he and his friends had remained silent for long afterward, held by the beauty and savagery of the cry. Now he tried to imagine the cat there in the darkness, an animal much better equipped to live in the woods than himself. He wondered if the panther had a mate, then wondered at the thought. He himself had not given much thought to mating until the past few weeks, when he began to feel the urges that occasionally troubled his sleep. He had gone to Tawodi with the questions and gotten all the answers, but he was not ready to make any kind of commitment to a girl. It would be nice to have a girl to talk to, if she would leave him alone when he wanted to be left alone. Tawodi had told him of the kinds and ways of lovemaking, but he had warned that girls always wanted to talk about it, too.

He stood up and leaned on a tree, a confusion in mind and body. There was a mild ache in his genitals. Heavier than he could remember. There was a weariness in his head as well, because he could not stop his mind from racing. After a long time he lay back on the pine boughs and tried not to think about anything at all. Shooting stars, above the trees. He saw the false dawn and then daylight, dawn coming with the stirrings of thousands of birds. He moved, stretched, and finally yawned. Maybe he could sleep through the heat of midday and catch Tawodi at the cabin before dusk. Not that far. He was hungry again.

Waya wrote:

> *this is the land of wolves you can see through,*
> *a place of two moons, one in the sky, one in the water.*
> *this is the land of the aniyunwiya, the real people,*
> *who one day will disappear*
> *like the wolves in the fog,*
> *like the moon in the water when the ice comes.*

1947

How often, thought Tawodi, have I seen him do this? And he looked with real affection on his grandson.

The boy was standing on the grass by the bank of the river, slowly taking off his clothes. When he was stripped he stood on the bank, he and the old man both listening to the surge of the water across and around the smooth, gray-white rocks of the river.

Here the Ocoee was hardly more than a stream, not the torrent it would become farther downriver, before broadening into the lake. Here it was thirty yards of gently flowing water moving among the rocks. But the water was deep and cold, and the old man looked with amusement at Starlight's son. How time flew! The boy was growing quickly to manhood. Already his body was taller and heavier than most full bloods'.

He smiled as his grandson moved over to the beginning of the rocks, where the rocks began their path across the river.

The boy studied the rocks intently, then stepped firmly onto the first rock and closed his eyes.

"Hey-yeh," called Tawodi, "the river is waiting. She has cold arms for you."

The boy smiled and stepped.

He was on the second rock, eyes still closed tightly.

"Give a man luck," called Tawodi, "and he can have shit for brains."

The boy grinned, took another step, and found the rock.

"So far, so good," he called to his grandfather.

Tawodi smiled and waited.

Another step. His left foot searched and found the rock. But when he brought his right foot up the left one slipped and he twisted violently, trying to stay on the rock. He hung for a moment, just long enough to hear his grandfather's gleeful "Hey-yeh!" and then he felt the cold water up and over him.

He was up in an instant, gasping at the cold, eyes wide and hands scrambling for a rock. He found it and pulled himself out, still feeling the numbing cold on his neck and wrists. Damn! He looked over at Tawodi, who was standing on the bank, laughing. The boy began to laugh as well.

"It's the white blood in you," the old man teased. "It makes you do crazy things."

The boy sat on the rock and grinned across the water at his grandfather. He could feel the cold wearing off, and the warmth of the early fall day was enough to put him in an easy mood.

"I tell you, grandfather, I will make it someday. You have to have a little faith."

The old man threw back his head and laughed again, then he sat in the grass under a tree, watching the boy's easy grace as he dressed. The boy's body was developing all right, and Tawodi knew that he could, indeed, move wolflike when he needed to. The boy was well and aptly named. But he wondered if the boy's spirit was evolving as well.

"Do you know how the little water spider brought man the first fire?" he asked the boy abruptly.

The boy looked up. It was a story he had heard many times,

but he thought Tawodi had his reasons for asking. "Yes," he said.

"And the legend of Ataga'hi, the magic lake?"

He walked over and sat near his grandfather. "Yes."

"And the story of Tsali, and the Trail Where They Cried?"

"Yes." He was watching Tawodi's eyes.

"And," the old man said slowly, "the story of Starlight of the Aniyunwiya, and how she loved a foreign man, and how he left her with a son?"

At last. "Not all of it, grandfather. There are things Starlight will not tell me yet."

"Then I will," said the old man, and the boy stared.

"Please," he whispered.

"You are old enough and you have been named. So listen."

The boy lay back in the grass. He could feel the pulse in his neck beating fast. Behind him was the gentle noise of the river, and he looked up to see the sunlight filtering through the crowns of the trees.

"From the beginning I called her Starlight," Tawodi began.

"It was for her eyes, which reflected the light. You could not see into them, and you never knew what she was thinking. She was straight and tall, graceful as a willow. She could ride a horse, shoot a rifle, and when she moved across the meadow with her long black hair swinging, it reminded me of her mother, and she was a delight to the eye.

"She was strong-willed and there was sometimes a need for discipline, but when I crossed a line and hurt her pride, she became like a wounded animal. Like many fathers, I wondered how to handle a daughter of beauty and fire. I did the best I could. In an earlier time the Aniyunwiya traditions would have kept her in line, but that was an earlier day. I did the best I could."

He paused, looking away from the boy. His voice was soft. The boy could see the deepening lines of his grandfather's face and it occurred to him he did not know Tawodi's age.

"She grew from a child to a woman. The young men of the village knew it before I did. Trailed her. She liked the attention, but she was half afraid. One day there was great excitement in the village and in the town. Many white men were coming into the area to camp. These were not like the merchants from Chattanooga or Atlanta. Some were foreigners, and all were going to build great dams so the whites could light their houses. They would harness the rivers and make power. It was a time that troubled me much, for I did not know what would happen to the river spirits if they became offended.

"For Starlight, it would change her life.

"One of the young white men came from Denmark. She had great trouble saying his name, so she called him Dane. The first time she saw him he was standing in the middle of the village, trying to find out about buying whisky. When she walked closer he stopped and looked at her, and she told me later, she was something in his eyes she wanted to see in a man. She was afraid of him then, because she knew he would change her life, that she would not be the same woman."

The boy stirred.

"In two weeks they were meeting secretly. She told me she led him up to the old cabin near Dry Pond Lead, where you killed your first real squirrel a long time later. You remember?"

He nodded. A single shot from the Winchester, a plummeting body, a prayer of thanks, and stew for dinner.

"They were several days in the cabin. When he returned to the camp of the whites, she came home to face me. Our beliefs do not forbid love, only lies, so she was not afraid and I was not ashamed. I think the old ways are best in these things. The old beliefs are the strongest. Strongest.

"I do not believe in a single spirit, either, in the way of the whites. No matter how you look at it, having several spirits is better than having one. What if you are in a place where the single spirit does not live? Then you must appease the spirit of that place. They talk of gods; I believe there are spirits in all things and together they make one spirit."

Tawodi paused. The boy watched him patiently.

"The spirits did not frown on Starlight for doing what her body told her to do. She was with child and very happy about it. She knew there would be trouble in her school, but she was almost finished, and she was a good student so she thought the trouble would be small. She would look into her mirror in the mornings and smile, and her step was light.

"Dane was busy. Dams were rising across the rivers, and he was in charge of placing the steel rods to hold the concrete. Now and then he could slip away to see Starlight, and it was on one of these visits that I talked with him."

The boy stiffened. "You met my father?"

"Yes. He was much like you, as you are now. You are darker, but I can see him in you. He had light eyes. It is because of him that you have eyes that change from brown to black sometimes. He had a very pleasant voice, and he was trying to learn the language of the Aniyunwiya.

"Starlight did not tell him of the child, and I could see it was something she did not want to hold him with."

Tawodi looked down at the boy. Waya was lying very still.

"One day Dane's boss sent him out of the hills to negotiate for supplies at the settlement down below, at the place you know along the Benton road. I remember that he promised to bring Starlight a present. So he went, with a few men, and he never came back."

The silence stretched out. Finally the boy asked, "What do you think happened?"

"At the settlement there was some trouble about supplies. Dane and his men had bought the things they were sent to get, but the merchants then tried to charge them more, in the way of many white merchants. There was a scuffle and someone held up a rifle and fired it into the air. In a little while your father and his men left with the supplies, at the original price. The merchants of the settlement were very angry.

"Later, when Dane and his friends were coming home with the pack mules, they were shot at by men higher on the mountain, in the trees. There were many shots fired and of your father's men, only one, badly wounded, managed to escape. Your father was never seen again.

"Some said he ran away and was too ashamed to come back. Others said he was still carrying a lot of company money and decided to disappear with it while he could. I believe the Dane was killed in the fight and that he fell into this very river and was washed away. I believe his spirit is still somewhere in a life of this forest."

Waya was silent. The old man looked down at him, but the boy's face was turned away, toward the river.

"He was a good man," Tawodi said gently. "He loved your mother. He would be here now if he could."

"But he is not," the boy said, "and his killers live."

"How do you think Starlight has felt all these years?"

"I understand," the boy said.

"Well, and what do you do now, Waya?"

The boy turned to look at him, and Tawodi could see the confusion in his face. Then he saw the face harden, the strange eyes go dark. When the boy spoke he was calm.

"I want to go to the upper cabin for a few days. I want to think."

"Good," grunted Tawodi. "I will tell Starlight you have gone. Take the Savage; you may have to hunt. There is salt in the cabin, and flour."

The boy rose and stood facing him. "Thank you for telling me," he said simply. "Starlight must have loved him very much, and now I believe I do. I, too, believe he died in the fight. I will never tell Starlight this, but I will tell you, grandfather. Once I wanted to find my father very badly. I wanted to find him and kill him for deserting us."

"Hey-yeh," said the old man. "You hate hard. And you are well named. But go now and think it all to the finish. Come back soon and we will fish a little. There are many bass in Hiwassee this year."

Waya wrote:

> *tawodi is an old man and filled with years*
> *but he is free of lies.*
> *there are no clouds over his eyes or in his mind.*
> *there is no dust on his heart.*
> *it is said of him he can summon the animals with his will.*

One morning they heard geese overhead, and the winds began to grow sharper. In the late afternoon the lazy village dogs had found warm places, readying for the coming night. The next morning, like the dropping of an icy curtain, winter descended on the mountains.

Tawodi was busier than ever in winter. It brought out the hunters, who paid the old man very well to find them game to shoot, and it was his work as a guide that made him well known in Chattanooga and Knoxville and Ashville.

Starlight, too, was busy. She was working in the town's post office and studying at night. She had decided that one day she would go to college, perhaps when her son was older. Her son. She smiled when she thought of him. He was such a typical boy, yet unlike the others. She loved him very much, but she worried about him, too. Quieter than most. Secretive, almost. He was ambitious and she wondered if there were limits to it.

He was competitive. She remembered the time when he was very young and had gone through the town picking fights with boys his size. He won them all and was bragging about it when she hit him. He went down and came up, startled. She hit him again. He got up with his hands clenched and she reached through them and hit him again. It went on until he couldn't get up anymore. Then she went away and threw up and cried. It had hurt her terribly, but he needed the lesson, and Tawodi was away. If only Dane had been there.

She also remembered his fight with the McLaren boy who lived in town. He was a large, tough boy, also a mixed blood, and he was ready with his fists. He and her son had gotten into a fight at school—she could not remember what it was all about—and her son had come home with his ribs aching and a cut over one eye. The next day he came home again with one eye swelling shut. She bit her lip and waited. Two days later the McLaren boy had rushed at her son again and Dane had hit him with an axe handle, dropping him like a felled tree. When McLaren finally got up, her son had hit him again. It continued until McLaren lay on the ground and asked for mercy. Her son had walked over and kicked him twice, viciously, in the ribs. Then he walked away. It was the last time she had heard of him being in a fight.

Yes, he was growing in many ways. Lately he had been seen a lot with the Boudreau girl—what was her name? Once she saw them walking by the post office, very deep in conversation, and she smiled and remembered. A few days later he and the girl were sitting together in the village's lone café. She thought they were holding hands, but could not be sure. Well, it was inevitable. But she thought nothing would keep him from the mountains very long, not even a girl. He was happiest when he was in there with Tawodi, hunting for wild turkeys in the pine flats, for deer across the spine of Big Frog Mountain, or gathering chestnuts at their secret tree. He was wild and free as any full blood and as much a young man of the Aniyunwiya as any of them. And yet, he was different.

Dane was ambitious and eager to learn. He listened to music, trying to decipher it. He listened to words the same way and often disconcerted people by looking at them very directly, with those eyes capable of revealing so much. It put people off. Good in school, but missed a lot of classes. When Tawodi sniffed the wind and smiled at the boy she knew they would be off for days. She really must try to keep him in school more. He was good in sports and played football and basketball for the school. In summer he sometimes played baseball for a white team from below the mountains; they gave him ten dollars a game. He put the money in an old leather pouch under the mattress. The pouch soon grew thick, for he also got a job as a janitor in the town's bank, and in the morning he delivered newspapers. She was afraid he would exhaust himself, but when the woods called him he hired others to do his work.

As he made money, he shared it. He never gave the money directly to Starlight, but with a fine sensitivity he brought home groceries or things for the cabin. Starlight was grateful, but never pressed him. He bought his own clothes, boots, moccasins. He had bought another rifle, a secondhand, octagon-barreled Marlin, which he said would be valuable someday. His proudest possession was the knife Tawodi had given him.

He carried it everywhere and nobody cared, because it was the kind of place where hunters carried guns in town. Starlight knew he slept with the knife under his pillow. It had become a habit. She wondered if the Boudreau girl would become a habit. With a French father and a mother of the Aniyunwiya, the girl was a beauty. She hoped her son would not be hurt too badly.

Spring came. A quiet explosion of freshness.

Dane sat at the river's edge, waiting. She would be coming from the town, that ugly town that was in such contrast with the woods that surrounded it. He would have to wait until school ended for the day.

The school was a curious one by normal standards. It was designed as a college but failed to get accreditation and so was used as the local high school. It brought together the Aniyunwiya who did not go to the reservation school for one reason or another and the children of the town. There were a few children of rich parents who had been brought down from the north to supervise the dreary copper mines, but most of the students were of the same economic class, which was, by almost any standards, poor.

The woods that Dane enjoyed were set aside as the Cherokee National Forest, but even beyond their boundaries were other mountains and woods, a variety of mountains, jumbled by glaciers. One dark spot, though. In the whole abundance of trees and lakes and rivers there was that large denuded spot. Miles of bare, eroded countryside. It would be years before the forest could reclaim the wounded land.

Most of the townspeople were miners, with habitually dirty fingernails and dark circles under their eyes. Some of them went down in deep shafts before sunup and stayed until after sundown, working double shifts for the money in spite of the hazards. They seldom saw the sun. Their bodies were pale and their eyes spoke of endless fatigue.

Their children were as hard as copper ore, and all grew with a single ambition: to leave town as soon as possible and escape the grinding poverty of their lives and the drudgery that claimed their fathers. Many of them succeeded, and the town's population ran in cycles. Some years there were hordes of young people, but at other times the only people on the streets were the wintry oldsters. It would have been a depressed area by most standards, but it was a classless society. Dane had friends in the town and he visited them from time to time. He was conscious that he was different from them, not so much in appearance as attitude. They talked constantly of escape. He talked of deer trails, secret coves, a magnificent eagle he had seen, sacred to the Aniyunwiya.

She came quietly through the trees, smiling at him, and walked straight up to where he stood. She kissed him quickly.

"Why are you nervous?"

"I am going to try the rocks today," she said, "maybe you will, too." Her face was innocent, alive. It was a small and delicate face and he wondered how he had gone so long without getting to know her.

"You first, Cissy," he said.

Moments later he sat on the riverbank, watching as Cissy Boudreau slipped out of her jeans, the last of her clothing. Already the erection had taken over and he knew it was useless to fight it. She was beautiful as she stood in front of him now, small and light.

He found his voice. "I've done it before. Let's see you."

She looked at him, her face all innocence. Body like a magnet, drawing him.

"How many times did you practice?"

"Until I could do it." He tried to hold her eye, but he was compelled by her body. The erection throbbed strongly.

She smiled. "Have you ever seen a girl with her clothes off before?"

He started to tease, but had been taught never to lie. "No," he said.

She turned and walked from him then, standing where he had stood so many times, at the edge of the first of the river rocks. She paused only for a second and stepped up on the rock. She took a last look, closed her eyes, and stepped confidently to the next rock.

He jumped up, surprised and grinning. She took another step and came up firmly on the third rock and then for the first time hestitated. Finally she stepped again and found the next rock. He was amazed at how gracefully she moved, and he watched her naked body with great longing.

He raised his voice so she could hear it over the running water. "Give a man luck and he can have shit for brains."

She looked back over her shoulder. He was fascinated by the curve of her hips and the clean brown line of her legs. Her skin shone in the sunlight, young and clear.

She took another step, and another, and then she was over.

From across the river he could see the triumph in her face. She raised her arms in a victory signal and he could hear the tinkle of her laugh over the sound of the water against the rocks.

With a grin he started to run across the rocks, knowing in advance he would not make it. Halfway across, his foot slipped and the sound of her scream was drowned in the sudden, icy grasp of the water. He went down and up, hurrying, scrambling to get on the rocks. He sat there, wiping water from his face. Her laugh had become raucous, and he joined it.

He got up and walked, eyes open, across the stepping stones to the other side of the bank, and as he looked down at her in the warm sun, he started to take off his wet clothes. She was still smiling.

He got out of his pants and stood in front of her. He felt the erection swelling again, and she reached up and touched it. She left her hand there, and he thought he would explode.

"Time," he said. "It's time."

She turned and walked from the river, through the tree line. He followed her until she found a place where the sun fell in a golden column through the huge pines and firs. He watched as she sank down on the needle-strewn grass and marveled once again at the grace of her body, the suppleness of her movements. He stood over her for a moment and again she reached up to touch him. His genitals felt heavy as lead. He dropped to his knees beside her, and for a moment she searched his face.

"Come," she said and opened her legs.

He went into her with more speed than skill, and in a moment he was pulsing inside her. Then he felt a sensation like a dam bursting, and a great, lifting, golden lightness. In a matter of seconds it was followed by the feeling that he was lighter than air. In a while he pulled out of her and rolled over in the grass, looking up at the treetops. Nothing at all below his waist. Nothing.

She reached over and rubbed his chest, and he came back to her from the other side of the sky. "There is nothing like it that I've ever known," he said.

"I'm glad." She grinned. "But there *are* things to teach you. You were too fast. It's better for both of us when you're slower. Rest a while. I'll show you."

He might have slept. He was aware of her arm, her hand rubbing his chest. She began stroking him, very slowly. He reached for her.

"Like this," she said and lay back with her eyes closed. A long time later, when he had learned many things, he was in her body again and discovering how right she was. Better, slower. When he felt her shudder and heard her quick half-laugh, half-bark, like some wild thing, he felt a flash of pride and manhood. He had done this to her, and for her.

When they walked back to the rocks the sun was sliding into a gap over the hills like the open sight of a gun. The air was very still, the late afternoon gold and soft. He was tired, and content.

He left her at the river's edge and, carrying the Winchester, set off for a rendezvous with Tawodi. He had taken only a few steps before he broke into a wide grin, and he began to trot easily along the forest path. Nothing like it in the world, nothing he had ever known.

"Talk to me in the language of the Aniyunwiya," Tawodi said. "What is the ceremony of the green corn?"

Solutsunigististi.

The friendship ceremony?

Atohuna.

The ripe corn?

Donagohuni.

The old man leaned back against the white oak tree in front of the small cabin, looking at his grandson. "When is the Nuwatiegwa?*"*

"October."

Tawodi smiled. "We will stop for today. Please bring the jug from the cabin. We will drink a little today."

Dane got to his feet, Tawodi watching.

"You are growing, Waya-unutsi. And changing. But some things must not change in you. Dignity. Honor."

"I will not change, grandfather," he said.

Waya wrote:

> *when i am old and passing slow,*
> *crawling through some dried mud bed in search of water,*
> *will i remember when i soared*
> *like tawodi the hawk? i was a hawk!*
> *will i remember the lifting wind and the long reach*
> *of muscles, and claws that opened as i struck?*
> *will i want to remember?*

1948-1950

Starlight knew she was being watched; she knew it even before she saw the two men in front of the copper company store. She was a woman, and of the Aniyunwiya, and she sensed the eyes on her as she crossed the street from the hardware store and moved up the slight rise. It disturbed her, because it was not the first time.

Walking with her eyes straight ahead, she gave no sign that she noticed the pair. They were brothers—large, white, and dirty. The Lawtons. It was said that they lived with animals in their cabin. They were notorious bootleggers, and although Starlight had no strong feelings about that, she had always felt a slight unease around them. In a place not noted for its courtly manners, these two were even worse. They stared at her openly as she passed, and she could feel their lust rising. She hurried on.

Soon the oppressive feeling left her and she began to smile

again. It gave her face a pleasant but secretive look, and she found passersby looking at her strangely. Never mind. She felt very good, because she thought she might be in love again. She wondered if it were true, if she could let those feelings she thought lost forever rise again with Nathan Bird. And she wondered how Dane would react. And Tawodi.

He was a good man, she thought, this one. He was a mixed blood, a very gentle man whose family came from Etowah years ago. He had moved into the area to become a merchant and had set up a small store. He had kind eyes and a soft voice. Large, and a bit slow in his movements, he had deep lines around his eyes that crinkled when he laughed, which was often, and he had a habit of looking at everything very gravely, even when he was close to laughter. It was that suddenness in him that caught her eye—the grave manner, the quick laugh. And he could make her laugh, something other men had failed to do since Dane's disappearance. He had been a friend of the family for years, but now, suddenly, they were shy with each other. She was attracted, but she was frightened, aware that this man, too, could change her life. She thought in practical terms. Where would they live? How would Tawodi and Dane adjust to someone else in the house? But, then, the boy was growing quickly and would be a man before long. She might consider waiting that long before making any kind of commitment. As for Tawodi, it was like trying to tie the wind. He would come and go in any house, or none; he would be there and then he would be gone. He did not exactly live anywhere except in the little cabin he had built with Dane, or in some cave he knew, or somewhere else, a dozen places perhaps in the deep woods. Tawodi hated having a roof over him anyway, and she knew it was his secret longing that he die outside, not under some man-made roof. He wanted his spirit to have plenty of room once he died.

She reached a corner, still smiling slightly to herself. On an impulse she turned and looked back down the street. The Lawtons had stepped off the porch of the store and were standing in the street staring after her.

Where is it you go, when you are off like that?
Everywhere. Nowhere. I am here with you.
You scare me sometimes, Dane.
Why?
Because I can't understand you. You never stop. We meet here and we do it and most men would just get sleepy. I can hear your mind working.
What do you know of most men? How many men do you sleep with?
You know what I mean. You don't relax.
I'm relaxed.
No, you're not. What are you thinking about?
I am thinking that Tawodi was right. Girls want to do it, but then they want to talk about it.
What do you know of girls? How many girls do you sleep with?
Ah-hah! You're learning how to debate, Cissy.
Every woman knows that.
Yeah, I believe it.
But why can't you relax?
It has nothing to do with you. It's just that sometimes I can't stop thinking about things. I can't shut my mind down.
What do you think about? Oh, I asked you that.
Who I am, where I'm going, what to do about college. Sometimes I just think about Starlight and Tawodi, and how lucky I am to have them. I think about how my life will be, and where I will go.
Don't you ever think about us?
I think about that first time, by the river. How your legs shone, how brown you were. I remember the good talk we had down by your folks' barn a couple of months ago; I felt really close to you then. I remember everything we do, Cissy.
But that's remembering. Don't you think of the future. I mean, the future, and us? Oh, God, now you get quiet. No, leave me alone. I want to go home. I'm going home.

Late on a Sunday afternoon in April. Still cool, higher up. He was so deep in the woods now he could not make it back by nightfall, and he would miss another day of school tomorrow. Starlight would be upset.

He was moving easily, carrying the Savage. In his pocket

were fishhooks and some salt. He also carried a compass that Tawodi had given him, an antique made in Colorado before the turn of the century. He carried a small blanket roll, having left the larger sleeping bag up in the high cabin a few days before. He wore his old boots instead of moccasins, taking no chances that the snakes would still be sluggish from winter. The boots already bore one set of fang marks from a young rattlesnake—a creature considered sacred by the Aniyunwiya. It had bounced off his ankle the year before, then struck again before he could move, scarring the leather of his left boot. Then it was gone into the bush, and he had stood there for a moment, looking at his boot and laughing. If the snake had been a copperhead he would have tried to kill it. He thought about that. A little lesson in knowing one's place in life.

Knowing who and what you were, knowing what to do with your life, seemed to him the most important thing. The spirit that was his inside this body could guide him, give him some directions. It could tell him how he felt, how to react. But he would have to make some decisions rationally, purely from the standpoint of practicality. He could be whatever he wanted within the framework of what he decided to do. He would be Waya, no matter how he spent his life.

He walked on through the woods, thinking about it. He liked writing poetry. He liked music, but he had no desire to play it. If he were involved with music he would want to create it, to write it for others to play. He thought Sibelius's Second Symphony one of the cleanest, purest, and yet most melodic of compositions. He liked the Ravel Pavanne and everything by Brahms.

And he loved the deep woods. How could he ever give this up? If this life could go on forever he would be content. But it could not. He sensed it, knew it. He could see changes— Tawodi would grow older and die. Starlight, now very lively and interested in Nathan Bird, might marry. He himself would probably go away to school. The changes were exciting, but they were sad as well. To arrest time, to hold this moment as he walked quietly and easily through the forest, to keep Starlight young and bright, to catch Tawodi forever in the present ...

He froze at the sound of a noise in front of him and to the right.

He stood very still, listening, lifting his head and trying to catch any kind of scent.

Again the noise, a slight creaking, like leather being twisted. Then he heard a horse strike a stone and a man's voice, low and hard.

He moved then, cutting to his right toward a thick stand of trees and at the same time trying to get a feel for the wind direction. He wanted to be downwind but on higher ground to look over the old road he now remembered, a road he believed made by the game warden to help him get his Jeep deeper in the woods. The noise again.

He reached the trees and went down, crawling toward the underbrush but still listening. He could see the road curving to the right, and with great caution he rose slightly and looked to the left.

The horse had stopped and was picking at grass along the roadside. The rider sat in the saddle, his face turned away from Waya, a canteen raised to his lips. Waya could easily see the dark green pants, the lighter green shirt, the blocked hat. The sheriff, from below the mountains. What was he doing here?

The rider lowered the canteen and screwed the cap back on and hung it carelessly from the pommel of the saddle. He stretched in the saddle and the horse looked up briefly, then went back to grazing.

Waya watched as the sheriff dismounted then and threw the horse's reins through a fork in a tree. The sheriff sat beneath the tree, shifting the gun on his belt to make himself comfortable. Waya waited.

A long time later—he saw the sheriff look impatiently at his watch twice—Waya heard the sound of an engine above the noise of the insects. He heard it before the sheriff did and shifted his position slightly so he could not be seen from the road to his right. He still had a clear view of the sheriff, and he saw him suddenly stand up and dust off his pants, looking down the road toward the sound of the engine.

When the Jeep came in sight Waya knew it at once. It was

the battered old Jeep that belonged to the Lawtons. He lay very still now and slid the Savage up to where he could reach it quickly. There was a lot of talk about the Lawtons, none of it good.

The Jeep stopped and the two brothers got out. Waya thought he could smell them, they were so close. The older one was heavier, dirtier, and more menacing than his younger brother, and he plodded over to where the sheriff stood waiting for them. Waya could hear them easily.

"Sheriff," said the older one.

"You're late," the sheriff said.

"We're here," said the older brother. "Let's talk."

"Let's not be all day about it," the sheriff said. "It's dangerous meeting you like this."

"Better than town," the younger Lawton spoke for the first time.

"Get on with it," the sheriff said testily.

"Well, we got a good batch and we can deliver. Whatever you want," the older brother said. The younger brother walked away and started to urinate a few feet from where the sheriff was standing. The sheriff looked at him in distaste.

"How much you want?" the older brother asked.

"Fifty gallons?"

"We can do that, sheriff. Soon as you pay."

"Pay on delivery," the sheriff said. "Same as always."

"Pay now," the older one said. He reached inside his jacket and the sheriff stepped back, startled. The older Lawton grinned and pulled out a plug of chewing tobacco. The younger brother walked back and stood watching them.

"Half now, half on delivery," the sheriff said. "I ain't carrying a lot of money when I come to meet you two."

"Damned smart, sheriff," said the younger Lawton, watching the sheriff with cold blue eyes. The older brother bit a chunk of the flat plug and offered it to the other two men. The sheriff shook his head. The younger brother bit into the plug, twisted it free, and handed it back to the older Lawton. Both men gazed at the sheriff in silence.

"Let's get on with it," the sheriff said again. The Lawtons clearly were making him nervous.

"Same price as always," the sheriff said into the silence.

"No," said the older brother flatly.

"You holdin' me up for more money, Lawton?" the sheriff asked. Waya could see the red creeping up the back of the sheriff's neck.

"Twenty cents a gallon more, sheriff. You see, we know what you're sellin' it for. This time you owe two hundred and sixty dollars. Take it or leave it."

Waya saw the sheriff's hard stare hold for a moment, then fall away.

"Shit," said the sheriff. "All right. But half now, the rest when you take it where you're supposed to."

"Same place, sheriff? Your lake cabin?" The younger one asked.

"Yeah," the sheriff replied and brought out his wallet. He stood there counting out bills into the older Lawton's outstretched hand.

"One hundred dollars. All I brought. You get the rest when you deliver."

"Have it tomorrow, sheriff," said the older Lawton. "We'll be at your place about midnight."

The sheriff nodded.

Deliberately, the older Lawton leaned forward and spit a long stream of brown tobacco. It splashed in the dirt in front of the sheriff's boots, sending a fine spray across his right boot and onto his pants leg. The sheriff's head jerked up, his face flushed.

"You just remember one thing, sheriff," said the older brother. "We got a deal goin' here. We're partners. Anything ever happen to us, we're goin' to fry *your* ass as well."

"I hear you," the sheriff said in a choked voice.

The Lawtons climbed back in the Jeep and started the engine. They swung the vehicle around, backing it once on the narrow road, then drove away without looking back.

Waya watched as the sheriff stood there for a long time,

looking down at his boots. Finally, the sheriff seized the reins and swung up into the saddle. He looked after the Jeep for a moment, then jerked the reins viciously, turning the horse around in the road. Waya heard the force of his kick as he slammed his boots into the horse's side, throwing the animal into a quick trot. In a moment the road was empty.

Waya stood.

It was an old story in the mountains. It was not something he was going to worry about. The only thing he had to do was keep quiet, for if he told anyone that the sheriff was buying moonshine from the Lawtons, he would have to deal with the Lawtons. They would surely come looking for him.

He stepped out from under the trees and into the sunlight. The birds, which had gone silent because of the men on the road, began to call again, their voices clear and clean. Waya turned away from the road and moved as a wolf would move among the trees.

He spent the next days in the mountains, the sheriff and the Lawtons forgotten. The hill cabin was in good shape, the cache of ammunition intact, and no more than the usual number of spiders, which he did not molest. For the propped-open wooden window of the cabin he could see down the slope and across to the next ridge and feel the soft breezes through the window. Beyond his field of vision but less than a day's walk was another lake, a sanctuary for the wild geese. He had seen them only a few times in his life, but perhaps they had always come to the lake. He remembered the precision with which they flew and their raucous honking as they bent to the lake, hundreds of them, their wings moving slowly and with grace, unhurried as they settled into the water. Tawodi, although he often hunted for food, had never killed one. There were fewer of them each time, the old man had said, and who could kill a race that was already dying? There would be a time when they would not come at all, the old man continued, a time when the deer would be gone and the foxes, the bobcats, too. Perhaps even the woods would go and be replaced by buildings. And one day the whole world would simply be buildings with people in them, and no forests or animals or rivers. He would be dead by then, Tawodi said, and the boy, too, perhaps—for which they should both be grateful. Well, he would be grateful, all right. But death was so remote from him he hardly thought of it.

What he did think of that night was Cissy, and he felt his erection rising under the rough blankets. She was becoming more difficult lately, but their times in bed were as wonderful as ever. He wished she would stop trying to decide their future.

Tawodi, half dozing, was sitting back against the rocks of the well, which was on a direct line with Starlight's kitchen. The Winchester lay across his lap. His chin was tucked in, eyes closed, and his ears accustomed to the humming of the large green flies and the nearby chattering of sparrows. A warm day. Little wind.

He sat so still that Starlight did not see him as she walked with Nathan Bird on the other side of the well. They were holding hands and talking in low voices. Tawodi tried to ignore them.

"In the summer, then," the storekeeper said. "A June wedding. But I don't want to rush you."

"No," he heard Starlight say, "you aren't rushing me. I know what I'm doing, Nathan. I'm sure." Tawodi heard the silence that followed. He thought of the storekeeper.

Nathan Bird, a member of the Paint clan. His little store was doing well at Postelle Station, and he was an honest, hard-working man. Tawodi respected him for his gentleness and his ability, and for the way he treated Starlight. But he thought Starlight, without meaning to, would dominate him. No matter. It would all work out. It would be good for Starlight to be married. He wondered what the boy would think of it all. Why not find out?

He stood, rising quietly from the other side of the well. Starlight gasped and stepped back and Nathan turned, startled. Starlight recovered first. "You heard."

"Yes," said the old man.

"And?"

"Good."

Nathan stepped forward and started to shake hands in the manner of the whites. Then he stopped and smiled at Tawodi.

"Will you come to the wedding?" he asked.

"If it is outside."

Nathan grinned. "Starlight will decide that, I guess."

"Who will tell the boy?" Tawodi asked.

"He may have guessed by now," Starlight said. "I don't think it is a big problem. Do you want to do it?"

"Yes," said Tawodi. "I think he is at the upper cabin. I will tell him," and he left without saying good-bye.

He stopped long enough to pick up a jacket. It could be cool higher up and he was getting no younger. Then he left the cabin and turned across the dirt path and headed north and upward.

He walked steadily, noting signs, watching the clouds building farther to the north. A few deer signs, a few hickory nuts cut by squirrels. A good day to be alive.

He came to the hill cabin straight up from the south, down from the ridgeline, and across the stream. It was early evening, but growing dark quickly. There were no lights in the cabin, but he walked steadily upward.

He never heard the boy, but he sensed someone in the trees to his right. He stopped and softly called Waya's name. The boy stepped out at once and lowered the Savage. In the darkness Tawodi smiled.

"It is good to see how well you learn. Let's go into the cabin, Waya. I have much to tell you, and I want to see your face."

Inside, they sat at the rough table with a kerosene lamp between them. Quickly, simply, Tawodi told of Starlight's wedding plans and was pleased to see that the boy was not upset, not even particularly surprised.

"I am happy for her," he said, meaning it. "But I will not think of him as my father."

"There is no need for that," his grandfather said. "But I believe the Dane would be glad, as I am, as you should be. Now we must think of a wedding present. No, tomorrow. I need sleep." And the old man rolled into a bunk and was asleep almost at once.

Waya sat in the dim light of the kerosene lamp and tried to weigh his feelings. In the end he decided that he was truly happy for Starlight and Nathan Bird. He blew out the lamp and sat in the darkness for a while listening. Finally he climbed into the other bunk. A cool night. An owl somewhere called a challenge. He remembered Starlight's soft touch when he was a child and how she always listened to him, always made time for him. She had dark eyes, like his, and a direct look. He would insist that Nathan Bird take good care of her. He was glad that she had someone. One day he would be gone, somewhere, for there were many things he wanted to see. He wished he could take Tawodi with him. He slept, not knowing that in the night the old man awoke and sat up and, sitting on the edge of his bunk, watched the boy as he slept. When Waya woke at dawn his grandfather was already standing in front of the cabin waiting for him.

They spent the next two days at the cabin, wandering a mile or two away and coming back, content with the warm days and the starlit nights, feeling very much at peace. In the late evening of the second day Tawodi turned up a small jar of moonshine, and they sat sipping it on the grass in front of the cabin. Waya told the old man about the meeting between the sheriff and the Lawtons, and Tawodi grunted his displeasure. He didn't like any of them, he said, but he was not surprised at the sheriff's dealing in moonshine. "He is no damn good," Tawodi explained, and the boy grinned.

They stayed a third day at the cabin before Waya began to feel slightly guilty about missing school. On the morning of the fourth day they began to walk down from the hill cabin.

They had crossed the stream and started toward the ridge beyond when Tawodi stopped suddenly and stood very still. Waya became alert, listening and waiting, not talking, facing the opposite way from him to extend their field of vision.

After a while his grandfather turned to him, and Waya could see the anxiety in his face.

"What is it?" Waya whispered.

"I do not know," Tawodi said. "Nothing I can see or hear. But I have a bad feeling." He stared into the distance. "I think we should hurry."

Starlight was badly frightened, but tried not to show it.

The brown Jeep had suddenly turned up in front of them and blocked the dirt road. There had been no time to run, and as far as Nathan was concerned, no reason to. But there were the Lawtons getting out of the Jeep, and this stretch of road was seldom traveled. She and Nathan had gone into the woods to look for grapes, unsuccessfully as it turned out, and were walking back. They were not far from town, but it was an isolated place. And the Lawtons were walking up to them. She gripped Nathan's hand, and he looked at her in surprise. Before she could speak to him, the Lawtons were there, looking at her, the older one spitting to one side and turning to squint at Nathan.

"Evenin', folks," the older Lawton said. She could see crooked teeth and tobacco stains. Even at this distance she could smell him.

The younger Lawton—she suddenly remembered his name, George, George Lawton—simply stood watching her, his eyes cold but bright.

"Nathan," she heard herself saying calmly, "these are the Lawton brothers, George and—I don't know your first name. This is the man I am to marry. His name is Nathan Bird."

"Bird, is it?" the older Lawton said. "Can you fly, little bird?"

The smile left Nathan's face. He felt Starlight's hand tighten. Lawton suddenly spit tobacco juice on his pants leg.

Nathan felt an enormous pressure in his chest and he fought for control. "We are walking around you, Mr. Lawton. We don't want any trouble with you." He nudged Starlight to the right to start her around the Jeep, but George Lawton stepped in front of her.

"It's no use," Starlight said, her voice tight. And at that moment the younger Lawton grabbed her by the shoulders.

Nathan hit him then, hard and direct, and saw Lawton's

head fly back and his hands drop from Starlight. Before he could turn he felt the weight of the older brother and the clasp of his arms as he was grabbed from behind. He was jerked off the ground and then slammed down, hearing the air come from him in a grunt. There was a sudden, devastating blow to his right side and he thought he heard something tick in his body. When he looked up, Lawton kicked him in the face. He lay stunned.

Lawton turned to see his brother standing in front of Starlight. She was holding a large rock and there was blood coming from the younger Lawton's face. Most of Starlight's clothes were torn and he could see her fine breasts.

"Indian bitch," he said and moved to help his brother.

They circled her, cutting off her chance to escape. George Lawton suddenly feinted and then closed on her, moving quickly.

Starlight was quicker; she saw the feint for what it was and held her ground. When he lunged she swung the rock with all her strength.

She felt it connect with a force that jarred her arm all the way to the shoulder. She saw the head snap back and the body hurl backward to the ground. Then she felt the hands behind her around her breasts, tightening, felt the large, dirty body and its incredible strength.

She was thrown to the ground and rolled roughly onto her back. The last of her clothing was torn away and her thighs were pinned by his knees, the weight of them pressing painfully on her and the rough hands holding her arms. The stench of him was overpowering and she knew he was still chewing tobacco.

Lawton let go of her left arm for a moment, moving his hand down to unbutton his pants. She jabbed her fingers at his eyes, but he was too quick and her arm was slammed down again. She looked in his eyes.

"I will kill you for this," she said in a strange, quiet voice.

"You bitch," he said. "It's too late for you."

She felt him starting to force his way into her body, and she began to writhe.

"Now," he said. "Now." She closed her eyes.

Suddenly, he was gone.

She felt the weight disappear and heard him scrambling to his feet. She opened her eyes and sat up. He was running for the Jeep. She turned to look for Nathan.

He was propped up on one elbow, his face streaked with dirt and blood. She was still staring, speechless, when she heard the other voices and looked up.

A group of men were getting out of a pickup truck and hurrying toward her. She knew most of them, especially the driver, a full blood who had worked as a watchman on one of the TVA dam projects. She watched as they ran to her.

"Lord have mercy," one of them said. "What's happened here?"

She couldn't talk. Someone put a jacket over her. She was aware that two men were bending over Nathan, helping him to his feet; he was standing now with his face in his hands, but calling her name. She walked, with help, to where he stood.

"Nathan," she whispered, and he reached out for her.

They stood holding each other for a few minutes, before someone pulled them gently apart. She felt an oilskin raincoat being slipped around her, and she held it gratefully. She was being helped toward the truck, and another man was leading Nathan. She wondered suddenly if he had been blinded.

It was in the truck, as they were hurrying away, that she remembered the full blood looking down at George Lawton. *"This one's dead," he had said.*

"Nathan?"

There was a reassuring hand on her shoulder. "He's lying down in the back, don't you worry," a voice said. "We're goin' to the hospital. He'll be fine. Did that son of a bitch rape you?"

"No," she said. She tried to talk about how close it had been, but then the tears were there, surprising her, and she put her head on the back of the seat and cried.

At the hospital they took Nathan directly to Emergency, but they put her in a small room and gave her a hospital gown. After a time she awoke, surprised that she had fallen asleep, and asked for Nathan. A nurse told her he was in surgery.

She wanted to bathe, but the nurse said no, not yet, and in a little while a young white doctor came to examine her. There were no traces of semen, he told her; she was badly bruised over much of her body. She asked if she could stay in the hospital, near Nathan. The doctor said yes.

After that she stood for a long time in a shower in one of the rooms. She scrubbed herself several times, put the hospital gown back on, and went back to the little room to wait.

After an hour the same doctor returned to speak to her. Nathan would recover, he said, but he had lost the sight in his right eye. He also had a fractured rib that had caused some damage to his lung, and there was suspicion of a mild concussion. Starlight cried again, weeping softly into her hands while the doctor stood by, uncomfortable and preoccupied. Finally she asked him to leave her alone.

She lay on the bed in the room wondering what would happen next. She had killed a man. No regrets. She thought then of Tawodi, and of Dane, and sat up in bed. How would they handle this? She thought she knew.

She nearly ran down the hallway to the night nurse, sitting in the glow of a soft light. The nurse looked up at Starlight's distraught face and voice.

". . . must find my family."

The nurse was soothing. "We're looking for them now, dear," she said. "You go lie down. We'll let you know when they get here. By the way, the sheriff's on the way here. He wants to talk to you. Are you up to that?"

"Yes," Starlight said. And she went back down to the room to wait again.

She was awake when the sheriff strode into the room, and almost instantly she sensed danger again. It was partly his face, immobile and cold, and partly his manner.

"All right," he said, "let's get this over with. You ready to talk?"

"Yes."

"Well, first off, we need a quick answer. You kill the Lawton boy?"

"Yes. With a rock."

The sheriff looked down and started writing. "So you admit it."

"He was trying to rape me. His brother almost did."

"That's your story. We'll have to check out the facts."

"You listen to me, sheriff—what's the matter with you, anyway?" Starlight was getting angry. "They tried to rape me. They almost killed Nathan. He'll tell you that when he can. Why aren't you out looking for the other one?"

"You don't tell me how to do my job," the sheriff said, standing stiffly. "Don't forget who's the law here. I'll come back and talk to you again. Don't you or the other Indian leave town, you hear?" And he was gone.

She spent a restless night, but the next morning was able to talk with Nathan, although she could barely find a face through the bandages. "I'll be all right," he kept assuring her, but it broke her heart to hear the pain in his voice.

In the late afternoon Dane and Tawodi suddenly turned up, carrying rifles. One moment the waiting room was empty, the next moment they were there. Starlight could almost smell the deep woods on them and smiled at the way they stood like two wild creatures. They saw her and moved quickly to her, Dane pulling her into his arms, then holding her at arm's length to look at her. Tawodi merely reached out and patted her shoulder.

"We heard," her son said. "Are you all right?"

"Yes." She smiled. "You must talk to Nathan, too. He will be glad to know you're here."

They led her to a bench in the waiting room. "Tell us," her son said.

She told the story, in detail, watching their eyes. She saw her father's face assume its expressionless look, but she could tell he was furious. As for her son, his eyes had gone from brown to black, a sure sign that he was deeply moved. When she got to the part about the sheriff she saw the two men glance at each other and she thought some understanding passed between them.

When she had finished they sat there for a few minutes, her son absently patting her hand. Neither of them looked at her, and again she thought some secret was working between the two of them.

"What is it?" she asked finally.

Dane glanced again at Tawodi, who nodded. Dane spoke: "The sheriff's been buying moonshine from the Lawtons and selling it, and if the word gets around he'll never be elected again. He'll also face charges maybe. He's not going to bring in Lawton because Lawton will tell everybody what's been happening."

"How do you know this?" she asked. He told her briefly about the meeting he had chanced upon on the mountain road.

"So what is he going to do?"

Tawodi said, "He will have to help him escape. From the way he talked with you, he will try to blame you for what happened, and then Lawton will be free, perhaps. It is the way of the whites."

"But," Dane said softly, "we will not settle this as the whites would, but as Aniyunwiya."

"Hey-yeh," said Tawodi. "Well spoken."

"You listen, Dane, I don't want you—"

He put a hand on her lips softly. "*You* listen, Starlight. We will do what we have to do. There will be no justice otherwise. You are a woman, and I am a man now, and this is not simply your problem anymore."

"Be careful," she said.

"Go home when you can," Tawodi told her. "Take Nathan. Do not open the door for anyone but us. It may be that the sheriff will become desperate and come back to you for some reason. Talk to no one until we come back."

She nodded, and they were gone as suddenly as they had come.

Now it was out of her hands. She turned her attention to Nathan, and when they left the hospital a day later, she took him straight to the house and did exactly as Tawodi had told her. She had no idea how long it would be before she heard from her son and her father again. But she had no doubts she would hear.

* * *

At first he could not understand his grandfather. The old man, instead of hurrying directly after Lawton, insisted that they stop, and sit, and think. And at first he could not think, he could only remember. Mostly he remembered her thoughtfulness, the way she kept his clothes clean. The way she always remembered Christmas and his birthday, even when they were very poor. Deeper in his memory, there were images of cold nights in the cabin when she came to him and cuddled him for warmth, while he listened to the howling of the wind and the splintering of tree branches.

And that son of a bitch tried to rape her . . .

"He will not go to his cabin," Tawodi said suddenly. "So we will not waste time there. He will not leave by the roads because he believes they will be watched."

"So, grandfather?"

"We know something he does not know we know," Tawodi said. "He is running because he is frightened, but he is not a stupid man in some ways. He will remember no one knows about his dealings with the sheriff."

"The sheriff's lake cabin?"

"Yes," the old man said, "it is there he will stop and resupply himself. Then he will try to cross the lake and into North Carolina. He will think he is safe there."

"And he will be," Waya said after a pause. "The law here won't go looking for him, and there are many places he could go."

"But he will be looking for the law, because he will think the sheriff must put up some show of searching for him, for appearances."

"So, while he stops at the cabin, we might catch him."

"Yes, or cross the lake ourselves and find him on the other side."

"It would be easier at the cabin."

Tawodi grunted. "It will not be easy anywhere. So, we go. Travel light; we will be running. No lights, no food. Only water, ammunition."

"What are you carrying?" Waya said.

"I will take the Savage."

"And I the Marlin."

Waya went into the house and picked up the Marlin he had bought. It was made at the turn of the century. The stock was old, dark walnut. It was a lever-action .44 caliber and heavy. But he wanted it on this hunt. He left behind the bright mackinaw and slipped into a dark green jacket. When he slipped the knife Tawodi had given him onto his belt he had another thought; he slipped on the headband Starlight had made for his name day. He filled a canteen with water and dropped extra ammunition into the right front pocket of his jacket. He felt strangely light, and cold, and ready.

His grandfather appeared in the doorway holding the .30 caliber Savage, his face blank. Without a word they turned from the house and began to trot toward the nearest trees. All at once Waya knew why Tawodi had wanted him to pause before beginning—it was to clear his mind, to prepare him mentally. It had worked, for he was now cold and calm inside; the fires had been banked and he was able to think clearly about what they must do.

They went along the ridgelines where possible, using the thinner brush on the crest instead of fighting through the denser thickets along the sides of the hills. Somewhere crow calls, very loud and insistent. Once a noise that could have been a bear moving from their path. They trotted steadily, the old man showing no signs of strain. When the sun disappeared they stopped and waited for moonrise, hoping for a hunter's moon. It came large and clear over the crest of the distant mountains, and the night was suddenly the color of frost. Tawodi grinned. "Lawton doesn't have much luck, does he?"

They had decided to take the longer route to the cabin, ignoring both the paved roads—because they did not want to be seen—and the shorter but more difficult route to the east of them where the hills were more gentle, but there were many streams to cross. Tawodi was sure Lawton would have taken the more direct route, but he also could be setting an ambush along the same path he had taken. Crossing the higher hills was longer, but surer. Waya agreed, noting to his own satisfaction that he was making calm and rational decisions despite the cold fury he felt.

Now with the moon rising in the night sky and the night sounds around him, he settled into a kind of shuffle, matching Tawodi's pace and marveling at the old man's endurance. They had covered at least seven or eight miles, much of it up-hill, and still his grandfather pressed on, occasionally stopping to find the quickest way through a stand of trees or brush. Sometimes they heard animals moving in the night, startled by the two passing men. Once a chattering, as if they had awakened a family of squirrels or chipmunks.

Finally, Tawodi stopped. "Rest," he said, and they lay down facing in opposite directions and not talking. Just as he thought Tawodi had fallen asleep, the old man stood and stretched and turned his face again toward the lake. In a moment they were off again.

At moonset they paused, waiting for light, but it was a long time coming, and when it came they saw clouds gathering to the east. For the first time that night Tawodi took a drink of water, and the boy followed, sipping slowly and sparingly. He felt the water swelling in his stomach, shrunk by very little food in the past few days. The water tasted good, but he screwed the cap back on and stood, smelling the morning. It was light then, and with daylight came a breeze that had the taste of rain in it, and all at once the clouds were much heavier and much deeper across the morning sky. Waya knew exactly where they were, just a mile or two from the cabin, and he knew that Tawodi had done a marvelous job of getting them through the woods, guiding them most of the way with instinct and a powerful sense of direction. Had he been alone it would have taken longer.

They pushed on across flatter country and in a half hour they crossed a trail that led to the cabin. A few minutes later they were in sight of the cabin itself.

Tawodi went down on one knee. "Tell me what you see," he said, as he had done so many times with the boy.

"There is the cabin," answered Waya. "There is no smoke coming from the chimney. There is the outhouse and a shed. There is a small corral, but no horses there for some time. There are tire tracks, but old ones."

"What is it you cannot see, but feel?"

Waya paused. "Because the cabin is on a lake, there must be boats behind it, tied up somewhere."

"That is reason," the old man said. "What does the wolf in you say?"

"That Lawton is in the cabin."

"Yes," said Tawodi. "I believe it. Now, we must decide what to do with him."

"I will kill him," Waya said simply.

"No."

"No?"

"We take him back to the whites. If there is no justice, *then* we kill him."

Tawodi watched the boy's face. He was still a boy, too young to be killing. But he hated hard.

"Move closer," Tawodi said. "Watch for a while."

They circled to their left, coming up behind the rough outhouse and crouching behind it, gaining a closer look at the cabin. It was a lapstrake design, very sturdy, with wooden shutters instead of windows.

There was no noise coming from the cabin.

"I will go to the back," his grandfather whispered. "If there are boats I will sink them. You will hear gunfire. Lawton may come out of the cabin. Foolish if he does. If he does not, we may have to go inside for him."

Waya nodded and watched the old man crouch and back away from the outhouse back into the tree line. Tawodi slipped through the trees and Waya thought once that he caught a glimpse of movement on the far side of the corral. He squatted behind the outhouse, watching the front door of the cabin.

The Marlin was loaded, a round in the chamber and the safety on. Earlier that night he had felt the weight of the old weapon, but now he was reassured by its size and balance. He shifted his knees, sat down, and put the rifle across his lap. It would take Tawodi some time to reach the boats. He did not think Lawton had time to cross the lake yet.

There were two sudden, loud gunshots.

He rolled to his feet and stood pressed against the side of the outhouse, watching the door, feeling his heart beat, but glad that his hands were steady. The door remained firmly closed.

He stood there a long time with nothing happening. He felt someone behind him and wheeled, throwing up the Marlin, but it was only Tawodi, a few feet behind him.

"Now he knows we are here," the old man said. "But he has no boats, and he cannot swim the Hiwassee. We have much time, but he has little, so he will come through that door sometime. We wait."

A shadow passed across the sun and Waya looked up. It was almost entirely overcast now and the clouds had a bleak, ponderous look. Smell of rain on the wind. Wild creatures in the brush, looking for shelter.

After a time he felt Tawodi nudge him. The old man was gesturing—he would go to the other side of the cabin, and Waya instantly saw the logic in it and nodded. In a moment Tawodi had wriggled backward and was gone. Waya settled down to wait.

An hour passed, and it began to rain.

He turned up his collar and pulled the Marlin down to cover it with his jacket. The rain began to build, like something alive, growing in intensity, hammering the leaves and dancing on the lake behind the cabin. With the water running down his face, Waya had to squint to watch the cabin door.

Now it was early afternoon. Waya wondered how much longer they would have to wait and what, in fact, Lawton was waiting for.

Lawton knew he was being hunted. He knew the boats were useless.

He also knew that his hunters were not a sheriff's posse, or men from the town; they would have called to him to surrender by now.

So he had reasoned that it would be Starlight's people— Tawodi for sure, perhaps himself.

Waya knew then that Lawton would wait for dark. After dark he would throw open the door of the cabin and run through it, taking his chances, hoping to blend into the night and escape.

And if the rain continued, it would be a very black night.

It was a cold rain and showed no signs of stopping. There was some protection against the side of the outhouse, but not much. At least he was keeping the Marlin relatively dry. But if he got inside the outhouse . . .

The thought made him sit upright, and when he did he felt the whistling of a bullet near his ear and heard it splintering the old planks of the outhouse; as he threw himself down again he heard the noise from the first shot, then a second, and again he heard its impact. By the time a third shot came he was well behind the outhouse, his throat dry and his hands tightly gripping the Marlin.

After a time he crawled back to his first position, noticing how Lawton's shots had nearly destroyed the side of the old outhouse, knowing it was a heavy-caliber rifle. When he settled in again he looked back at the cabin and got a start.

Tawodi was sitting against the cabin wall, cradling something in his lap. Even through the rain the thin wisp of smoke from the coals was visible. Waya saw him look toward the outhouse and gesture emphatically toward the nearest window of the cabin. Waya understood.

He stretched into the classic prone position and worked the lever of the Marlin, feeling a sudden exhilaration. Then he fired directly into the center of the window, feeling the slight recoil. Then he fired again and again.

Tawodi had crawled around to the other side of the cabin and out of his line of vision. Waya put two more shots into the window, but the heavy shutters were holding firm. He wondered how his grandfather had been able to get a fire going in such a driving rain, or how he could keep it alive.

Then he noticed the cabin's overhang, something the old

man must have seen and thought about. The cabin walls would be dry enough.

He reloaded the Marlin and waited. After a while he put two more rounds into the window, and this time he saw the shutter move slightly. There was another booming sound and he heard the round smack into the wood above him, but closer than the first two. He fired one more round and worked his way around to the other side of the outhouse and waited.

He did not know how long he waited, but in time he saw smoke streaming out under the overhang. Tawodi had gotten the back of the cabin to burn, and it was now a matter of time.

A longer time than he thought. Lawton must be trying to fight the flames and watch the front at the same time—an impossible task. The roof had not caught because of the rain, but the cabin walls were blazing and Waya could smell the burning wood. Then the cabin door swung open, and Waya saw a rifle fly out and land in the mud in front of the cabin. Then Lawton walked out, his hands in the air.

Waya stepped out from behind the outhouse and walked toward him. From the corner of his eye he saw Tawodi closing from the other side. Lawton walked straight out, and seeing the two of them, stopped and put his hands down, hunching up against the rain. Close to him, Waya could see the small, mean eyes squinting through the downpour. Lawton stood very still, without speaking.

Tawodi gazed at Lawton, his face impassive, but Waya could hear the hate in the old man's voice. "We will take you back," Tawodi said. "If you try to escape we will kill you. If the whites let you go free again, we will kill you."

Behind them the cabin roof suddenly fell in, with a great shower of sparks and a wrenching noise. Waya, involuntarily, glanced at it, and Tawodi must have also, because Lawton, facing them, lowered his head and threw himself at Tawodi. Waya looked back to see the two of them fall heavily, Tawodi twisting away and starting to rise again. But Lawton was already on his feet and Waya saw the handgun he had pulled from somewhere, saw the gun rising, knew that in the next instant his grandfather would die. The old man was between the two of them, preventing a clean shot, but there was no time to move, no time to think.

He threw up the Marlin and shot Lawton in the face.

It's not that I'm afraid, Dane, it's just that my pa will beat me if we're seen together. And it's no fun slipping around like this, hiding all the time.

No fun?

You know what I mean. Sure, this is great, but I want to go to dances and movies with somebody, not just meet in some damned old barn.

I see.

You don't see. I can tell by your voice.

Cissy, I don't know what your father is worried about. I was acquitted.

Pa says you'll have a record all your life.

I haven't done anything wrong.

Pa says you and that old man shouldn't have gone up there, that you should have left it for the law.

I'm getting sick of hearing what pa says. What do you say?

I told you, I want to go out some, and I can't go out with you without pa beating me. Unless.

Unless what?

Unless we get married. He'd have to go along with it then. If we were married— Where are you going?

Good-bye, Cissy.

Oh, God. Just like that. Aren't you even going to kiss me?

No.

Starlight was married in June, on a day of high, lazy clouds and a gentle wind that rustled her full dress and pushed her hair back. Waya could see her shining eyes and the way her body trembled slightly during the ceremony. She was as taut as a bowstring, but he knew she was happy.

Nathan Bird stood beside her, wearing a new suit and a black patch over his right eye. Waya watched him as he touched Starlight gently, escorting her to her place in front of the minister.

It was a wedding in the manner of the whites, something Starlight had wanted for reasons none of them could fathom.

She wore a beige dress with a darker sash and carried a bouquet of mountain flowers. Waya knew that underneath she was wearing moccasins, and that the necklace she wore was made from seeds, in the old way, before the Europeans brought glass beads to the mountains. In deference to Tawodi—they were afraid he might not attend otherwise—the wedding was held in a small glade outside of town. Waya, wearing his only suit because Starlight had wished it, stood near the wedding party, but the old man was standing under a tree on the edge of the glade. Waya thought he was pleased, nevertheless.

The others were a mixture of whites from the town, most of them miners, and full bloods who had known of Tawodi's reputation. The full bloods, down from their cabins, wore work clothing but had decorated themselves with feather necklaces. Here and there he could see high deerskin boots of the old design, and an older woman had trimmed her skirt in turkey feathers. As he looked over the people he saw several of them staring back at him, and he knew what they were thinking. He knew what they said about him, among themselves.

He looked at his mother. He had never seen her more beautiful, and perhaps she now was finished with the Lawton thing and it was behind her. He knew that for long nights afterward she had lain awake, but whether she was reliving the experience or was worrying about him he would never know. He did know what they said in the town: that his family bred killers, because now all of them—Tawodi, Starlight, and himself—had killed. He let his mind drift.

The heavy slug blew away the back of Lawton's head and the thick body jerked backward. Even as he fell Waya was working the lever of the Marlin, and then Tawodi recovered and was bending over the body. Waya walked over and looked down and felt his stomach turn over. He clenched his teeth and swallowed and forced himself to look. There were brains and blood everywhere, and the scent of death.

"... do you, Starlight, take this man, Nathan ..."

They buried Lawton where he lay, putting him in a shallow grave. Afterward, Tawodi took a tree branch and raked the spot, turning the fragments of skull into the mud. All the while they worked the rain kept

beating down, making the day darker. When Lawton was buried they
marked the head and foot of the grave with rocks, certain that the sheriff
and his men would want to dig the body up again.

"... till death do you part?"

He and his grandfather spent a wet and cold night huddled under the
shed, the last part of the cabin complex that was undamaged. It housed a
few tools, which they threw out into the rain; then they sat upright
against the wall of the shed and dozed. Sometime before morning, the old
man asked him quietly how he felt. He said he did not know.

"It is a hard thing to kill a man in such a way," Tawodi said. "But it
is harder if he kills you." And the old man had not mentioned it since.

"... man and wife. You may kiss the bride."

Then Starlight was hugging him, and Nathan had his arms
around him also, and there were people crowding around. In
the middle of the confusion Tawodi had slipped up quietly and
put his arm around Starlight and placed his hand on Nathan's
shoulder. The old man turned to him. "Tell me what you see,"
he demanded.

"Much happiness, grandfather," he said, grinning. The old
man leaned over to whisper in his ear. "And what does the wolf
in you see?"

"That my father's spirit is happy right now." He saw the
hawk eyes glittering, felt the old man's strong grip on his arm.
"I will wait at the hill cabin," Tawodi said, and then he slipped
out of the crowd.

There was a reception at the home of one of Starlight's
friends. Waya stopped by long enough to see that the young
bucks were starting an old game on the grass outside. It was
called *tsungayunyi*, a game in which makeshift spears were
thrown at a rolling disk. From the noise inside the house he
knew that some of the older men were drinking already, and he
hoped the friendly fights sure to follow would leave them relatively unhurt. He left his wedding gifts, a gold chain for Starlight and a fine pair of moccasins for Nathan Bird. He kissed
Starlight again, holding her tightly and feeling the love and
happiness in her, and she smiled at him, knowing he was about
to slip away.

Darkness found him far to the west, near a creek that had been stocked with trout. In the dusk the crows had come to sit in the trees. He built a small fire, rolled in a blanket near it, and lay watching the stars come out and shimmer through the tops of the bending trees. He thought of Tawodi and how the old man had sat in great dignity in the courtroom answering directly in a steady voice. He knew the old man had no faith in the whites' system, and somehow he had managed to convey this to judge and jury without giving them enough provocation to do anything about it. He thought of how Starlight had described what had happened in such a simple straightforward way that you could not help but believe her. His own testimony was the worst of all. He had become strangely detached and could hear the coldness in his own voice, describing the shooting as if it were something he had read about, and he could see the jurors looking at him in a kind of shock, staring at him the way they would look at a mass murderer. At first he had tried to explain too much, then lapsed into noncommittal answers, finally projecting an air of controlled coolness, almost boredom. But he was acquitted, and Starlight had not even had to stand trial for George Lawton's death. It was all over—or should have been. He wondered how long it would be before he would forget the sight of Lawton's head disappearing in the mushroom of a .44 caliber bullet. Still, the bastard had tried to rape Starlight. He watched the fire die and felt the chill of midnight.

He pulled his knees up and rolled tighter in the blanket, the Winchester beside him and the stag-handled knife under the jacket he was using as a pillow. He hoped Nathan Bird would be very good for Starlight. He slept.

I don't know, grandfather. Everything has changed.

But you will need to go on to school. To get all the learning you can must be a good thing. How could it be otherwise?

I can't afford a big college. I'd end up in a state university . . . if they'd have me.

You can write good anywhere. The state university, would it not teach you to write better?

I guess.

Then tell me what it is that bothers you. Lawton?

Yes.

If you had not acted we would not be talking here.

I know. That isn't what bothers me.

What, then?

I don't have any friends here anymore. People are avoiding me. The colleges will ask if I have any kind of trouble with the law; I'm not even sure I can get into the state university. Besides, I just don't seem to care that much now.

The Aniyunwiya respect you for what you have done.

Okay, but let's face it, we aren't in charge here anymore. Look, Tawodi, I didn't mean it that way. I just meant I have to function in a white world, too.

What do you plan to do?

I think I want to go away for a while. Not just to another place nearby. Someplace far off.

How will you do that?

I have an idea.

He enlisted as John Dane, just turned eighteen; father deceased, mother remarried; high school diploma; no mental or physical problems. He had to get a waiver from the Sheriff's Department because of his record, but the sheriff gave it willingly, happy to see him leave. He knew his record would follow him through the service, but it no longer mattered. They had taken him. Tomorrow he would board a train in Chattanooga, change trains in Dallas, and arrive finally at Camp Pendleton, in California. He hoped they would send him even farther, and it seemed to him then that the world wasn't big enough. He would come back, in time, and everything would be all right again.

Starlight had cried. Nathan shook his hand over and over, telling him how proud he was. Tawodi took him on one last foray into the mountains: they walked all the way from the ranger's tower down Dry Pond Lead to the river, then followed the river and doubled back to retrace the famous panther walk, where the panther killed a man near the knob of a mountain.

They turned north and came out of thick woods above a lake, and camped, and talked. It was a sad, happy time, and he wondered why it could not simply go on forever. But nothing ever stayed the same. He looked at Tawodi, wondering, as he had wondered before, how long the old man had to live. Tawodi was incredibly tough, but he was mortal. The old man sensed the boy's stare and turned his hawk eyes on him. He felt his grandfather looking right through him.

"When you come back," Tawodi said, "we will hunt and fish, and you will tell me about the places you have seen, and about the war."

"I don't know if I'll see the war, grandfather."

"Why wouldn't you? Who shoots better? Can the whites track better than you? No." The old man shook his head. "They will use you in the war because you are young, and good at what you do. But you must come back to us. The mountains would not be the same without the Snow-wolf."

"I will be back, grandfather. You be here."

To his surprise, the old man leaned over and hugged him.

On the day he left they gave him presents, but he left them with Starlight. He left his prized knife with Tawodi, not wanting to risk losing it. He wore the wolf's amulet, having sworn to himself never to take it off, and he carried a minimum of clothing in a small bag. Other than Starlight, Nathan, and Tawodi, no one came to see him off.

The bus came that would take him to Chattanooga. It stopped in front of them as they waited by the roadside. Starlight was crying again and Nathan was comforting her and trying to give him advice at the same time. His grandfather stood a little to the side, looking like something carved out of rock. Waya said his good-byes and got on the bus. He heard the door close behind him and the driver engage the gears. He sat by a window and looked down at them, his eyes dry but feeling his breath coming faster, hearing his heartbeat. He felt the smooth rolling of the bus and sat back in the seat, his eyes straight ahead.

It was as John Dane that he enlisted. But no matter what came to him, he would be Waya-unutsi.

Dear Family,

There is little news, here. My DI is a good man, as I have told you, and we are quickly becoming marines. The days are long but not as difficult as some of the others here think, and I am enjoying myself, which the city boys here find hard to believe. At night I can hear concerts on a classical music station, and I think I am the only one in my company to actually gain weight during this time. Grandfather, I am the top marksman in the company and we've outscored all other companies in camp, so I think I have outshot several hundred, if not several thousand, others. I owe it to you. I don't know if I mentioned it earlier, but after boot camp I am going to a special recon school to become a sort of scout, and I'm told that I may get sniper training here. I have stayed out of trouble here except for the one incident I mentioned to you, the time they wanted me to take off my amulet, as being nonuniform. It was painful, but it got straightened out and I'm still wearing it. This is strange country; there's very little game in the hills, and the desert where we sometimes train is full of snakes. I have been into town twice, but it is just another city. Things are going well. I hope this finds all of you well also.

Dane

1951-1954

He lay the carbine in the scrub brush and stretched out beside it, keeping his eyes on the terrain before him. To the right was a mine field left by the Chinese as they hurriedly pulled out. No time to plant the mines; the damned things just sat there, glinting in the sun. To the left, a slit trench. It ran from a bunker down to an observation post, beyond the OP the ground dropped off and reached across a small valley to rise again in a range of hills he estimated to be about eight hundred meters high.

Almost halfway across the valley there was a rise in the earth with a few bushes on it. Dane watched it for a few minutes, then got out the binoculars he had been issued, taking care that the sun did not reflect off the lenses. The rise was a perfect place for a sniper; it was too obvious a target for the Chinese to place mortars, but they would risk slipping a man out there at night to hole up during the day, then harass the marines the following night. It was what he would have done himself.

He pushed the carbine in front of him and wriggled a little closer to the top of the hill. He looked up at the sun; no problem there. Sky starting to become overcast. Promise of snow. A wind, born on some far flat plain in Manchuria, kicked up small dust devils in the still air of the morning. *The land of the morning calm.* He unbuttoned the top of his field jacket in spite of the cold and lay there thinking about the problem. It was very open country, but he had to get in range.

He slid his carbine back now, and worked his way backward from the crest of the hill. Protected by it, he walked around until he reached the back of the bunker and dropped into the adjacent slit trench. Keeping low, he hurried into the OP.

There was a lone marine in the OP, a large black man. He did not seem especially surprised to see Dane, and he greeted him in a soft southern accent, glancing at him diffidently and turning back to the range finder.

"I heard you was here, Dane."

Dane nodded. "What do you see out there?"

"Shit, not much. We had a recon out last night and they didn't see a damn thing." He gestured toward the range finder. "Can't see nothin' through this, can't see nothin' through the glasses, either."

"I'll take a look in a while," Dane said.

It was cozy in the OP. The big black sat on the ground, leaning against the wall of sandbags. There was enough room for Dane to sit as well. For a moment he felt like surrendering to the warmth and safety of the OP, but he knew he couldn't stay anyplace too long.

"You not all white, are you, Dane?" the black asked suddenly.

"No."

"Mexican?"

"Indian."

"What kind?"

"Aniyunwiya."

"What?"

"You know it as Cherokee."

There was a pause. "Funny, you know?"

"What?" Dane asked, stretching and shifting his position.

"You an Indian. Me a black. White officers makin' us fight a war against a bunch of Orientals."

"I guess that's funny."

"Look at this," the black said and went into an inside pocket and brought out what looked like a Christmas card. He handed it to Dane. It read:

> *Greetings from the Chinese People's Volunteers*
> *Whatever the color, race or creed.*
> *All plain folks are brothers indeed,*
> *Both you and we want life and peace.*
> *If you go home the war will cease.*

Dane laughed. "Where did you get this?"

"It was all over the place when we moved up. Shit, I don't believe nothin' they tell me. But I don't believe much of what anybody else tells me either."

"Well, I guess it's a strange war."

"Shit."

"Listen," Dane said, "I'm going to move out there on that little mound. You do me a favor?"

"Sure."

"Pass the word to all the line companies that I'm out there. No patrols till I get back, no H and I fire anywhere near the rise."

"Okay. That it?"

"Tell them I said I'll shoot anything that moves out there."

"Okay," the black said. He paused. "You kind of a hard-ass, ain't you?"

"Just tell them what I said."

He went out and down the hill to the left, using the sage grass as a cover. It was the best cover he would have, but it wasn't much. He took off his helmet and put his binoculars in it and left them both in the grass, noting the spot. He hated the helmet; it gave him headaches.

He studied the ground in front of him for a long time, then began to crawl.

An hour later. Seventy-five meters. The sky was getting darker and he thought he could smell the snow coming. He thought of Tawodi and the snow; the old man loved it, claiming it was the best time to hunt, to be alive. Well, he was alive and hunting now, but he wished he could talk to the old man again for a little while.

It is not so much they will see you, or smell you, Tawodi had said. You can learn to avoid that. They will sense your presence if you are out of place. The deer will sense that you are here. So it is the instinct that you must overcome, and to do that you must belong totally to your time and place. You must be one with the forest and the deer, one with the gun and the earth.

Another hour and he stopped. Harder now, the ground rolling away slightly. He tried to figure the elevation, whether he was moving into an area where he could be seen from higher up. Time to move quickly now. He would be seen, or he wouldn't.

He got to the bottom of the rise in a kind of low, shuffling run and lay panting and listening. It was a strange land where you couldn't hear birds, he thought. *Don't think about it now . . . belong totally to your time and place.* He had to get up on the rise a bit, near the crest, but he would work his way around it instead of going over the exposed top. He started to crawl again and stopped, something inside freezing him.

He lay still, thinking.

If a Chinese scout had the same thought he ran the risk of meeting him head-on, or having the Chinese come up behind him as he crawled. Either way he didn't like it, nor did he want to sit still and wait for a movement to either side. Finally he crawled straight up the side of the rise, rolled over on his back near the crest, and listened.

For a long time he heard nothing but the wind, and then, ever so softly, a sound like metal scraping against something, perhaps a rock. It was to the left. Head immobile, he cut his eyes to the left just in time to see the figure move below him, not twenty meters away. It was a Chinese, crawling slowly and packing a long rifle. He was so close he could see the stitching in the thick, quilted coat the Chinese was wearing.

Gently he eased the carbine into place, still lying on his back. He waited for a few seconds, wondering if the Chinese had heard him move. He looked at the Chinese again just in time to see the man's eyes come around and meet his. Before he could move, Dane fired.

The Chinese jerked violently and dropped the gun.

The shot was still echoing when another rifle fired and Dane felt the round rip through the sleeve of his field jacket.

Two of them!

He threw himself up and over the rise—nothing to lose now. Another shot kicked up the dirt at the crest and he kept rolling toward the bottom, trying to end up in a firing position. He ignored the crest, knowing the second sniper wouldn't follow him over, and started on a low run around the side of the rise.

The place seemed to explode. Rounds from automatic weapons were kicking up dust around him. His mind was a blank. He ran out of instinct and went around the side of the rise, looking for protection. He threw himself around and under the sheltering earth of the other side, only to see the second Chinese, facing the other way. Without pausing, he took a snap shot that caught the sniper high in the back and turned him around. He was still rolling when Dane shot him again.

All hell was breaking loose on the other side of the rise. Dane kept low and slithered to the Chinese he had just shot. The sniper was lying on his back, blood streaming from his mouth. He looked like a boy. Dane quickly went through his pockets and in an inside shirt pocket found a packet of folded papers. He stuffed them in his pocket. The Chinese was not wearing dogtags.

He looked up and listened. The firing had stopped abruptly, but he ruled out going back around to search the first Chinese he had killed.

Now he was conscious of the cold, and it seemed to be getting darker. He couldn't stay on the rise, because the Chinese would be looking for him there after dark. He would have to make his way back through the sage, a long and tedious route under the guns of the Chinese, but it was better than staying at the rise. No choice. He began to crawl. Soon afterward, enormous snowflakes began drifting down and he hoped for a heavy snowfall that would cover his trip back. In half an hour the visibility was no more than a few feet and he smiled to think the snow had saved him.

He passed the OP and went back to his bivouac area. The intelligence officer was Major Crawley, a burly career marine whose quick mind was hidden in a country-boy manner that he had worked hard to perfect. He was Dane's boss as far as operations were concerned. Dane trudged through the snow without stopping for a parka, and delivered the packet he had taken from the dead Chinese. The major was impressed when Dane briefed him succinctly on the recon.

Dane stood just inside the tent while the major went through the papers, looking for any quick references or identifications that might be understood and used before the packet was sent back to the translators. The tent had only one stove, but it was warm and comfortable. There was a table and two chairs and the major's cot, and a large footlocker. Someone had put a crude shade around the dangling light bulb and the lighting was softer than the glare in the command post. He felt himself growing sleepy.

The major put the packet aside and, against all regulations, began pouring whisky into two canteen cups. He handed one to Dane, who took it gratefully.

"Thank you, Major."

"Sure," the major said. "Sit down for a spell."

Dane sat in one of the two wooden chairs, unbuttoning his field jacket and crossing his legs. The major sat on his cot, leaning forward for balance and sipping the whisky with satisfaction.

"This a violation of some rule or other, Major?"

"Sure as hell is. But I have my reasons."

Dane watched him silently.

"How long you been in Korea now, son?"

"Nine months. Why?"

"That's about a tour."

"I suppose."

"You anxious to get out?"

"Not especially. I guess I don't feel much of anything right now, Major. You have a reason for asking?"

Major Crawley shifted on the cot, not looking directly at Dane. "Well," he said, "you've done a helluva job. Half the Corps knows about you, and it wouldn't surprise me if the Chicoms had a wanted poster on you in their post offices."

Dane sipped and remained silent.

"Tell me what happened out there today."

Slowly at first, Dane began to talk about his movements around the rise and the killing of the two Chinese. The major did not interrupt, but when he was finished he leaned forward and whistled softly. "You came close out there."

Dane shrugged.

"Look," the officer said, "this isn't my place at all, and God knows I have enough to do, but I want to talk to you . . . about you."

"I don't understand."

"Dane, let's relax and drink a little."

Dane set the canteen cup down carefully. Major Crawley poured more whisky into it and Dane picked it up again without speaking. It was pleasant in the tent and the whisky was having a wonderful warming effect. It wasn't as strong as the moonshine he used to drink with Tawodi, but it was good, it was good.

"Tell me about your home, Dane." the major said.

He sat back and closed his eyes, looking at a quick image of Starlight, and then Tawodi, and then Nathan Bird.

It is unlike anything you know, for it is big, wild, and untamed. My people move through it all their lives and when they die they become part of it, so that all their lives the Aniyunwiya know they are one with the forest and the earth, one with the wind and the lakes. Our souls are united with the spirits of the rocks and trees. We are the Real People. Our lives are real because we do not lie. Starlight, my mother, is a famous beauty who once killed a man, and before that had the courage to love a foreigner. My father died in battle. My grandfather is part hawk, part spirit. I my-

self am a brother to wolves. Our land is free, but the Aniyunwiya, most of them, are confined to reservations. Not my family.

Dane stopped, suddenly remembering where he was.

"Is there a reason for all this?"

"Yes," said the major. "Go on."

In the summer the land is gentle and green and there is laughter, and games. We play very rough games. There's a lot of contact and some injuries now and then. None of it in anger. We are a peace-loving people now, but once we were one of the most aggressive peoples of North America. Our sacred symbol is the eagle; only designated people could catch or kill an eagle, and the feathers were sacred, used in special ceremonies.

There's also the town, and the miners, and the tall, narrow structures above the mine shafts. The miners go thousands of feet into the ground, looking for copper. The town is ugly and the countryside around it is bare, where the smelting acid outdoors has killed all the plants and trees. In spite of that, it has a certain hard beauty.

They breed men in that part of the world.

In the winter the snow comes, deep and clean. Tawodi is my grandfather. He likes the snow, and so do I. We used to hunt in the snow. We did a lot of winter camping, which is the best kind if you know what you're doing. It is a high, clean world up there when it snows. Where, exactly? Well, it's where Tennessee and North Carolina and Georgia all run together—still Appalachia, I suppose. It's wild country sometimes. Brush so thick you can't get through it in places. Many, many lakes, built by the TVA, and lots of streams and rivers. We used to portage the Ocoee. Have I told you about Tawodi?

"You're falling asleep," the major said.

Dane looked up. "Sorry. It's because it's warm in here. What's this all about anyway?"

"Your records have finally gotten here, Dane. No wonder they wouldn't let you hand-carry them the way everybody else does."

"What do you mean, Major?"

"I think you know what I mean. The fact that you killed a man is all over your service jacket."

Dane stood. "I've hidden nothing from the marines, from

any commanding officer I've had before, or from you. Did you look at the rest of the record?"

"Yes, I did. And I have to admit, it's outstanding. It only convinces me I'm right in what I started to do before your record ever got here."

"And what's that, sir?"

"You've been in Korea too long, and doing what you do too long. I want you to take some R and R in Tokyo, when you get back we're gonna pin another stripe on you, Sergeant."

"Well. Thank you, Major."

"Pick up your orders in the morning. I don't want to see you until six days from now. And watch the firewater."

Tokyo's Ginza caught him by surprise—much larger, noiser, and more crowded than he had expected. There were neon signs everywhere, of all shapes, and music blasting from speakers mounted on the streetlight poles. The music was either full of tones he hadn't heard before, or was country music straight from America. He didn't like any of it. He thought the scene was exotic, but he hated having to walk down the wet, rainy streets protecting his eyes with one hand, watching out for the ribs of the sea of umbrellas that poured toward him.

He felt strange in his uniform after being in combat kit for so long, but he was glad for the raincoat. He kept to the edge of the sidewalks in an effort to avoid the crowds, but the rocketing taxis came so close he moved back to the other side, nearer the buildings. When he did the doormen in the myriad nightclubs tried to coax him inside to see the strippers. He felt detached from it all. He crossed the street, but found it pretty much the same. Smell of burning charcoal. Somewhere, fish cooking in a strange sauce. From the bars he could hear an occasional American or European, knowing them by their laughter, louder than the Japanese. He wished he were back in Korea, where there was less confusion, where the real things became real again. He wasn't having a good time here. He wondered what Tawodi would think of this torrent of people sweeping toward him. The old man probably would cut and run; the thought made him grin.

He rounded a corner and came up to a park with a sign in both English and Japanese: HIBIYA PARK. He almost ran to it, an oasis of green trees and grass and shrubbery in the middle of the busy streets. Even at night he could appreciate its size and beauty, and he pulled the raincoat about him and sat on one of the wet benches, enjoying the sight of trees in the glow of the streetlights.

"Hello."

He looked up, startled that she had been able to get so close to him.

"Hello," she said again.

She was garish in the light falling from the streetlights; she was short and heavily bundled against the rain, and she was wearing a ludicrous bright pink scarf. When she smiled he could see the gold teeth the GIs all joked about.

She was smiling as she sat on the bench close to him, and when she began talking rapidly he had difficulty with the heavily accented Englilsh. Then he realized she was asking him to go home with her. She was a whore and old enough to be his mother.

He had a quick vision of Starlight reduced to this.

"Where do you live?" he asked.

"Short ride, short ride," she said.

On an impulse he stood up and reached for her arm, and she snuggled against him as they walked out of the park. They had to stand in the rain for several minutes before one of the thousands of small taxis splashed to a stop. She spoke to the driver in a staccato burst of Japanese, and the small car shot out into the traffic, weaving dangerously in the flood of cars. From the back seat Dane could see nothing but a tide of flickering lights.

It was a good twenty minutes before the taxi finally stopped. She had given up trying to make conversation, but he hardly noticed. As he paid the driver she went ahead of him through a low gate.

It looked small from the outside. Locking the gate, she hurried into the overhang from the house, but he stopped to look around. On one side there had been an attempt at a rock garden. The house itself was small and unpainted, but he liked the look of it, with its upswept corners and baked tile roof. He followed her through the doorway and she turned and smiled and bent to help him off with his shoes.

"I've never been in a Japanese house before," he said, and she looked up, pleased that he had spoken. Gesturing, she led him into a room sheltered by another door. There was an opening in the floor and a charcoal brazier glowing in a cast-iron pot. The room was warm and pleasing, more so because it was almost empty. He noticed the bedding on the floor and felt the soft tatami mat beneath his feet. "A good campsite," he told her, and she smiled again, the gold teeth very pronounced.

The room had electricity at least, for there was a small lamp burning in one corner. He saw a small alcove of some sort with a scroll hanging in it, and a jar with reeds on the floor under the scroll. The scroll itself showed a group of long-legged birds—herons, he thought—about to take off from a marsh. He studied it for a time and turned to see what she was doing.

She had folded the bed covering back and was sitting on her heels with her knees on the floor, looking at him quizzically.

"I'd like a bath," he said.

"Good," she said. "Come."

He followed her through another sliding door into a smaller room. It was dark in the room, but he sensed a large shape in the corner, and as he walked by it he saw it was a piano. Before he could ask her about it she was leading him into yet another room containing a large wooden tub.

She began to undress him and he helped her, feeling no sexual excitement at all. She sensed his mood.

He stood shivering slightly in the cool night as she began heating water and filling the tub. She paused and asked, "You like drink?" and he nodded. She went away and came back in a few minutes with a glass half full of a clear liquid. He sat on a small bench and sipped it. He liked the taste.

"What is it?"

"Vodka."

He sat with the drink and watched her fill the tub with a long wooden ladle. He began to feel warmer with the slight steam in the room, and he thought suddenly of the sweathouse, and how old Tawodi had taken him there once when he was very sick. He wondered how the old man would react to getting a bath from a Japanese whore who had a piano hidden in one room of the house. Tawodi would, of course, react with dignity.

She motioned to him and he put the glass down and got into the tub. It was fiery, but he kept his face emotionless and slid all the way into the steaming water. She watched him with approval, then motioned him out. Surprised, he got out of the tub and stood in front of her, then smiled as she began soaping him with a round, hard soap. She covered him thoroughly, then washed him off with the same wooden ladle and gestured him back into the tub. He got in gratefully and sat while she began to massage his neck. The water that had seemed scalding now felt like a comfortable old friend, and he closed his eyes.

He saw a small puff of dust on the back of the North Korean officer's uniform where his .30 caliber round had entered. The officer lurched forward and went down on one knee. His second shot entered within an inch of the first one and the officer went down on his face and lay still. When he turned him over to search him, he saw that both bullets had exited the chest, and he could see right into the man's body.

"Let's stop," he said and climbed out of the tub.

Once again they passed through the room with the piano and entered the room with the fire. He was wearing only his undershorts now, but he was comfortable enough, and he had remembered to bring the drink with him. He sat on the blankets on the floor and looked at her. She started to undress in the soft light.

"What is your name?"

"Kazuko. You?"

"Dane."

"Is hard name for Japanese. Dane."

"Kazuko, you play piano."

"Yes. I teach."

"You teach piano? But look for GIs, too."

"Yes." She lowered her eyes. "I must have money."

She was out of her clothes now, but slipped so quickly into a kimono that he hardly saw it happen. He was watching her face.

"We have not talked about money," he said.

"I like Dane-san face. No worry about you."

"Kazuko, will you play for me? Anything you like."

"I play?"

"Yes."

"You like music?"

"Very much."

She stood and pulled the kimono tighter around her and fixed it at the waist, then led him back to the other room. She left the sliding door open so that some light fell across the piano. He sat on the floor near the piano as she pulled the stool closer.

The first notes were soft and melodic, and he recognized a Mozart theme. She played with a calm authority and then with a concentration that made him believe she had forgotten him. He bowed his head and lost himself in the music.

He did not know how long she played, only that the notes leaped into the cool night and shimmered there before disappearing in the rush of yet other notes, and that he fancied he could see things in the music as well as hear them, and he thought of sounds casting shadows in the dimly lit room.

After a while she stopped and bent to look at him. Even in the dimness he could see the slight smile at the corner of her lips and the ever-so-slight bending of her thick eyebrows. At that moment she was almost beautiful, but he was still held by the purity of the music and as long as he could he wanted to hear it in his mind.

She sat quite still, watching him. After a while he said, "It was beautiful," and she stood and gave him a slight, practiced bow.

"Thank *you*, Dane-san."

They went back into the other room and looked at each other. She began to take off the kimono. She seemed hesitant. *For a whore,* he thought.

He saw the small breasts and the prominent nipples, then the body, a bit too thick and soft. Her pubic hair was coarse and black, and her legs were shorter than he imagined. As he stood before her he thought the most striking thing about her was the dark splotches of varicose veins around her ankles, and now he noticed the lines etched into her face. She must be twice his age.

And now he noticed something else. She was looking at him with an unease that was close to fright. She was afraid, and for a moment he almost misunderstood, almost went for his clothes. Then he realized she was afraid he would not take her and it went beyond the money. She wanted him to want her— for herself.

He reached down and stripped off his shorts, and she came to him at once. With both hands she gripped his penis, then suddenly bent and took it in her mouth. He felt himself beginning to swell. She left him then, got into the mass of quilts on the floor, and opened them for him. He slipped in beside her and she was over him almost at once, and he gave in to it. He was aware of her smell, a peculiar smell unlike the whites, but not offensive. She moved around under the covers and he felt a marvelous sensation, as if the very essence of himself were being pulled into some sort of mainstream, and the stream welling up within him. She turned again and her face appeared, and he felt her slide down on him, felt her mass of hair, felt her begin to move slowly, and then faster and then with a rhythm that began to match the pulsing he felt. He heard her cry out once, but he was too lost to think about it, and all at once he was bound up in a great, soaring relief that almost lifted him from the floor.

She lay on top of him and he looked down at the top of her head and her body stretched away; she still held him, her legs tight together, as if she would never surrender that vital part of him. He closed his eyes and lay still. Finally, she released him and got up. He heard her pad away, then come back. He could smell the scented towel and feel its warmth as she rubbed him clean. He thought he might sleep. He had never felt so sleepy. He slitted his eyes to see her as she came back to bed. She was wearing some thin, cotton garment, very modestly, as she got under the cover again. She was almost motherly as she pulled the quilt over his chest. He closed his eyes again. She said something in Japanese, but he didn't hear it.

When he awoke the room was glowing with morning light and he reached for the knife that he kept beside him. When he realized it wasn't there he began to think about where he was, and what had happened. He stretched under the smooth quilt and suddenly turned, but she was gone.

She was somewhere else in the house; he could hear her moving around and he thought he could hear her humming. He got up and dressed and found the bath area again. He washed his face, drying it with his hands and then shaking the wetness from them. When he passed the piano again he stopped and tried to recapture the taste of the music he had heard there, but it eluded him.

He found her straightening the quilts and smiling to herself. It was a youthful smile on a face that, he could tell in the morning light, was definitely middle-aged. He almost pitied her again, but he knew it was the worst thing he could do for her.

"*Ohayoo goziemasu,* Dane-san," she said softly.

"Good morning," he said.

"You sleep good?"

"Very good."

"*So, desuka.* I glad." She smiled at him again, and he returned it, and they both enjoyed the moment.

She served him hot tea, fish cakes, and rice, and he ate with gusto. When he found out she did not have to teach that day, he invited her for a walk and lunch somewhere. She had a better idea.

Two hours later they were somewhere on the outskirts of Tokyo in an area of tall pines and a fresh wind. He felt glorious; the press of humanity in the streets and on the electric trolleys had been almost more than he could take, but she had brought him out of the city into a green and uncrowded place, and he felt very good about her insight. In the distance he could see the walls and moat of an old castle. She said it had belonged to a prince, and now his heirs were living in it but were very poor. They sat under a tree and she told him stories of Japan.

"You must be a good piano teacher," he said.

"Yes?"

"You tell stories very well. You make learning interesting."

"I like talk *you*," she said, nodding slightly and smiling.

"Will you play for me again—the piano?"

Her eyes clouded. "I do not know, Dane-san."

"Why not?"

"I must not see you much times."

"Why not?"

"You not understand."

"I'll try."

"It very sad and Japanese. You American and not understand."

"I am only part of what you think of as American. I am first of all one of the Aniyunwiya."

"Never mind," she said. "Only Japanese understand."

"Give it a try," he said.

"Very *sabishi*—very sad, and beautiful. Girl much older than you, little Japanese whore, you make feel very good. But you cannot stay. I cannot go. If I see you much, I get very *sabishi*, maybe kill myself later. You make me ashamed what I am."

"You are a piano teacher who does what she must do."

"I am a whore, and older than you."

"Kazuko—"

"I am decided," she said and stood with an air of defiance, watching his face. He saw the determination in her eyes.

"All right," he said. "Let's go."

All the way home, she avoided his eyes. When they got out of the taxi in front of her house, he kept the taxi waiting. They stood beside the low gate and when he looked her full in the face, he saw she was crying.

"Kazuko, I want to thank you," he said and tried to press some yen into her hand. The tears were streaming down her face now, and she shook her head. All at once she bolted for the door. He turned and got back into the taxi.

The car dropped him at the Rocker Four Club, an enlisted man's bar where the prices were low and the food good and the drinks perilous. He had several, sitting by himself at the bar and trying to sort out his feelings. There was an element of rejection, which gave rise to a sardonic smile, and there was a feeling that he might have learned something in that half-light, with the music strangely sweet and compelling. But he would learn nothing here.

He headed for the door, past the tables where sergeants and petty officers were laughing, red-faced and slightly drunk. There was a band, somewhere, and a female vocalist, Japanese, trying very hard to imitate the current American star, and too much smoke in the room, and finally too much of everything— too much food, liquor, laughter. Too many people.

Dane wrote:

> *i bead a string with my illusions,*
> *placing them as carefully as any suicidal mind, unknowing,*
> *coordinates its failures.*
> *prayer beads, rounded glass, trinkets of a life—*
> *when the string breaks the beads will vanish.*

On his first day back in Korea he climbed down from a C-47 and felt the wind and dust kicking up around K-16 airstrip, across the Han River from Seoul. He caught a ride into Seoul in a Jeep driven by a fat Armenian sailor. As they crossed the long steel bridge spanning the Han they saw a body swinging from a rope around one of the higher girders. "A North Korean spy," the sailor said, but didn't elaborate. The sailor had been a gunfire spotter on the bombline and was deaf in his right ear. Dane gave up trying to talk with him.

The Jeep dropped him at the Navy-Marine Corps liaison office at the headquarters of EUSAK, the Eighth United States Army in Korea. The headquarters was in a former university, and it occurred to Dane that at last he had gotten on a college campus. A harassed sergeant endorsed his orders and said he would try to arrange transportation on to Dane's unit, now pulled back a few miles to a point near Uijonbu, in central South Korea. That night Dane slept on a cot in EUSAK's headquarters compound, enjoying the comparative luxury and the fact that he had no duty to pull until he reached his unit.

The following morning he was up early, tasting the phenomenal stillness that seemed to characterize each new day in Korea. It never lasted long, but it was distinct and pleasant. He stood outside the headquarters, back in his battle kit again, and watched the calmness of the morning come and go, and then he went for a walk through the city.

Seoul had changed hands and showed the effects of it. There were miles of nothing but rubble, and through it wandered starving children and rats. There was a grayness over the city that was only partly the color of the building stones—it was also an aura of despair, the dry-mouthed, bloated-belly look of a city ravaged by shellfire. Once, when he rounded a corner, a girl of five or six hurried up to him begging for food and carrying a younger child, as if the smaller child would bring more sympathy. When he looked at the infant, he saw that it had been dead for days. He wasn't carrying food and showed his empty hands and pockets. The little girl left him quickly, shuffling off in filthy rags to look for someone else. She carried the dead child with great tenderness. He wondered how long she would carry it.

That night he slept at EUSAK again, but he had not been able to bring himself to eat. The next morning he went to breakfast and carried most of it out with him, looking in the same area for the little girl, but not finding her. He gave the food to a couple of other young beggars, then he went back to urge the sergeant to find him a ride up to his unit; the city was sickening him.

But the countryside did not. Other marines thought Korea a hellhole; he thought it fascinating. He was captivated by the miles of relatively uncovered land, blanketed by sagelike grass and scrub trees. The trees and rocks, even the hills, had a sculptured look, a look of antiquity. The small villages were full of homes built in a square around a small courtyard for animals. The houses were simple but adequate, and when he was able to explore one, abandoned in an exchange of artillery fire, he felt right at home. It wasn't too unlike the hill cabin he and Tawodi had built.

And he was interested in the people, who seemed to him very basic and sensible compared to most Westerners he knew. He liked watching the old men in their high, conical hats and flowing robes and white beards. They could carry incredible loads in the A-frame wooden packs, and when they smoked their long pipes with the small brass bowls they projected a kind of dignity that reminded him of his grandfather. He could look beyond the savagery of the war on their lives and see that they were a cultured and artistic people.

At night he lay on the cot and thought about what was happening to him. He knew that he had to be honest with himself if he reached any conclusions that made sense at all. He wished he had Tawodi to talk with.

It seemed to him that when he went out on patrol and he knew that there were others out there, the important things became important again. His senses became acute; he thought faster and better. His moves were so coordinated with his mind that he was not conscious of thought, but of movement, instinct, and action. Combat brought its own ironies and its own despair, but as he inched closer to the possibility of death, he also moved deeper into an appreciation of life, and he was fired with the beauty and wonder of life itself. In the rear areas, surrounded by regulations and confusions, he seemed less attuned to life, and he chafed at confinement, or at being moved as one of thousands of others, from place to place. It lacked dignity, as Tawodi would say. But out of the rear and up on the line, or even in front of the line on a recon mission, all the extraneous things fell away and he became as vibrant as a darting arrow. If someone had asked him then why he kept going back into combat he could have told them: *for its clarity.*

On the third day, when he arrived at his unit, he found the Fifth Marines spread over a group of low hills with a South Korean Army division on one flank and a Canadian unit on the other. He also learned that Major Crawley had wandered out of his tent one night looking for the latrine and stepped on a mine that blew him almost in half.

Dear Folks,

If you're following the truce talks at Panmunjom, you know that things are dragging on. But not for me. The big news for me is that I'm being shipped out, due to my upcoming discharge date. I'll leave here in another ten days, probably by the time you get this. Stage through Japan. I'll be back in the States and discharged in six weeks or so. I've spent twice as much time in Korea as the average marine rifleman. For a time I seriously considered reenlisting, but they told me I'd probably end up teaching back at Pendleton, and I couldn't stand the idea of that.

I plan to come home for a while and then I might travel again. I'm considering coming back to Asia. I may go to school somewhere—I know you want that, Starlight—but I don't want to go just yet. I want to learn a little more.

First, though, I want to feel and taste and smell the mountains again. I hope, grandfather, that you're ready to walk a little and hunt a little and fish a little. Korea is strange and beautiful, but I missed the mountains. We have much to talk about.

Dane

1956

And now you are a man with two hearts, Waya-unutsi.

It would seem that way, grandfather.

Tell me.

It's not simple, grandfather. You know how I feel about the mountains. And yet . . .

Are there mountains where you were?

Of a different kind, and the people are different, and still the same. I will always feel that these mountains, this place, is my home. In my heart I will always be here . . . and there. And there are some things that seem the same. There are men there with great dignity, but there are many poor people as well. I hear a lot of stories about Asia. I want to see more, to see for myself.

The Aniyunwiya were wanderers; I can understand. But we will miss you here.

I will be back, grandfather.

Tell me about the war.

It's not something you talk about easily. If I tell people I liked being where the action was instead of in bivouac, or even back in Japan, they think I am some kind of weird killer. I don't enjoy killing. And I think wars are stupid. But there is a feeling you get, grandfather; it's like stalking a deer. You become very conscious of the sky and the wind, how glorious the day is, the feel of warm clothes, the taste of water. Everything comes down to basics and the things that are important, really, become important again. All the shit drops away to the point where living becomes a goal in itself, and every breath feels like a victory.

Go on.

Well, the best meal I ever had, before or since, came one early spring morning in Korea. We were down off the line after several weeks of little food, no baths, and lots of activity. I was asked to go over to the Navy-Marine liaison office at Eighth Army with another marine to pick up some aerial maps, and we drove over early in the morning, without breakfast, without baths. We had just pulled back the evening before, a little beat up and awfully scroungy. Anyway, we turned up at this army headquarters, and just inside the door was hot coffee and some big crackers and a pot of jam. We were invited to help ourselves. I sat on the hood of the Jeep and ate crackers and jam and drank the coffee. The morning was crisp and cool enough to make a field jacket feel good. I remember sitting there thinking I had never, in my entire life, enjoyed eating more.

What else?

There was a time when we were trapped by Chinese mortars on a hillside and there was no way out of it. We thought we were dead in the next few minutes. The Chinese never learned to use the mortars properly; they just walked them up to you, a click at a time. The last shell dropped in front of us and we waited for the next one to land in our laps. It never came, and we never knew why. They just stopped. Maybe they ran out of ammunition.

You were wearing your amulet?

Always. I tell you, Tawodi, the sixty seconds or so after we realized the mortars had stopped, that we were going to live, there was a taste of air in my lungs like nothing I had ever know. And it seemed the whole world was in my field of vision, that I could see not just distance, but time. And I think that's what was happening to me—I was seeing time in front of me, where a minute ago it was all ending, there was no time. I felt I could see over the horizon, right into the future. It's a feeling that I never would have known if I hadn't been in that time and place. It was a great piece of luck.

So now, Waya-unutsi, every day, every moment, is a gift.

Yes, a bonus.

How will you use it?

I don't know enough yet to make that decision. There are things I want to explore. Taekwondo, for one.

What is that?

Literally, the art of the hands and feet. It is a form of unarmed combat, but much more. A way of life, a form of disciplined existence. It toughens your mind as well as your body. And I want to read the Asian writers. They aren't known at all over here, but I came across some great poetry. They have a way of saying a lot in a few words. A Chinese poet named Li Po once wrote about life passing. He sat on a stream bank and watched blossoms fall into the stream and be carried away and wrote, "The peach blossom follows the moving water."

Men who make songs are very special, and much honored by the An-iyunwiya.

Yes. And there is a style of Korean poetry, the classical sijo *form—you can say it or sing it. There is an anonymous sijo that I heard once that reminded me of you, Tawodi.*

Can you say it?

Yes. It goes:

> *In the waters a reflection fell;*
> *on the bridge a priest was passing.*
> *Tell me, I asked, where are you going?*
> *He did not answer nor turn his head.*
> *But he raised his cane and pointed*
> *to a herd of white clouds passing.*

Hey-yeh!

Yes.

You have told Starlight you will go to college.

It will happen, grandfather. The government will help because I was in the war, and I will earn more. But there are schools in Asia, and I think I might consider one of them.

Waya, it seems to me we are going to lose you to that other place. Each man must find his own way. I ask you to keep the Aniyunwiya alive in your heart. And come home to us when you can. We will be here, your mountains and your family, and your memories.

PART
TWO

At the end of the train spur he had gotten a ride in an ox-cart, simply by walking alongside and repeating the name of the Uijonbu temple. After a few miles the young boy with the cart said something to him in Korean, then turned and pointed up to the hill above them. Through a gap in the hills he caught sight of a temple roof and began to walk.

It was bitter cold, and he was grateful for the parka he had saved from the war. He had seen a lot of GI clothing, especially here in central Korea. He was bareheaded but he had good boots and felt strong. The recent year of training had hardened him far beyond his expectations.

He went up through scrub brush and a few trees made grotesque by the relentless winter wind. The clouds were almost touching the earth and held the promise of snow. Then the temple loomed above him, a large, rectangular structure made of some kind of stone. It had a massive wooden door, and in front of the door hung a rope. He tugged it and heard a deep, vibrant tone from somewhere in the temple. In a few moments the door opened.

A young monk stood there in a gray robe, tied about the middle. He looked at Dane without surprise, then gestured him inside. Dane stepped through the door into a large, square courtyard and his eyes took in a jumble of structures, some of them two stories high.

"I am here to see Master Kim," he said.

The monk nodded. Dane knew he had caught only the name, Kim. He followed the monk around the corner of a structure and headed deeper into the temple complex. Around him monks were moving, some of them carrying bags of rice or other foodstuffs. They came to one of the larger structures and the monk opened the door. Dane followed him into a small anteroom. There was a wood carving of Buddha on the wall and a small pan of coals. Dane felt the warmth of the coals but stood away from them, looking curiously toward the inner room.

"You may go in," the monk said, and turned away.

Dane stepped into the room. It was at once strange and familiar. He recognized some of the devices, the stretching bar, the boxes of sand, the hanging punching bags, the boards. But this was different, too. There were weapons in the room. All about the walls there were javelins, chains, knives—and some throwing implements of an odd design. He stood there taking it in, feeling the power of the room. Only then did he look at the seated figure at the other end of the *dojang*. He bowed deeply to the sitting man, then straightened and looked at him curiously.

The man was not young, but not old. He looked to be an average size but his hair was long and he had tied it in the back with a plain white strip of cloth. The rest of his dress was the familiar white cotton *ghi*, the pants and shirt of a student of taekwondo. Around his waist was a long black cotton belt, tied in the traditional manner.

"Master Kim?"

The seated man looked at him and answered. His voice was unaccented, a low, growling sound.

"You will speak only when spoken to. You will do exactly as you are told. You will not address me or any other instructor unless you are asked to do so." He paused, and in that pause, Dane bowed again, but stayed silent.

"Sit down."

Dane sat cross-legged on the floor, aware suddenly of the force of the wind outside and of the silence in the gray room. He was a good thirty feet from the other man as he sat waiting.

After a while, the other man began: "I am Master Kim. This is the temple of the monks of Uijonbu. It has no other name, just as we have no other cause. While you are here, you will be a follower of taekwondo. If you think your black belt makes you proficient, you will find that here it is just a beginning.

"Master Song has told us that you are very good, technically, but that you lack humility. Here, we will teach you humility. Here we will teach you many things. We will help you to know what is inside of you. Do you understand?"

"Yes, Master."

"You are the only person who is not Korean who has ever been selected for this temple. Do not let that get in the way of your humility."

"Yes, Master."

"You are from the West. That makes it difficult for you to accept certain things, but you will, in time. You will learn that the hands and feet can move faster than the eye can see, and that to think a thing means to have done it, all without conscious effort. You will learn that this temple is unique; you will be taught to defend against weapons. You also will be taught to defend against other thoughts. Here you will not eat flesh. Here you will drink from the sacred spring, which produces, for us, cool water in summer, warm water in winter, as it flows inside our temple. You will learn meditation, that stillness that will allow you to refresh yourself without sleep."

Master Kim suddenly stood, like the uncoiling of a spring. Dane got to his feet and stood rigid, looking at the Master.

"Master Song has told us you are one of the best he has ever seen. He speaks of your exceptional gifts. We will see. We will push you very hard and very fast. If you break, it will be a waste. If you grow, taekwondo will spread, through you. Do you understand?"

"Yes, Master."

"Your training," Master Kim said, "already has begun."

The snows came to Korea in a sudden, violent burst. He awoke one morning and followed the monks out to the spring near the heart of the compound and dipped his bowl into the flowing water. The spring that had been providing him with cool water now was a hot spring, with steam coming from it. He looked it over carefully, trying to understand, but finding nothing about changed. When he looked up, he saw Master Kim watching him, his eyes unreadable.

A week later, he was instructed to begin his training, and was introduced to several instructors to whom he showed great deference. But to his dismay they started him with the First Form. He was back at the beginning again, but did as he was told.

In a few weeks he had progressed, covering ground he knew very well but not feeling any sense of challenge. Someone else was now cleaning the *dojang*. In another month he came under the tutelage of a monk who began to talk to him of meditation.

"I believe you in the West have a mistaken idea," the monk told him. "We meditate before practice in the *dojang* to clear our minds and help us concentrate. We meditate outside the *dojang* for inner strength and spiritual refreshment. It is not mysterious at all. We are not emptying our minds, or seeing with a third eye. In taekwondo, we meditate to put our minds and bodies in harmony, nothing more. If you want to achieve that harmony, do not struggle within yourself. Let your mind take itself, and you, where it wants to go."

"I think I understand," Dane said.

"You cannot understand in the Western sense of the word," the monk answered. "You must reach a state of calmness that can be always the same or never the same. You can think about everything, or nothing. You must allow the mind to wander, or to bring it into tight control. You see, the rule is: there are no rules."

Dane's worst problem was the cold. Through the long winter the monks never wore any more clothing, and he longed for the parka in his small chest, thought often of the warm boots.

A morning came when he awoke with a strange sensation, a feeling that something would happen. All morning he looked for it, looking for trail signs, searching for indications. He was not surprised, that afternoon, when Master Kim entered the *dojang* and ordered it cleared, except for him.

They stood alone in the *dojang,* a few feet apart.

"Time to continue your training," the older man said, standing very still.

"Yes, Master," Dane said.

"Light contact," Master Kim said.

They bowed. Dane took the ready stance in front of the older man. He thought he saw the Master smile, but he could have been mistaken. In moments he knew he was facing the best man he had ever faced in the long hours in the *dojang.*

Dane tried a side kick and missed; Kim had vanished, only to turn up on the other side, aiming a punch at his chest. Dane blocked and whirled to find himself under attack. He threw a desperate down-block and turned again to see Kim going away from him. No—he was in a spectacular turn-and-kick, touching Dane lightly on the chest before spinning away to assume a blocking stance. Dane attacked with a knife-hands cut to the throat, but the Master blocked and moved again. Dane had never seen anything like it—his opponent was constantly in motion, but a motion so swift, so controlled, that it left him intimidated. In desperation he threw a middle-stance punch that Master Kim turned off easily, almost contemptuously. Dane backed off and simply stood looking at the master instructor. Then he bowed deeply from the waist.

"You may speak," Master Kim said.

"You are the best I have ever seen," Dane said. And then stood in shock as Master Kim walked over and in a friendly, even intimate gesture, put his hand on Dane's shoulder.

"My young American friend," Master Kim said, "if you decide to be serious about taekwondo, you will go unchallenged. I have watched you for months, and I am impressed. Someday the pupil will outdo the master. Master Song was right about you. You can be as good as you want to be."

In the ensuing weeks he worked harder than he had ever known he could. His mornings were spent in serious but restrained combat with other black belts, and he found that he won far more often than he lost, and that when he did lose it was because he had broken his concentration. In the afternoons, he blocked and dodged a variety of knife thrusts, learned to shatter the wooden shaft of a javelin as it was thrust at him. He became adept at using those weapons himself. He rarely saw Master Kim.

One morning he looked up and it was spring.

The Korean countryside came alive, and where the grayness had been, there was now a mantle of green and growing things, still not the lush countryside of his childhood, but beautiful all the same. It was open, rolling lands, graced by numerous small shrines; in the villages the air became redolent with the farmer's use of night soil, but the odor also held the promise of growth, and enough food. The ox-carts were on the road again, and the old men with their conical hats and long pipes and their great dignity. The young people, dressed in new spring clothes, had come alive with the ending of the war and were out on the roads calling to each other. Dane eyed the girls with appreciation and thought it was true what he had heard: Korean girls have the greatest complexions in the world.

On a morning so fresh it seemed to crackle, Master Kim sent for him.

"It is time for you to leave us," he began, pausing, but Dane remained silent, watching him.

"You are the first of several men of the West to be trained in this temple. You are as good, or better, than any one of us, or any one that I have seen. To keep you here as an instructor is a great temptation, but to have you leave is better for the world's understanding of taekwondo. You may speak."

"What is it that I can do?" Dane asked, anticipating the answer.

"There is a great misconception about taekwondo. It is our

intent to send out instructors from this temple to teach, because from this temple will pour the spiritual qualities that are necessary for the true student, not simply the physical qualities. Because you are a Westerner you will be able to teach others from the West. It is our hope you will devote your life, or a great deal of it, to the teaching of taekwondo."

Dane had prepared his answer. "The movement, and the things I have learned in the temple, will be with me always, and will be an important part of my life. If I can convey this to others I will do so."

"It is enough," Master Kim said. "You will leave tonight."

He packed in the late afternoon, a simple procedure because he had so little to pack. He walked across the compound and drank for a last time at the strange spring. It was, with the coming of spring, ice cold.

He said good-bye to the monks he knew, and walked through the wooden door and down the hill. Partway down he looked back and saw Master Kim standing outside the temple. It was difficult to see his face in the quickening dusk, but he knew that stance, the way he held his body. He turned and bowed and when he looked up, Master Kim was bowing as well. Dane turned away and went down the hill. When he reached the road he looked back, but the temple had merged with the darkness.

1957–1962

*T*he door to the house was unlocked as usual, and it irritated him. He walked through it still in his ghi, as always grateful that he had found a place to rent so near the dojang. But he wished she would keep the house locked; there were enough thieves about.

"Is that you?" she called. The soft English accent. The vision of her long blond hair on the pillow.

"Come on up," she said, not waiting for an answer.

He went up the stairs and entered the bedroom. She was lying on the bed in a pair of bikini panties, listening to some kind of rock music. He hated rock music.

"You smell awful," she said. "Why don't you get out of those smelly clothes?"

"That's not the worst smell around," he said.

"I just smoked a joint, what's the big deal?"

"I hate it and you know it. And that damned music, too."

"You act like you're a hundred years old."

"Look," he said, sitting on the edge of the bed. She immediately moved to the other side, wrinkling her nose in mock disgust. He was struck, as always, by her raw sexuality and her undeniable beauty, by the passions she aroused and her eagerness to assuage those passions. She looked at him now, half mocking, half defiant, her gray eyes glittering, the blond hair spilling down over one shoulder and onto her large breasts.

"Look, I'm trying to understand you. You must try to understand me. I don't do things to my mind and body for the hell of it, and I don't like you doing it."

"A joint, a joint. Why do you carry on about nothing? It's nothing."

She turned from him in disgust and reached for the record player. She turned the volume even higher. He rolled off the bed and went into the bathroom and dropped the ghi on the floor. He looked at his watch. Yes, still time to shower and beat the water restriction.

He got into the shower and turned on the cold water and let the water wash away the Hong Kong heat and humidity. He knew he was lucky to be living here at Mid-levels, away from the unbearable heat of downtown, and not yet into the mists that hung around the Peak. It was a good place, near the dojang, and he was pleased to be instructing there. I should be happy, he thought. I have seen so much, learned so much. But there's always more.

He heard her padding across the bedroom, heard her kick the discarded ghi out of the way, then felt her hands on him as she entered the shower. She put her arms around him and started rubbing her pelvis across his backside. She had taken her panties off.

"The water's going to stop any minute," he said. Without speaking she dropped her hands from his chest and closed them around his groin, and in spite of his mood he felt himself stiffening. As he turned she raised one leg and locked it around him, giving him access, and he took it. Balancing in the small shower he began to move, and she joined him, and as he felt himself shooting and shooting he saw her face transform, eyes closed, lips drawn in a wide smile, and in her throat there was a soft growl.

She washed them both, and just in time, for Hong Kong's precious water supply stopped, to be turned on again later in the day.

"That was nice, darling," she said. "Aren't you glad I'm so good to you?"

"I need a towel."

"Don't be grumpy, darling. I won't smoke any more today. I promise."

They lay in the large bed with the ceiling fan turning slowly. Soon they would get air conditioning, something she wanted badly.

"What's happening in town? I don't get out that much. Are there any more riots? Those bastard communists."

"Yes," he said, "those bastard communists."

"Are you going back to the dojang today? We could take the ferry over to Kowloon and have lunch. There's a new restaurant on Nathan Road, an Italian place. Or you could take me to the Peninsula."

He propped up on one elbow. "Listen, I'm thinking of going away for a while. I have a job offer. It's interesting and I'm thinking about it seriously. I was going to talk with you later."

"What job? How long would you be gone?"

"I don't know exactly."

"Well, where is it?"

"I'm afraid I can't tell you. You'll simply have to try to understand. It's probably a matter of a week or two, maybe slightly longer. I really don't know for sure."

She looked at him stonily. "And you can't take me, of course."

"No, I can't. You wouldn't like it anyway. You'd be homesick for Hong Kong in a matter of hours."

She got out of bed and put on a nightshirt and sat in a wicker chair in one corner of the bedroom, staring at him. "How did you get this marvelous job?"

"One of my students."

"I see. Some filthy Chinese beggar offers you a job you won't tell me about, and you're going off for months. What am I supposed to do while you're gone?"

"It's your own fault. I've tried to get you interested in a lot of things. You don't seem to care. You could have your own life here, with me, but a life of your own."

"Some bloody Chinese, some bloody asshole Chinese, and you're going. What are you going to be doing? You don't know anything but taekwondo. Oh, yes, I almost forgot—your absolutely boring, boring, bloody courses at the university. What are you going to do about that? You might miss your marvelous graduation."

"I've worked it out," he said.

"Oh, God," she said, and put her head in her hands. "I knew you would leave someday." She began to cry.

"It won't work," he said calmly.

She looked up instantly. "You can be a son of a bitch when you try."

"Here we are," he said, getting up. "The happy couple. You realize it's been nothing but a fight since you moved in here? I've got a job offer and I'm taking it. Instead of trying to understand, you— What are you doing?"

"I'm about to smoke another joint, as you can bloody well see and if you don't like it you can bloody well bugger off."

"I'll help you pack," he said, pulling on a pair of pants.

"What?" She looked up, shocked.

"I've had it. Get your things together."

"You bloody bastard. You—"

He reached over and put his hand over her mouth. She tried to hit him and felt herself caught in a vise; she hadn't seen him move. When she looked up, frightened, his eyes had gone dark, and she became truly afraid.

"You still have a checking account at the Bank of East Asia. The last time I put any money in it you had about twelve thousand Hong Kong dollars, enough to get you started again here or take you home to London. Your choice. I want you out of here as soon as possible. Do you understand?"

She nodded, eyes wide.

He released her and she took an involuntary step back, rubbing her wrists. She watched him put on a shirt and sandals. "Get your things together. Your clothes. And especially those damned records." His voice was low, but angry.

"How can you just—"

He stood up suddenly and again she stepped back.

"I'll be back this evening. Don't be here."

He left her standing in the bedroom and walked down the stairs and outside the apartment. He breathed deeply; it had to happen sometime. He had seen it coming for several weeks. The growing incompatibility. Her marijuana. His long hours, first at the dojang, then at the University of Hong Kong. He had promised Starlight he would finish college, and it was also something he had wanted for himself. But it took time, and he knew they were growing apart. She was still the most beautiful woman he had ever seen, still enticing with her accent and her eyes and her in-

credible body. But the price was too high. There were things he wanted to do, had to do. And he was bitterly opposed to drugs; he had seen what they could do.

If it had to happen, this probably was the best time. The job he had taken was very secret and very dangerous. There was always the possibility he would not return to Hong Kong.

He went to his lawyer's office on Connaught Road. He was there for more than an hour. Back at the dojang *he gave careful instructions to his assistant, a tough young Korean. While most people in Hong Kong were having cocktails, he was interviewing a housekeeper, an amah, telling her how he wanted the apartment kept. The semester had ended at the university, so there were no problems there. He felt ready.*

When he went back to the apartment, she was gone. The furniture was scarred and the upholstery of the couch torn. The mattress on the bed had been slashed. The mirror in the bathroom was broken and his record player smashed. How could he have been so wrong about a woman?

He placed a telephone call to the dojang; *his assistant would replace the furniture and fix the damage. The thing that really annoyed him, though, was the lingering scent of the marijuana. She had left some burning in an ash tray, a final defiance.*

He packed and caught a taxi to the Star Ferry landing, Central. From the ferry the lights of the ships in the harbor had never seemed so bright, and when he looked back at the island he felt a familiar thrill. It was really one hell of a place.

He took another taxi out to Kai Tak Airport for the flight to Bangkok. He had put the knife in his shaving kit and so went easily through Customs. A small Chinese girl in a neat white uniform stamped his passport and he went into the lounge. In another half hour he was boarding a Pan American flight.

He sat in the first-class compartment, sipping an American champagne and watching, with approval, the long-legged American stewardesses. He thought about the girl. A waste. A pity. He thought about his work in the dojang, *and of Master Kim and Master Song. He wondered what Tawodi would think of his life now, if the old man would understand. Then he grinned; the old man was full of surprises, and few things shocked him. All he would want of Waya-unutsi would be that he would keep his dignity. Little else mattered.*

He sat back and tried to sleep. In a few hours he would be in Indo-
china. He wondered what it would be like. After a while, sleep eluding
him, he sat quietly in the seat, meditating. Afterward he felt much better
and he sat back, refreshed, and asked for a cup of coffee, and watched the
sun throwing wild colors all over clouds that were gathering over the
South China Sea.

Bernier sat in the lobby of the Hotel Asie and contemplated
his future with great satisfaction. The situation in Vientiane
could not have been more muddled, that is to say, more to his
liking. He lifted a glass of excellent beaujolais, noting the body,
the bouquet, the presence of the wine. He looked about him;
who could be more fortunate?

Out there, somewhere in the bush, the busy little communists were scheming. Souphanouvong was very active; plots
were thickening, great decisions being made. Out there too
were the rightists and the neutralists, the Souvanna Phoumas
and the Phoumi Nosavans. Somewhere out there, the American Central Intelligence Agency was running its airline, Air
America, with its black, unmarked aircraft and helicopters.
Somewhere out there in the incredibly tangled bush of Laos, in
the highland occupied by the fierce little Meo, loyalties were
wavering, men were being bought. And that was, Bernier
knew, exclusive of the very private situations, the opium con-
siderations, the vendettas, the family feuds.

He crossed his legs and poured more wine and sat back to pe-
ruse it all, very happy in its complications, for the more involved the situation, the more opportunity for profit.
Calamitous times called for decisive actions. Uncertain loyalties meant that one could shift sides without fear of retribution,
especially if one was careful.

The lobby of the Asie was a landfall in that great sea of jungle and river and hardscrabble farm that was Indochina. It was
managed by a French expatriate, which meant the bedding
was full of ticks but the dining room was as good as anything in
the Orient. It meant the sanitation left a few things to be desired, but that no one looked twice at the *jeune filles* who
trooped upstairs with the clientele. And what beauties they

were! French and Lao, a devastating mixture of sex and innocence. And there were so many of them.

The lobby had a high ceiling and wicker furniture, and a long bar at which correspondents were prone to congregate. It also had one of the four telephones in Laos, and in a great burst of sensibility, they were all connected with each other and none of them went outside the country. The real beauty of the Asie was that all of the business done in Laos was done in this little world, at these small tables. Bernier, who had lived in Laos longer than anyone he knew, had made the lobby his headquarters, his milieu, his domain. Others came and went— pilots, correspondents, opium runners, the occasional drug-riddled and bearded young expatriate—but Bernier stayed on, conducting his business with Gallic insouciance. He loved every moment of it. Negotiating with the fanatics, bargaining with those who had information to sell, double-crossing anyone who was stupid enough to leave themselves vulnerable, earning enough *kip* to keep him more than satisfied, Bernier was an institution, mistrusted by all, needed by all. He was a small, sophisticated man with wavy black hair and a languid air; it was his aura of boredom that first annoyed, then lulled the unsuspecting into his web. Bernier was not an actor playing a role—the blasé mannerisms were real, but not an overriding factor, for in Bernier's heart he was an enthusiastic schemer, an intriguer of the highest order. He was proud of his convoluted involvements in the land and its people, and he knew how fortunate he was. Probably at no other time and in no other place was there such an opportunity for enterprise.

And any moment now part of his latest innovative scheme would file through that door, out of the hot afternoon sun. There would be four of them, four of them recruited by his friends for a difficult and dangerous task.

Bernier knew the moment they had assembled in Nong Khai, just across the Mekong River in northeastern Thailand. They would have crossed the Mekong by now and be en route from the opposite river landing. They would be packed in a small taxi, sweating and swearing at the heat, and perhaps mistrusting each other.

"Monsieur Bernier," the barman called softly.

He looked up and they were there. He stood.

The four men filled the center of the small lobby. He knew them from their dossiers. He wondered which could be the most dangerous.

"Gentlemen," he called. *"Je suis Bernier."*

The four moved to his table and he smiled at each in turn and began to make introductions in English.

"The American, John Dane. My two English friends, Ian Clayborn and John Hensley. Ah, and my countryman, Gabriel Langé." The four sat awkwardly, watching Bernier.

"Quel vin prennent ces messieurs?" the barman asked.

"Water," Dane said.

Bernier turned to him. *"Voulez-vous de l'eau minerale?"*

"Evian is fine," Dane answered.

"A pleasant surprise to know you speak French, my friend," Bernier said.

"Not really. A few words here and there."

Clayborn sat back in his wicker chair and said, *"Une bouteille de Saint-Julien,"* and Bernier smiled. Already they were starting to compete.

"Tell me about yourselves," he said, to fill in the gap.

Clayborn was the first to speak. "You've seen our files or we wouldn't be here."

Bernier said smoothly, "But I'm paying to know a little more."

Clayborn crossed his legs and folded his fingers together.

"Ian Clayborn, ex–British Army. British parachute training. British demolition school. Worked in Africa, early on. Assumed rank of captain, seconded to the African Scouts. Wounded twice. A knack for languages." Bernier watched him talk, a tall, fair-haired, vaguely upper-middle-class Englishman who also had a criminal record he wasn't mentioning. When Clayborn finished, Bernier swung his gaze to Hensley, a shorter, darker man but with an accent strikingly similar to Clayborn's. Bernier wondered idly if they had gone into the military together.

"John Hensley, ex–British Army. British demolition school. Served in the Middle East as a sapper. Some tank experience.

Taught tactics to the Arabs, until we were all thrown out. Worked as a bodyguard for various sheiks."

The barman padded up and placed the drinks on the table and turned away. For a few moments they were busy with the drinks, then Bernier turned to the Frenchman.

"Gabriel Langé, former platoon leader, French Forces, Vietnam. A long time in Asia, *messieurs*. I prefer mangos to melons, and a single Asian girl to a roomful of European whores. Fluent in a few hill dialects, and Vietnamese. Also English."

They all turned to look at Dane.

"John Dane," he said. "Ex-marine."

In the silence that followed, Dane sipped his Evian and then sat back, waiting for the challenge that never came. Instead, Bernier was rubbing his fingertips together in front of his face and smiling slightly.

"Let us proceed," he said. Gesturing to the barman, Bernier got out of his chair and started out of the hotel, the others following.

Out in the blinding sun Dane squinted and looked up and down the street. Vientiane was in a building boom. Workers were scrambling over a hugh stone war memorial at one end of the street. The movement was covered in a maze of bamboo scaffolding. Other workers were widening the open sewers alongside one of the side streets, and Dane could see, farther on, a single truck in which there appeared to be at least a dozen men with scarves tied around their heads, but the truck was simply parked, the men just sitting there. Dane shifted his small bag to his left hand and followed the others.

Bernier led them to a room on a side street near the hotel. As they approached a young woman came out of the shade in front of the small flat. Bernier waved her away and said something in a harsh voice. As she walked past, Dane saw that she was very young and quite pretty, but she walked with the plodding step of the rice farmer.

Inside the apartment, Dane blinked several times before becoming accustomed to the shade. Bernier seemed to have adjusted immediately, for he walked quickly to a corner of the room and unlocked a chest. He brought a map back and placed it on the small table that stood in the center of the room. The four men gathered around him.

Bernier unfolded the map and spread it on the table. It was in French, obviously a French Army engineering map. Dane could see that the focus of it was on an area near the China border, a sector that appeared very hilly from the contour lines of the map. Bernier smoothed out some of the wrinkles of the map.

"To begin, *messieurs*. What you are going to do for me is take a number of men to this area"—he tapped the map—"and kidnap, for me, a high-ranking communist political and military leader from China, who makes frequent visits here."

No one spoke. Bernier raised his eyebrows. "Is it so simple, then?"

"We'll want to know a bit more," Clayborn said.

"You will leave here at night in a truck, carrying arms that I have readied for you. On the outskirts of Luang Prabang you will shift to another truck and also pick up the men you will take with you."

"How many men?" Dane asked.

"A dozen. You will, of course, rely on surprise to take the target, not on superior manpower."

"You must have him alive, I suppose," Hensley said.

"By all means. It is the single most important consideration. You may sacrifice whatever it is necessary to sacrifice, but bring me the general."

"General?" Dane asked.

"General Lam Kwai-sin. He commands the military sector just across the border, but he is frequently in Laos."

"Why?" Dane asked.

Bernier grinned. "He is a living example that the communes do not work. Our General Lam is engaged in an old capitalistic enterprise. He is busily ordering more materiel and supplies than he can possibly use, to support troops who exist only on paper, and he is taking the surplus into Laos and selling it."

"There are a hundred other questions," Clayborn said. "Is this the best briefing we can get, or is this merely an introduction?"

"Check into the hotel now and get some sleep. After dinner, return here and I'll tell you the rest. By midnight tonight you will be on your way."

"And payment?" asked Hensley.

"Half tonight, half when you bring me the general."

"What do you intend to do with him?" Dane asked.

"Sell him." Bernier grinned again. "To the Americans."

The night brought darkness but no relief from the heat. In the headlights of the battered truck the insects died in a final, rapturous surrender. Dane could hear noises in the night that he could not identify. He felt uncomfortable in the truck, and vulnerable.

Instead of sleeping in the afternoon as the others had done, he had wandered about the streets of Vientiane. In the celebrated White Rose whorehouse, a block from the Hotel Asie, he had stopped for a drink and sat watching the traffic, an incredible assortment of young and old men, pursuing demons and dreams in backwater ports and malaria-ridden interiors. He thought of Conrad's *Heart of Darkness*. He thought of Tawodi and vowed to go home for a visit when this was over. He watched the young whores and the old men wasted by opium, sailors far from seaports, and healthy young Americans, their very youth and vigor calling attention to themselves when they obviously wanted to avoid it. Was it necessary to have so many spies in this small, forgotten, unimportant part of the world? He watched the French planters, exiled now from Cochin and Tonkin and Annam, hoping to recoup in Laos what they had lost, probably forever. He watched a procession of saffron-robed priests en route to a funeral, riding carts, all drinking Coca-Colas, and one of them snapping his picture as the procession went by. He wandered into an enormous bookstore, surprised to find most of the volumes in English instead of French. He stood outside a Buddhist temple and watched a beggar, his own legs horribly deformed, grasp for the legs of passersby. He saw two incredibly beautiful young women, mixtures of French and Lao, wearing white dresses and giggling and talking under a frieze on which was the three-headed elephant that symbolized Laos, the storied land of elephants. He noted the feces in the open sewers, noted the incredible artistry of the temple carvings, and tried to sort out his feelings. He was not surprised to find that he had an immediate and enormous empathy for it all. It had been building in him for some time, the pull of the old, barbaric, splendid, murderous, opulent, mythic, and mystic Orient.

He shook his head and went back to the hotel to pack again, a matter of ten minutes at most.

Now, in a night so black that he could not distinguish the end of the tree line and the beginning of the sky, he rode north on a semblance of a road, squeezed into the cab of one of the trucks with Langé and a silent Lao driver. The two Englishmen were in the other truck. They had ridden in silence for a while, Langé dozing, Dane thinking about Bernier's briefing. It had been complete and professional. He had told them how and where to pick up the dozen men on a side road out of Luang Prabang, had given them a map location in which to hide during the following day, and where to pick up the road on to the north the following night. The Frenchman had offered them a rather extensive choice of weapons and Dane had picked the ones he knew most about, a carbine with a banana clip and the standard U.S. Army-issue .45 caliber handgun. They were not the most exotic weapons Bernier stocked, but they were reliable.

It occurred to him that almost nothing else was reliable, they had only Bernier's word for the presence and location of the trucks and troops. It was General Lam's pattern to be in Laos at this time, but no one could verify he was actually there. Bernier indicated he had only a verbal agreement with the American Central Intelligence Agency that they would be interested in a Chinese general. And they were committed to a strategy that, if it didn't work, left them very few options. The actual taking of the general would be up to them, Bernier sid loftily; he would put them on the scene with the required number of men, and then get them all back to a prearranged drop point northwest of Vientiane. If they failed to take the general—well, there were possibilities of unpleasant consequences, not the least of which would be forfeiture of the remainder of their pay.

Dane had been thinking about the operation for several miles. The truck bounced and jostled over a road that seemed not to bother the driver, and Langé went back to sleep after every hard bounce. Finally Dane nudged him awake.

"Langé, I want to talk to you."

"Ah," Langé said, looking at him sleepily, "you *have* got a tongue."

"There are things I don't like about this."

"So? You want to catch the next flight home?"

"No. I want to know what you know about the political situation here. Not in depth, just a quick look."

"Why?" Langé demanded, searching now in his kit for something to drink.

"For my own reasons. What can you tell me?"

Langé took a pull on a flask and Dane could smell the cognac. He offered it to Dane, who shook his head.

"Laos," Langé began. "Laos. Land of elephants. Land of plotters, too. You would think that with all the farming, the opium, the lovely whores, the festivals, this place would be too busy to care about politics. Out here are three million people and four million ideas. Most of the people are Buddhists, of course, and very religious. And gentle, a gentle people. But they get stirred up politically and seldom agree.

"Have you been here before? No? Well, much of it is inaccessible. The damned roads are awful, as you can see. There are no railroads. Airports open and close with the fortunes of the airlines. Up in the highlands are the *Meo*—they hate to be called that, but it is a word describing all of them. They would like to be known by their tribal names. A matter of pride.

"As you have seen from the maps, Laos is the high ground in the center of the Indochina peninsula. If you wanted to take it all, you would want to be strong on the high ground, *n'est-ce que pas?*

"Well, my friend. Everyone wants Laos. The Viet Minh— the Vietnamese communists—are in constant touch with the Lao communists, the Pathet Lao. I'm told those bonds are very solid. The key figure is a royal prince, Souphanouvong, very procommunist. So is a lesser-known but very powerful politician, Kaysone, who was a young firebrand under the direction of old Ho Chi Minh. They say Ho's people are now running guns to Kaysone. And that's bad news for the *other* royal prince, Souphanouvong's half brother, Souvanna Phouma. Souvanna is a neutralist—he wants everyone out of Laos and a return to the old life-styles. His personal life-style expanded a good deal while he was being educated in France, I presume."

Dane stared ahead at the torturous road. "So what is Kaysone doing with the guns?"

"He's waiting, my friend." Langé took another pull at the cognac. "Waiting. His day will come; he'll run this country someday, no matter how long it takes him to get there."

"You sound like you know him."

"Yes, I do. He's a capable, dangerous man."

"What's the Chinese involvement?" Dane asked, still bothered by something he couldn't identify.

"Well, you see, I am not sure. Bernier says it is a simple little smuggling operation, of a kind that goes on across borders all over Asia. Someone must want the general rather badly, I would say. I don't think getting him will be any big problem, but I think about getting him back."

Dane knew what he meant. The most dangerous sort of operation was returning to base along the same path you took to reach the objectives; everyone knew who and where you were and where you were going.

"Thanks, Langé, I think."

The Frenchman smiled and lowered his head again, and Dane lapsed into a semiconscious state in which he tried to roll with the bounces.

With the approach of morning they hid the trucks in a thick matting of trees, Dane scouting the area first. There were no signs of habitation, not even any trails. The drivers simply turned off the road at a point on the map and there were gigantic trees and a canopy of vines. Dane knew that no spotter aircraft would ever see them from the air.

The two Englishmen were still keeping to themselves. Dane drank a cup of tea brewed by one of the Lao truck drivers, while the rest of the Lao troops lay in the grass and fell asleep. Dane noticed no one posted sentries, perhaps not necessary, but assuming too much all the same.

It was a seemingly endless day. Dane slept as much of it as he could, ate a light lunch of rice and a piece of stringy chicken, and cleaned his weapons in the afternoon. Clayborn and Hensley spent much of the day talking between themselves, drinking tea, and sleeping. Langé, who obviously could sleep anywhere and as much as he wanted to, spent most of the day curled on his right side, snoring.

Finally Clayborn stood up and checked his watch and looked around the group. He's nervous, Dane realized suddenly. He watched Clayborn approach, followed by Hensley.

"Right," Clayborn said. "I think we should have a council of war. Plan tactics, as it were."

Dane nodded, watching him. Hensley awoke Langé and the four men squatted in a circle, Clayborn leading off simply because he had picked up a stick and was drawing in the dirt.

"Bernier said he would be here, in a hut, his car probably parked here, so I think our first move should be to surround the hut with half our force while the other half takes up positions in case the old boy has troops with him. Any disagreement?"

"Yes," Dane said quietly. "Our first move should be to immobilize the car and driver. If we miss the general here, he'll have to walk home, and we have another chance at him."

Clayborn looked at him coolly. "We won't miss him."

"So you say, Clayborn. *You* surround the hut; I'll take care of the car and driver," Dane said steadily. *Clayborn's a fool,* he thought.

"Right," Clayborn said testily. "On with it, then. We surround the hut, and take the general, if possible without any shooting. We put him in the second truck, with me guarding, and troops in the back. The first truck leads us back out in case there's firing on the road. We don't want the general damaged, do we? Dane, you can follow with the general's car, or you can ride in the back of the second truck. We need to keep a careful eye on the road behind us."

Dane nodded. *But they won't follow us down the road because they'll be expecting us to ambush it. They'll take some other road, some trail, to head us off. The danger will be ahead of us, not behind.*

"Don't forget, Clayborn, there's more than one hut in that complex, according to Bernier," Langé said. "We must not mistake, eh? Surround the wrong hut?"

"We'll hear him, I'm sure," Clayborn said.

There was talk about the optimum use of the Lao troops, with Langé assigned to give them their orders because a few of the Lao spoke French. They selected one of the truck drivers to be the leading relay and would keep him close to Langé during the operation. The start of the operation would be when Dane flicked the car's lights on and off.

Afterward Dane lay back and thought about the coming operation. He had to empty his mind now and concentrate on the events to come, bring his Korean experiences to bear, plus all that he had heard. He wore no deodorant or after-shave; it could be smelled as far as fifty to a hundred yards in the jungle. He did not smoke—smokers could be smelled easily—and nothing in his clothing would rattle or bump against anything else. The radium dial of his watch was covered. He would black his face shortly before moving in. He would flex all his joints violently before beginning, to keep a joint from cracking at a crucial moment. His weapons were ready. He was ready. He had serious doubts concerning the two Englishmen, and Langé was so casual he was either very brave and experienced, or too stupid to know what could happen to him. Dane hoped Langé would survive the night. He was beginning to like him.

With the coming night the mosquitoes swarmed and Dane could hear movements in the bush. Pigs, he guessed, too noisy to be men. They had one final, quick discussion, made sure the Lao troops were ready, then loaded onto the trucks again. Before they left, Dane went off by himself and sat down to meditate, thinking of his *dojangs* and Master Kim, and for a moment of Tawodi. Then he was stretching again, feeling refreshed and confident. Someone lit a match and called to him, and he boarded the truck. For twenty twisting miles they rode in silence, then parked the trucks off the road and formed up in two columns. They walked along the road, Dane feeling his heartbeat increasing slightly, knowing the adrenaline was flowing. He walked as a wolf would walk. He tried to think as a wolf would think.

The columns moved off the road at some point Clayborn had selected. Dane knew that the Englishman had assumed command simply because they had let him do it. Dane didn't mind the chain of command, but he wondered about Clayborn's competency. But now he was hunting as part of a pack, so when Langé dropped back, motioned to the left, and stepped off into the bush, Dane waited a heartbeat, then followed. Langé was moving very quietly for his size. Behind him, Dane could hear some of the Lao troops, spread nicely in a semicircle they now started to tighten.

He saw the car, an old French Citroën. The driver was sitting on the hood, smoking a cigarette. With Langé beside him, Dane lay and watched. After a while he could make out the complex of huts, and now his eyes made out the larger hut with a candle burning inside. He thought he could hear voices. He touched Langé and whispered, "Let's move up."

They tightened the circle again, crawling through the brush, passing over soft and smelly earth and leaves. Dane hoped there were no snakes. He was pleased with the quietness in which they were able to get closer.

Now he could see the huts quite clearly, some with candles burning in them. He counted six huts and some sort of a bunker, probably ammunition storage. He saw no movement in the camp, but heard voices from several of the huts. He waited.

The driver of the car finished his cigarette and walked around the car. He opened the door and lay down on his back on the front seat, his head near the steering wheel. Dane knew the driver would try to sleep then. He turned to Langé. "I'm going for the car," he whispered. "If it goes wrong, follow me and flick the lights."

"*Certainment,*" the Frenchman answered, and Dane turned back toward the car. He started to crawl. He was almost to the car when the place erupted.

There was a tremendous banging noise on his left and he felt the ground under him heave. He rolled with it, going to the right and coming up in a crouch and trying to get his bearing on the car. A machine gun opened up off to his right and across the camp and he heard running feet and the sudden bark of a Chinese submachine gun, a sound he had heard before in Korea. He went flat again, holding his fire and trying to make sense of the situation. His first thought was that Clayborn had committed his forces without waiting, but even Clayborn wasn't that foolish.

There seemed to be men running all around the camp now, amid the crackling of the guns and the deadly whine of ricochets. He wheeled on the car and fired at the tires, the windshield, and the engine and watched the old Citroën almost come apart. There was another blast to his left and he thought someone was looking for him, for the source of the fire, and using grenades. He quickly moved off to his right, still in a couch, trying to make sense of what was happening. When he did, he felt a sudden chill.

There were soldiers in the center of the camp, having set up a fire base and starting to return the fire of the attacking Lao troops. But there was also a ring of soldiers behind the attackers. He could hear the stuttering of the guns off in the bush. For all the firing, there seemed to be few casualties. He knew then, with certainty, that it was a classic ambush and that the general's forces were attempting to take prisoners. *But why?*

There was a noise behind him, but instead of looking back he threw himself to the right, turning as he moved. As he turned, he fired, and saw the surprised look on the face of the man who might have captured him. The man went down and back, his weapon falling to one side.

Dane started moving then, knowing he had to slide back out between the closing ranks of soldiers. He couldn't go back into the bush without getting captured, so he ran parallel to the tightening rings, looking for any opening, any break. He knew it increased his possibilities of getting hit in the crossfire, but he kept running.

He could feel his heart pounding, hear his own breath, but he was running quietly and low, trying to use the darkness that was, itself, an enemy. The firing was growing weaker on his left, stronger on his right, and he thought the outer ring of troops was moving in.

He moved to his left slightly and ran headlong into someone else in the dark. Recovering, he dropped lower to the ground and swung the carbine in a short, savage arc. He felt it connect with the man's legs, felt the man fall heavily in front of him. With an almost unbroken motion Dane swung the carbine again and felt it slam against the man's head. He stood in a crouch again and looked around. Then he started jogging, using the hut with the candle as a bearing. From what he could see he had moved almost all the way around the back of the camp.

He began to edge toward the bush again, still in motion. All at once there seemed to be a concentration of men there, so he turned back toward the camp. What he saw then caused him to pause.

Unless it was a shadow, a trick of the darkness and light, there was a shallow ditch running near the back of the main hut, and the ditch seemed to be unoccupied. There were stabs of light in the darkness behind it, and again on the other side, where positions had been set up, but the ditch was empty. He hoped. He turned and leaped into it, and with the carbine in his right hand, began to crawl.

The firing had intensified and he heard a grenade again. Something about the fire fight bothered him and then he realized he had seen no one hit, and he was sure now that the soldiers guarding the camp, guarding the general, had been told to take as many prisoners as possible.

He scurried on through the ditch, hearing the singing of rounds above him but no longer particularly worried about getting hit; his fear now was getting caught. But if he could reach the hut, hide in it somewhere, they would never look for him there.

He estimated he was now halfway and he risked a look at his watch. Another hour or so before dawn. He put his head down and kept going, glad that the ground was as soft as it was.

Above him the firing continued.

He reached a point where he could make out a large bulk in

the darkness. It was the corner of the hut, not more than ten meters away. He crawled out of the ditch and went for it, still in a crawl. When he had gotten to the point where he could almost touch the hut he got up on his hands and knees and started to look around. It was then that someone pounced on him.

He went down with a grunt, feeling the man's knees in his back, knowing the man would go for his throat or put a knife in him. He feinted to his left, rolled right, and felt the man adjust his weight, as Dane knew he would have to do; when he did, Dane bent, swung his arm back, and hit him hard in the crotch. The man's head snapped downward, and with the same hand Dane swung up and hit him in the face. He felt his attacker slide to the right and go down, but start up again, a recovery so quick it caught Dane by surprise. The man's hands suddenly were reaching for his throat.

Dane slid Tawodi's gift out of its sheath and as the man fell heavily on him again, he swung it viciously into his chest and held it there while the man shuddered and was still. He pulled the knife out, wiped it on the back of the dead man's shirt, and replaced it in the sheath. He lay panting for a moment, then turned and dragged himself the last few feet under the thatched overhang of the hut. He wondered if anyone had heard the struggle outside. He leaned back against the wall of the hut, listening. There was no noise from inside, and even outside the firing was beginning to slacken. He had to move quickly.

He ruled out going under the hut; they would look there. He had to hide inside somewhere, get in while it was dark, perhaps hide up in the roof. He might at least throw them off until the ambush rings dissolved, then make it back to the bush.

He looked up and saw the bamboo supports holding the thatching. If he could get up there . . .

He straightened and looked around. It was still dark enough. He slung the carbine, crouched, and jumped. His hands closed around the bamboo, and using his impetus, he swung his legs up and searched for support. His legs locked around more bamboo struts, and he slithered up and into the thatching. He was now inside the hut and his next moves had to be very deliberate. He stretched out along the bamboo supports and waited, waited for dawn, or at least a lessening of the blackness. Somewhere in the darkness below him other men were waiting. Beyond the hut, the sounds of gunfire were growing more sporadic. He hoped, again, there were no snakes.

In a half hour he was cramped. He risked some flexing of his arms and legs, trying to keep them responsive to that explosive moment that would come at some point. As he shifted slightly into a new position, the firing suddenly stopped.

The silence seemed to go on and on. He waited.

Below him there was the sound of a chair scraping on the floor. Someone coughed. A match flared to life and Dane watched as an oil lamp was lit and light suddenly flooded the room. He drew back as far as possible into the thatching, but he knew if someone looked for him there they would find him. He put his finger on the carbine and waited.

The light fell on a group of men in the room. Dane instantly picked out General Lam Kwai-sin, a small, dapper man in a general's field uniform. The general also wore a sophisticated and slightly condescending look, and with reason. Beside him the other men, all Lao, looked slovenly. Dane watched as the general fitted a cigarette into a long holder and lit it. He said something sharply in a dialect Dane did not recognize, and the men arranged themsleves in the low chairs around the table. Dane looked for weapons; there didn't seem to be any in the room, although he thought the general might be wearing one that he could not see.

The group had no sooner sat than the door burst open and a Lao soldier stepped into the room, looking worried. He stood stiffly and addressed the general, looking down at the general's feet as he talked. The general's voice had a whiplash quality as he cut short the soldier's talk. Then he barked an order and the soldier fled. A few moments later, Langé, Clayborn, and Hensley were thrust into the room, their hands tied.

Dane studied them. Hensley appeared to be wounded badly; there was a blood stain all over the upper right portion of his shirt. Langé stood very still, listening, and looked to be more annoyed than hurt. Dane could see a large bruise under his left eye. Clayborn, apparently untouched, tried to appear disinterested. It was Clayborn the general spoke to in excellent English.

"Where is the American?" he said softly.

"I'm sure I can't tell you. In the bush somewhere, I should think."

Langé stirred. "How do you know he's an American?"

The general moved to stand in front of Langé, looking up at him through the cigarette smoke. "Gabriel Langé, French Forces, Vietnam. You lived in Hue for two years, spent some time in Da Nang. You preferred the *langouste* at the old La Maisonette near the canal in Dan Nang before being transferred to Saigon and other places. You missed Dien Bien Phu because you were on sick leave, recovering"—the general smiled—"from what we call the French pox."

"That *cochon* Bernier," Langé said disgustedly.

"What?" Clayborn started. "What's that you say?"

"Only Bernier could have found out that much and told these people. Haven't you seen it yet, *monsieur?* We've been betrayed."

"But why?" Clayborn gasped.

The general turned to answer him, but at that moment Hensley fell forward onto the table, knocking the lamp over and plunging the room into darkness again. Dane used the time and confusion to move his aching muscles and flex his ankles and wrists. Then he lay quietly and waited.

They got the lamp going again and Dane could see that Hensley was still on the floor. One of the Lao soldiers bent over him, then straightened up and spoke tersely. The general replied angrily. In the light of the oil lamp Dane could see Hensley's face already taking on the waxy appearance of death.

Langé, who seemed to be more than a few steps ahead of Clayborn, turned to the general. "And then there were two, *mon general,*" he said. "Not as valuable as four."

"What are you saying?" Clayborn asked.

Langé shook his head. "I'm too thirsty to talk," he said and stood with his head bowed, a look of supreme disgust on his face.

The general barked an order and a Lao soldier began cutting Langé's bonds, then moved on to Clayborn. At a second command, a young Lao appeared with an earthen bottle and a few glasses. At the same time, two soldiers picked up Hensley and carried him out of the room. Dane heard them move out and around to the side of the house; apparently they had put Hensley's body on the narrow deck around the house and were sitting with it.

Now the group was around the table. General Lam had poured some amber-colored drink into the glasses and they were sipping it. Clayborn still appeared stunned. "What is this all about?" he asked again.

The general sipped his drink delicately. He had taken his hat off and Dane could see him more clearly. He was young for a general and seemed very self-assured.

"You see," the general said, as if lecturing a lower-school class, "the People's Republic of China tries to assist its brothers in other countries in their revolutionary struggle. We support the Pathet Lao, as you obviously are aware. In many ways. One of those ways is through the dissemination of information of varying kinds, information to the right publics."

"Propaganda," Langé said, rubbing his wrists and taking a large drink.

"Propaganda," the general agreed. "Internal and external. Through out friend Bernier we found that we could locate some white mercenaries. You are going to help us a little bit with our program."

"Doing what?" Clayborn asked sullenly.

"Clayborn," Langé said heavily, "don't be stupid all your life. They're going to use us to show the world that white mercenaries have been recruited, probably by the Americans, to fight against—let me see if I can get this right—the legitimate aspirations of the struggle of the people of Laos to overthrow the yoke of imperialism. Or something like that."

"Correct." General Lam grinned. "You will be photo-

graphed in the jungle, leading troops against the struggling
Lao people, you big white mercenaries from the West. Neocolo-
nialism should figure in there somewhere, as I'm sure it will."

"But there are only two of us left," Clayborn protested.
"Surely that's not enough."

"Because your friend is dead does not mean he cannot be
photographed, killed by the valiant Lao people as he attempted to insure their subjugation." The general took another
sip. "It will work out all right."

Dane noticed with a start that he could see much better in
the room. In a few moments there would come that quick, hard
light of Southeast Asia, and right behind it the heat.

"Yes," General Lam said again, "I think it will work out."

Langé grinned broadly. "Perhaps," he said, "perhaps not."
And he suddenly flung the table over and dived for the rifle of
the nearest Lao guard.

The room was in an uproar. Langé collided with the guard
and began wrestling for the weapon; both fell heavily to the
floor. From somewhere in his tunic General Lam produced a
pistol. Clayborn bolted for the door and slammed into two
other guards rushing in.

Dane dropped from the ceiling, carbine at the ready. Lam
fired one shot at the guard and Langé as they thrashed about
on the floor. Dane slid up behind him and pushed the muzzle
of the carbine into the general's back.

"Tell everyone to calm down, General," he said quietly.

The general didn't bother to turn around. He yelled an order
and the room got very still. Dane saw Langé getting up with
the rifle, a broad grin on his face. Clayborn too was rising,
staring at Dane and looking as if he were about to say something.

"No talk," Dane said. "I want it quiet in here or I'll start
shooting. That means you, too, Clayborn. Just shut up and listen."

In the pause that followed General Lam turned slowly,
hands in the air. He stopped in a frank appraisal, apparently
unafraid, but Dane saw a slow flush growing in the general's
neck.

"Sorry to spoil everything for you, General, but we're doing a new scenario for your films."

The general held his eye. "The American, I presume."

"Tell everyone to sit down. I want the guards' hands where I can see them. If there is any sudden movement, anywhere, I'll shoot you first. Clayborn, collect all the weapons you can find. Search the guards. Put the weapons in the far corner of the room. *Move, goddammit!*"

Dane turned to Langé. "Gabriel, sit by the door and watch the outside. If anyone starts in, let them come in and disarm them. Above all, let's keep the noise down."

"*Oui, mon ami,*" Langé said. "I knew we were all right when I saw you hanging in the rafters like some great bat." He grinned hugely.

"Sit down, General," Dane said. "Start talking. How was the connection made? Why this particular group of men?"

Slowly General Lam sank to a chair, one of the few left upright. Dane stood over him, the carbine leveled at his chest.

"Bernier was to sell us mercenaries for propaganda purposes," General Lam said. "You know that much. The fact that you're of different nationalities would be used if necessary, later on, in broadcasts in your native tongue. Eventually you would have ended in prison in China, examples of the deviousness of the West. What else do you want to know, John Dane? I don't know how or why Bernier selected you four, just that he would deliver. He has been very helpful to us in the past, in various ways."

Dane smiled thinly. "Bernier is going out of business shortly, General, and so are you."

"I think not," the general said calmly. "If you kill me here I will simply be replaced. If you try to take me back to Vientiane for whatever reasons ... well, it's a difficult trip. One of us would not make it back. As for Bernier, he is both expendable and easily replaced."

Langé walked over and began to whisper in Dane's ear. Dane listened, nodding his head. At one point a broad smile covered his face.

"Gabriel," Dane said, "right the table and pour a round of drinks. We will discuss that idea with the general in a proper atmosphere. He is a ranking officer, after all."

In a few moments Dane was across the table from General Lam. *The general is not stupid.* "We have a proposition, General," Dane said.

"I was sure you would," General Lam answered, his dark eyes locked on Dane's face. "You appear to be resourceful enough."

"As I told you, Bernier is going out of business," Dane said. "The new man in Vientiane will be Gabriel Langé. From now on, you will deal with Gabriel. There are limits to what we will do, however. If it rubs us the wrong way, ideologically speaking, you can forget it. If there is an area of mutual advantage, and enough money, we will work together in the future. Our gesture of good faith will be to let you walk out of here alive."

General Lam smiled. "The king is dead; long live the king."

"Precisely," Dane said.

"And you think we Asians are devious!"

"Yes, but I admit to learning fast."

"What will you do now?"

"We're going back to Vientiane to persuade Bernier that France is better for his health. Langé will assume his quarters, position, connections, and so forth. You can communicate with Gabriel the same way you did Bernier. We'll be happy to service your account." Dane grinned.

General Lam looked into his drink. "You are a strange man, John Dane. How do you reconcile dealing with the People's Republic of China? Aren't we sworn enemies?"

"I don't know, General. Maybe. But I make my own rules, and that's usually on a situation-by-situation basis. I hate the same things in America that I hate in China or anywhere else."

"And what would those things be?" General Lam asked, his eyes never leaving Dane's face.

"Anything that takes away my individual freedoms. Bureaucracy. Taking a lot of shit from anyone. Dishonesty. I must tell you, I fought you bastards in Korea, but there were bastards on my side as well. Look at Clayborn there. He's about to wet his pants in this situation. But he likes to throw his weight around."

"I say—" Clayborn began, but Langé said tersely, "Shut up," and he closed his mouth.

"Do we have a deal?" Dane asked the general.

Lam leaned back in his chair, his eyes amused. "What choice do I have? When I go across the border am I to tell them we bungled it? Or that we made a better deal, found a better set of partners?" He broke into laughter. "When you dropped out of that ceiling, John Dane, you dropped into a whole new life."

"It's beginning to look that way, isn't it?" Dane said pleasantly.

1963

Starlight heard a soft knock and opened the door. Her son stood there.

The tears formed immediately in her eyes and she threw her arms around him. She whispered his name, embracing him tightly. Then she stood back for a look.

He seemed taller to her and also changed in a subtle way. There were small lines around his eyes, but the eyes themselves were calm and confident. He seemed self-assured, without saying a word.

"You're too thin," she said, and he laughed and stepped inside.

It was more than a cabin now. Nathan had made many changes, all for the better. He noted the improvements, and the happiness that his mother seemed to project, and he was glad again for the marriage.

"I'm happy to be home again, Starlight," he said. "Where is Tawodi?"

"At the hill cabin. Let me get you some food."

He laughed again.

"I will find Tawodi and eat later."

"He will find you," she said. "He will know you are here."

"Maybe," Dane said.

"Let me tell you about him before he comes. He has not changed in many ways; you will see the same man. A little older. But he is more . . . spiritual, I guess you would say. He sees visions. He hears things in the wind."

"You mean he's—"

"No," Starlight said quickly. "Who can argue with it? When he says he hears voices in the wind, maybe he does. Who am I to challenge it? I only tell you this so you can be ready for it. He talks to spirits and they talk with him, he says."

"So you think he will find me, eh?"

"Dane, I would bet you that within the next few hours he will come through the door. You will never hear him or see him come; he will just be there. So don't be surprised."

"All right."

"You have changed, my son."

"For the better, I hope."

"I don't know. You have changed and yet you are the same. Tawodi will know what to say to you."

"You're doing all right."

"I want to feed you!"

"Let's do it," Dane cried happily. "It's good to be home."

After lunch he got back in the rented car and drove through town. In that quick drive he found it depressingly the same, the same tall mine shaft towers, the same dust blowing through the streets, the old men sitting on benches in front of the stores, swapping lies. There was an impoverished air about the town that made him want to get into the woods quickly. But he stopped in the store at Postelle Station and greeted Nathan Bird, a greeting filled with genuine warmth. Nathan told him things were going well. The store was prospering, the future bright. The killing of the Lawtons was still remembered and always would be, but the feeling seemed to be now that the Lawtons probably got what they deserved. At any rate, they weren't

146

having any problems. Nathan asked Dane if he could stay for a good, long visit.

Dane returned to find Starlight at an old-fashioned sewing machine, but she put away her sewing and came to sit with him. She asked him about his life and he told her part of it. She asked him if there was a girl and he said no. She asked if he would marry someday. Probably not, he said. He saw the faint shadow of anxiety cross her face, so he tried to tell her about Asia, concentrating only on the sights and the shopping and the customs of the various people. He paused and in the silence he suddenly heard a voice calling his name.

It was a soft call and he knew it at once. He opened the door and looked out into the yard, but saw nothing. Then he caught the slight movement of what he thought first was a part of the tree line.

Tawodi stood there holding a rifle and watching him. He could see a broad grin on the old man's face, and he ran to his grandfather at once, hugging him. In his arms the old man was still hard and sinewy.

"Hey-yeh," Tawodi cried softly, "it has been too long."

"You have changed very little, grandfather," he said, meaning it. Tawodi still moved with a spring in his step. His remarkable eyes were bright and wise and calm all at the same time. The face was heavily lined but in a kind of symmetry, so that the eyes seemed to be watching from a mosaic that made him appear younger. The old man's body was as slim as a youth's. He wore an old pair of jeans and a plaid shirt with the sleeves rolled up. At his right hip was the Randall knife Waya had sent him a few years before. He also wore a new headband Starlight had made, the old one with the raven motif having worn out. Waya noticed the same design was in the new headband. For a moment he thought about the fact that his grandfather had never told him his true name, and thinking about it, smiled again. The old man was not done with being a warrior.

Waya studied his grandfather for some sign of displeasure. After all, he had been away for several years and once or twice had received scolding letters from Starlight. They did not hear from him often enough, she wrote, and he knew it was true. Tawodi seemed truly glad to see him, but the old man's first question startled him.

"Are you writing verse, Waya-unutsi?"

"No, grandfather. Not anymore."

"I thought so. It is because you live on the edge of death."

"How do you know this?" Waya asked.

"A wind came out of the west, from the place where you stay now, and told me many things. You know our ancestral home is to the east, toward sunrise. I am mistrustful of things from the west. But I listened, and I learned. Come, pack your things. We will go for a few days to the hill cabin and talk."

Starlight, too wise to protest, helped him unpack, chattering away about his expensive clothes. But he put on some of his old clothing. The shirt, though, was too tight and he selected one from his bag. He took his knife and the Winchester, a few matches, a pinch of salt, some fishhooks and line, and joined Tawodi in front of the house. The old man nodded and started walking.

For the rest of that day and into the night, they simply enjoyed each other. They talked about the woods and the season and about the hunting season to come. The hill cabin was unchanged as far as Waya could see, and the night's sleep he got on the old bunk was the best he had known in a long, long time. In the early morning he put a fat earthworm on a hook and went fishing in a backwater cove, pulling out a fine small-mouthed bass that made their breakfast. Through the middle of the day they walked in the woods, Waya suffering from a deep nostalgia, wondering why he had ever left. For the first time, he felt a sense of time rushing past. Where was the youth who had walked in these woods? Now he lived in a bright, hard, often magnificent, dangerous world, a world in which he had learned to adapt, a murderous world still with its splendors and its beauty. But far different from this.

They emerged near the cabin again and Waya could tell by the way the old man sat on the hill in front of the cabin, by the posture of his body and the look on his face, that they would talk now. He made himself comfortable near his grandfather.

"You have changed, Waya-unutsi."

"Does it show so much, grandfather?"

"You are larger. Not a big man, not small, but larger than when you were here last. You were late in getting your full growth. Now you are a man, without question. Hey-yeh, it seems a long time ago you were a boy in these woods."

"Yes, grandfather. I feel that, too. What else do you see?"

"That you are, by turn, happy and unhappy. Your life is exciting but sometimes empty. Perhaps you do not talk enough with the spirits of the place where you are."

"Fair enough," Waya said.

"The jug is in the old place. Let us drink a little and talk."

Waya got up and went into the cabin. He found the jug and brought it back outside, sitting on the ground close to Tawodi. Before them the woods were deep and green and filled with the sounds of birds. The pale sun, dropping light but not heat, was sliding toward a cloud bank that hung over the ravines and coves below them. Waya could hear the hum of bees nearby. The tensions he had felt in the past weeks seemed to be dropping away, but there was a sadness, too, a sense of the seasons coming faster, of something passing beyond his grasp.

"Talk to me of what you do," Tawodi said.

"You know what I do, grandfather. I manage a *dojang*, a training place, and teach martial arts, principally taekwondo. I have written of this to you."

"But it is not all you do. Are you wealthy, Waya-unutsi?"

"By some standards, grandfather."

"You do not have a wife." It was not a question.

"I am in no hurry. If it comes, it comes."

"Many women, though."

"Many, grandfather."

"They are as different as trees," the old man said. "Some are strong, some are rotten. No tree is like any other, no woman like any other. When you take one to wife you must be sure of her."

"Can anyone be sure?" Waya said.

"Hey-yeh," laughed the old man, "there is wisdom in the

question." Tawodi grew serious. "Now tell me what else you do."

Waya smiled. "You are as wise as always. I am a professional soldier. A mercenary."

"You have chosen a warrior's way. Not an easy life."

Waya took a pull at the jug. "No, but not bad, either."

"How did this come about? Your letters did not mention it."

"I didn't want to worry Starlight. It came about more or less by accident. I was in a place called Laos to kidnap a Chinese general. I did it, not just for the money, but because I had some idea that it was for the right cause. As it turned out we were betrayed. The man who betrayed us escaped, but I left my friend, Gabriel Langé, in his place, and we took over operations in Laos. We now do only the things we feel comfortable with, and we get paid very well."

"And what is the rightness or wrongness of this?"

"I have found," Waya said slowly, "that morality depends on what you really want. Most countries are alike; they're after their own interests. Most people, too. I found that when you sift the words and phrases out and look at what's really happening, there are great similarities in the way people and nations go about getting what they want. I try not to work for bad people no matter who they are, what country they represent. I do not work against good people. Sometimes who I consider good and bad does not agree with others, but that's their problem. I would not fight against the United States, but I tell you, grandfather, I feel no great love or loyalty for the nation that crushed the Aniyunwiya."

"Hey-yeh," said Tawodi. "You still hate hard."

"When I work it is not just for the money, but also because I can use my skills and training. Because I do not want a boring job. Because I can travel, and because it gives some meaning to my life."

"And in doing this, you are happy? You will do this with your life?"

"Laos was a kind of beginning, although I think I was being led in this direction. I believe it is what I will do until I am too old."

"When you were very young you hated hard. Once you wanted to kill your father before you knew the Dane's story. Later you were forced to kill Lawton, to save our lives. I believe these things may have set you on this path."

"Does Tawodi the Hawk disapprove?"

The old man stared, unblinking, at the forest. "I would disapprove only if you enjoyed killing. The hunt itself, the chase, the using of your skills against another—these things are in the blood of every Aniyunwiya hunter. How could I disapprove? But I think it is wise not to tell Starlight. She will worry."

"I agree," Waya said.

They sat in silence for a time, passing the jug back and forth.

"I have heard what you told me," the old man said suddenly. "I think there is something else. I think it is this: that a man, if he is true to himself, probably does in life the thing that he is best at."

Waya thought. "You are right, as usual."

"And because you are doing what you do best, you will be misunderstood by others, who cannot or will not do the same."

"Yes," Waya said. "It happens."

They were silent for a time.

"How long will you stay?"

"A while, grandfather."

"Will you be here for deer season?"

"No, not that long."

The sun dropped swiftly behind a cloud and the shadows disappeared in a kind of blue light. A sudden breeze came from the valley below and they could smell the scent of the woods, an odor of mystery, a kind of musk.

"It may be when you return, Waya-unutsi, that I will not be here. No—hear me. All things die. I have told Starlight that at the time of my death I am to be burned and my ashes thrown into the wind from some mountaintop. My spirit will be gone, but my ashes will be a part of the earth of the Aniyunwiya. Do you still wear the wolf amulet? Good! And the knife I gave you on your name day? Ah, good. When I am dead you will have this cabin and the Savage and the good Randall knife, which I have treasured. You also will have a memory. As long as I am alive in your memory, my spirit will be happy. It may be at the time of your own death our spirits will join. It may be someone will have a memory of you."

"I hear you, Tawodi."

"It may be that your ashes will be thrown elsewhere, if you are killed in some strange place. You must remember to talk with the spirits of that place, to placate them. They will talk for you with the One Spirit who guides the lives of the Aniyun-wiya, and of all things on the earth. One who chooses to be a warrior must be prepared to die in a strange place."

"I hear you, grandfather."

"If you die before me you must send your mind to me at the time of your dying. I will try to comfort you."

"It is a huge gift, grandfather. I thank you for it."

"We will try not to need it." Tawodi smiled. "But we were close at least once, not long ago."

Waya started. "How do you know that?"

Tawodi looked out at the darkening forest. "Once in the winter, I was here at the time of a deep snow. I looked out of the cabin door and saw you."

"Saw me?"

"I saw you in the snow, struggling. You were favoring your left arm and there was much blood. The snow was beating in your face and you were close to death. I told the spirits of this place who you were. I gave them your name, Snow-wolf, and suddenly the snow was behind you, pushing you onward toward the shelter of a large tree. Even though one arm was useless, you made it through the snow, and as you reached the tree I heard the long, glad howling of a wolf. Whether it came from you or from one of your brothers, I could not say. I only know that you survived. I think you survived because I saw you and spoke with the spirits, and perhaps because there was a wolf watching over you. But the snow turned and pushed you to safety. When you reached the tree I closed my eyes and offered a prayer. When I looked up you were gone. But I knew you were not dead."

Waya had stood slowly as the old man talked. He unbuttoned his shirt and slipped it off. As his grandfather finished speaking, he turned so that Tawodi could see his back.

"It was just as you said," he spoke over his shoulder. "Except it wasn't snow; it was water."

"Where did it happen, Waya, and why?" asked the old man. And as he waited for his grandson to begin the story, the old man looked without surprise at the long, dark scar across the younger man's left shoulder.

"It was in a place on the China coast, grandfather, an island the Chinese call Chinmen Tao and the rest of the world calls Quemoy . . ."

He had walked through a long tunnel to see the garrison commander, a colonel in the Chinese Nationalist Army. He reached the island on an even-numbered day, because in one of the more bizarre facets of the communist-nationalist conflict, Quemoy was shelled only on odd-numbered days. On the days of even numbers the people of Quemoy City went about their business as usual. They marketed, made love, played golf, traded, slept, quarreled, played Mah-Jongg, had babies. On odd-numbered days, they went underground, into the maze of tunnels that reached in all directions from the heart of the island.

Quemoy lay less then a mile from the communist gun batteries at Amoy, across a stretch of water that was relatively calm except for the boat traffic. Communists and nationalists alike had boat patrols all over the water, the communists looking for strays, the nationalists trying to aid the Chinese who were escaping, making the swim from Amoy to Quemoy.

When the batteries on Amoy fired, the island of Quemoy trembled. There were not enough shells fired to do widespread damage, but even a few shells in the wrong place could destroy a home, blast apart a rice crop. The tunnels were a great protection.

It was through one of the tunnels that he made his way to see the colonel, soon to be general, in command of the Quemoy garrison, the island's defenses, counterintelligence, propaganda efforts—launching propaganda balloons toward Amoy—and anything else that moved on Quemoy.

The colonel had read the orders he brought and frowned; he did not like mercenaries, he explained. Unless China solved its own problems it would always be using colonialists.

Not a colonialist, Dane had said, but a businessman. A contract with the Republic of China to develop a better program to get escaping civilians to the island instead of seeing them shot in the water, as was happening all too frequently. The colonel had spoken in broken English; Dane in broken Cantonese, which he had been studying.

In the end Dane knew he would have to go to Amoy himself and see what the organization looked like. The colonel insisted there was a foolproof system; people were killed in the water because they deviated from the system—it was not his responsibility if fools did not do as they were told. Dane knew there was no point in arguing with one of the more fundamental facts of life in Asia: all life is cheap, but my life is more important than yours.

So he had gone to Amoy in a lorcha, *lying just under the gunwales as the boat crossed at night. He sweated every meter of the crossing, but at last they were on Amoy, meeting as prearranged with a group of Chinese ready to flee. By Chinese standards they were a sorry lot, having too little money to bribe their way across. The women and children would go by boat, the men would swim. It was a fairly long swim, and the water was cold, but Dane thought they could make it. Anyway, it was the way they did it, so he would go along for the learning experience.*

They were more than halfway, the boat well ahead of them, when the Chinese patrol boat found them in the water and began shooting. The first burst of machine gun fire missed them all; the second burst brought screams and a thrashing in the water. As the firing continued, Dane moved through the swimmers, pushing them apart, forcing them to scatter.

He had turned once again for Quemoy when there was a ripping in his shoulder and a sudden searing pain. He had never known anything like it; it numbed him a moment later and he felt a nausea that he fought to control. When he looked at his shoulder all he could see was blood, being washed away by the seawater. He thought of sharks. He looked toward Quemoy, gauging the distance. The patrol boat had passed and was a hundred meters behind him, looking for stragglers. He turned his face toward the island and began to swim, feeling the strength flowing from him with every stroke.

A long time later he knew he was going to die. He was stroking with one arm, kicking as best he could, but he knew he lacked the strength to make it to the island. The water was beating in his face and seemed to be pushing him back, back, and he felt he was losing headway with every stroke. He would died here, now, in this uncaring sea. He felt a great anger.

Suddenly he heard a voice speaking his name, his true name. He looked toward the shore and saw the old man there, his eyes calm, calling to the Snow-wolf. He felt the tears stinging his eyes. Tawodi.

Then he felt the current change. The sea lifted him and pushed him toward Quemoy, hurled him toward the island so swiftly and surely he hardly had to swim. It seemed only a few moments before the island loomed before him in the growing morning light, and all at once he was near some kind of dock. He could see the great pilings before him, and he reached out with his right arm and grabbed the piling and held on, held on . . .

The island's hospital was more than adequate. In a few days he had been out again in a battered Jeep, studying the landing sites on Quemoy. He had made a detailed report on what was right and what was wrong with the system of aiding the escaping Chinese. He felt that he had fulfilled the conditions of his contract, which called for him to take a look, nothing more. Again on an even-numbered day, he flew back to Taipei. He went down to the Friends of China Club to stay overnight and catch a Viscount back to Hong Kong the following day. At the club that night he had sat in the bar, talking to the permanent guests—the Armenian poet, the American correspondent, the White Russian hooker. It was after midnight when he went to his room. In the stifling heat, staring up at the ceiling, he felt the hair on the back of his neck rise as he thought of the image of Tawodi, calling his name in the confusion, in the night, in the gunfire, in the dark blue waters of the South China Sea.

He promised to write more often. He said good-bye to Starlight and Nathan in their home. He drove again through the town, as if confirming something he was thinking. He walked again in the woods.

He said good-bye to Tawodi in the same small glade where Starlight had been married years before. His grandfather, of course, did not say good-bye. He merely hugged him and turned and walked with that surprisingly young stride into the forest and disappeared from sight. Waya turned and watched him go, feeling his heart beat faster, listening to some inner voice. When the old man stepped through the tree line there seemed to be a pause in time; he found he was holding his breath.

He drove the sixty miles to Chattanooga and turned in the car. He flew to Denver and changed planes. He flew to Honolulu and changed planes again, and a long time later he stepped down from the aircraft at Kai Tak Airport, smelling the smells of Asia, listening to the blending of sounds that struck him as vividly as the clanging of a gong. He looked off in the distance toward Lantau Island. Outside the airport complex one of the most beautiful children he had ever seen wanted to shine his shoes. He took a taxi to the Star Ferry landing, and then took a ferry over to the island, watching it rise up before him like something out of a storybook, drinking in the ambivalence, the beauty, the ruthlessness, the charm, the deviousness, the ambience of Hong Kong. He looked at the junks in the harbor, at the rusty, hunchbacked freighters. He turned toward Mid-levels and wondered if his apartment was intact. He closed his eyes and breathed in through his nose. *Here it is,* he thought, *my other uncommon home.*

1964

Ashton sat at a spartan desk in a very tidy room, staring out the window, his mind far beyond the oddly shaped trees in his line of vision. Behind him was a wall map with an acetate overlay on which he had marked in crayon the positions of his various units. Those positions occupied most of his mind, but part of it remained annoyed with the stack of papers on his battered metal desk. He loathed paper work. He had done his share of staff work, but he hated it all the same. He glanced around the room, as if seeking relief.

The room was small, but had two open windows through which he could hear the distant sound of recruits on the rifle range. Hardly recruits, though. Most of them had been in one army or another, which accounted for some of the paper work on his desk. He had assured the general that none of his troops would cause trouble here in Thailand, legal or otherwise, and there had been nothing beyond the occasional skirmish over a bar girl. But now one of his soldiers was being sought by French authorities for a killing in Marseilles a few months ago. The notice gave him no discretion, if he took it seriously, because it did not *request* the presence of the man now known as Loder—it *demanded*. What was his authority in this case? This wasn't the French bloody Foreign Legion, after all. He would have to discuss it with the general, and he hated to bring him problems of this kind when he was, literally, fighting for his own political life. Ashton had been summoned to help, not to hinder.

The other stack of papers consisted of a number of requests by foreign journalists, some of them well connected apparently. The stack grew daily and he would have to deal with it soon. Refuse them all? Grant them all? How to be selective? Would it be good for the troops, his own reputation, the government's war on the bandit armies in these hills?

He had arrived in Thailand in the dead of night on a special aircraft, having been summoned with extreme haste and secrecy from a cruise boat then anchored in the loveliest bay he had ever seen, in Bora Bora. The cruise was a gift for his wife, who had endured many long and difficult separations when he was on active service, and who had been giddy with relief at his retirement. He had left the ship in Tahiti without luggage, for his wife had locked him out of their cabin in her supreme disgust. He would make it up to her later, he had said through the locked door. He had tried to explain that the summons had given him a new lease on life, a chance to be useful again. His last few postings with Her Majesty's forces had been staff positions that smothered him in details and removed him from contact with troops. Retirement had been less a solution and more a final blow, placing him among civilians, a world removed from the thrill of soldiering.

The cable from Thailand was a reprieve; it offered him a job, and a command. His wife was unimpressed, and silent.

Armed insurgency had broken out in northeast Thailand. Bandits were everywhere and it was difficult to transit the countryside. To combat the menace, the Thai government was pulling in advisers, to be placed under the overall command of a prominent Thai general who had risen politically, only to fall again in the chaotic milieu of Thai politics. Ashton was to organize the advisers, recruit as necessary, put down the insurrection, and find out, if possible, if the communists were behind it, as everyone suspected.

Old acquaintances—a kind of working soldier's version of the old boy network—plus previous experience in Thailand had brought his name up in the barracks in Udon, then a field headquarters at Korat, and finally the army's headquarters in Bangkok.

Ashton could visualize the process, the time it must have taken, and the soul-searching. The Thais were conspicuously proud; every step leading to his hiring would have been matched against national pride. And the obvious solution had been reached. Hire advisers. Recruit mercenaries. Put a Thai general in charge, and make it a general who, if he failed, could easily be ostracized because he was not politically too well connected to cause a problem.

All right, thought Ashton, *his* mercenaries would be the finest field soldiers he could assemble, but they would not be flamboyant adventurers. They would be disciplined, tightly held, and would do their job and depart. He was not programming failure.

"Major Ashton."

He looked up from his desk, pulling his thoughts back to the moment.

"A message from the general, sir. He wants to see you at thirteen hundred." Ashton nodded his dismissal and watched the orderly depart. Much more formal than he would have demanded. The orderly was a former police officer in Leeds; no one had ever known him to smile, nor had ever seen him in a rumpled uniform.

Ashton thought about the general.

By the time he reached Thailand, Ashton had formed his own broad ideas about the organization of the mercenaries he would have to hire. Fortunately, the general had agreed, easing them both over what could have been a formidable obstacle. The general's own professionalism had prevailed, and he ac-

cepted Ashton's general organization plan because it made
sense and because it made no sense to hire an expert and not
listen to him. Ashton recalled that first meeting, in a hot, close
room with an inoperative fan—the electricity was always failing here in the north—and the bodies pressed closely over a
map on the table.

"We will build strike columns with organic artillery, engineering, and medical support," Ashton had said. "We will
make each column independent because we cannot have long
supply lines. We can't police the entire north of Thailand, so
we will strike at the bandits' vantage points. Use air drops as
the columns go deep. And rely on a lot of local intelligence."
He paused, and the general stepped into the pause. "All must
function as a part of the Royal Thai Army Counter-Insurgency
Force. My command."

"Agreed," Ashton said. "But they will be under my direct
control, General. Is that your understanding?"

The little general smiled up at him. "There is no need for
misunderstanding. I command the force, you direct the troops.
I believe that is the prime minister's perception and I believe he
made that clear to you. When you have left Thailand with
your mercenaries, the Royal Thai Army will still be here, keeping the peace. It is important to our future to establish their
presence as a force for peace and stability in this country and,
in particular, this region."

Ashton thought he might have had a mild rebuke, but he
had gotten what he wanted. His would be the guiding hand
over the mercenaries.

Recruiting had been the first problem. He called on fellow
officers, now also out of the service, for assistance. At one point
he simply ran an advertisement in several newspapers around
the world and was astonished at the results. Within six weeks
his second problem had been one of selection, not recruiting.
For weeks he had interviewed each man personally.

And there were a few men with growing reputations whom
he wanted to interview.

Some men came for the money alone; he could live with that,
if they could soldier. He devised small tests to see what they

knew, how much experience they had. And despite their experience, he organized a training program designed to accustom them to his type of command. From his questioning came the determinations of rank, pay, and jobs. He looked for specialties: bazooka men, medics, radiomen, even men with combat engineering skills. He looked for psychological quirks. He weeded out the psychopaths, the criminals.

Applicants were screened by his contacts in London and Durban, in Sydney, New York, and on the Continent. His own judgment was final and when he was unsure the questions became technical.

All other things being equal, the major extracted views of communism, which probably was the cause of the unrest here in the north.

In the end he had his mercenaries, and the training progressed with speed and discipline. From the start, some of them stood out. There were the Germans, Prien and Hartmann, disciplined and motivated and well qualified to be captains. There was the former Turkish cavalry officer, cashiered because of a gambling debt, but good enough to be a leader in any army, and now a lieutenant. The major had rejected, then changed his mind and accepted, a hard-drinking Finn because of his combat engineering experience. Loder had signed on a month ago, a loud, swaggering bully who was the most physical mercenary in camp—but an expert with any weapon and a man obviously willing and able to fight. Ashton had made him a sergeant. There was an assortment of Australians, some South Africans, a large and affable metalsmith from Glasgow, and the American.

His orderly loomed in the doorway again. "It's twelve forty-five, Major," he said.

Ashton started, looked at his watch. "So it is."

He stood, whippet-thin and straight, pulled on his beret, and smoothed out his shirt. Almost as an afterthought he pushed the requests from the journalists into his frayed briefcase and zipped it shut. He strode across the room, leaving his orderly at attention as he passed, and stepped out into the glare and the heat. He took his driver's salute and stepped up into the Land-

Rover, his mind still occupied. Should he hand Loder over to the French or fight to keep him? What to do about the journalists? Damn all paper work.

A few minutes later he was entering the general's compound. He hurried up the steps and into a high-ceilinged, whitewashed room where, miraculously, the overhead fans were working. With hardly a pause, a Thai noncom ushered him into the general's office.

The general stood up to receive him. His uniform showed no signs of wrinkles or sweat. Ashton suddenly was aware of the dark ring around the armpits of his camouflaged jacket, and of the jacket clinging wetly to his back. He came to attention and waited for the general's invitation to sit. Instead, the general walked from behind his desk and looked up at him.

"I believe the press is in touch with you?" the general asked, without preamble, in his excellent English.

"That's correct, General. I have a number of requests for interviews, and reporters wanting to go into the field with the troops."

"You've turned them down?"

"I haven't responded."

The general walked around his desk and sat down, leaving Ashton standing, a sure sign of his annoyance. The general lit a cigarette with an expensive gold lighter, then tossed the lighter carelessly onto his desk.

"I hate the damned press," the general said. "The prime minister, on the other hand, believes we can use the press to tell our story. To identify the communist menace. I think that is a mistake, but I am not the prime minister, merely a soldier." He took a long, slow pull on the cigarette and watched Ashton, standing stiffly in front of him. "What do they ask you for, precisely?" He emphasized the last word.

"They want to interview me, General," Ashton said unhappily. "They want to go into the field with the mercenaries, and they want to interview specific people in the force."

The general looked his distaste. "They have not asked to go on operations with any of our Thai forces, engaged in the same operations? To interview any of *our* leadership?"

162

"Regrettably, General, they have not."

"I see," the general said and let the silence hang.

After a while he gestured for Ashton to sit in the wicker chair facing his desk. Ashton sat stiffly and waited. The general extinguished his cigarette and lit another.

"Just how good are the mercenaries at this point?" the general demanded. Ashton knew it was not a casual question.

"I don't know yet," Ashton said truthfully. "Individually, rather good. As units, we'll have to wait and see, I'm afraid." In the next few seconds he listened to the soft turning of the ceiling fan, waiting.

"It seems," the general said finally, "the same press that has contacted you has convinced the prime minister of the value of publicity. We are *ordered,* therefore, to allow some journalists to accompany our missions. Inevitably, it is the English-speaking press that must concern us." The general looked at Ashton out of the corner of his eye. "That will not always be the situation, as I'm sure you are aware."

"I wouldn't know about those things," Ashton said, knowing how false it sounded.

The general took a long pull on his cigarette, stubbed it out, and reached for another. They were American cigarettes, Ashton noticed; they went well with the little general's vaguely American accent and his penchant for revealing his displeasure. It was a Western trait, odd in this small Thai. Ashton wondered if the general had studied or trained in America.

"You think I am prejudiced," the general said.

"I wouldn't know," Ashton said again.

"You Caucasians are wonderful," the general said, leaning forward, "with your lawn parties and upper-class accents and sanitation and your belief the world *owes* you something. And yet—and yet—I am *not* prejudiced, Major. Envious, perhaps."

Ashton remained silent, watching the small man.

"Never mind," the general said suddenly. "We will work together for the betterment of Thailand."

"And ourselves, I hope," Ashton said.

"And ourselves, of course. Now to business. A number of journalists will be selected to accompany some of your units.

You must accommodate them as much as possible without jeopardizing your mission." Both men stood.

"How far do I have to go with these people?" Ashton asked.

"Provide all assistance, once they are here," the general said and picked up his lighter. Ashton understood he was being dismissed.

Back in his own office he looked at the list. Bloody nuisance. He walked over to the wall map and stared, feeling the size, the physical features, feeling the old stirrings of Asia with its beauties and its mysteries. He should be out there instead of in this damned office. At least it was better than rattling around in the London flat, bored senseless, snapping at his wife. His poor wife.

He sat again and looked out into the hot compound, the shadows directly underneath. He should be out soldiering somewhere, not in a damned office.

The situation was fluid, to say the least. The general—hardly anyone called him by his name because everyone knew who the general was—had to be watched. Was there a coup in the making? Ashton wanted no part of these machinations, if machinations they were. He wanted to be out in the field. Still, it was insidious. By a word, a glance, a smile, a moment that you were invited to share, you were pulled into it. He bloody well would not take sides politically.

Restless, he went back to the map, running a hand through his short, thick graying hair, pushing his fingers over the clipped mustache. He saw the disposition of his forces. Christ, they were spread all over! It made his work at headquarters essential, the coordination alone a mammoth effort.

It was manageable, though. Especially with the quality of the forces he had now. He paced the office and thought of them. Prien was good, damned good. But the American was, or would be, the best he had ever seen.

Once again he turned to the wall map. The American was up there now, a deep penetration mission against a bandit stronghold. By Christ, Ashton said aloud, that's where I should be.

All that day they had walked down a road covered in large, gray-green fruit and vast hordes of dark and angry flies. The flies would hurl themselves up from the rotting fruit, attack the passing column, and return to the fruit when the column moved on. All along the column there was swearing and slapping at the flies.

He looked back down the line, pleased that it was moving in good order, pleased with their performance the day before, the first time they were bloodied as a unit.

Flankers were out and the point man was moving with caution but no slower than necessary, striking the right balance between speed and safety. Near the center of the column was the radioman, Kretschmer, carrying the PRC-10 with half the antenna missing, shot away in the fight the previous day. The German was probably the oldest man in the column but very steady during the fire fight.

As he walked he watched the ground in front of him and on the flanks, but he felt safe enough to let his mind wander over the previous day's action.

Late in the afternoon they had taken positions outside the bandit camp, moving with urgency because there were reports the bandits had taken hostages. There were often such reports, usually untrue. Somehow the Thais always assumed the mercenaries would not go into the bush unless there was hope of recovering hostages, who would be grateful, or finding caches of gold or jade, or seizing high-ranking prisoners who could be ransomed. Perhaps it was because the Thais themselves would need such motivation. At any rate, in his opinion, any hostages taken by this particular bandit group would have been killed by now, for his unit was pushing them hard. And then the bandits made the fatal mistake of stopping to rest, so he had set a blocking force on the other side of the camp and positioned the main body of the column to take advantage of the slightly higher ground. He thought his opposite number might be a good man in a strike situation, but he hadn't the experience to set up a fortified camp properly. He thought that, given time, the bandit chief would panic and abandon his position. If that happened, he thought, he might save some lives. So he sat the column down, in position, to wait.

"Herr Kapitan?" Kretschmer called softly. "Sergeant Loder reports it is very quiet in his area. He says he is moving the blocking force closer to the camp."

"Tell him to hold his position."

After a while there was a sudden burst of covering fire and then a movement in the bush in front of them.

"Fire," he yelled and began to shoot.

They came on a run and the front ranks went down and were leaped over by others in a fanatical charge. Behind him a smoke grenade went off and there was a prolonged scream that momentarily rose above the gunburst near him. There were explosions on both sides and then the machine guns on the flanks opened up with almost a textbook field of fire, and he heard the shrieks of pain and the hammering of the guns on all sides.

There was a grunt and a curse and he turned to see Kretschmer staring at his radio, its antenna shot in half. Ten feet away lay a dead bandit. He turned back and saw that the fire from the column had crumpled the attack, and the bandits were panicking, running back toward their camp. He thought they would pass on through it now, knowing there were not enough of them left to defend it. Strung out along the back trails they would be easy to find, which was why he had not wanted Loder's blocking force so close to the camp.

"Cease fire," he ordered.

No sooner had the firing stopped than it erupted on the other side of the bandit camp; the bandits had encountered Loder's group. He sent two small patrols to the right and left, hoping to find stragglers and take prisoners. Then he formed up the column and moved it in skirmish lines toward the camp. Eventually they had trapped the remaining bandits and destroyed them, with only the patrols taking prisoners.

After dark the column had settled into campsites. Sentries were posted and he had ordered the prisoners interrogated, expecting to get very little real information. Their leaders seldom told them very much, simply expecting them to fight for money and drugs, and to die when necessary, another expendable resource of Asia.

Later in the night he had sent for Loder.

The sergeant appeared before him, large and fully armed as always. Loder was a giant of a man, his face hard and expressionless, the eyes extraordinarily deep and cold. There was about him an air of violence, which he made no effort to conceal or deny.

"I'm breaking you to corporal," he told Loder, looking at him steadily. "To move the blocking force would have been stupid and would have cost

us lives. Anybody can make a mistake, but you're experienced enough to know what it would have meant—more casualties."

"Casualties are part of war," Loder had said, in a thick accent, and with no attempt to conceal his insolence. "If you are not prepared to die, you should not be here." Loder meant it personally, he knew.

"If you cause the unnecessary death of any man in this unit," he had answered, "I'll teach you about casualties. I'll shoot you myself." He saw Loder's eyes shift, then focus on his. Loder smiled a tight, ugly smile.

"Then you had better look to yourself."

"Don't threaten your commanding officer."

"Pardon," Loder had said, sneering.

"You're dismissed."

Loder had left without looking back, but he knew the man's reputation. He knew he would have to be careful and slept very lightly that night.

Now, on the following day, they had left the camp behind and were making for a rendezvous point to support the probe of another unit into bandit country. He looked at his watch. They would be early; he could risk a slower pace and keep his men fresh in case they were needed. He halted the column, put out sentries, and ordered a two-hour rest, no fires, no leaving the area. Sitting back against a tree, hoping there were no ants, he put his map case beside him and took off his beret, stuffing it into his belt. He took the Luger out of its holster, flicked the safety off, and placed it beside him. He made himself comfortable against the tree and prepared to doze. Just before he fell asleep he reached down and unsnapped the leather sheath housing the knife Tawodi had given him on his name day.

Ashton was, by turns, elated and furious.

The elation came from the action report he had been able to take over to the general. He had returned in a nasty temper because the general had maneuvered him into a corner without so much as a by-your-leave.

Ashton's helicopter had gotten him to the scene in time to participate as an observer. With a fine sense of protocol he had not attempted to take command after all the prestrike work had been done by the men in the field. He had remained at the command post and watched the action develop. Later, he had commended those who deserved it, shown himself to the men, accepted a drink of some fiery liquid from the man they now simply called Finn the Engineer, and returned by helicopter to headquarters.

Standing in the little general's cramped office, Ashton was gratified to see the general's expression of pleasure and reflected that there could be more riding on the mercenaries' success than he had considered. At any rate, the general was smiling and patting him on the shoulder, something he had never done before, and a very un-Thai gesture. Not only a military victory, the general said, but a propaganda victory as well. It demonstrated the government was doing something about the bandits—and with the attack on Khun Sa, something about the opium growers as well—and it couldn't have come at a better time, what with the foreign journalists arriving soon.

"What?" Ashton had barked.

They would be here at any moment. He looked about the small room and wondered if he should cover the map, with its overlays clearly showing the positions of the columns. No need; that operation was finished. He turned his attention to the list. There was the usual paucity of detail: R. Manning, Reuters, out of the Bangkok bureau; L. Jamieson, the Associated Press in Singapore; S. Sunderland, "pooling" for a group of smaller American newspapers; J. Marino, writing for a prominent New York magazine; and M. Becker, a free-lancer widely published in Europe. The meager data noted only that their names were pulled out of a hat in a sort of lottery. There would be others later perhaps, God and the prime minister willing. He sighed and thought about having a stiff whisky in spite of the hour and the heat, and at that moment his orderly announced the arrival of the newsmen.

He stood to greet them and had to conceal his surprise. One of them was a woman.

Not just a woman, he noted with a quick second glance. A stunning woman, lithe and tawny. She seemed to glow. She was wearing loose-fitting jungle fatigues and her hair was brown and full of waves, which had streaks of light in them. Her eyes were a startling blue in a face that featured small bones, good design, perfect teeth—she might have been a highly paid fashion model. Whatever else, she had a fine sense of timing, because the moment he realized he had been staring she stepped forward to shake his hand and smile.

"Major Ashton," she said, "I'm Sara Sunderland. We understand we have you to thank for getting us here." Her voice was low and pleasant and he found himself smiling politely in spite of a sense of forboding.

"We weren't expecting a woman."

"I'll try not to cause you any special problems," she said, and her smile reached her eyes. He suddenly wanted to like her. "May I introduce my colleagues?" she asked, and Ashton shook hands with them, not really seeing them.

"Look," he said finally, "we're a bit cramped here. Perhaps you'll come over to my place and let's have a drink or two and talk about this."

"I don't think you have a thing to worry about, Major," Sara Sunderland said. "But I, for one, will be happy to accept a drink later on, perhaps while you're briefing us."

"Right to it, I see," the major said.

"Just ready when you are," she said evenly.

Ashton looked at the others. The Reuters correspondent was a tall young man about the same age as the New York writer, and both of them considerably younger than M. Becker, freelancer. Jamieson, the Associated Press, was a middle-aged man with a weary look. Ashton had the feeling it wasn't the first war for some of them, and he felt his mistrust slipping away.

"Let's go to my quarters for a drink or two. I can brief you in the morning. For now, I'd suggest you settle in and meet me for a late dinner at the mess tent, and then get some sleep. Tomorrow morning, early, you'll get a full account of what the government's trying to do here." He saw a couple of smiles of relief.

Later, over drinks in his quarters—thank God the fan was working—he probed them for more information, trying to decide how to place them with his units. Sara Sunderland got quickly to business.

"Are there any Americans here?"

"I don't know if I should answer that," he said, not un-friendly.

"Oh?"

"You see, America, unlike a lot of countries, won't permit you to serve in a foreign army. It costs you your citizenship. *If* I were to have an American, and *if* you were to interview him, he could lose his citizenship. I don't know if he'd like that."

"I see. Is he working out? I mean, does he fit in with this kind of life?"

"Oh, yes. He's one of my finest officers—providing he's actually here. Would you like another drink, Miss Sunderland?"

"Please. And more about the American. What if I interviewed him without using his name?"

"No pictures either?"

"Well, it won't have the same impact, Major. Is he the only one here?"

"The only Yank, yes. A very good man he is, too. I'll speak to him about it. If he agrees, it's all right with me. I assume you will want to do it here?"

"No. In the field. Wherever he is."

Ashton sat back and chewed on his upper lip for a moment. "Miss Sunderland, if I may say so, you have a rather disquieting way of saying outrageous things in a very nice voice."

"Does that mean you don't want me out in the field?"

"Well," he said, anticipating her argument, "although you are, I'm sure, a competent journalist, there are simply no, uh, arrangements for you out there. There are no other women out there, for example."

"Do you mean there are no women in Thailand?"

"You know what I mean. There are no women with the mercenaries."

"I wonder."

"What does that mean?"

"It means that if I can't see for myself, I can't be held responsible for any errors of fact. Someone told me your mercenaries were rapists, that they captured the bandit women and kept them for their own amusements."

"Ah, now you're teasing me."

"Yes, I am, Major. But I'd like to ask you to think in terms of putting me with the American's unit. What's his name anyway?"

"You'll have to wait until I can talk with him."

"When will that be?"

"Soon. Now, let me freshen that drink."

After dinner, when they were settled in quarters, he went back to his office and spent some time on the field telephone. He went as far as he could and then relied on the radios. Dane was somewhere in the north, active as usual, handling reconnaissance-in-force missions until the next operation. Yes, the major was assured, Captain Dane would be in touch as soon as they could reach him. He cradled the telephone and, not surprised, looked up to see Sara Sunderland standing in his doorway, wearing some thin summer dress in deference to the heat, but still looking cool and composed.

"I saw your light," she said.

He reached in the bottom drawer of his desk and pulled out the Scotch. Rummaging in the same drawer he found a glass, slightly dirty, and an old canteen cup, U.S. Army issue. "Your choice," he said.

"The cup."

She sat across from him as he poured the drinks. He was aware of her understated sexuality. She was not the type to flaunt it, but she bloody well had it, all right.

"Health."

They sipped the Scotch, straight, and studied each other.

"Tell me about the American, Major Ashton, or can we get on a first-name basis?"

"It's Bill Ashton . . . Sara. Have I your word?"

"Of course."

Ashton leaned back, remembering the day Dane walked into his office.

"He came in like he owned the place, very sure of himself. A young man, well built, a kind of grace about him. He walks like an animal. He has strange eyes—they're brown but at one point in the interview they went much darker. Never saw that before. I think I made him angry."

171

"What did you say to him?"

"I can't remember exactly, but I think I might have been prying too much. He's a curious case. We try to find out as much as possible, but I think my curiosity may have gotten the better of me."

"Go on."

"As I started asking questions he handed me a resumé, anticipating the questionnaire that Thailand requires of us. It was detailed in some ways, very careful in others."

"Can I see it?"

"Sara, I can't allow that. We try to protect these men as much as possible."

"Tell me what you can." She leaned forward, sipping the whisky delicately from the canteen cup.

"He was a marine in Korea, a sniper. Afterward he stayed on in Asia, but didn't tell me why. He's built a small but significant little mercenary force of his own. And sometime in the past ten years he got a degree in literature from the University of Hong Kong."

Sara sat up. "Literature?"

"Yes. Quite remarkable, I suppose."

"What else do you know?"

"He's thirty-one, five feet eleven inches tall, about one hundred eighty pounds, not a big man but not small. He has no physical impairments; in great shape, in fact. He has a scar across his left shoulder and a scar on his left foot. He says he speaks a smattering of languages but none with fluency."

Sara sat back, musing. A strange animal. Might be a very good story. Or not.

"What motivated him to become a mercenary, do you know?"

Ashton indulged them in a little more Scotch. "Interesting question. He'd had experience here in Indochina and I gather he plans to stay here, but he did go off to Africa. He's something of an anticommunist, I gather, but no great—what's that expression of yours?—no great flag waver? I guess he has about the same motivations as any mercenary."

"Yes," Sara said, quietly. "That's what I'm here to find out about. Why a man will fight just for money."

"Wait a minute, Sara. It isn't *just* for money."

"Isn't it why you're here, Bill?"

"Of course not. It's much more complicated than that. I suspect it's complicated for your American as well." He was feeling testy. "I don't really expect you to understand."

"Perhaps my readers won't either, unless I explain it to them."

Ashton looked at her coolly. "That sounded a bit ominous."

"I just want you to understand that the image of mercenaries is one of men who fight for money. If that's wrong, you'll have to convince my readers."

"And you?"

"I think it's probably a true image. We'll see."

"I think we'd better call it a night. Miss Sunderland."

She stood and smiled at him. Were her eyes mocking him? "Good-night, Bill," she said.

Sara saw John Dane for the first time on a hot, windless morning, with heat waves rising and the sound of a helicopter hammering in her ears. She stood out near the matting, feeling the sweat beginning on her back and forehead and under her arms. She wore a khaki shirt and pants and carried her two cameras, both around her neck, and a small purse with a notebook in it. She wished she had tied a scarf around her head to hide the sweat, or at least soak it up. She felt rumpled.

The rotor blades threw dust far past the matting and she squinted into it, watching the handful of men leap down from the helicopter. She picked out Dane at once—he looked younger than she knew he was, almost boyish, with a very clean-cut appearance in spite of the grubby, shapeless uniform. He was carrying a rifle slung over his shoulder, and a musette bag, and when he was down from the helicopter he took off his beret and wiped his forehead with his hand. He glanced toward the waiting group, put his beret back on, and began to walk toward them.

Ashton was right; he walks like some kind of wild animal. Very graceful. Very sexy, too. She frowned at the thought and waited.

Dane walked up to the little knot of people, seeing her but not giving her more than a glance. He saluted Ashton, who returned it and broke into a wide grin and grabbed Dane's hand, shaking it.

"Rather good job up there," Ashton said, and Dane returned his smile. Only then did he turn to look directly at Sara.

"Miss Sunderland, may I present Captain John Dane. A countryman."

He doesn't look all that much like a countryman. Darker skin, strange eyes. Good-looking. Dangerous, maybe.

"How do you do, Captain?" She put out her hand. He looked down at his own grimy hands and nodded pleasantly, without touching her. "I appreciate your taking the time to talk with me," she said.

"Major Ashton suggested it," Dane said, watching her. "He said it would be useful. Let the world know what's happening here. I hope you can keep me out of it, personally."

"We can discuss it," she said, "but I understood there were no restrictions."

"Except," Ashton said, "as I told you. If he wants to protect his identity you'll have to honor that."

"Is that going to be a problem for you, Captain?"

"I don't know," he said. "Let's get into it and find out."

"Let's get out of the sun," Ashton said, and the three of them walked toward the shade of the mess tent. Sara watched Dane; after the major he was the only real mercenary she had ever met, but he hardly looked the part. He was no whisky-soaked, undisciplined brawler. Quite the contrary. He looked very much the disciplined professional. It annoyed her a little.

"Where are you from in the States?" she asked Dane as they walked.

"Tennessee."

"Ah, a southerner."

"Not exactly."

She looked up at him again. It might take some time to peel the layers away. But she would do it.

They sat in the mess tent and sipped tea, Sara watching Dane as the major asked about a recent operation. She noticed he answered the questions directly and completely but without offering much more. But then Ashton was only interested in the details of the operations; she wanted to delve inside the skin of a mercenary and see what made him tick. She noticed how completely he relaxed, seeming to be at ease in any situation, but she also noted the hard body and the quick eyes. Yes, a dangerous man.

"Well," Ashton said finally. "He's all yours. At least for a while. I've got to run off and take care of the bloody paper work. I'll see you later today, Dane. Miss Sunderland." They watched him leave the mess tent and there was an awkward moment before Sara could begin. It bothered her. She was seldom awkward, especially during an interview. She knew she was a good journalist, but something about Dane disquieted her.

"Well, Captain. Tell me about yourself."

"You'll have to do better than that," he said quietly.

She looked at him sharply. "Most men love to talk about their work."

"You ask the questions and I'll answer the ones I can."

"It might be easier if we knew a little more about each other. I don't want this to be a formal interview. I'm interested in telling my readers what makes a man—especially an American—become a hired gun."

A beauty, Dane thought. "You said we should know each other. How about telling me about yourself first?"

She didn't hesitate. "My name is Sara, without the *h.* I'm twenty-six years old. I write for a group of small American newspapers. I was born and raised in Hawaii. My father lives there; my mother's dead. I have a degree in journalism from the University of Missouri; always wanted to be a journalist. I am not, nor have I ever been, married, but I've had some offers. This is my first time in Asia." She smiled at him. "You're my first mercenary."

"And am I what you expected?"

Oh, no. No. "We'll see," she said.

"I more or less specialize in features," she continued. "The human interest stuff. I've covered my share of hard news stories from the police beat on up, but I like doing features—it lets me explore the reasons people do the things they do. I'm hoping to get syndicated. I want to do a book sometime. Which leads me to ask about your degree in literature—from the University of Hong Kong, right?"

"In 1962. It was simply something I wanted to do, and besides, I had promised Starlight I'd do it."

"Starlight?"

"My mother."

Sara sat back. She reached in her purse for the notebook. "Starlight. What kind of name is that?"

"Aniyunwiya," Dane said. "Starlight is the English equivalent of her name, Noquisi Igagati."

Sara stared at him. "My God," she said. "We have a lot of work to do."

He has touched me and I'm not sure I like it. From that moment in the mess tent he—and his story—became more and more fascinating. But he won't tell me all of it. He talks about the mountains and Starlight and Tawodi, but there's more he won't say. I'll write that I can, but I hate it, writing while knowing there's more to him than he will say. We've had, let's see, four sessions now, and he's opening up a little. But he's still hiding a lot. And a strange thing is happening. I like him. He's a damned mercenary and a girl would be crazy to get attached to him. But I like him all the same. Where are my notes? Ah, yes.

I need to know more about the taekwondo years, and there's a big chunk of time missing somewhere—although he's done quite a bit since Korea. He hasn't mentioned women. I'll bet there were a lot of women. He's very attractive. I need to know about Quemoy; he isn't saying much about that. And he's told me practically nothing about Indochina.

He has a certain southern charm, but he definitely isn't a southerner. My God, a Viking-Indian! No wonder he's stubborn. Must ask him again about his decision to join the marines; you'd think a man like that would never leave the mountains. He's a mass of contradictions, though. A mercenary with a degree in literature. An Indian who loves Asia. An attractive man, probably with a little money, unmarried and no steady girl friend. He's killed people, mustn't forget that. But when he helped me into the Land-Rover the other day his hands were very gentle, and despite the dangerous eyes, his smile is quite nice and easy.

In any case, I've got to wrap this up and get going. I can't devote all my time here to one mercenary, even if he is the only American. American? He certainly doesn't act it, sometimes, but who can blame him? Why didn't my history books tell me about the Trail Where They Cried?

Dane smiled and thought of the last time he had seen Sara Sunderland: stamping her foot and yelling at poor Ashton, who wouldn't let her go on this mission with them. He had leaned out from the front seat of the Jeep and waved the column forward, then caught the look of desperation and anger on her face, and something unexplainable in her eyes.

Just as well she wasn't along. This wasn't exactly a piece of cake. He glanced down at his watch. Soon.

Then he heard the chopper overhead and a few minutes later he saw smoke grenades, followed immediately by an eruption of gunfire.

"Now," he yelled, and they started forward.

Gunfire to his left and right, and a new sound. He turned to Kretschmer, raising his eyebrows inquiringly. "A 7.62 millimeter Degtyarev—light machine gun made in Russia." Dane nodded and kept moving. He topped a small rise and looked across an area of interlocking paddies and several farmhouses, then waved his company forward. He started down the dirt path that led to the first house when a figure jumped onto the path. Dane ran laterally and fired, dropping him. The action was becoming confused and he looked for his radioman. Kretschmer was down, but unhurt, and waved to him. He paused to get his bearings and saw his men sweeping the far side of the paddies and the action shifting more to his right. Dane squatted and listened to the sporadic gunfire, then moved up near the first house, large as farmhouses go in this area, he thought. He saw two of his own men come out of it, then swing on down the path. Satisfied, he reached back for his canteen, a move that, later, he knew had saved his life, for when he turned he felt the air crackle, heard the low buzz of metal, and felt chips of wood flying from the edge of the hut where the rounds had made impact. He threw himself down and forward and rolled up, carbine ready, in the direction of the shots, knowing they could not have come from in front of him. He turned in time to see a form vanish in the trees behind him. A large man, wearing battle kit like his own.

He turned his attention to the scene in front of him. Medics were moving among the bodies, and Kretschmer was hurrying toward him, sweating under the radio.

"My regrets, Kapitan Dane," the older man said. "I couldn't keep up."

"It's all right, Kretschmer," he said. "Have you been in touch with both units?"

"Yes, sir. A good operation. They lost many, we lost a few." Kretschmer shrugged. *"C'est la guerre."*

"Have you seen Corporal Loder?"

"Earlier, on the right."

Dane nodded and walked forward. *I wonder if she will still be there,* he thought. *She said we weren't quite finished. And she was pretty upset with Ashton. Enough to keep her around?*

"Kretschmer, get me a full report from platoon leaders. Ask all officers and noncoms to meet me in one hour for a debriefing here. Any wounded too bad to make it in the trucks, let me know and we'll try for a helicopter. And find Corporal Loder. Tell him to meet me on the other side of that house there in fifteen minutes."

He went around the other side of the house immediately, so he would be there before Loder. He found the high ground and sat there, making sure he could see in all directions.

Loder came from the left instead of straight on. Dane watched him push his bulk through the underbrush, the AK47 assault rifle he fancied carried low and ready. He could see Loder's mean eyes. At the right moment he stepped behind the larger man and pushed his carbine into his back.

"Put the piece on the ground and walk forward, and be very careful how you do it."

Loder gently placed the rifle in front of him. Dane removed

his Luger and put it on the ground beside the AK47. "Stop," he ordered. "Turn around."

Loder turned and stood easily, unafraid, staring coldly into Dane's face. "Now what, *mon capitaine?*"

"You shot at me back there, you son of a bitch."

"You'll never prove it."

"I'll never have to."

Loder stiffened. "What do you mean?"

"I mean you're finished here. I'll charge you with attempted murder, but there won't be a trial. Ashton wants to get rid of you anyway; you're a problem. You'll be out of Thailand in two days, as an undesirable alien."

"I kill you someday, Dane."

"This is your chance. No weapons. No rank. You and me."

Loder charged.

Dane waited. *Master Kim had said, "You will know why you run up Sul Ak Mountain. It is for the legs, for the stretching, and the strength."*

Loder was on top of him, but he spun away and kicked the big man full in the chest. Loder went back and down like a felled bull, but then was on his feet again with surprising quickness. Dane watched him, standing in the classic ready position of tackwondo. Loder came at him again.

"No one can know all there is to know about taekwondo," the Master had said. *"But one word is important:* concentration."

Dane looked at a point on Loder's chest, grabbed the big man's swinging arm, and pulled him over. As he toppled, Dane pulled on Loder's arm and put his foot on the massive neck. "You'll have to do better," he said to Loder.

The corporal got up, moving cautiously now, assuming a boxer's stance. Dane let him close. When Loder suddenly leaned back and kicked, Dane stepped into a down block with his left arm, then went forward, throwing the punch from just above his hip, twisting his arm as he hit in the most fundamental tackwondo attack. He caught Loder in the throat and watched him go down. Loder got up again, gagging, his face red, and lurched forward, swinging as he came.

Dane stepped into him, turning at the same time. His right elbow slammed Loder in the sternum, his right hand then swinging down to hit the big man solidly in the crotch. As Loder started to crumble Dane pulled his fist straight up and smashed him full in the face. Then he stepped back, caught the sagging Loder, and hit him as hard as he could, an old-fashioned punch without any finesse, just a satisfying, arm-jarring right to the jaw. Loder went down heavily and stayed there.

Dane picked up the weapons and walked back to his unit. Kretschmer was waiting. "Send a detail for Loder," he told the radioman. "I want him stripped of his uniform; he doesn't deserve to wear a uniform. Put him in civilian clothes. He is a prisoner and I want him treated as such. If he tries to escape, shoot him, and let him know I said that. You'd better have a medic look at him, too. I think he's hurt himself in all the excitement."

Kretschmer nodded and grinned. He went away and Dane could hear him barking commands. Dane saw a detail double-time down the path where he had left Loder. He turned his attention to the details necessary now in the wake of the action. Ashton was right. There were always too many details.

Ashton stood in the small room, watching the general light another cigarette. The general appeared more dapper than usual, but he detected an annoyance in the cultured voice.

"Have you seen Sara Sunderland's newspaper articles?"

"No, General. I didn't think I would. She writes for a group of small newspapers in America, I believe. I don't expect we will ever see them here."

"But they *are* here. They were reprinted by a news service. A series of five articles on mercenaries in Thailand."

"I see." Ashton was sure of the annoyance now.

"Somewhere," the general said, his voice turning sour, "somewhere in the series there is an incidental mention that, oh, yes, there may be some problems with bandits in northern Thailand."

"I see," Ashton said again.

"She does not exactly glorify the mercenaries, but she does not put them in perspective either. She fails to point out they were simply one organization, under the overall command of the Royal Thai Army. She fails to point out they are just another combat team."

"General—"

"She does not go into elaborate detail, if I may say so, about the extent of the problems here. She has so understated the political situation that it is difficult to reconcile why the mercenaries are here at all, except the poor Thais cannot manage this problem by themselves."

"General—"

"She has not understood that the mercenaries were an experiment. An experiment"—the general lifted his head—"that is coming to an end, as far as the official Thai position is concerned."

"If you will just let me—"

"And she writes quite a lot about this unnamed American. She seems taken with him. Did she sleep with him here?"

"I'm sure I don't know, General. May I say that—"

"You realize, of course, that the most serious breach is that she makes the mercenaries look like they have saved the little brown men from all sorts of problems, caused, of course, by other little brown men. Can you imagine how this will look across the rest of Asia? I am sure the world will never be rid of mercenaries, but I can assure you it is the last time *this* government will hire them."

"If you will just let me finish," Ashton said coldly.

"Go ahead, what's stopping you?" the general snapped and sat back under a thin layer of smoke. Ashton took a deep breath.

"First, I'm sorry she concentrated on the mercenaries as opposed to the causes of the bandit problem here. Second, that was the chance you took when you invited the mercenaries here and then invited the press. You could have kept all this under wraps, as it were. I told you I was against it at the time."

"And so was I," the general said. "But the prime minister

was not, and now we are stuck with the image, for the time being at least, of a people who need help from outside."

"It's not so bad, General. Mercenaries have been used for centuries. The practice will outlive the both of us."

The general grunted and stared up at Ashton.

"General, we mercenaries have done an outstanding job here. We came to help you, and we have. Furthermore, we've been very disciplined and orderly troops, barring a few incidents."

"By the way," the general said, "that fellow Loder—"

"I've turned him over to authorities in France, General."

"Good."

The general sat, deep in thought. Ashton stood patiently.

"Good," the general said again and suddenly stood and stretched. He flashed an uncharacteristic smile. "Yes, we will survive it all," he said. "You are correct. The mercenaries have been a big help. But you will go and we will be left to solve the problem ourselves, which is the way it should be. You know that Thailand has never been conquered totally? Never been the vassal state? Our history is long and honorable, and admittedly violent. Yet we have survived. We have neighbors who are not completely trustworthy. We have dishonorable politicians. We have bandits, smugglers, and opium growers—all problems. But you will go and we will stay and solve our own problems. You know, my dear Ashton, as much as you have helped, I look forward to the day when the mercenaries are gone."

"General, I've never forgotten why we're here."

"Yes, you've been very loyal. It's why we are giving you a promotion in rank, Lieutenant-Colonel Ashton." The general smiled again, a smile this time of genuine warmth. Ashton was astonished.

"I hope you can use the rank in some other army, some other time?"

"Yes, General. Thank you. It's very much appreciated, sir."

"By the way," the general said casually, "was that American as good at his job as Miss Sunderland seems to think he was? In spite of her obvious inability to make up her mind about mercenaries, she was rather definite about *him.*"

Why are you so angry?
They told me you came close to getting killed this time. One of your own men.
It's dangerous business, Sara.
Why do you do it?
You've asked me that before.
I'm not convinced by your answer.
I'm not sure why you want to be convinced.
You're not stupid. I think you have an idea.
Sara, I'm a mercenary. A good one. I am experienced now. I have my own little organization, just beginning to grow. I have no quarrel with my life.
I can't believe you fight just for money.
I don't fight just for money.
The glory? The adventure? The chance to carry guns and play soldier?
Don't get cute, Sara.
Tell me again. I want to be convinced.
I'm a professional soldier, an ancient and honorable calling. I help people who are too weak to fight for themselves and I take pay for it because money is necessary to survival. At least I can choose, Sara. I can go in or out of a war. Your American army can't do that. And incidentally, how long do you think the U.S. Army would fight if nobody got paid?
Once you wanted to write poetry. I simply can't reconcile that kind of contradiction. The poet, the man with a degree in literature . . . a mercenary.
You aren't trying very hard. You're hung up on semantics, on a word. Let me try again: the wisest man I ever knew once told me that a man who is true to himself ends up doing what he does best, no matter what it is.
Well, maybe. But I want to know more about you before making up my mind.
You can't possibly use all this in a newspaper article.
Knowing you better makes it more authentic.
Then you would have to go all the way back with me, to Tennessee.

Maybe I will someday. God, does that sound like I'm throwing myself at you?

It sounds like we've wandered a little from the point of all these questions.

Do you mind terribly?

I don't know yet.

Well, I deserved that, I guess.

Sara, you're a beautiful woman, and intelligent. I think we could be very close, but I don't want you to have any misunderstandings. Eventually, I'm going back to Hong Kong, and then there will be other jobs, just like this one.

I'm not asking you to change. I have no claim on you.

Well, maybe a small claim? Ah, it's nice to see a smile.

So, if you're visiting in Tennessee you'll have to pass through Hawaii, either going or coming, right?

Yes.

Why don't you stop off and visit me, and my father? We don't live in Honolulu, though. We live down on the island of Hawaii; we call it the Big Island. It's totally unlike Honolulu. Come and spend a few days.

Sara, I would like that very much. Would your father mind?

He'll be suspicious at first, but he won't mind.

But are you sure you'll be there when I come? You're a journalist, you have commitments. You might be somewhere else.

No. I'll be there. Hurry.

PART
THREE

1965

*S*ara lay on the sand at Anaehoomalu, watching the two men and smiling faintly; they were so different.

They were at the end of the beach just beyond a little grove of coconut palms, standing on the jumbled ruins of an old concrete quay. Dane was looking intently at something her father was pointing out in the water. Her father was wearing his customary shorts and ragtag aloha shirt and his planter's hat low over his eyes. She had given him the hat on his birthday and he had thrown away the old, disreputable one he had worn for years. The new one made him look a bit rakish in spite of the inexorable paunch.

On Dane there was no sign of a paunch. He stood as dark and as trim as any beachboy, and as he bent to look at where her father was pointing, she noted the grace of his movements and the quickness of his head. Even in relaxation, he looked like something wound very tight. She wondered what he would be like drunk, or stoned, or satiated. She tossed her head.

Her father was a big man, standing two or three inches taller than Dane and needing every bit of it for his weight. She had been after him for years to cut down on his intake, but he loved the Hawaiian foods—the poi and lau-lau and lomi salmon and haupia—and she had resigned herself to a losing battle. Kona Sunderland was one of those *haoles* who had come out to the islands and thrown himself with happy abandon into the local life-styles. When her mother died of cancer, very young, Sara expected her father to marry again, and marry some Hawaiian girl who would give him a brood of children and the kind of happy, loose household that he so admired. To Sara's surprise, he had not. He was uncomfortable talking about it when she was younger, but on one trip home from college he had told her of his deep love for her mother, how no one could take her place, how he believed such loves were rare and he owed it to her memory not to marry again. Sara noted the small bits of evidence that women had been in the house, but she said nothing. It was her father's decision, her father's affair. Affairs. She knew that her father had been deeply in love, and perhaps it was the only love he could give, permanently.

Sara thought of her mother, dying so young. She had died in the small hospital in Hilo, having been transferred back to the Big Island from Honolulu, where she was pronounced incurable. She had stayed at home as long as possible, then they had taken her to Hilo, where drugs eased the pain and allowed her simply to leave them, like closing a door. One moment she was smiling at them, the next moment she was dead, a frail, blond, pretty woman whose eyes, in spite of her bravery, had carried a dark hint of the injustice of her death. Sara had cried for days. Her father had comforted her for a while, then he left her with a neighbor and went off to climb Mauna Kea by himself, in the middle of a sudden winter snowstorm above the ten-thousand-foot level.

Sara turned to look at Mauna Kea. It was afternoon and the top was covered in clouds. She had seen it in various moods most of her life, a massive volcano towering nearly fourteen thousand feet. Incredibly, a second volcano almost as tall stood across from it, visible from the Sunderlands' kitchen window. From that same window they could see Hualalai, yet another volcano, rising to some eight thousand feet. And beyond Hualalai was the ocean, and off to the right the Kohala hills, and upland pastures dotted with cattle—a far cry from the world the average tourist expected. Sara had been told that her home looked much like Wyoming. She had never seen Wyoming, but thought it must be beautiful.

She heard her father's sudden laughter and looked back. Dane was holding a small fish. He had simply caught it in the water, a movement so quick it had made her father laugh. She saw Dane gently put the fish back into the water and straighten up again, turning to look down the beach toward her. She could see his flashing grin, and she smiled and waved. The two men turned and walked down the beach toward her. She sat up and pushed her hair back and turned to the cooler to check the beer. When she looked up again something in the water had caught their eyes again.

Kona Sunderland was named for the section of the Big Island where he first made his landfall from the U.S. mainland. He had fallen in love with the indolent, tropical stretch of coastline and become one of its biggest boosters. Although he regarded tourism as a mixed blessing, he had helped Kona blossom in many ways, not the least of which was his favorite pastime, running a small weekly newspaper. It was here that Sara had gotten her start in journalism, and she remembered every moment of it, from the days when her father had let her have her own paper route to the day she wrote her first story for it. Without forcing her, Kona Sunderland had guided her into a career they both loved.

She watched him now, turning to come down the beach once again, smiling, she thought, but it was hard to tell through the grizzled beard he wore. He seemed to be getting along well with Dane, once he had made up his mind to have a look at this strange young man.

"But what's the point?" he had asked her a few days ago, sitting on the *lanai* of their breezy house in Waimea. They were wearing sweatshirts against the wind that had blown unchecked across thousands of miles of ocean to be funneled through the mountains and across the little cattle town in the shadow of Mauna Kea.

"The point is," she had answered, "that I like him. I find him very interesting."

"Are you falling in love with this character?" Sunderland asked uneasily. "A mercenary doesn't exactly have a long life span, Sara. And it must be a very unstable kind of life."

"He doesn't bore me," she said.

"That's not an answer," he replied. "Or maybe it is."

"I just find him an interesting man, and yes, he's attractive. I thought if he stopped over I might get to know him better. And I wanted the two of you to meet, for no particular reason."

Sunderland had looked at his daughter, a smaller, prettier version of her mother. He felt his heart stir with the old love he had felt for the two of them. Now there was only Sara.

"Sara, the one thing we've always shared with each other is honesty. And I respect your intelligence. I'm not going to lecture you about this guy, and I'll try to keep an open mind. I just want you to know that I don't think making your living as a mercenary is a very honorable or very stable way to live. To say nothing of the dangers involved. I'd hate to see you hurt."
As I have been hurt.

"Dad, I don't think he has a permanent interest in me. I don't think you have to worry." But her father looked worried all the same.

They had picked Dane up at the small Hilo airport. He had stepped down from the aircraft and looked about him curiously, then walked across the concrete to the small building where dozens of people of various races were holding great wreaths of flowers. When he saw them and walked over, Sara put a lei of carnations around his neck, reached up, and kissed him softly on the lips. A moment later Kona Sunderland was shaking his hand and asking about his luggage.

In the hour-and-a-half drive up to Waimea along the winding Hamakua coast, deeply indented with coves covered in a variety of trees and flowers, Sara thought about that mild kiss. Dane was looking at the spectacular scenery and being very attentive to her father. She wondered if Dane had felt anything; his brown eyes had been unreadable at that moment. She had been very conscious of a hard body and very gentle lips and she wondered if she had blushed.

Then they had piled out of Sunderland's old station wagon in front of the ranch-style house in the middle of rolling cattle pastures. Dane had liked the place immediately. She could see him staring at the volcanoes, at the sea, at the vividness of the green earth and a clean blue sky. Already it was cooler than down in Hilo, and the evening promised to be one of those clear, cold nights in which the stars were low and brilliant. Somehow, she wanted it to be perfect.

It had been, too, she thought, stretching now on the towel she had spread in the soft sand of Anaehoomalu, that great, curving beach of palms and gentle waves. Evening in Waimea was a special time, a moment in which everything took on a kind of sparkle. The evening sky had been as astonishing as she could remember, with deep blue fading to black and stars appearing like lanterns, and her father serving vodka martinis so cold they nearly numbed the lips, and later they had introduced Dane to the fine local fish, mahimahi, and he had enjoyed every moment of it. Before the evening was over she thought her father looked much more relaxed, and over cognac he was as charming as if he had been entertaining an old friend. She found herself smiling at the two of them as they probed and answered and got to know each other. In the process, she learned a few more things about Dane, but not a lot. She still wanted some time with him.

She heard someone approaching and looked up to see her father smiling down at her through the beard and under the hat. "I think we've lost him," he said, and she sat up to look for Dane. She saw him far out in the water, right on top of the reef, his snorkel bobbing up and down in the waves. He had positioned himself head-on to the surge of the water over the reef and rose to meet it as it poured across the coral, managing to stay more or less in one place.

"He's a natural," her father said. "He does very well in the water. Could make a beachboy out of him, if you want."

"I like him the way he is. Want a beer?"

Sunderland accepted a beer and sank to the sand beside her. They sat in silence for a while, watching Dane move about the reef.

"I'm worried, Sara," her father said suddenly, still staring out at the reef.

"But I thought you liked him. You seemed to be getting along very well."

"I do like him. That's the problem. I've seen you with a lot of young men from time to time, but this one's different. He's going to hurt you, Sara. That's what I'm afraid of."

"I don't think he's going to hurt me."

Sunderland sighed. "Let me put it this way. You'll never tame him and you'll never change him, and if you get involved you're going to be damned sorry someday when he's off in the bush earning his paycheck with a gun."

Sara turned to look in her father's face. "You don't like mercenaries, that's all."

"I don't like the idea. I like Dane well enough. It doesn't seem right to me to fight for money."

"I feel the same way, but I'm learning some things. Money isn't the only reason they fight. Besides, I don't want to change him. I don't know if I even want to get closer to him. He frightens me a little, too, you know."

Her father reached out and closed one huge hand over her wrist. "Then be careful, my dear. I couldn't stand to see you hurt." And then he leaned over and hugged her, as he used to do when she was a little girl. She smiled at him and was startled to find tears in her eyes. What was going on here?

Dane came out of the water at last and walked to where they were sitting. It is incredible, thought Sara, how easily he blends into wherever he is; he looks like he's been a part of this beach all his life. *I wonder if he would ever want to live here? Not much work here for him.* Still, it was a nice fantasy. She shook her head and looked around to see Dane watching her curiously.

"I thought you were asleep," he said.

"Daydreaming." She smiled. "And working on my tan."

They stayed at the beach until after sundown, watching the sun drop suddenly into the ocean in a scattering of wild colors that highlighted the white clouds drifting far behind the beach and the mountain. In the darkness they drove back to Waimea, feeling the quick drop in temperature as they crossed the two-thousand-foot level and met the sharp buffeting of the wind.

It was cold enough that night for a fire in the fireplace. The three of them sat in front of it, the flames sending sparks up the lava-rock chimney. Sunderland had served the cognac again and Dane sat quietly, getting the feel of the house. Sunderland, wearing a thin blue cardigan, sat in a chair near the fireplace and stared into the flames. Dane could feel Sara's presence, could sense when she turned to look at him. Wearing slacks and a plaid shirt that looked old, faded, and comfortable, she sat leaning back, her ankles crossed, looking quite at ease. The house itself also looked old, faded, and comfortable, a happy marriage of lava rock and wood, with a high, beamed roof and the luxury of plenty of space. The hill cabin where he had last seen Tawodi would fit into this living room with room to spare, Dane knew. Still, it felt warm and dry against the wind and the blowing rain that had come up long after sundown. Sunderland had told him it only rained at night, and why else would the hills be so green and the cattle so fat?

Sunderland stirred and put down his glass. "Well, if you'll excuse me, time to turn in. You folks stay up late as you like." He punched at the fire with a long poker and said good-night.

"Would you like more cognac?" Sara asked. She got up and took his glass and filled her own as well before coming back to the couch.

"Sara," Dane said quietly, "this is very pleasant, and I want to thank you for inviting me here. I hope your father didn't mind too much."

"Not at all," she said. "He was curious, in fact. A real, live professional soldier. That's a bit exotic in Waimea, even for an old newspaperman."

"And does he find me wearing horns and a pitchfork, killing babies and burning houses?"

"You know the answer to that. He likes you."

"I like him."

"That's nice."

"Neither of you know quite what to make of me, though, do you? No, don't answer. I don't want to get into this right now. I'm a little tired of defending myself."

Sara watched him. "Do you want to tell me about the visit home?"

He stretched and put his head back on the couch.

"Starlight looked older to me, and so did Nathan, but they looked good, happy. Starlight is concerned about me but doesn't pry too much. She would, of course, prefer it if I lived back in Tennessee again. Somewhere close."

"And could you?"

He hesitated. "Yes. I could, if all I had to deal with was working somehow in the deep woods. But I wouldn't want to live again in a place that didn't offer me more opportunities to get into other cultures. Being an Indian, Sara, has suddenly turned into a great advantage. You can get under other people's skin, really get to know them. Somehow the mixed blood makes it easier for me."

"So you've fallen in love with Asia. Does it look like a lasting romance?"

He rolled his head to face her. "Yes," he said. "I don't think I want to live anyplace but there. Strange, isn't it?"

"No, not so strange. You could blend into anyplace. You're a chameleon."

"Asia is so alive, Sara. It's old, but it changes all the time. You get a sense of both time passing and time standing still. You get involved in something and look up and years have gone by. It's never dull. Besides, I'm doing very well there financially. Asia can actually make me rich one day."

"Would that interest you a lot?"

"Only in passing. What it really does for me is let me do what I do best."

"Dane, you haven't mentioned Tawodi."

Dane grinned. "I have to tell you, that old man is amazing. He looked better to me than when I saw him last—younger somehow. We hiked all day once, and he nearly ran me into the ground. I think he will live forever, if he wants to. His eyes are remarkable. His hands are steady and strong, and he's as slim as you are. He's got to be in his eighties now, but he doesn't show it except for the lines in his face. He's still a hell of a shot with a rifle."

"But what does he think of you living in Asia?"

"Well, he misses me, I guess. But he knows that I'm inclined to go wandering around. He says it's the white blood, but he knows that the Aniyunwiya were wanderers, too. He misses me—and I miss him, Sara—but he knows we have our individual lives to lead."

Sara shifted on the couch and leaned on one elbow, studying him.

"He is," Dane continued, "becoming more spiritual, even more so than on my last visit home. He talks more to me now about listening to trees, or lying on the earth to feel its spirit. He talks about drawing comfort from the sunrise. He told me that last October he had a talk with a fawn, and that the fawn had been a deer in some other place in a previous life, but now she was happy to be growing up in the forests of the Aniyunwiya, where she would be respected."

"Do you believe in a lot of that mysticism?"

"I believe there are people in touch with the earth and sky and animals, and that other people—most people—aren't. I think Tawodi knows more than anyone I ever met. We are all animals, Sara."

"And some," she said, "are predators."

"All of them necessary in the scheme of things," Dane said, looking at her. "If you can think as an animal thinks, if you can have the pure vision of an animal, a hunter, a predator if you will, then things begin to make sense."

Sara set her cognac down carefully on the table beside the couch. "Do you always obey your animal instincts?"

He reached for her and she slid across the couch to meet him. He took her in his arms very gently and kissed her. Then he released her, but she stayed in his arms and looked questioningly into his eyes. He kissed her again. When they pulled away he could feel desire building in him. And he saw it in her.

He pulled her over him and began to rub her back, gently at first, then with more pressure. Her breathing was becoming faster and more shallow. He stroked her hair.

"Is this right for you, Sara?"

"Yes. Oh, yes."

He slid onto the floor in front of the couch, pulling her after him. Still holding her, he unbuttoned her shirt and moved his hand inside. He began to undress her, and himself.

Outside the wind hummed and gusted against the sides of the house. He could hear it above the popping of the logs in the fireplace, above the drumming of her heart and the beating of his own. They were naked on the floor in a small circle of fire-light, and he was held by the beauty of her and by her intense sexuality. He was suddenly very light and happy with her, en-joying her as a woman in a way he had not found joy with a woman for some time. She looked happy as well, and along with the laughter in her eyes was a rush of passion. She lay be-side him as his hands moved gently over her, and she reached for him.

The wind sang and the fire warmed them and the whole world shrank to that circle of light, which was world enough. They moved past self-consciousness, past inhibitions, and reached for a moment of freedom that each found in giving, and in giving received. In those final few seconds Sara found an excitement she had never felt before, and with it an unmistak-able taste of pure joy, and she knew that he had found it too.

Hey-yeh, the old man had said, tell me what you see.

I see the deep woods in late afternoon, grandfather. Perhaps it will snow soon.

On such a day we named you.

Yes. I will remember, always.

And has the name served you well?

Very well, grandfather. I thank Tawodi of the Aniyunwiya for giving me my name, and my purpose.

When you are across the ocean, does your name work for you there?
Extremely well.
Then I am glad. The spirits were with us that day. Do you wear the amulet?
Always, grandfather.
Then you will be safe, the old man said.

They walked in the pasture, at one point being intimidated by an enormous bull before moving around him and crossing a fence. It was one of the more spectacular days Dane could remember, with fine, high white clouds just enough in evidence to make the blue sky seem deeper and more intense. Sara walked beside him in jeans and a scruffy pair of hiking boots and a windbreaker, looking marvelous, her cheeks glowing. All across the pasture she had been talking, pointing out landmarks, the various *puus,* the hills, the ranches, and the homes of people who had lived there for generations. Dane listened to the song in her voice.

They crossed a fence, Sara first, and in helping her Dane slid his hand along her tight jeans. She smiled at him, enjoying the intimacy, and his touch. When they walked beyond it she put her arm through his and swung along beside him. She was humming some song he couldn't identify, and now and then she would look up for no reason and smile.

She is enchanting, he thought. *A gamin, a waif. Beautiful and smart. Her father worries about her, as well he should. Kona Sunderland worries about me, too. As well he should.* He turned and hugged her, kissing her on the forehead.

"Well," she said, "that was a nice, friendly kiss."

"I can't kiss you the way I want to, out here in the open."

"Dane, I want you to know. I have no regrets."

He grinned at her. "Well, you seem to have survived it all right."

"Listen," she said. "I damn well enjoyed it and I want to do it again."

"Christ, woman, don't you have any shame at all?"

"None at all, at all, at all . . ." she started singing it, throwing her head back, and when she did she saw her father's station wagon, bouncing off the dirt road and onto the pasture and coming toward them.

"What's going on?" she asked and began to run toward the fence, Dane beside her.

They reached the fence by the time Sunderland had gotten out of the car. His face was gray.

"What is it?" she called. "What's the matter?"

The three of them stood there for a moment. Sunderland was staring at the ground as if trying to decide what to say next. "What is it?" Sara asked again.

"There was a call from your editor, what's-his-name, Harrison."

"Well, that's no big deal," Sara said, relieved. "What does he want?"

"He wants you to go on an assignment. Right away, he said. He wants you to telephone him when you get back to the house. I think you'd both better come back with me."

"So what's the problem?" Sara asked, a note of irritation creeping into her voice. "We all knew I had to go back to work sometime. Does he want me back in the office?"

"No," Sunderland said slowly, his face sagging. "He wants you in Vietnam. A hell of a lot of marines have landed in a place called Da Nang. This country's at war—again. They want you to cover it."

"Damn," Dane said. "That's one they'll never win."

"I don't want you to go, Sara," Sunderland said. Sara knew that the vision of her mother was there between them. She knew she would hurt him.

"I have to go," she said. "It's my job. And it's my chance, too." She turned to Dane. "Why do you say we can't win it?"

"The Americans won't have the patience. And they don't know Asia."

"You talk about them as if you weren't an American," Sara said.

"I know who I am, and I know where I'd better be shortly."

"Going to make some money out of it, are you?" Sunderland asked, suddenly bitter. He had aged in the past hour, Dane thought.

"Mr. Sunderland, I just think it's time I got home to Asia. I don't look at this war as any great moneymaking enterprise. I'm not even sure I want to get involved, or involve any of my people."

"Well," Sunderland said slowly, "one of your people seems to think you ought to get involved. I had a second telephone call, relating to the first one. It was Western Union with a message for you from somebody named, I think, Lang."

"Langé," Dane said. "What did it say?"

"It said—I wrote it down—'Large cargo arriving. Need your presence here. Meet you where we last parted. Leave golf clubs at home.' Does that make sense to you?"

"It certainly does. It means I'd better saddle up, too. Sara, maybe we could ride out together, at least part of the way?"

"Yes, I'd like that." She turned to her father, the three of them moving slowly toward the station wagon. "I'll be very careful," she told him. "But you must see this as a newspaperman. It's my chance to make a name, to do some good stuff. I hate the whole thought of a war, but it's a chance for me to break out, do some real writing. It could lead to better jobs. I could find out whether I'm really any good at this or not."

Dane saw Sunderland absently pat Sara's shoulder. His mind was thousands of miles away. *He knows she will go, and he'll worry all the time. Well, he has reason to. I'm not that thrilled by her going myself.* He hoped she would learn quickly; Asia did not suffer fools very long, nor show a great tolerance for mistakes. She would have to adjust to a lot of things. Perhaps he could help.

"Listen, Sara," he said, "fly out with me. We'll talk on the way, to make it as easy for you as possible before you get there. Besides"— he grinned—"I'll need a chess partner on the plane."

They both turned to look at Sunderland. He had reached the car and was standing by the open door, staring absently toward the front of the car. He had not heard anything they had said in the last few minutes. Sara put her hand on his arm. "Don't worry," she told him. "Please. It'll be all right." Sunderland nodded and looked up at Dane. There was fear in his eyes.

* * *

Langé waited on the veranda of the Peninsula Hotel, a Hong Kong landmark. It was old, taut, managed with the efficiency of a ship of the line, which it somehow resembled. On the Kowloon side of the harbor, it was a magnet for Englishmen and a source of constant wonder for the Chinese. Teatime was rigidly observed; formality was the order of the day. In space-conscious Hong Kong, the Peninsula offered large lobbies and high ceilings, and somehow seemed less bothered by the nagging problem of water than most other institutions in the British colony. Langé had no idea how they did it, but he felt the British had moved a little section of London to the edge of the China mainland. He admired the hotel's white and pale blue interiors, and its quiet efficiency. It lacked the Gallic charm, of course, but it was adequate.

The veranda of the Peninsula served some of the finest Chinese food in Asia, or so Dane had insisted. Finishing a lunch of sautéed scallops and an ice-cold white wine, Langé was inclined to agree. He was also inclined to wonder what had delayed Dane, usually very punctual. On the telephone that morning, Dane had agreed to meet him for a noon lunch, but had been nowhere in sight. Ah, well, Langé was a real Parisian when it came to lunches. He could enjoy one by himself if it was good enough and if there was no need to hurry. He ordered an espresso and watched the harbor.

He was conscious of someone behind him and turned to find Dane standing there in some sort of white suit with an open collar. With him was one of the prettiest girls Langé had seen in a long time, and he got to his feet, smiling.

"Sara," Dane said, "this is the one to watch out for. This is my good friend Gabriel Langé. And this lady"—he turned to Langé—"is Sara Sunderland."

"Ah," said Langé, "who can blame you for being late?"

"Not too late for lunch, I hope," Dane said. "I'm starved."

Langé signaled for waiters and seated Sara as Dane settled in a chair opposite.

"You look marvelous," Langé said to Sara. "A model? An actress."

"A journalist," Sara said firmly, then grinned. "But you sure know how to talk to women."

"I told you to watch out for him. It wasn't an idle comment," Dane said and went back to studying the menu. In a few minutes he ordered lunch for the two of them and insisted on buying Langé a drink. Langé, meanwhile, was pointing out some of the Hong Kong sights to Sara.

Dane studied Langé. He was unchanged, a burly, bearded, and highly cultured Frenchman. He admired Langé's openness and ease. He also thought Langé very good in the bush and extremely competent to handle things in Laos. And from Langé's veiled comments on the telephone that morning, things were going to heat up very soon.

". . . but for days I was brushing my teeth in Bordeaux blanc," Langé was telling Sara. "After a while you say what the hell and start drinking the water and eating the local food and taking your chances. If you live through the first few attacks of dysentery and malaria, and of course if some husband doesn't corner you in his bedroom, you can survive very well. I have. Dane has."

"And has he ever been cornered in a bedroom by a jealous husband?" Sara asked.

"He is very adept at survival," Langé said.

Sara turned to Dane. "I hope so," she said. "What is happening now? What brought you back? Can you talk about it?"

"Langé and I haven't had a chance to discuss it," Dane replied. "We'll know more this evening when we meet with some people who came here to see us. I'm not sure who they are, and I don't think we should involve you, Sara. You have other things to think about. The next few days are going to be traumatic for you."

Dane turned to Langé. "Sara's going to Vietnam to cover the war."

Langé glanced at Sara and looked back at Dane, his face suddenly somber. "It will be a very nasty business, you know."

"Will I see you two there?" Sara asked quickly.

Langé grinned at her. "Who knows, *cherie?*"

The waiters brought chicken in a green pepper sauce, egg

rolls, rice, and tea, all served from enormous silver dishes. Sara was delighted with the lunch, the hotel, the busy street outside, and the junks in the harbor. She talked happily about being in Asia.

"Sara," Dane said, leaning forward, "I'm going to stay here for a while and talk with Gabriel. We'll have an early evening drink, if you're not still shopping, and after we do some business tonight, I'll take you for a dinner you won't forget."

"A deal," she said, rising. She smiled at Langé. "He's right, you know," she said to Langé. "You're as dangerous in your way as he is in his."

"*Cherie,* I adore you for saying that."

"*Au revoir,*" Sara said. They watched her free-swinging walk as she moved across the veranda toward the elevators.

"Well, you said she was a beauty," Langé said and sighed.

"Tell me about this evening," Dane said.

"I was approached in Vientiane," Langé began.

He was back from a trip through a group of Hmong villages. He had gone just to show the flag, to let them know he was still around. The mission had no particular focus, but he did discover a girl in one of the upcountry villages, an absolute beauty. He had just gotten back to Vientiane and the Hotel Asie when two men came to see him. Both Americans. One was a tall, sandy-haired man with a habit of pinching his right earlobe when he talked. The other was a smaller, darker man whose name was Shaw and who spoke perfect French.

"They thought they would have to translate, I guess," Langé said to Dane. "The other man, who said his name was Kinnan, seemed very nervous and worried about talking to me. They kept looking around as if they were going to be overheard. I tried to put them at ease, of course, but most Americans don't know how to relax, as you know."

Dane ordered a round of drinks for them both and sat back, knowing Langé would tell it his way.

"Finally they got to the point," Langé continued. "What they want is a lot of work." He paused for dramatic effect, then lowered his voice.

"They want, *mon ami,* to organize a private army. They want operations against the Pathet Lao north of the *Plaine des Jarres* and elsewhere, as necessary. At the same time, they want us to help with a paramilitary operation in the Mekong Delta. I told them it would mean more money than they knew and they just shrugged. I told them it would involve hundreds of men and they just looked at me as if to say, 'So what?' Then I told them you were in charge. They asked many questions about you, none of which I answered, of course. That is why they want to see you this evening."

"Where are we meeting?"

"I have to let them know. They're registered at the Repulse Bay Hotel, and they are waiting there for my call."

"Good. We'll see them there around seven and I'll take Sara on to dinner from there, in Aberdeen. What else?"

"I asked them why they needed us and they almost laughed. It seems that Pathet Lao are doing a lot of damage in the villages, something I can turn around with a little help. They also are concerned about riverine warfare in the delta. The Americans are sending a few navy officer advisers to some of the more remote places; they want us to fill in the gaps and to work with them as required."

"It doesn't sound all that complicated, but it still leaves me a little puzzled. I have the same question you have—why do they need us? They've got the manpower."

"My feelings exactly. There must be more. That's why I held them off until you got here."

"Tell them I'm here and we'll meet on the terrace of their hotel at seven," Dane said. "Let's meet here again for breakfast, say oh-nine-hundred, for a little evaluation, eh?"

Langé nodded. "Still strange, isn't it?" he said. "But one of the last things they said to me was, 'We can afford it.' So, my friend, let's see if they can pay for what they want. Could you put together such a large group if we have to?"

"I know just the man who can," Dane said. "See you later."

In the lobby Dane picked up a copy of the *South China Morning Post*. Vietnam was riveted by the presence of U.S. Marines. Other nations were considering sending troops if requested to do so. In one corner of the page Dane noticed that a police ac-

tion had resulted in the arrest of several Cao Dai priests in Tay
Ninh, in the western part of Vietnam. A news analyst was pre-
dicting a quick end to the Viet Cong infrastructure now that
the United States had made its commitment to support South
Vietnam.

He put the paper under his arm and walked to the desk and
pulled out a telegram form. He wrote:

POSSIBILITY OF LARGE ACTIVITY HERE. MAY NEED YOU AND
YOUR ORGANIZATIONAL AND RECRUITING ABILITY. COULD
YOU HANDLE IF DEAL SOLIDIFIES? CALL COLLECT, PENIN-
SULA HOTEL.

He signed it and penciled in the last address he knew—Lieutenant-Colonel William Ashton, Beaconsfield, Buckingham-
shire, England. Then he went up to Sara's room, knocked, and
entered.

She was in the bedroom. He tossed the paper onto a table
and went in and looked at her. She was lying, undressed, on the
large bed, letting the ceiling fans push cooling air over her
body. Through eyes half closed she stared up at him. "Come to
bed," she said.

He dropped his clothes on a chair and lay beside her, wel-
coming the cool air. They lay not touching, enjoying the silence
and the coolness. After a while she spoke, without turning her
head.

"You know I have to go tomorrow. I suspect you do too."

"Probably."

"Do you want to hear about the dream I had, about all
this?"

"Tell me."

"I was a little girl again, in a park somewhere, or on the
range in Waimea, someplace green and open. The sun was out
and it was very hot, so hot that I ran toward some trees, for
shade."

"And?"

"Some men came from behind the trees and grabbed me.
They started beating me. All I could see was that they were

Orientals. They beat me until I couldn't walk, then they went behind the trees again. I got up and started to run, but I was too sore, hurt too badly. I kept falling down, crying for someone to help me. There was no one else around. I was terrified. My dress—I remember that dress, it was a party dress my mother bought me when I was little, a white dress with a blue sash, very old-fashioned and pretty—the dress had blood all over it."

"It was just a dream, Sara."

"There's more. Once when I tried to get up the Orientals came at me again, and I started screaming. Suddenly they turned and ran and I looked behind me to see what had scared them. What I saw then really frightened me, but in a different way." She sat up in bed and put her arms around her knees and put her head in her arms. Dane lay quietly, but he felt his pulse quicken.

"I saw," she said, "a man. He was a dark man and he was holding something in his hand, something that he pointed toward the men who were beating me. Dane, I think what he was holding was that amulet you wear. And I think the man was an Indian."

Dane sat bolt upright. "Tawodi," he whispered.

"Yes," she said. "I think it must have been." She turned to face him. "For the first time since I've known you, I'm a little afraid. I really don't know what to make of all this. I don't believe in that superstition stuff. I don't like having dreams like that; I've never had them before."

He took her in his arms and lay back on the bed. She shivered once, slightly, and buried her face in his chest. "It's just a dream," he told her. "When you think about what's in your mind these days, it's a quite logical dream. All of this is coming a bit fast for you. And I know you're a little scared of the Vietnam thing. I can tell you I am damned well scared about it. I don't like you going in there. It isn't going to be the picnic everyone seems to think."

He heard her sniff and looked down to see tears glistening in her eyes. "Hell of a thing," she said. "I come across you and before we can do much about it we have to be apart. Are we going to stay in touch? How do I put this delicately—do you care enough? Goddammit, I don't want to lose you before I find out more about you—and me."

"What do you think I am," he teased, "a one-night stand?"

She rolled on top of him and kissed him, dropping tears on his cheeks. He held her very tightly, losing himself in the moment, and then feeling his body take control, and her body begin to respond.

The excitement came to him then, quick and intense, and he lifted her slightly and pulled her back so that he entered her and felt her moving over him. He simply let himself go then, abandoning all thought and giving in to sheer pleasure, feeling it roll in him like a wave and then the wave crashing on a beach with a wild and joyous noise, and somewhere in the middle of it all he heard her cry out. A few moments later she rolled to one side, as limp as a rag doll, her breathing beginning to slow again. He watched the tiny mist of sweat forming on her forehead in spite of the ceiling fans. Her lips were parted, showing her perfect teeth, and her face took on a look of contentment. While he was watching, she fell into a deep and untroubled sleep.

He closed his eyes and rested. He might have slept. He was shaken into consciousness by the sound of a gong in the corridor outside. He grinned. At the Peninsula, by God, you observed teatime, no matter what.

The terrace of the Repulse Bay Hotel was exposed to the sea breezes, whenever they came, and in all seasons afforded an unobstructed view of the magnificent, star-filled sky over Hong Kong. Most of the tables were filled with an odd assortment of people. Dane guessed at occupations and came up with journalists, salesmen, honeymooners, a con man, visiting Kiwanians, a British artist down on his luck.

Langé sat beside him. Both men were sipping drinks, but Dane's was a club soda. He wanted a clear head to talk with Kinnan and Shaw. He glanced at his watch. Time they were here. Beyond the terrace wall the highway wound round the bay and disappeared, and out in the water he could see the lights of the junks. Water people; some of them spent their lifetimes aboard the boats. He wondered what a life like that would be like.

"Here they come," Langé said.

He watched them approach the table, Kinnan the taller one, as Gabriel had described. Shaw, looking somewhat out of place, trailed Kinnan by a pace as if to acknowledge the other man's seniority. Both men wore suits not cut for the tropics, and were tieless. As they neared the table Dane noticed Kinnan looking around, ostensibly enjoying the view, but checking, Dane knew, the persons closest to them. Dane had selected a table to put them out of earshot, and by the time Kinnan reached them, he seemed more relaxed.

Dane felt a mild tension, and an active curiosity.

They stood and shook hands with the two men, Langé making the introductions. Kinnan gave Dane a long, appraising look before taking a chair opposite him. Then the tall man sat and pulled on his earlobe and began to talk in a quiet voice with an accent that Dane put at somewhere around Atlanta.

"I understand, Mr. Dane, that you have an organization, or at least the nucleus of one, that can perform a variety of tasks out here in this part of the world."

"A variety of tasks is a delicate but accurate way of putting it," Dane said. "We're mercenaries. What do you want us to do and how soon do you need it and how much can you pay?"

Kinnan sat back and smiled. "About the only thing you haven't asked is who you-all would be working for."

"With your accent it certainly isn't the Mexicans or the Egyptians. I think we all know who you are and what you want. Why don't you just spell it out?"

Kinnan shifted and glanced at Shaw, who had not spoken since the introductions and looked like he wasn't going to.

"We—and I mean America—we're heavily involved out here, but we don't have a lot of expertise. We are smart enough to know it. Now we have a number of needs and priorities involving a bit of staff work and a lot of training and a certain amount of taking troops into combat. It has been brought to my attention that we could buy this kind of experience and put it on-line at once. Is that right?"

"At once," Dane said, "cranking in the usual screwups."

"What do you see as the big problem?" Kinnan asked.

"The big problem is getting you people to tell me exactly what you have in mind."

Shaw cleared his throat, catching them all by surprise. "We want you to organize the villagers of Laos into effective troops, establish bases both north and south of the Plain of Jars, and keep the Pathet Lao busy around the clock. At the same time, we want you to intercept any Viet Cong supply lines through Laos and cut them, permanently. We want you to do this because, for political reasons, we can't put American troops into Laos."

"What else?" Dane asked.

"We want you to put non-Asians into American uniforms and into the Mekong Delta to augment the riverine warfare forces. We simply don't have enough people with enough experience. We're hoping you can find them and insert them faster than we can start from scratch and train them."

Langé rubbed his beard and turned to face Shaw, Kinnan forgotten for the moment. "How many men? How long a period?"

Shaw answered, "I would guess you will need about thirty professionals to be the cadre for as many as three or four hundred Asians, who you will organize and train. Getting the right thirty or so men is the expertise we're willing to pay you for. Then, of course, you will be responsible for their success or failure. How long is anybody's guess, but I would estimate we'll need something more than a year. It depends on how quickly the Pathet Lao and the Viet Cong realize the error of their ways and cash in their chips."

"They aren't going to do that," Dane said quietly.

"I think they will," Shaw said.

"What about the pay?" Dane asked.

Kinnan stirred. "Ah, yes, the pay. What would you need to do the job?"

"Make us an offer," Dane countered.

"We've thought it out," Kinnan said. "We would recognize your position as more or less that of a battalion commander. Consequently, we'll give you the pay and allowances of a colonel and that rank, unofficial of course, but we'll use it for protocol and command purposes."

"What about the rest?"

"We can authorize equivalent pay for a couple of lieutenant-colonel positions and that of a major, figuring you'll need two distinct commanders in two different places, plus somebody in charge of a base command area. The rest of the men you recruit will be recognized and paid, all unofficial as I said, at the rank of a captain."

"No," Dane said.

"Then what do you want?" Kinnan asked, pulling his earlobe.

"You add up all those allowances we'll never collect and put a dollar value on them. You add that to the pay. Then you arrange for all of this to be tax-free. You set up insurance policies for any man killed or crippled. You add a little sweetener, such as an occasional R and R somewhere—maybe right here—and we can deal."

Kinnan looked at Shaw, who nodded.

"All right," Kinnan said. "What else?"

"You pay transportation costs for the people I bring out. And you don't argue with me about my choices."

"We don't even want to know your choices, that is, we don't want to know more than we need to know. Just get them together. We'll set up a pay system as you put your people in place."

"There's more," Dane said. "We're going to put together troops from these mountain villages, as you say. They're unsophisticated, unused to modern weapons. But they are Hmongs, some of the finest people in the world, the most honorable, the most fearless. They are not afraid to die, but they love life. I want them paid the same as you would pay any American soldier in this situation. Just because they're Asians is no reason to buy them for pennies. When they work for me I want them paid what they earn. Otherwise, we're all wasting our time."

Kinnan had trouble with that; Dane could see it in his face. He felt himself growing cooler. "Listen, Kinnan. An Asian puts as much value on his life as anyone else. He may view death differently from most Americans, but he isn't rushing toward death. It isn't a minor thing out here, despite what you may have heard." He leaned closer to Kinnan. "We're not concerned with color here, we're concerned with abilities. Give me a few Hmongs and we'll make Sherman's march to the sea look like a stroll through the garden."

Kinnan flushed. "Don't be abusive. We haven't said we wouldn't pay them."

"Then make up your mind," Dane said.

"Take it easy," Shaw broke in. "I'm sure we can meet the terms."

Langé suddenly laughed. "Then do it, *mes amis,* and let's get started. The war isn't going to wait forever, you know."

Dane settled back. A waiter came and Kinnan and Shaw ordered drinks. Dane shook his head, noticing that Langé had hardly touched his drink. Out in the water some junk sailor was calling, and there was a sudden burst of laughter on the beach. The night was still warm.

"There are still some unanswered questions," Langé said, as if he had just thought of them. Dane smiled. Langé had a great way of dissembling; ideas that were deep in his mind seemed to suddenly float there, catching the unwary by surprise and leaving them unsuspecting of the cunning that lay just underneath. It had taken Dane a while to discover that in his friend, but now he knew it was always there.

"Will we have liaison? Do we operate independently?"

Dane was glad Langé had asked the question. It was in his own mind, but now it was out on the table.

"There will be a certain amount of coordination. You'll have two Americans as liaison, just to make sure we're all facing the same direction if the shit hits the fan."

"The two of you," Dane said flatly.

"Yes," Shaw said.

"Knowing the American system, then," Dane mused, "I'd say we were in the presence of Major Shaw, probably a West Pointer, and Major Kinnan, from VMI or Clemson or some such."

"Close enough," Shaw said. "Right about the ranks."

"What kind of Asian experience have you had?"

"None, but don't let it bother you," Kinnan replied.

"I won't," said Dane, "providing you understand that in all—and I mean all—operational situations, Gabriel or I will call the shots. Not you."

"You aren't the only people we can turn to," Kinnan said hotly.

"Fine," said Dane, rising. "Lots of luck. Let's go, Gabriel."

"Jesus Christ, Dane," Shaw protested, "don't be that way. We aren't giving you a hard time. These situations are fluid, and we'll simply have to play a lot of this by ear."

"*Merde,*" said Langé. "Our way or not at all. We haven't got all night. He has a lovely girl waiting, and I have one or two, I forget which."

"Please sit down," Shaw said. "I'm willing to give you an unqualified okay to all you've asked for. Now let's take it from there."

Dane smiled at Langé as they sat. Kinnan looked up at the stars, face flushed. *He's holding back a pretty good temper.*

"There's one more thing," Dane told them, sitting back. "What you've outlined for us is the kind of projects your own people could do eventually. We can buy you time, but I know you could do it on your own. Let me tell you the real reason you've come to us."

Kinnan was watching closely. Dane thought he saw the ghost of a smile on Shaw's face and a slight narrowing of the man's eyes.

"First of all," Dane continued, "you want us to operate in Laos because you've correctly worked it out that nobody knows the territory like we do, and second, because Laos is not at war you can't put troops in there. You will deny any one of us that gets killed or captured, so we're really on our own. I don't mind that; we can live with it. But what you're not saying is that the type of mission you expect of us is the kind you also don't expect us to come back from. Well, don't count us out. We'll do the job."

Langé sipped his drink and then stared into the glass, lost in thought.

"As for the Vietnam end of it, you've got hell's own number of troops in there, so you want us for something you don't want to soil the hands of the GIs. Something that you believe runs against the grain, something immoral from the American point of view."

"And what would that be?" Shaw asked in a quiet voice.

"Kidnappings, assassinations, general terrorism against the Viet Cong infrastructure all down the line, including some deep penetrations. A bag of dirty tricks you don't want to have to admit to later on."

"I underestimated you," Kinnan said.

Dane grinned at him. "Maybe you just don't know enough about us."

"Does it cause you problems?" Shaw asked.

"No." Dane was emphatic. "Wars are so stupid anyway that whatever you can do to get them over with is all right with me. Personally, I'd rather take a shot at a high-ranking officer than one of the grunts any day."

"Well spoken, *Colonel*," Kinnan said sarcastically.

"You select the operations—we can see the necessity for that. But don't try to take command of any of the mercenaries after we're dedicated to the mission. Gabriel and I insist on that."

"How do you want to proceed?" Shaw asked.

"Gabriel and I will talk. Then we'll meet with you again. I suppose your orders are to stay with us until everything is operational? I thought so. All right. I have things to do here, so let's meet again tomorrow night."

"Here?" Kinnan asked.

"No," said Dane. "Same time, but let's have a drink in the Gloucester Lounge. We'll iron out some of the details and at least set up a timetable and a table of organization. Then we'll start putting it all together."

"Time's a factor," Shaw said.

"Don't get too excited," Dane told him. "Whether you believe it or not, it's going to be a long war."

How much time do we have?

We'll leave for Kai Tak in an hour.

God, I'll miss you.

One thing's for sure, we won't be that far apart. I'll find a way to get to you whenever I can.

I wish you would tell me where you're going to be. At least I'd have something.

Sara, this whole thing is something I just can't talk about. Especially to a reporter. . . . Ease off, I'm only teasing you. But I really can't talk about it.

I know you're going to be in Southeast Asia, Dane. I just know that. I won't pry anymore, but I'm going to think of you being somewhere close to me.

You can do that and you'd be right.

I want to ask you something.

Go ahead.

Is it always like this before you go into a war zone? I mean, I'm scared stiff, I don't mind telling you.

But you're going to go, right?

Yes.

Because it's your job. It's what you do.

Yes.

You are going to deliberately put yourself in a position where your chances of getting killed increase dramatically—because it's your job.

Yes.

I rest my case.

Then answer the question: is it always like this?

It's different for different people.

What about you?

I always consider the possibility that I will not make it back. I also consider the possibility of not going in. And then I go, because it's what I do. Sometimes, I wish it were some other way. Maybe it's selfish, or egotistical, or some psychological quirk. But I know it's not. I do what I do very well, as well as anybody I know. There's a certain satisfaction in doing it well, even a kind of exhilaration. I guess I'd have to answer the question by saying that I lose myself in my job until it's over.

At least I'll have that.

Yes. You're going to be busy. I don't want you to go crazy in there. I know you're out to win your spurs, like most of the rest of them will be; but keep your head down. And your nice ass as well.

Dane, we haven't made any commitments.

Does that bother you?

I don't know. Maybe. I know what I feel when we're together. I'm not sure how you feel. Dammit, we need more time.

If this is good, and lasting, we'll find out. If it isn't, we'll find out. Don't force it.

I guess you're right. But I'll miss you.

And I'll miss you.

At least that's something, isn't it?

1966

D ane sat in a thatch-roofed hut, parts of his carbine scattered on the rough wooden table in front of him. He was smiling at the uninhibited snoring coming from the sleeping bag on the floor in one corner of the rectangular hut. He could hear the snoring even above the sound of the rain battering the roof. *It's always something. During the day it's the rain, at night it's the rats. And Donovan's snoring.* He pushed the two thirty-round magazines to one side and began to reassemble the carbine, now cleaned to his satisfaction.

It was evening—Donovan sleeping after a long patrol, cooking fires in the compound banked against the driving rain, which seemed somehow cold in spite of the heat of the delta. He could smell the residual smoke from the fires. He could, in fact, smell the entire country.

He got up and walked over to another rough-hewn table and unscrewed the cap to a bottle of Scotch. He poured some of the

Scotch into a canteen cup, replaced the cap, and went back to his seat with the cup. The drink was a treat. He drank less than most people, and even less than that when operational. But there was no patrol for him this evening, so he could relax.

What a place to relax, he thought. A thatched hut with wooden sides, decorated functionally with assorted tools of the trade: ammunition boxes; a semioperational, apartment-size refrigerator they had stolen from the air force at Vung Tau; a huge jug filled with evil-tasting cough medicine for the Vietnamese junkmen, who were very susceptible to respiratory diseases; various articles of clothing in various stages of repair; a wide range of weaponry, including two deadly Vietnamese crossbows; extra sleeping bags, which could be spread on the dirt floor to make an instant guest room.

Not that we get many guests. Even the pilots flying the supply drops into the compound hated to make the trip; they were shot at by the Viet Cong almost every time, sometimes with deadly success. The pilots would bring the choppers straight in from the sea and drop like a rock into the compound. Without shutting down the engines they would offload any cargo, then go up and out as quickly as possible. It was during the liftoff that the Viet Cong found them most vulnerable.

The compound was a triangle of mud walls with .30 caliber machine gun emplacements in each corner, and beyond the walls was a ring of concertina wire. Empty C-ration cans were tied to the wire to rattle if disturbed, and here and there were the devastating antipersonnel mines, the Claymores. Dane had seen to their placement himself since he didn't trust Donovan's judgment or experience. Donovan was, after all, a navy officer. He could tell you all about naval gunnery, fire control, navigation, and the niceties of the wardroom, but he was just cutting his teeth in bush warfare. Still, he was coming along. Dane knew that in other sectors of the delta there were highly experienced navy advisers to the junkmen, and he respected their abilities and their results. Donovan, although not a novice, still had some catching up to do.

For a few hundred meters beyond the wire and mines, there was relatively open ground. Dane had ordered that one wall of the compound face that direction so that any attack from that side could be met by two machine guns in a crossed field of fire. The second side of the compound faced the ocean, where their chulucs, thirty-foot junks with lug sails, were anchored and where at least two of them were on a constant and interlocking patrol pattern. The compound's third side of the river was the village, still hotly contested by Dane's junkmen and the Viet Cong. Generally, the junkmen could move freely about the village during the day, but at night it belonged to the Viet Cong, a situation Dane determined either to remedy or use to his advantage. The village would be an area of concentration in the near future. The past five months had been spent putting the base together, establishing their presence, and starting the patrols. In all that period, it was the river that had held Dane's attention.

He got up and walked, canteen cup in hand, to the doorway and stood under the thatched overhang. The Song Cua Dal was swollen with rain and dark with silt, a brown, turbid, winding spur, one of the tributaries of the great Mekong. Deep in-country it widened and narrowed with each rainy season, flowing around an island that was a Viet Cong sanctuary, and leading on to the important delta town of My Tho. Each season's rain changed, however slightly, the whole network of waterways in the delta, sometimes creating new rivers in the low-lying areas, making it impossible to move about except by shallow-draft sampan. At other times the river would simply disappear, dried up or funneled back into the main watercourses. In the best of times the river would be unreliable; in the worst, a danger. And all of it a part of the mighty Mekong, the river that was so much a part of so many Asian lives. He wished he could see the origins of the Mekong, sixteen thousand feet high on a Tibetan plateau, fed by snows, producing what the Tibetans called the Water of the Rocks. Roaring down through China the Mekong was called the Lan Tsan Kiang, the turbulent river. It rolled on, a total of twenty-six hundred miles, spilling through Vietnam, where it was called the Cuu Long Giang, the River of the Nine Dragons (for its nine major tributaries). The Cambodians called it Tonle

Thom, the Big Water. Sharing a common tongue, the Lao and Thai all spoke of the river as the "mother river khlong," with "khlong" having an imprecise definition. The impatient Westerners contracted it and called it the Mekong. And this little finger of a portion of it now rolled through Dane's area and was going to be very important to him. Even now, he was trying to mesh an idea of his with an operational requirement that had been placed on them a week ago, and the river might provide the answer.

It was still raining. He leaned against the bamboo door support and looked idly about the compound. Nearby was the communications shack, and across from it the cramped huts of the junkmen and their families huddled under the beating rain. In the center of the compound was a device that made Dane grin each time he looked at it. It was a large, flat, wooden arrow on a swivel. The idea behind it was to give the junkmen an air-strike capability. Nailed to the top of the arrow was a row of cans containing kerosene. At night, when an air strike near the compound was desired, the cans could be lit and the arrow swung to point toward the Viet Cong attackers. It was primitive but necessary, because the compound had no way of communicating with the aircraft—they simply had to point the arrow. They were fighting here much as they had fought along this coast from time immemorial; their fanciest weapon was the one he had just reassembled, a gas-operated .30 caliber Garand carbine. Still staring out into the rain, he wondered what the M-16s were like; that rifle had yet to make it down here to the paramilitary forces, so he refused to carry one himself. When his troops got them, he'd carry one.

He was conscious of a silence behind him, and he turned to peer back into the hut, now growing dim with the onset of evening. Donovan was sitting up in his sleeping bag, looking at him through half-closed lids.

"Well, *Dai Uy* Donovan," Dane said, using the Vietnamese word for officers of the rank of army captain, "about time, I'd say."

Donovan ran his hands over his thick blond hair. "How long have I been asleep?"

"Where's your watch?"

"Somewhere between here and a twenty-mile stretch of coastline. I dropped the damn thing overboard. By accident of course."

Donovan got out of the bag, wearing only a pair of shorts. He looked at Dane's canteen cup and walked over to get his own. "Attitude readjustment hour," he said and poured himself a Scotch. He sat at the table and looked gloomily out into the rain. "Must be around nineteen hundred."

"Right."

"What's up?"

"Shaw's coming early tomorrow. We got the word while you were out practicing your act with the disappearing watch. I've asked him to come and brief us on the goings-on in Saigon, and I want to talk to him about an idea I have."

"Oh, shit. Every time you have an idea it results in a lot of banging around and me wetting my pants."

"You'll love this one. I'm going to make you the center of attention."

"Colonel, I'd just as soon phone it in."

Dane grinned. "If you only knew."

"Oh, shit," Donovan said again.

Dane turned to stare into the gathering darkness. Rain sometimes meant a Viet Cong attack. Two could play that game, though. He would launch his idea in the next big rain. "I'm going to get some food. Want to join me?"

Donovan shuddered. "How can you eat that stuff?"

"I'll be back before it gets too late. If I'm in the village past, say, twenty-one hundred, send in the cavalry."

"Papa Dat's?"

"Yeah."

Dane slipped on a field jacket and an old bush hat he had gotten from an Australian at Ben Tre. He strapped on the heavy .45 sidearm and picked up his carbine. He put the two clips in it, taped back to back for easy changing, then he went out the door and across the compound.

Passing through the gate on the river side, Dane motioned to one of the junkmen, who ran in front of him and untied a small sampan. In moments he was being rowed across the river, no more than fifty meters here, but flowing swiftly from the rain. *Probably flooding upriver.* He gestured for the junkman to wait, then walked swiftly toward the lone street that wound through the village.

The village dogs went into their usual hysterical barking as he strode down the dirt street; he knew they were too cowardly to attack, but they told the world he was here. Never mind. He hurried toward the center of town where the village's single café was marked by the glow of candles. He went through the door.

Papa Dat looked up, startled by a late visitor. When he saw Dane he nervously blew out one of the three or four candles and hurried forward, pointing Dane toward a table. By long habit, Dane shook his head and moved to another part of the small room, squinting through the dim lighting. There were two other people in the café, both elderly men, and they were deep into bottles of "33," the potent Vietnamese beer. He sat and pointed to the beer and nodded to Papa Dat, knowing the old man would bring a beer and join him.

Papa Dat came over with the beer, his deep eyes glistening in the candlelight, his face a mass of wrinkles. The only smooth place was his skull, shaved bare and looking strangely youthful. From his chin dangled a few wisps of beard, which kept getting into his glass as he sipped his beer. Dane watched him with interest. Papa Dat was a man of great curiosity, hence a great source of information. Between the old man and Dane had grown a close but not necessarily friendly relationship. Dane didn't trust him.

"*A votre santé,* Papa Dat," said Dane, raising his glass.

"*Santé,*" the old man answered.

"What is the news?"

"About what?" asked Papa Dat, guileless, his voice smooth and his English very competent.

"Are the VC still harassing you at night?"

"You do not hear anything from where you are?"

"I cannot hear the striking of a knife, or the young man who disappears to turn up in the VC. Tell me about them."

"We have had no problems that I have heard," the old man said, his voice low and emphatic.

"And your young girls?"

"Nothing since the rape three weeks ago. Of course, we never knew who that was, Colonel."

"Not one of mine."

"So you say."

Dane sipped his beer. He decided he wasn't hungry.

"You seem," he said, "a little nervous. Is something bothering you, my friend?"

"No, nothing."

"You said that rather too hastily."

"It is just that you have not been here so late before."

Dane smiled thinly. "You have said nothing of importance, but you have told me what I need to know. I will leave you now, Papa Dat. I thank you."

The old man bowed his head, his eyes glittering. He was still sitting there as Dane went through the door and out into the evening and the rain.

Back in the hut, Donovan was working on another Scotch and had found a battered paperback novel with a lissome brunette on the cover, almost wearing a dress. He was reading avidly.

"*Dai Uy*," Dane said, "the Viet Cong are moving about tonight. I don't expect trouble, but double the sentries and make sure the chulucs stay in motion out there; I don't want them still in the water."

"Aye, aye, sir. Anything up?"

"No. Just precautions."

Dane lay down in his sleeping bag. He put the carbine on the floor beside him and the .45 under his pillow. He unbuckled the sheath of his knife, thinking of Tawodi as he always did at such a moment. Then Sara's face floated in front of him. He heard Donovan turn another page and cough. He closed his eyes.

Morning brought clear skies and a blazing sun and about the time the heat was really setting in, a young Vietnamese junkman ran out of the communications hut and reported contact with the helicopter. A few minutes later Dane and Donovan stood in the shadow of the hut and watched the chopper come in high from the sea and plummet to the heart of the compound. It was a battered Huey, and out of it popped Shaw, in uniform and carrying a briefcase and an M-16. He ducked his head and held his cap and trotted away from the helicopter. The pilot gave a perfunctory wave and lifted off immediately, hurrying toward the open ocean, leaving dust hanging in the still air of the morning.

Dane led Shaw through the dust into their hut and offered him a semicold beer from their off-and-on refrigerator. Shaw took it gratefully and took a long pull.

He looks older, Dane thought. *The war isn't treating him properly. He thought he'd be out of here long before now with a chestful of ribbons and some war stories to dine out on, and silver leaves instead of those gold ones.*

"Well," Shaw said finally. "What do you want first?"

"The news from my base camp," Dane answered.

Shaw grunted. "Langé is well to the north, very active along the Ho Chi Minh trail. The Hmongs are doing a great job. You were right about them. Langé has reported he's in a no-win situation as far as permanently interdicting the trail goes. It's too easy for them to simply divert the supplies. He's fought a couple of set-piece battles with the Pathet Lao and believes they're being resupplied through Viet Cong liaison offices and regional headquarters. He said to tell you the tax collectors were busy in the villages, that you'd know what that means."

"Yes. Go on."

"Ashton sends his regards and reports no problems at base. He's stamping around complaining about the paper work, though."

"I wouldn't expect otherwise," Dane said, grinning.

"And he passes on a bit of personal information, he says."

"Which is?"

"He said to tell you that Miss Sunderland is well and apparently quite prolific. He sees her by-line regularly."

Dane nodded. *Sara.*

"Any problems with the pay system?"

Shaw looked annoyed. "No. Everybody's getting paid on time."

"Okay," Dane said. "Localize it."

Shaw looked relieved to be on more familiar territory. "I've been to the other junk bases. We now have the dozen that you set up and control, plus the dozen staffed by the navy, the black beret types. It's going all right, a few problems here and there, but in general the bases are working and we're doing the job. Each base situation is different, of course. As you know a patrol out of Da Nang is quite different from going upriver here. All I can say is that it's going well."

"What else?" Dane asked.

"Our friends have given approval for your mission upriver. They think it's a good idea, in fact. They want to know what you need to pull if off."

"I need them to leave us alone for a while. We're going to ease off the patrols in preparation for this and I don't want any crap from Saigon about our patrol statistics, all right?"

"That's easy. What else can I do?"

"Arrange some R and R for me. After this mission I'm going to get out."

Shaw looked at him curiously.

"Look," Dane said. "The bases are functioning. You don't need me here any longer. I'm going to pull off this one job, leave young Donovan here alone unless the navy wants to send him a partner, and get the hell out. In sounds like Gabriel could use some help. How's he getting along with Kinnan, by the way?"

Shaw smiled for the first time. "Like oil and water, I would say."

Dane nodded.

"A lot of this is going over my head," Donovan interjected, then got up to get more beer. The heat was building inside the hut, and all three men were covered in a light sweat. In an hour their camouflaged fatigues would be soaked.

"Tell your friends it's my intent to leave this force in place and take some R and R. I'll go to Hong Kong or Singapore, then I'll go to the base camp. From there I'll hook up with Gabriel and see what can be done."

"What the hell is all this?" Donovan asked.

"You're regular navy," Dane said to him. "There are things you don't need to know, and shouldn't know. Just be happy with the fact that you're going to be the *dai uy* in charge here very shortly. Providing, of course, we pull off this last job together."

"What is it?"

"Later," Dane said and turned to Shaw. "What about the big picture?"

"Where to begin? Well, Nguyen Cao Ky has promised to hold a referendum for a new constitution, all leading toward a civilian government."

"Another one?"

"The Tet holiday passed with the ceasefire in effect, generally. The VC mortared the shit out of a Special Forces camp at Khe Sanh. Lots of casualties. A lot of brass, including President Johnson, met in Hawaii for talks, and Hubert Humphrey came back with Ky to Saigon. The Koreans are sending another regiment; the Aussies are beefing up, also. We took a pretty good hit up in the A Shau Valley and pulled out. And there's a lot more activity in Tay Ninh, near the Cambodian border."

"What's the political news?" Dane asked.

Shaw looked uncomfortable. "Not good. There's a hell of a lot of unrest in Saigon. Some troops took over a pagoda. Turns out it was headquarters for a bunch of dissident Buddhists. The government claims it's a victory, rooting out the troublemakers, but a lot of people are rather pissed. And, of course, we had another immolation. A young priest set himself on fire and burned to death, a few minutes after he had passed out a press release to the correspondents in the Caravelle Bar."

"What's going on in the countryside?"

"Ky has given the Minister of Rural Construction authority over a new concept, revolutionary development cadre teams to work in the hamlets. An evolution from the people's action teams, which, uh, have phased out."

"Search-and-destroy tactics still in effect?" Dane asked.

"Yes."

Dane looked away. "I told you we were settling in for a long war, Major. You'll be a full colonel, maybe even a brigadier, and I'll be retired and swilling vodka in Kowloon before this one's over."

"We haven't even begun to use the force available to us," Shaw protested.

"You've got nearly four hundred thousand men here now. You've been bombing the Ho Chi Minh trail for a year. Nothing has changed. Nothing will. You ready to do this for another ten years?"

"No," Shaw said. "I don't think the American people will stand for that. They want this war to end."

"Or the Americans out."

"Christ, Colonel. Why are you such a pessimist?"

"I know the patience of Asia," Dane said slowly. "And you've just told me Gabriel is up to his ass in Laos. That means we aren't having all that powerful an effect."

"Do you advocate just pulling out? Leaving these people to their fate? Letting the communists simply take South Vietnam and Laos and the rest of Indochina?"

"I hate the communists as much as you do," Dane said. "Maybe more. That's one reason I'm here. But overall, we're doing it wrong. We've alienated everybody—the Hoa Hao, the Cao Dai, the civilian leadership, the top army echelon, the American people, the people of the hamlets. Do you think the Vietnamese give a shit who's in charge, as long as the shooting stops?"

"I think they do," Shaw said. "I think they're anticommunist."

"I think they're antidying, myself."

"Listen," Donovan said. "What I want to know is what would happen if we did simply pull out. Say that the war's over and we're all going home."

"Absolute chaos," Dane said, and Shaw nodded agreement.
"Then what's the answer?" Donovan asked.

Dane looked at the young navy officer, almost envying him his innocence. "There may not be an answer," Dane said.

Tawodi took his only meal of the day that morning, sitting on a bluff overlooking the Hiwassee, watching it flow swiftly around a slight bend and drop suddenly, creating a small amount of noise but making a curtain of water through which he thought he could see lights shimmering, like the spirit of the water, signaling him.

He drank from the river. He ate some roasted corn from a small bag he carried and then lay back and looked up at the sky.

How many days, he thought. How many nights. Life is as quick as water dropping over stones. Somewhere in the mountains the snow dies so that the river can live, and that life flows through the path that has been made for it. It mingles with other waters and disappears, and one day runs its course. But the next year there is snow again in the mountains and water in the watercourses.

He could die on a day such as this, when all the world glistened, when the spirit of things touched the earth and set it on fire with beauty. It would be easy to die on such a day, having his ashes scattered somewhere in the trees, becoming a part of the earth while his spirit waited to start life again. He wanted to die in the mountains so his spirit could stay here and become one with a life that lived here. He could not do what Waya had done—venture far from the mountains. For Waya, it was right. For himself, he intended to die outdoors, and up here somewhere, where his ancestors had died and where he felt their closeness.

He slept.

He awoke in the midafternoon and sat up. It was bright and there were highlights in the river now with the changed position of the sun. In places the river's surface looked like hammered silver, opaque and heavy. He went down from the bluff and got another drink from the river, saying his thanks in a courteous manner, and climbing back up the bluff, feeling the strain on his aging muscles.

Waya had told him once about some of the strange customs of the people where he now lived, and he had marveled at the diversity of life and the splendor of it. Men came in all sizes and colors and spoke languages that made no sense to any but themselves. They ate things other men would consider unclean. They had many wives, or none at all. But one thing they shared: all men died.

He shook his head. It was sometimes easier to die than to live. Many tribes had been enslaved by the whites and had died in great numbers, even as the Aniyunwiya had died. Better to die than to live in a stockade, to live as if your paw were caught in a trap.

He wondered how much longer he would live, and as he had the thought, a wind came from behind him and brushed across the back of his neck. He grew very still. For long moments there was nothing more, and he relaxed. Then he heard the cry of a strange bird from somewhere across the river. Was it really the voice of Adanundo, the Great Spirit? He looked across the river and sent his mind to speak with the Great Spirit. He said: Starlight and Nathan are well, and they are flowing in their own course. Waya, whom I love and miss terribly, has set his own path, wherever it will take him. I am alone, and so it does not matter much to me. But, O Great Spirit, the trees are beautiful on a summer's afternoon and the water of the river is as quick as all my dreams; the cries of the birds gladden my heart and the woods sing a song that stirs the blood and brings a great pleasure. Tonight is a night of a full moon. The earth will look like frost. I will feel young again, as if I were a boy as quick as lightning among the coves and on the hillsides.

Sara was in front of her mirror at a table in the small, dingy flat above the store where a Vietnamese family sold copperware. It was said of that family that they had a Laotian slave, and Sara always saw a man there she knew was not Vietnamese; he was very thin and dirty, and he slept on a pile of rags in front of the door, just inside the store. During the day he polished all the copperware, so that his hands were always gray, and eventually it seemed he was gray all over. Sara pitied him, but she did not know if he was truly a slave or just a servant, or how he had come to be with the family. The members of the family refused to talk about him.

Yes, she pitied him, as she felt pity for the entire country, north and south, it didn't matter anymore. She was becoming totally apolitical, and all she wrote about now was the people. She had said to hell with the troops, the politicians, the generals—yes, even the clerks and the bureaucrats. She would no longer write about anything but the plight of the Vietnamese people. It had wrung her heart in a way that had startled her, and over the months she had grown quieter, more introspective. She had started learning Vietnamese, as quickly as possible. She read everything, devouring books on Vietnamese history and culture and thought processes. It had taken its toll. Dane had warned her.

She stared into her mirror. The cheekbones were more prominent and there were shadows in her eyes. To herself, she looked older. More interesting perhaps, a few character lines here and there, but definitely a little older. She seemed tired much of the time, and now and then she wanted to throw it all over and go somewhere and dance and drink and perhaps go to bed with a man, and forget the children with their bloated stomachs and liquid eyes, the old men in their great dignity curled in the streets, some dead, some soon to die. She wanted to forget the priests and the deliberate way they chose a clean part of the street on which to sit, just before spreading their robes and soaking them in gasoline, and then, with absolutely passive faces, striking a match and setting themselves on fire. She wanted to forget the high-ranking officer's wife who had cracked that she'd be glad to provide the priests with matches. She wanted to forget. . . .

She touched her hair. She would be twenty-nine soon, and then thirty. Where would she be at thirty? In Vietnam? Where would Dane be, and where was he now for that matter? It had been weeks since the last cryptic message. An army officer had written her a note that he had seen Colonel Dane and that he was well. Colonel Dane! She smiled. Not bad for an ex-marine grunt. The note hadn't told her where he was, but she assumed he was in Vietnam. She had heard rumors about a lot of little sideshow wars here and there, in Laos, in northern Cambodia. But she had a feeling he was in Vietnam. She stared back at herself. It was difficult to admit, but what was happening around her took most of her thoughts these days. Even Dane got crowded out by these homeless, helpless people. They came streaming out of the countryside, swelling the city, looking for food, shelter, work. Looking for a way to stay alive.

Her popularity was growing; it was small consolation. She had come to Vietnam for the same reason many of the other reporters were here. It was the only game in town and a chance to make a name. She had admitted it to Dane and to others—why lie about it? She had worked hard, slept very little, taken some chances, and tried to be honest and objective. After a while objectivity was impossible. You got caught up in the horror of the war and what it was doing to people, and to the land, and to whatever beauty there had been. Where ancient, lovely temples had stood there were mounds of rubble and bloodstains. The graceful terraced rice fields were full of poisoned pungi sticks, sharpened and baked bamboo on which the Viet Cong had defecated, to go right through the sole of your boot and infect your foot. The old man on the corner carried a string of grenades under his robes, ready to die along with you, ready to give up the order of his life and the serenity that should have been his in old age. The children poured out of doorways and alleys and old pipes, stealing anything they could, fighting each other like animals. Still others became something much worse—they robbed at knifepoint, pimped for their sisters, stole anything not nailed down from shops and stores. Some of them were Viet Cong spies, some of them spied for both sides. The bar girls came, pouring in from the hamlets and taking off the lovely *ao dais,* that utterly feminine Vietnamese clothing of long slit skirt and trousers underneath, and replacing it with cheap imitation Chinese slit skirts cut to the waist, enticing the troops and making as much money as they possibly could, trying to escape poverty, loneliness, hunger. There were venereal diseases loose in Saigon that had yet to be identified, much less treated. But the worst disease of all was the war itself and its impersonal, uncaring, remorseless inhumanity.

Yes, her copy was widely read now, but it was hardly any comfort. No one seemed to care. The big story about Vietnam in America was the fact that the war was pulling America apart at the seams, brother against brother, father against son. Kids were fleeing to Canada and Sweden, burning their draft cards, telling anyone who would listen, "Hell no, we won't go." And other kids—yes, the same age, a hell of a lot of teenage grunts—went and got killed or maimed. And while a lot of them were protesting the unfairness of it all, a lot of others were doing what *they* thought was right. After a while it didn't matter, Sara thought. After a while the immensity of it all overwhelms you, and you find salvation in work, hard work, in filing stories that let you vomit up all the ugliness on the page, sharing it with the readers. (And then Luke Harrison, her editor, asks her, among other things, if Da Nang was on the outskirts of Saigon. Couldn't they *read* back there? Didn't anyone look at a map?) Dane had been right; few Americans cared about Asia, and even fewer knew anything about it. She had a growing feeling he was equally right when he said the Americans had no patience for this kind of war.

Her image in the mirror was darkening with the coming night. She could hear the night sounds outside her flat. The "white mice"—the Saigon policemen—were blowing whistles on the corners of Tu Do Street and the incessant noise of the motorscooters and bicycles infiltrated her window. She heard the slamming of the iron grill in front of the shop downstairs; the Laotian slave was closing up. Through the window she could smell the charcoal cooking fires. She thought she could scent the evil that was aboard in the night. She felt a trickle of sweat down her back; it was useless to try to do anything about that, everyone suffered from the heat. In the half-light there were great shadows under her eyes, giving her face a witchlike appearance. She thought she might cry and determined not to; she wondered if she had tears left after these few months in this grand, awful, complex, exciting, terrifying, and beautiful country.

Where was Dane? *Ah, you see, a tear after all.*

Dane went up to Saigon, hating having to go back into a city that depressed him. He hated the noise and the confusion, things that had delighted or interested him in other Asian cities. But this was a different kind of noise and a type of confusion that smelled of corruption and inefficiency. He sensed that, more than any other conflict he had seen, there was division in the leadership that ultimately would bring it down, even if the Viet Cong and the North Viets did not—and they certainly would unless something was changed.

He also hated going back into the headquarters where he was to meet Shaw. It lay between the city and Tan Son Nhut, the sprawling air base, and was both well hidden and well defended. He would take the borrowed Jeep into an alley, where a gate would mysteriously close behind him; after a winding drive he would emerge at the porte cochere of an old villa, be asked to disarm by two marines, and be hustled into a large drawing room. It was in this room that he had first met the large, florid civilian who started out by treating him as a part of the domestic staff. By the time Dane had gotten him out of that frame of mind, he had made an enemy.

He swung the Jeep to the right and around a long column of priests, walking silently. An image flashed in his mind: *barefoot, in the temple at Uijonbu, following the others to a session in the* dojang, *or to a silent meal, or to the mysterious spring.*

He turned the Jeep again and the gate closed. A few minutes later he had turned off the ignition and was walking up the steps, already unbuckling his sidearm and handing his carbine to the marines. Shaw was waiting just inside the door.

"Everything all right?" he asked.

"Yes. What's the story here?"

"Everybody's inside, waiting for you. You're late."

"The war isn't running on time. Let's go."

They walked on into the large, formal room. Dane thought it had once housed a French family of wealth and position. The furnishings were old and scarred, but of quality, and over a mantel hung a faded and torn portrait of what was undoubtedly a French nobleman. No one else, smiled Dane, could manage such hauteur.

Three men stood in the room, all sipping drinks. Before he could reach them a young Vietnamese in a white jacket asked him if he wanted a drink. He ordered vodka and walked on in, trailed by Shaw.

Three of the men he recognized. The tall, red-faced civilian with the large, pitted nose was the one who had given him an argument last time he was here. His name was Barton; his cover was some obscure assistance program in Saigon. Dane thought he probably was not military, probably Central Intelligence Agency or Defense Intelligence Agency. It didn't matter. He was the conduit for both the funds and the political strategy in the delta. The second man was Kapitski, reportedly an expert on the Viet Cong infrastructure. He was a small, pleasant-looking man who seldom ventured an opinion unless pressed. The third man was a navy captain, a military aide at the U.S. embassy.

Barton was the first to speak, talking in a loud, grating voice.

"Well, at last. Maybe now we can get started."

Dane merely stared at him, breaking it off when his vodka appeared. "Let's get comfortable," Barton said, and the men arranged themselves on the couches and chairs in the center of the room. Dane realized he had taken the chair nearest the door, facing the others. Good. It was the way he felt about them.

"Start it, Kapitski," Barton commanded and took a long pull of his drink.

Kapitski cleared his throat and glanced around the room. "All of you know something of the Viet Cong organization. It's far superior to the army of Vietnam, as you could guess. The VC have taken what was essentially a vertical system of communications and flattened it out, so that no longer does a peasant talk only to his immediate superior, his immediate inferior, or his immediate family. By a system of 'education camps' they've managed to break a lot of old traditions and create units capable of independent actions and operations. In other words, they're no longer the dull peasants who only respond to orders, usually accompanied by brute force. Today's VC are led by people who can innovate and experiment."

"All right," Barton interrupted. "None of us got here yesterday."

Kapitski lowered his head for a moment and then began to talk again, a bit more swiftly. "Through a system of regional headquarters and some support bases, the VC organization is now complex and interlocked. It has one serious flaw. Whether by design or accident, one man becomes indispensable if he is the man in command."

"Explain," Barton said harshly.

"In the operation we are about to discuss, the target is one man who is regarded as vital to VC operations in this sector of the delta. He is commander of the VC combat units. He is the tax collector for the villages. He is the commissar for political thought and action. And he wears a number of other hats: he commands the headquarters area where he locates, and he's also in charge of the VC hospital, the recreations site—in short, he's a one-man band with enormous power. And he has counterparts elsewhere in the delta. We believe there are five other such headquarters, meaning five men with the power and influence in their area that Nguyen Phong Hoan has in this area.

"We propose," Kapitski said, "to terminate Hoan. It will take weeks or months to replace him, which they will of course do. But we will have broken up their timetable for operations, disrupted their organization. We—"

"All right," Barton interjected. "I think they've all got the picture."

Dane sipped his vodka. "Why not capture him?"

"We don't think it's possible," Barton answered, "not even for the hired guns." Dane let it pass.

The navy captain spoke for the first time. "If we're ready to talk operational details?"

"Yeah," said Barton. "I'd love to hear an honest-to-God plan instead of somebody's reaction." He scratched his nose and looked slyly at Dane. "You got any ideas?"

"Yes, I have, Barton," Dane said mildly, "but I'm not going to tell you about them. I don't think you can keep your fat mouth shut."

Barton leaped to his feet, his face reddening. Dane gently set his vodka down on a table and watched him. If Barton came close to him, he would hit him. Instead, Barton stood where he was, his face beet-red, searching for words.

"I have to report to you as a matter of both protocol and practicality," Dane said, looking him in the eye. "It doesn't mean I have to take any shit from you."

The captain tried to intercede, but Dane waved him into silence.

"Now I have a plan, Barton," Dane continued. "I'll give it to you in general terms, but not the details. If you don't like it that way, I'll just ease on out. My contract is more than met, and incidentally, after this operation I'm going to join the rest of my group elsewhere, so you'd better plan to insert some more navy types down here."

Barton sat down, still glowering. The other two men relaxed a little.

"I'm going to send a patrol up the river and attack the island that lies opposite Hoan's headquarters, as a diversion. He'll recognize it for what it is and try to get out another way. I'll funnel him into my own position and, if possible, take him alive. If not, I'll kill him for you. That way, you people won't have to soil your hands in an assassination—although your morality escapes me for the moment."

"It's why you mercenaries were hired," Barton said in a strangled voice.

"I know," Dane said. "You don't want to have to tell the people at home that you engaged in actually assassinating the enemy leadership. As I said, I don't understand the morality, and frankly, I don't care."

"Is that it?" Barton asked. "That's all you intend to tell us?"

"That's it." Dane nodded.

"Can't you even tell us when?" the captain asked.

"That I can, and will. Exactly eleven days from now we'll go into a ready status and begin the operation with the next heavy rain. I want no air strikes or unusual artillery activity in that sector to spook Hoan, so you could arrange that for me."

"You know I have to approve or disapprove these operations," Barton said.

"It was your idea to go for Hoan, not mine. Are you telling me now you might disapprove it?"

"No," Barton said. "It's a go."

"You just wanted me to remember you had the authority, right?"

Barton's face began to redden again. "That's right, Dane.

After all, you are a hired hand. That rank isn't real, at least not as far as the U.S. is concerned. We all have our niches, and you have yours."

Dane stood. "I'll do this job, as I said. Then I'll go to my base camp and eventually join my partner elsewhere in Indochina. I'll check in with the embassy in my area, to fulfill the rest of the contract. But I'll tell you this, Barton: don't get in my way anymore. If I'm not an officer as far as you're concerned, neither am I a gentleman. Which is a roundabout way of saying that if you continue to piss me off, I'm going to knock you on your ass."

In the silence that followed, Dane smiled at all three men and walked from the room. He heard Shaw hurrying after him. To hell with them all. He was sick of Vietnam and its futility. He fought for money, true, but he also fought in causes he could support. The war was unwinnable unless the Americans changed their tactics, unless they began to pay attention to Vietnam's history and Indochina's tradition of malice toward neighbors. Vietnam was going under and there was damn little anybody could do about it, short of starting over and doing it right, and it didn't appear likely. And if Vietnam went, what about Laos and Cambodia? Even now it was impossible to keep the war away from them. He thought of the proud highlanders in Laos, and the gentle Khmers in the towns and small villages. God help them when the Viets finally took over all of Vietnam, because everything in their history pointed to more conflict. Well, he would do what he could in Laos, at least. Maybe Gabriel was making some headway against the Lao communists. Must be a bitch up there, though, trying to fight the Pathet Lao, trying to cut the Ho Chi Minh trail where it snaked through northern Laos.

Shaw caught up with him. "I'm coming with you," the major said. "That was a hell of a show back there."

"Meet me in the delta, then," Dane said. "But I won't be there for another eight or ten days."

"Right," Shaw said happily. "See you then."

Dane got into the Jeep and cranked it up. Now to find Sara. As he pulled away from the villa he caught sight of the three men stepping outside, Barton leading them as usual. He hoped Barton would cross him again someday, just for the pleasure of taking him apart.

How to go about finding Sara? Start at the Caravelle, perhaps, or meet her outside the five o'clock follies, that daily briefing that had become so infamous throughout Vietnam. Or simply go to her place, if he could find it.

Sara. He smiled. He had truly missed her.

A long time later he had turned in the Jeep and gotten a ride in a battered Citroën to Sara's place; the Citroën was driven by a correspondent for a Washington newspaper, and Dane was astonished at how young the correspondent was. Or was he just getting older?

He found her place in the charcoal dusk of evening and took the stairs two at a time just as the grille was being closed over the front of the store. That was the Laotian slave that Sara had mentioned. Dane put it out of his mind.

He found the door at the top of the stairs and paused. From inside came the sound of a typewriter, and he smiled. Sara, at last. He knocked gently and stepped back.

Sara opened the door and he smiled down at her, trying to hide his shock. She rushed into his arms and held him desperately, while he held her very gently and let her sob into his shoulder. She had aged; she was painfully thin and there were lines on her forehead that he had not noticed before.

"Come inside," she said. "There's someone I want you to meet."

Frowning, he stepped inside. On the bed of the small room a child was looking at magazines. She was a Vietnamese girl with large dark eyes and wearing an American dress.

"This is my friend Colonel John Dane," Sara said formally to the child. "And this young lady is my very close friend Huyen," she said, turning to Dane and looking at him anxiously. "I had no way of telling you she was here," Sara said apologetically.

"What's the story?" Dane asked.

"I found her in a pile of rubble in Cholon. The VC had rocketed the place. She was the only thing left alive."

"So you brought her home," Dane said, sitting down on the edge of the bed. The child watched him carefully.

Sara ran her hand through her hair, gesturing helplessly with the other hand. "I just couldn't leave her there."

"Have you gone to the Vietnamese authorities?"

"I've done everything. You know what it's like. She's just another mouth to feed."

"Yes, I know."

"And a girl at that," Sara said bitterly. "That gets her even less sympathy from the bureaucrats."

"Sara, are you about to tell me what I think you are?"

"That's right. I'm going to adopt her."

Dane got up and walked over to the small veranda overlooking the street. He could not blame her. It happened to a lot of people here. You came out to do a job and got caught up in the immensity of Asia, its cruelties as well as its splendors. If you were young or idealistic, or both, you had a terrible impulse to do something about the poverty and the callousness and the agonizing traditions that bound many Asians to a remorseless past and future. Westerners came to Indochina, some to plunder, some to preach, but all got ensnared by it, inexorably bound in its subtleties and its diversity. And some, like Sara, felt they had to try to change things—but never could.

He felt her come up behind him, felt her arms going around his waist. He reached down and covered her hands with his. "How long have you had her?" he asked.

"A couple of months. I've started the paper work. It could take a while."

"Anybody asked for squeeze, yet?"

"No. I'll pay it if I have to."

"What does Kona Sunderland think of the idea?"

"He's all for it."

"And the girl?"

"She's still bewildered, but she knows what's happening. She's learning English from a private tutor who comes here every morning. She knows her family is gone."

Sara turned to the child. "We think she's four years old, right Huyen?"

The child nodded, watching Dane gravely.

"She knows we'll be taking a long trip together someday, and that she'll have a new home. And no bombs or guns, right, sweetheart?"

The child nodded again.

Sara smiled up at Dane. "She's a little shy at first."

Dane stared at the child, lost in thought. *Who needed a father, he had once asked himself, if you have Tawodi? But mixed in with the answer there was still a sense of loss. I'll be around if my son ever needs me, and obviously that's the way Sara feels about this child.*

Dane heard himself sigh. "Now what, Sara? Are we going to have any time alone?"

She answered quickly, "Of course. I can get a baby-sitter this evening. The family downstairs will be glad to take care of her for a while, especially for a few piasters."

"I was thinking of taking you to Singapore for a few days," Dane said. "I think you could use a rest. Get away from the war for a while."

"Oh," Sara said quietly and sat down on the bed. Dane waited.

"I don't think I can leave her," Sara said, her voice almost a whisper.

"Sara, you've got to go away for a while. I think the war is getting to you."

She looked up and to Dane's surprise there were tears in her eyes. "I know what you're saying. I look awful. I can see it myself."

"You don't look awful. You look tired."

The child walked over and stood by Sara, frowning at the tears she saw. Sara put one arm around her and drew her close, and the child put her arms around Sara's neck. Dane walked back to the veranda and looked out again. The evening had brought darkness, but little relief from the heat. There were no stars visible. He hoped the rainy season would last at least another eleven days.

He turned back into the room, where Sara had turned on a table lamp. The glow made the flat look softer and more inviting, and it took some of the lines out of her face. Huyen had climbed onto the bed again, sitting with her arms around her knees, watching Dane.

"I've forgotten to offer you a drink," Sara said and managed a smile.

"I want you to come with me to Singapore," he said. "If nothing else, you just need a rest."

Sara looked away, then looked back. "Maybe I can do it," she said. She walked to him and put her hands on his chest. "You're right. I need to get away. Some bad things have happened here. Could we go for just a few days? I don't want to leave her too long."

"Bring her," Dane said. "It might be awkward, but we can manage."

"No," said Sara. "I'll leave her with the family downstairs for four or five days. If that's all right? Is that enough time?"

He ran his hand gently across her hair. He thought some of the tension might be leaving her, but he couldn't be sure. "We'll go for just a few days, Sara. We'll eat very well and drink champagne and take real baths. We'll stay in an air-conditioned room. We'll make love slowly and with great care, and great frequency. You won't think about Vietnam for even a moment."

"Oh, God, Dane. Let's do it. Yes."

"How soon can you leave?"

"I'll start making arrangements tomorrow morning. What about tonight?"

Dane glanced at Huyen, still staring at him.

"I can get into the Majestic for tonight. Long as I wear these colonel's eagles, everyone thinks I'm real."

"Damn," Sara said. "I haven't seen you in months. Tonight you're only going to be a mile from here."

"It's all right."

"Do you want to have dinner?"

"No. You'd better spend this evening telling her what's happening. I'll start working on the flight and see you here about noon. Maybe we can have lunch somewhere."

She stepped outside the door with him and he bent down to her. He kissed her, a long, lingering, hungry kiss. When he straightened up he saw her eyes were glistening again. "Damn you, John Dane, I've missed you terribly. What are we going to do about each other?"

"We'll talk about it over a real Singapore sling."

He walked through the streets of the city, headed toward the river. The streets were packed with people, cyclists, motor-scooters, beggars. There was a great deal of noise and a variety of scents, of incense and dung, drugs and cooking fires. He went up the steps to the Majestic and spent a few minutes checking in. A Vietnamese man old enough to be his father insisted on carrying his bag up to his room. He tipped the man and got rid of him, washed his face, and turned on the ceiling fan to cool the room. Then he took the one workable elevator up to the top floor of the hotel and walked out on the terrace. It was crowded with military men and civilians, and a Filipino vocalist was mimicking the latest Stateside singing style. He got a vodka at the bar and went over to a small table by himself. Behind him the band had struck up a new tune and the vocalist was throwing herself into it with forced suggestiveness. He could hear the tinkle of ice in glasses and the laughter of the men on the terrace. He sat very still, listening, and looking out over the river and over the city and into the countryside beyond. As he sat there he could see flares dropping and watched the flickering of artillery in the distance, lighting up the hot and dangerous night.

Ashton was content this morning. He had breakfasted well and early, and now he strolled through the base camp with a mug of hot tea. It could be some moments yet before the camp came alive and when it did it would bring the usual joys and the usual problems. But now dawn came out of China, not like thunder but like a whisper, delicate and beautiful, and a slight breeze began to stir the leaves to life. He stopped, one foot up on a rock, and sipped the tea.

The camp was in the foothills of the Luang Prabang Range, which dropped north-south out of Laos. It was well chosen; Dane had a genius for picking his spots well. To the southeast

lay Udon, with its airstrip and its strategic position on a junc-
ture of workable highways. To the northeast was Nong Khai,
perhaps the most important town in northeast Thailand by its
location on the Mekong directly across from Vientiane, the ad-
ministrative capital of Laos. To the north was the Mekong, and
a thousand places where it could be crossed in secret if necessary, and to the west was the mountain range and the protection of miles of friendly Thai territory. *Friendly for now, at least.
In this bloody part of the world friends often became enemies and enemies
became friends.*

Inexplicably, his thoughts turned to the morning's mail.

There had been a letter from his wife. God, he still thought
of her that way. His *ex-wife*. The divorce had been very painful
for him and, he thought, for her. It had been only a few months
ago and he had known immediately it was a mistake. Obviously, she did too, for the mail had brought the letter from
her that had given him much encouragement. It had hinted
that having him now and then, between jobs, as it were, was
better than nothing at all. It also had suggested that she had
been a good army wife throughout his career, and she supposed
she might be able to do it again, and how did he feel about it?
Well, he felt wonderful about it, and he would tell her so.

There was a message from Langé; he would be pulling
back as planned and would arrive in base camp in another
week.

He went back to his tent to find the in-tray piling up again.
He took off his beret, ran his hand through his cropped hair,
and plunged into the rest of the paper work. He was engrossed
in it when he sensed someone else in the room. He looked up.
Dane was standing there.

"My God, what a surprise! I thought you were in Singapore." He grinned and reached out to shake hands.

Dane shook hands briefly, removed his own beret, and sat in
a folding camp stool opposite Ashton's desk before replying.

"Well, as you can see, I'm here. How are things going?"

"All right, no problems. But what are you doing here? We
didn't expect to see you so soon. How was Singapore? How is

Sara? Ah, I'm sorry, Dane. That's it, isn't it? Didn't go smoothly?"

"No," Dane said shortly. "Let's drop it. What do you hear from Gabriel?"

For long minutes Ashton sketched in Langé's last few messages and his morning message that he would be back in a week. As he did so, he watched Dane carefully.

The American looked tired. He sat opposite Ashton like a coiled snake; his face was drawn and the dark eyes looked shadowed. Somehow, he still gave off that air of absolute confidence in himself, and a hint of menace. It struck Ashton then that Dane was as much a victim of those attributes as he was aided by them. The Old West analogy occurred to Ashton again. Dane was the gunfighter hired to chase the outlaws out of town, the man who could get the job done but remained friendless and, later, an embarrassment to the town.

". . . so, other than having a mild case of Ho Chi Minh's revenge, Gabriel is in good shape. He should be in camp in another three or four days."

"I'll miss him, then. I'm going back to the delta for a final operation, then I'll be back here for a while. Is Kinnan with Gabriel?"

"Yes."

"Are the troops getting paid on time? Any problems with the embassy? Any logistics problems?"

"No, rather good shape, actually. We try to remain unobtrusive and just do the job. I think everyone's pleased with us."

"Not everyone," Dane said softly.

"Beg pardon?"

"Nothing," he said. "It's nothing. I want to look around the camp before leaving. I'll stay overnight and leave at first light. I'll need a Jeep and driver. And with Ashton beside him, Dane began his inspection of the camp.

It's no use, she had said; I can't relax. I'm so sorry, Dane, but I want to get back.

You haven't given it an honest shot. We've only been here two days.

I want to go back. Oh, God, I've loved making love to you. I love this wonderful old hotel. I want to come back to Singapore someday with you, my darling. But I can't get Saigon out of my mind.

You mean Huyen.

Yes.

I told you to bring her, dammit.

I know, but it didn't seem right. The Phan family downstairs will take care of her.

Then what are you worried about?

I feel guilty. I feel I should be back there. I don't know, I guess I feel there's something wrong with lying around in Singapore, drinking and screwing—as much as I've enjoyed it.

Sara, it's going to be a hell of a long war. I can't seem to get anyone to believe that. You'll have enough time in Vietnam to get sick of it before all this is over.

I'm glad I don't believe that.

You can use your eyes, can't you?

You're saying the war will go on another two or three years?

Or longer.

And will you be around for all of it?

No. I'm getting out in less than a month.

Oh?

Look. The Americans aren't going to win it, any more than the French could, because they're making the same mistakes. The night and the countryside belong to the Viet Cong. The daytime and the cities belong to the Americans. I don't have to tell you which one frightens the people of the hamlets more, and which one is going to outwait the other.

So you're leaving because it looks hopeless?

No, I'm leaving because I don't believe in it.

My, my, you're now on the side of the antiwar protesters.

No. You're not trying to understand.

Explain, then.

I don't think America was evil for coming in here. The U.S. came with the best of intentions. But the strategy is wrong and the tactics are wrong and it can't be won unless there are drastic changes, and I don't believe there will be. So I'm taking my people and getting out. I told you, we don't fight just for money; we fight when we believe in what we're doing. I can't follow orders from people who are doing it wrong.

Look at us. In this enormous suite at Raffles, in Singapore. A bottle of *champagne, a cool ceiling fan, two nights without being rocketed. And all we talk about is the war. It's my fault. You see how it is with me? I just can't let go of it.*

Huyen.

Yes. I simply have to get back. I worry about her, about all of them. I'm really, really sorry, Dane. I think I love you. I want more time with you, away from the damned war. But not like this, not when I can't get rid of it. It simply lies there between us. I want to go back to Saigon and get Huyen and get her out of there as soon as possible.

And then?

Then I'll go back. I'll leave her in Hawaii and go back until I feel I've done all I can. Then I'll get out.

All right, Sara. I think we just turned a corner, don't you?

I don't understand.

Well, you've had difficulty understanding what I do, and now I'm having a problem with you. Maybe sometime in the furture . . .

I'm so sorry, Dane.

It's all right. I'll see about getting a flight. This afternoon all right?

Oh, God, I suppose. Are you angry with me? Did I hurt you?

I'll survive.

They caught a ride with two CBS cameramen out of Tan Son Nhut air base into Saigon. The cameramen asked Dane what unit he was with and he used the cover story that had been worked out for him. Sara sat stiffly beside him, lost in thought, as silent as she had been most of the trip back from Singapore. The few days away had made no recognizable changes; Dane felt the same miasma he always felt in Saigon. He glanced at Sara. The few days away had made little recognizable change in her either, for the lines still creased her forehead and she was becoming as thin as any hungry peasant. He looked out the window, keeping a wary eye on the bicycles nearest the car. The Viet Cong were wont to drop grenades in cars, using young girls on bicycles who would close on the cars in the dense traffic and simply flip a fragmentation grenade through the open window. He was distracted by the bicycles and was looking away when he heard Sara gasp. He looked back just as she put her hand to her mouth and started to moan.

A military police unit had cordoned off the entrance to her street. Beyond the barricades and the handful of military policemen, Sara's block lay in ruins.

The car lurched to a halt. As quick as he was, Sara was out of the car ahead of him and running toward the barricades. He was right behind her when he saw the MPs close and start to raise their weapons in a blocking stance. He charged in front of her, yelling.

"I'm Colonel Dane. Let us through."

The MPs drew back at once and Sara rounded the barricades and flung herself down the street. Dane paused to get a feel for what had happened, and then he heard Sara, half moaning, half screaming with every breath as she ran toward the rubble where her flat had been. By the time he caught up with her, she was standing very still, her face deathly white, staring at smashed concrete. Nothing of the two-story building was now more than two or three feet high. They stood, staring at the wreckage. He left her standing there, trancelike, and went back to the nearest MP.

"What happened?"

The MP was a tall, composed black.

"Well, it was a VC mortar attack, Colonel. Some terrorism, too. Man in that house there"—he gestured toward Sara's place—"he killed the family in there and set some charges. When they went off the VC started blowing other buildings around here. Sure made a mess."

Dane felt himself growing cold. "Where's the report on this?"

"The Vietnamese police did the investigation, but we did one, too. Ours is better, I guess. You can see Colonel Vandermeer. I guess you know him."

"Yes," Dane said. "I know who he is."

"Happened last night," the soldier said and turned to look down the street. "That the lady that lived there?"

"Yes," Dane replied.

"Colonel Vandermeer's trying to find her. You want to take her down, Colonel, or shall I get someone to do it?"

"Get us a Jeep if you can. I'll bring her."

He turned to go back down the street. Sara was running again, this time toward him. Her eyes looked enormous in her thin face. Dane felt a great sorrow welling up inside him.

"Dane—"

"We don't know anything yet, Sara. Come on, I'll take you down to headquarters and we'll see what we can find out. Don't jump to conclusions."

"She's dead. I know it."

"We don't know yet. Come on, here's the Jeep."

A few blocks to the east they entered a low, concrete building in the center of a compound filled with MPs. Colonel Vandermeer was a heavy, balding, businesslike man who saw them at once.

"Excuse the clutter in here," he said. "Can I get you coffee?"

Sara was still ashen. "What happened?"

Vandermeer looked down at the report on his desk.

"Perhaps you'd better sit down, Miss Sunderland," he said gently.

Sara screamed and would have fallen. Dane caught her and eased her into a heavy wooden chair. She had both hands to her face and her eyes were wild. She started to sob.

Vandermeer cleared his throat and looked resignedly at Dane, who stood beside Sara's chair.

"There was a servant of the Phan family—"

"The Laotian slave," Sara said, her voice rasping.

"He was a terrorist. He shot the family—"

"Oh, God. Oh, God." Sara buried her face in her hands.

"—and then planted charges throughout the building. It seems the Phans were politically connected and had been marked for assassination by the VC. He blew the building as a signal for a VC mortar attack. It was a suicide mission, of course. They did a hell of a lot of damage, but none of them got out of it. I must admit, they terrorized the city, though. It was a hell of a psychological victory for them."

246

"Colonel," Sara said, in an awful whisper, "who was killed in the Phan family?"

"All of them," the colonel said. "One grandparent, an elderly male. The parents. The wife's sister. Three children, two boys and a girl, all in their teens. And the little girl, age three or four."

Sara fainted.

Dane carried her to a couch and loosened the buttons of her dress. She had never looked more vulnerable. An MP brought a basin of water and a towel, and Dane began pressing the wet towel to her forehead. In a few minutes her eyes fluttered and she opened them wide suddenly and looked at Dane, and then her eyes grew cold.

"She's dead."

"Yes, Sara. It appears that way. I'm sorry. I'm sorry."

She propped up on one elbow, then swung her legs and sat up on the couch. Her face was still pale and he thought she might faint again, but when she spoke it was with a voice of steel.

"We should never have left her. We should never have gone."

"Sara, you can't blame yourself. Or me. We had no way of preventing this. It would have happened with you here."

"I would have protected her. She'd be alive if we hadn't gone to Singapore."

"You can't know that. I don't believe that for a moment."

"You—what do you care? You're used to this. You just take your fucking pay and kill people."

"Sara, don't."

"We're responsible. I'll never forget that. I'll never put that out of my mind."

"You're wrong. We couldn't have prevented it. The only thing that's different because we went is that *you're* still alive."

She stared up at him. "I don't want to see you anymore. I'm going to try to not even think about you."

"Come on, let's find you a place to stay tonight. Vandermeer will want to talk with you later. We'll get you into the Caravelle for tonight and tomorrow things will look different. Believe me, I know what you're going through. But you'll make it."

"Don't touch me," she said coldly. "Leave me alone."

"Sara—"

"Get out of my life. I'm sorry I ever knew you." She stood up suddenly and screamed, "Get out, get out, you heartless bastard, you goddamned *mercenary.*" She started to scream hysterically.

He slapped her. She grew still immediately, like the slamming of a door.

He turned and walked out the door, knowing he would never see her again.

A half hour before the junks were to sail, Dane called a final briefing. It was attended by Donovan and the chuluc commanders, six of the most trusted men in the compound and, Dane knew, six of the highest paid. They met in Dane's hut, all of them wet from the rain outside, which washed over the compound and turned it into a quagmire. It was absolutely the rottenest weather Dane had seen in days, and he welcomed it.

In the gloom of the hut he lit a kerosene lamp and looked at the faces around him. Donovan looked anxious but unafraid; he was gaining experience by the day and Dane thought him reliable. A couple of the chuluc commanders he had doubts about, but the others were impassive and apparently ready to go out and do the job.

"Let's do it all once more," Dane said.

Donovan spoke: "Upriver on the engines, hidden by the sound of the rain. Stations in a broadside pattern—crossing the T, as it were—on the left, or west, shore of the island. At twenty hundred, open up with the mortars and small arms. Every second junk close on the beach to put men ashore. The beach party to dig in and not try to advance. Then we wait."

"All right so far," Dane said.

"At twenty hundred plus fifteen minutes the other junks close and begin evacuation of the beach party, providing the secondary attack materializes and we hear it. If we do not, we advance at best speed and try to close on the headquarters, inflicting all the damage we can.

"Because"—he grinned—"if we don't hear the secondary attack, the thing is damned well blown."

"You'll hear it," Dane said. "Tranh?"

The Vietnamese sitting near Donovan answered in broken English: "We take north end, across island. Wait for Hoan. Shoot as soon as VC come. Then go in island, join beach party."

Dane nodded. "And I'll do the rest," he said.

Back out into the rain, they filed through the compound and out the end facing the river. Dane had ordered a couple of junkmen to stay at Papa Dat's and give the impression of another quiet night on the river because of the weather. But he knew the VC would have spotters out in spite of the rain, and he would have to beat them upriver. He had the advantage of knowing where he was going, but the VC couldn't know.

He boarded the last of the dozen junks and heard the engine kick to life, saw the spurt of light smoke disappear in the driving rain. He crawled into the low, thatched deckhouse and lay down and closed his eyes. It would be at least an hour before he had to move again. After a while he gave up trying to nap; every time he closed his eyes he saw Sara's face, her eyes filled with hatred, accusing him. He went through a weapons check again, just to have something to do.

He carried the M-16 now, because his men did. He had two grenades in a small pouch on his belt. He wore the black pants and shirt of the junk sailors, and a black beret. Nowhere did he wear insignia; no point in attracting fire. His stag-handled knife was secure in its sheath, and underneath his shirt was the wolf amulet he had worn for twenty years now. He wore a pistol belt with an Army-issue .45 and ammunition pouches. On his feet were the new jungle boots the Army was trying. He wasn't sure about them yet. Hell of a place to experiment or, more accurately, hell of a time.

He stuck his head out of the deckhouse. The next junk was only twenty or twenty-five meters in front of them, but it was almost impossible to see, for which he was grateful. Surprise and confusion were going to be essential tonight, or the whole operation would simply unravel.

As he looked upriver he saw the sudden glow of a cigarette and swore under his breath. He had insured radio silence by leaving all the PRC-10s back at the base, but that would be useless if they were spotted. The VC would know they left the base all right, but there were a hundred tributaries and small channels they could take, so no signal would be sounded until someone knew where they were, and where they were going. *Get rid of that damned cigarette!* In a few minutes, the smoker did, and the river was dark again. He pulled his head back inside the deckhouse, rain streaming down his face, and tried to concentrate on the mission. Hoan's dual military-civilian capacity made him a prime target, and if Kapitski had been right, his removal would disrupt the infrastructure for a time. Dane also had gotten an understanding from Shaw that if they collected any money in the operation, he could spread it among the junkmen, a kind of accepted looting that Shaw and the others were prepared to condone. Dane would have done it anyway.

He had no illusions about Hoan. The VC would simply replace him with some other qualified man from the COSVN— the Central Office for South Vietnam of the Lao Dong Party, the link between Hanoi and the Viet Cong. COSVN was located in the Plain of Reeds near the Cambodian border and, he suspected, it actually shifted over the border when things got hot. But eliminating Hoan would serve notice that two could play the assassination game, and it might slow some of the more brazen acts of terrorism. He thought of the rubble of Sara's building, the dead family, the building shuddering apart, and then the mortars falling indiscriminately on the street. He had little respect for people who made war on women and children, but would readily admit that terrorism of that sort was effective and might spell the difference in the outcome of the war in the long run. Well, there was going to be one terrorist less.

The junks slipped smoothly upriver in the darkness and hammering rain, no lights showing and the engine noises blotted out by the rain. He felt ready, but decided to meditate for a few minutes. He smiled when he thought of Master Kim, then he sat in silence for the next ten minutes, freeing his mind and finding a level of peace. When he looked up again, he felt even more relaxed and the old confidence came to him, the feeling that he could do anything demanded of him on this mission, the sense that he would not, could not, fail. He got up and left the deckhouse and moved easily to the forward section of the chuluc, ignoring the rain. He was, at that moment, a bad-weather animal, Waya-unutsi, a warrior of the Aniyunwiya.

He heard a soft call from the junk immediately in front of them. It was time to start. He went back and spoke softly to the helmsman, and the junk dropped off and swung to starboard and cut its engine. It drifted gently up onto the river bank, and he eased over the side, feeling his weight push him into the mud. But he could walk. He slapped the side of the chuluc and heard them start the engine again and back away from the bank. They would rejoin the others. He was on his own now, in the pitch-dark night and the rain, deep into the enemy camp. He turned to his left and began to ease through the jungle, operating on his sense of smell and feel, and on instinct.

It was slow going, but he simply moved around obstacles, sometimes going crab-wise to the side until he could pick up his direction again. He was in no particular hurry, and he had time to think about what he was doing. He liked the premise on which this raid was based, being both Asian and subtle, and bold and typical Aniyunwiya strategy.

The raid by the junks would be a diversion; Hoan would see through it immediately. The second raid from the north would be considered the real raid. Hoan would hold out in his camp until he became convinced that the second raid was real, then he would turn to the southeast to escape. It would not occur to him that so few forces would be raiding so strong an outpost. So he would run, and run straight into Dane. Hoan would not think the Americans would be bush-wise enough to provide not one but two diversions. And the rain and darkness would confuse everything, and confusion was Dane's ally.

As he moved around a thick clump of brush Dane noticed a lighter area off to his right, possibly a clearing. Now he was getting close, and the things to worry about were guards and trip wires. He squatted and thought, in his mind picturing the lay of the land and roughly his position on it. He thought his speed was good enough, and if he was as close as he thought, his target wasn't far. Now he moved with great caution, stopping every step to feel the ground in front of him for wires and trying not to touch any of the branches that jutted out at him in the darkness. He was astonished by how much noise the rain was making. Hoan would never believe it, Dane grinned, never believe the Americans would be out in such weather.

He felt a wire, and careful not to pick it up, he ran his hand along it very gently until he felt it curve upward. *Something in the tree.* He stayed low and stepped over the wire and waited. All at once another image came to him: months ago, in a disputed village, a junkman had walked in front of him to a gate and stopped to check it for booby traps. First the junkman took off a trip wire that would have blown the gate, and them. Then he searched again and found a second wire to still another cache of explosives. Gleefully the junkman removed the second wire. Before he started through the gate the junkman made one more cursory search—and found a spring-loaded pungi stick that would have snapped directly into the chest of anyone coming through the gate. Laughing, the junkman dismantled the trap and opened the gate and stepped through it. And stepped on a personnel mine just under the dirt on the other side of the gate. The concussion had knocked Dane backward and down, and they had found very little of the junkman.

So Dane squatted and waited for a few minutes, trying to *feel* what had happened here. He moved his hand slowly to the left and upward, very gently, and found the second wire, three feet off the ground and taut. He crawled under it, again feeling in front of him. A few minutes later he moved to the left and walked, crouching, parallel to the wires. If they had paid a lot of attention to this area, it must be well traveled, hence Hoan might decide this would be his way out. Dane wouldn't take any chances. He wanted to be closer.

He thought the rain was letting up. He looked at his watch.

Almost time. Out of long habit he changed his direction again and started doubling back to the right. And froze.

It was a very human sound; he thought at once of Donovan. Someone was sleeping very close by and snoring. He squatted again, riveted to the spot, listening. Then he knew where it was, and he crawled slowly in that direction. In the dark night he almost missed him, but there was a tiny bit of reflection on the guard's weapon. Dane sat and studied him, and after a long time could make out how he was lying. He couldn't leave the guard behind him once the shooting started. He had no choice. He crawled beside the guard and took the knife out. He brought it with all his strength down into the guard's chest, feeling the body lurch under him. He held the knife as the guard's body heaved again and was still. A few minutes later he had sheathed the knife and was moving once more, trying to decide where the second guard would be. Then he heard the night shatter with gunfire.

He hunched beside the guard and waited until he heard the pounding of footsteps; the second guard was coming by, probably to collect his fellow sentry. Dane backed off and stood behind a tree. In a moment the second Viet Cong came up and stopped, bending over the man Dane had killed. Dane swung the M-16 in a short, powerful arc and watched the second guard roll heavily into the bushes. He turned and stared toward the sound of gunfire, glancing once at his watch.

The junkmen were making a hell of a noise and the element of surprise was devastating. Dane could hear a lot of confusion and he thought he heard boats being launched. The first diversion was drawing support troops to the island, but he knew Hoan would not go. Someone in Hoan's camp stupidly lit a lantern, though, and in the quick light Dane could orient himself with the few huts of the camp. A moment later the lantern went out, and a moment after that Dane heard the second attack begin in the north. Things would heat up quickly now.

Someone finally got the camp organized, and there was a systematic return fire. The junkmen were still pouring it on and the raid had all the earmarks of a classic frontal diversion, flank attack. Dane waited for the third part of the plan to develop, and it wasn't long in coming.

A party of Viet Cong were moving in his direction. He was sure it was Hoan and his staff, moving records out, trying to melt into the night. Dane slid down behind the tree and took the safety off. They were quite close now.

He saw the bushes part and a group of men start out. At almost exactly the same moment the rain stopped like the shutting off of a tap; it didn't let up, it just stopped. For some reason the men paused and began to talk in low but excited voices. Still Dane waited. A few minutes later two other men joined the first four and in a night growing steadily lighter with the disappearance of the clouds, Dane knew one of the men was Hoan.

He stepped from behind the tree and fired.

The two men nearest him were blown backward and he kept traversing, but he thought Hoan had gone down too soon. He turned and moved behind the tree and off to the other side, looking for a new angle of fire, moving out of instinct. As he came up he saw the man believed to be Hoan slip into the bush. He looked like he was limping. Dane moved farther to his left and started to make a wide circle. He could hear shouting behind him and then he realized the firing from the junks had stopped. Donovan would be pulling the troops out now, a few minutes early. He's learning, Dane thought. The coming moonlight had better find them downriver or there'd be hell to pay, and Donovan wasn't wasting any time.

He heard the voices again and hurried in a direction paralleling that of Hoan, but not directly behind him. The damned moon will be out any moment, he thought. He might have wounded Hoan mortally, but if not, it was going to be a hell of an interesting night.

Donovan had the party off the beach and onto the junks in good order; the moonlight now would become his enemy and he wanted to get downriver before the VC could set an ambush. Although the river was a major one in the delta, it could widen and narrow remarkably, in places only a few meters from the junks. He couldn't wait for the secondary attack to be pressed, knowing Tranh would take his contingent and move them eastward to a friendly area, eventually making their way back to base.

In the brightening night he saw the casualties for the first time, the six or seven men who had been hit. None of them looked fatal and if they could get a medic to the base they could med-evac the worst of them. In any case, the casualties were much lighter than expected, and Donovan could appreciate Dane's insistence on total surprise. There were few things in life more demoralizing than to be attacked suddenly, at night, in bad weather, and not knowing the enemy's strength or intentions. He hoped Dane was all right.

With the last man aboard Donovan shouted and the junks began to turn downriver. He was on the lead junk and setting the pace, for if he ran the diesels at full power, he'd literally tear the junk apart. The lack of wind and the narrowness and curves of the river made the sails useless now, so he pushed the engine as far as he dared and lay down on the deck, facing the riverbank to his port. The attack, if it came, would come from there. It would also tell him something about the VC ability to regroup and rebound.

He looked back and saw the junks in line, a fine sight even in the middle of a war. They were of a design that had been popular along this coast centuries before, and his particular war was the kind of warfare that must have taken place here, with men on shore hurling missiles of one kind or another at men in boats. Donovan was still staring at the junks when it came to him that he could see them quite clearly. In the aftermath of the rainstorm, the moon was up and nearly full and the river and brush were taking on silver reflections, wet leaves shining in the steamy night, and highlights of the moon on the water. He could even see men on the other junks. Oh, shit, he thought, and the first shot came from the riverbank.

The low gunwales offered little protection, but Donovan hugged the deck and turned his M-16 toward the bank, looking for gunflashes. He saw them then and opened fire. Around him, all at once, the night seemed to explode with gunfire and the noise was deafening. In the next few moments he was in the heaviest fire fight he had ever known, and deep in his stomach he felt a great emptiness that was somehow linked to a tiny part of his mind that kept telling him this was a hell of a place for a nice Irish kid from Boston. He reloaded and kept firing.

From somewhere in the brush he heard a familiar banging sound, very close, and the water alongside his junk suddenly blasted upward in a great fountain. The junk rocked and settled and something Dane had told him flashed in his mind: the junks were uncomfortable, flimsy, and no protection in a fight, but they were impossible to sink without a direct hit. Even full of holes they would stay afloat.

The second blast came at the junk behind him, and he saw it, too, ride up and settle back. The VC were using a captured M-79 grenade launcher, good for some three hundred meters. It looked like a sawed-off shotgun and broke down and loaded the same way. It was a favorite weapon in the delta. *Too bad the bastards had it.*

The third blast found the range. The third junk in the line suddenly came apart in the middle, throwing men into the water, hurling debris, which seemed to take long moments to splash into the water. Donovan saw the fourth junk slow to pick up survivors, then he turned back to the fire fight.

Suddenly, it was over.

The junks were through the narrows and into the wide waters that formed part of the river mouth, opening on the South China Sea. Donovan sat back against the deckhouse, took off his beret, and wiped his forehead—and winced. He felt gingerly above his eyes; his forehead was pocked with dozens of tiny splinters, probably from the gunwale. He hadn't even noticed at the time.

They reached the base long before morning, but now it was a bright night and they had no trouble standing down from the long patrol. Donovan called a quick debriefing and an assessment of casualties. There were two men who would have to have a dust-off tomorrow morning, providing he could get a chopper to the base, but he thought they would make it. He called for a round of drinks for all hands, and finally he dropped gratefully into his sleeping bag. If all went well, it would take Dane a few hours to reach his pickup point, rendezvous with the helicopter, and be flown home. He, Donovan, probably would still be asleep.

Two days later he was still waiting anxiously for Dane.

Waya was tracking.

There were two trails, two wounded men. They had split up and were moving southeast in parallel courses, but separately. They knew they had been ambushed and were taking no chances. Traveling apart they would be harder to find.

He picked up blood signs, on a leaf, on a tree where one of them had leaned for support. From there they had parted and he now had the hard choice to make: follow which one?

There was no way to reason it out; it was all chance. He abandoned any hope of making the rendezvous with the helicopter. He had to hunt Hoan down and kill him, wherever he was and however long it took. He saw the broken tree branch and took it as an omen, and pushed off in that direction.

The night now was brilliantly lit. He hoped Donovan and the junks would get downriver all right, but the VC were good, and quick, and undoubtedly they would ambush. He had known that experience more than once.

He put it out of his mind. He was tracking.

Here and there he followed a bent branch, a footprint visible in the new mud created by the rain. He found another bloodstain and kept easing forward, knowing there were few other men in the world who could do what he was doing now.

An hour before dawn he came across a wide ribbon of blood. His quarry's wound was worsening and probably slowing him even more. He would have to be more cautious now, especially with the coming light. Depending on where they were, Hoan—or his companion—would either hide during the day or plunge on, counting on being found by friendly forces. It was a characteristic of war in the delta; there were no neatly drawn boundaries, and you could go from one point to another in a straight line and be, by turns, in friendly and enemy areas. It was one reason why the farmers and the fishermen of the delta tried desperately to remain friendly with everybody. But they couldn't understand that in Saigon, where they demanded absolute loyalty from the peasants. Absolute loyalty meant somebody in your family would be disemboweled as an object lesson. He couldn't blame the peasants for their efforts to placate both sides.

First light found him in a thick brush and facing a decision: move on during the day, or wait. He decided to move.

The delta was waking up. He thought he heard noises and moved cautiously. There were many natural sounds in the brush—the wind causing huge leaves to flap, tree branches rubbing against each other, heavy fruit plummeting to the ground and breaking up—and he listened to each sound, trying to identify it. Still he kept moving.

He saw his target an hour after dawn, drawn to the spot slightly to his right and ahead of him by a noise that sounded unnatural. He crept forward and stopped and straightened up. The Viet Cong had fallen forward. He could see the man's body heaving as he struggled to breathe. He moved forward cautiously, then bent and turned the man over. Even as he did, he heard the man give a small sigh and stop breathing.

It was not Hoan.

He quickly searched the body, finding what appeared to be a few letters and a rather impressive amount of piasters. He pocketed them both for intelligence, then stood up to take stock.

A decision was needed, and quickly. He took a small sip of water, then a longer one, and replaced the canteen. He could simply go on until he found a friendly base, then make it back to base. Or he could go back for Hoan.

He knew he would go for Hoan. It was the reason for all this effort. He got out the canteen again and poured a small amount of water in his hand and ran it over his face. He put the beret back on and turned to look at the way he had come. He would have to follow the track backward to the tree where it began, then start all over. It put Hoan ahead of him by several hours. But Hoan, too, was wounded. Perhaps he had lain up somewhere, waiting to see if he was being trailed. By now he would be feeling confident, perhaps hurrying carelessly, making noise.

Waya put the beret back on and turned and started back, shuffling through the brush in a ground-eating movement he could keep up for hours at a time.

He stopped once about midday to drink.

In the late afternoon he found the tree where he had started and began to search in a wide circle, being very cautious. He knew he was back closer to VC country and he didn't want to stumble into a chance VC patrol of some sort. The greatest danger would be at night, but he was careful all the same.

In time he found it, a few tiny specks of blood on a broad fan leaf. Keeping the spot in mind he widened the circle and moved again. When he found the second bloodstain he had a direction and started off once more into the brush. He was getting hungry and welcomed it, for it always made him feel lighter and somehow keener, more alert. He found the third bloodstain, and not far from it a broken branch, and not far from that another footprint. Hoan would appear to be badly wounded as well, and moving carelessly; probably looking for some quick medical aid, but afraid to go back to his headquarters, thinking it had been overrun.

By nightfall he felt he was getting close and slowed his pace. He didn't want to blunder into an ambush, even one by a wounded man. He kept finding the trail signs he needed, and unhurried now, he stalked Hoan as he would stalk a wounded deer. And for the same reason.

Near dawn, almost twenty-four hours after he had found the first wounded VC, Dane heard a crashing in the bush ahead of him. He was certain it was Hoan. He trotted off to his right in a circular path, keeping the noises to his left. In a few minutes he had found what he was looking for, a small rise with a dead tree that had been hit by lightning. It gave him a shield if he needed it, for now it had occurred to him that if Hoan wasn't wounded that badly, he might get him back alive. That bastard Barton had said it was not possible. "Not even for the hired guns," he had said. Well, we'll see.

Hoan came stumbling out of the bush, his clothes dirty, bloodstains all over his shirt, his right arm dangling uselessly. He had tied a strip of cloth around the arm just above the elbow, but blood was still running down his arm and dripping from his fingertips. He was going to pass close to where Waya was waiting. He watched him approach, a middle-aged man, large for a Vietnamese, wearing the peasant's trousers and shirt of the delta. Part of the shirt was sticking to the right side of his chest and up over his shoulder; it looked like a multiple wound. The man was strong to have gotten this far after losing so much blood.

When Hoan reached a spot a few meters from his hiding place, Waya stood and pointed the M-16 at his chest. Hoan stopped and sagged a little, then stood very still.

"Do you speak any English?" Waya asked him. Hoan remained impassive.

"Comprennez-vous français?" *Still Hoan did not react, but Waya was sure he understood. Hoan was a northerner, educated in the French colonial system.*

Waya looked at his watch and up at the climbing sun. He could try to make Tan An with its airstrip, but there were plenty of VC around there. He could walk Hoan back to the river and work down to his own base, at least a two-day trek, and Hoan might not make it. He could take Hoan to the original helicopter rendezvous point and wait, in the hope they would keep coming back for a few days. It was the nearest option, and Hoan might not last much longer if he couldn't get medical aid.

He pointed the M-16 at an angle to where they were standing and gestured to Hoan. The Vietnamese looked as if he were going to protest, but he turned and began to stumble in the direction Waya had indicated.

In the next ten hours Waya prodded, pushed, and then carried Hoan toward the rendezvous point. He knew he was tiring and he worried about how long Hoan would stay alive. He had looked at Hoan's wounds and decided it could go either way; they were bad enough but might not kill him if he could get to a medic.

At midmorning they heard the sound of rotors and the distinctive whine of a helicopter engine. Waya took a chance and dropped Hoan where he was, running quickly toward the noise.

He burst into the small clearing and was seen immediately by the helicopter pilot, who was almost lifting off. The helicopter settled back and he waved to them, signaling them to wait.

Back in the bush he found Hoan trying to crawl into a hiding place. He pulled him out and to his feet and pushed him in front as they got out of the bush and back to the clearing.

The helicopter pilot looked startled, but his copilot got out of the Huey and helped them into the chopper.

All the way back across the stretch of delta, he stayed awake, watching Hoan. He would see that Hoan got medical attention. Then he would deliver him in person to Barton. For the first time in days, he smiled to himself.

"Dai Uy!"

Donovan looked up to see his radioman running across the

compound. He rose quickly and stepped through the door of the hut.

"Huey come, Huey come," the radioman was shouting.

"All right, calm down," Donovan said and turned to look seaward, knowing it would be a few minutes before the chopper came into sight. Maybe they would have news of Dane. Whatever it was, Donovan thought grimly, it couldn't be good. Dane had been gone for days, and in a few more days they would have to consider him lost. *He was the best.* Donovan was already thinking of him in the past tense.

The helicopter came in from the sea and dropped quickly, in a welcome absence of sniper fire. Donovan and Tranh and the radioman stood in front of the commo hut, watching the helicopter settle in. Other junkmen began to gather.

A few bundles came flying out the door and landed heavily in the dust. Donovan grinned; an experienced pilot. Then Donovan's grin turned to elation. A man had leaped lightly down from the helicopter and was trotting away from it. Even the shambling run couldn't hide the man's graceful movement. It was Dane.

In a moment Dane was surrounded by cheering junkmen, and grinning broadly, Donovan grabbed him and hugged him. Dane was smiling, happy to be back in the compound. Someone broke out the beer and in moments there was a party under way. Dane and Donovan let it go—there was a time now and then when you had to let them cut loose, and this was as good a time as any.

They drank through much of the afternoon. In the early evening Dane broke away and took a bath and came back to the hut. The junkmen had a meal waiting for him, rice and fried pork and lettuce, all permeated with the strong odor of *nuoc man*, the fish oil in which the Vietnamese cooked much of their food. He ate it with gusto, calling for more beer. Donovan, now the worse for wear, disappeared with a pretty Vietnamese girl he had been seeing a lot of, and gradually the party wound down.

With Donovan nowhere in sight, Dane went on a final dusk inspection of the camp. In spite of the party, all was in order, the sign of good leadership. Dane knew that he could now leave Donovan in charge with no qualms. In a few days he would go to the base camp in Thailand.

Long after dark he was getting ready for bed when Donovan came in, looking a bit sheepish but considerably more sober. They opened a final beer and sat in the glow of the kerosene lamp, talking quietly.

"Let's have one more beer," Donovan said, laughing.

"Split one," Dane said, and Donovan poured.

"Christ, Colonel," Donovan said suddenly. "I almost forgot your mail!"

"You mean messages. Couldn't be important."

"No, this is mail. Only one letter, though." He got up and went to the table at the far end of the hut and returned with a letter. He handed it to Dane.

Dane looked at it in the glow of the kerosene lamp. It was crinkled and dirty and had gone to at least two other places before finally catching up with him. He recognized his mother's handwriting and opened the letter.

He read it twice and then stood abruptly and walked to the door of the hut, staring out into the night. After a while he heard Donovan clear his throat politely and inquire, "Bad news, Colonel?"

"Get me a helicopter, first light," he said. "And get ready to take over here."

Starlight's letter had been terse.

Can you come as soon as possible? she had asked. *Tawodi is dying.*

1967

He telephoned from Saigon, ignoring the time difference, and getting a sleepy Starlight out of bed. She was happy to hear from him. Yes, Tawodi was still alive; he would be alive until Dane got home. She knew that because he had said so. He had pneumonia, from exposure. He had taken to wandering about in the dead of winter with very little protection, sometimes not even a jacket. He was in bed, but it was difficult to keep him there. She felt he was waiting for Dane to take him into the mountains to die. Starlight began to cry.

He arrived in Los Angeles on the first day of the new year. The airport was insane, and flights were heavily booked. It would take him another six or seven hours to get out. He spent part of the time in a bar, the rest sitting in the observation tower and watching the aircraft, his mind far away, remembering.

Tawodi would be well over eighty years old, he thought. A

tough old man who had always been gentle with him, leading instead of shoving. He had a knack for saying the right things, for finding the right emotion, for being *right*. He had never known his grandfather to do an ugly or ungraceful act. He had never known the old man to show the slightest fear, either. He seemed more in tune with himself than anyone Dane had ever known.

They called his flight at last, and he boarded, going into the first-class section. He rebuffed the elderly lady in the seat next to him and she ignored him throughout the rest of the flight, which was what he had intended. He got off the plane in Atlanta, in uncommonly cold weather, and in an hour had rented a car and was driving north in darkness and a stiff wind from the northwest. After a few minutes he pulled into a service station to think. If he continued he would arrive at two or three in the morning, disrupting Nathan and Starlight. He would have to delay for a few hours, arriving at a more reasonable time. If Tawodi was waiting for him, he would wait. Dane knew the old man would not die until he was ready.

He drove the car north and crossed into Tennessee, turning up alongside the Ocoee River and following the road that snaked around the mountains. It was bitter cold, and the higher peaks had snow on them that he could sense more than see. He passed one or two trucks in the early morning, but no cars, and he drove leisurely eastward, then angled north again, taking in old landmarks. He came to the town and saw that it was still as he remembered, with its mine shafts and smelting plant, its railroad and its weatherbeaten houses. He drove through the town in a few minutes, seeing only a scattering of lights in a few shop windows. Beyond the town he turned the car northward again on a narrow, paved road and was once again out in rolling countryside. He was now within a few miles of home, but he kept driving and in another half hour had turned the car off onto a dirt road. He switched off the ignition and got out of the car.

It was a dark night with gusting winds that brought the smell of snow. Asia had thinned his blood, he thought, and wished he had something heavier than the windbreaker he was wearing. But then he hadn't owned a heavy coat in a long time.

He walked toward a spot at the end of the road, keeping, by habit, close to the trees and away from the center of the road. After five or six minutes he came to where the road dead-ended and sat down.

He was on a bluff and below him in the darkness was an expanse of trees that led away back toward the town, hidden in the distance. Underneath the canopy of those trees were streams, rocks, animals, birds, insects—and history. Tawodi would die in such a place and want him to scatter his ashes. And he would do it. He would do anything his grandfather asked.

The wind was shrieking now in the pines on both sides of the road; he heard echoes of it, long, sighing sounds, in the trees below. He thought of Sara then and felt a great sadness. He had lost her, and now he was losing Tawodi. There would be Nathan and Starlight someday, until all the people he loved were gone. Gabriel, that crazy bastard, would get knifed in some quarrel with a berserk jealous husband. He worried about Ashton as well; Ashton's wife had left him, and he was pressing to take over operations in Laos, relieving Gabriel.

What had it all been for? There would be wars in Asia long after all of them were gone. But then he had no illusions about ending the wars. He had simply done what Tawodi had said: he had gone out and found what he was best at, and it was something he could live with, so he had done it. His morality and his principles were intact. The people he had killed were people he felt deserved it, and they would feel no qualms about killing him. There was a certain sanity and reason in what he did, but it escaped most people because they got caught up in the emotionalism of it, not thinking it through. He was not a murderer; he was a soldier who fought for the highest of motives—he could join any cause he felt was right, and did so. There could be nothing more sensible than fighting for what you believed.

He thought of the child, Huyen.

He had no special feelings for her, because he hadn't known her. Instead, he felt for all of the children of Indochina, and for the old men and the farmers and the fishermen. In many parts of Asia, he looked into the faces of the elderly and caught a glimpse of Tawodi, the same dignity, the same quality. He hoped, when he was an old man, that he would have the same grace.

He thought of the women in his life. Starlight was there, strong and supportive, and filled with the same flinty resolve that he knew he had. She was a damned good woman, and he was proud of her. There were other women, none of them really important until he had met Sara. Sara had eclipsed them all, with her openness and her intelligence, her . . .

He shook his head and studied the sky. Morning coming, he thought, but not much lighter. Snow a real possibility. He shivered slightly in the dry cold, feeling the strange grayness, a world removed from the vividness of Asia. He stood up and looked over the bluff, able now to see more clearly. The wind began to drop and it grew still, as if the dawn were pausing somewhere over the rim of the hills, waiting for the proper moment.

Back in the car he found he still needed the lights, for safety. As he turned from the dirt road he saw the first flakes in his light beams, and by the time he reached Starlight's house, it was setting in heavily.

As he turned and parked the car in front of the house he saw a light come on in the bedroom; Starlight had heard him. He got out of the car and was getting his luggage out of the back seat when she flew into his arms, wearing a flannel nightgown and a robe, tears in her eyes. He hugged her and eased her toward the house, all at the same time, then had to go back and get the luggage while she waited, framed in the doorway. They stepped through he door and he heard Nathan moving about in the bedroom. Dane looked down at Starlight.

"You look marvelous," he said, meaning it. Her hair was mostly gray, but she wore it long and loose; and though there were fine lines in her face, the bones were strong; and her large, dark eyes were as expressive as ever. "I got here as soon as I could," he said. She hugged him again and he stood holding her until Nathan came into the room, smiling broadly and reaching out his hand.

"Come," Starlight said, "let's get coffee."

They went into the kitchen, a very warm country kitchen that looked much like the one Dane had grown up in. Starlight started busying herself with coffee while Nathan, wearing an old-fashioned nightshirt, kept smiling and patting Dane's arm. Every time he looked at Nathan's one eye, he was reminded of how and why it happened. It seemed a long time ago.

He turned to his mother. "Where is he?"

"Sleeping in the other room. At least he was. I expect to see him any minute. He'll know you've come home." She handed him a steaming mug of coffee, and one to Nathan. Then she sat opposite them at the table, pushing her hair back and studying Dane.

"Well?" he asked.

"You're older, as we all are. But you look very healthy, my son."

"It's true," he said, "I never get sick."

"Nor did he," Nathan said.

Starlight shifted in the straight-back chair. "He wouldn't listen to any of us. We told him to stay out of the deep mountains in winter, but it was like talking to a rock. He caught a cold, which surprised us all, and it turned into pneumonia. The doctor said he might live if we were extremely careful, but Tawodi told us one day it was time, and to get you if we could."

"That means," Dane said slowly, "that he's been hanging on for at least two weeks."

"Closer to three weeks," Nathan said. "A man in his eighties."

"It will end now," Starlight said in a whisper. "He wants you to take him out to die—and not just outside. He wants to go deep."

"How do you feel about it?" he asked her.

"You must do it. No question about it. It's what he wants."

Dane looked into his coffee cup, watching the heat rise. "How soon does he want to go?"

Starlight looked up, fighting for control. "As soon as you're here."

"You mean now?" Dane said, startled.

"Tomorrow," said Tawodi from the doorway.

Dane turned. The old man was standing there barefoot and shirtless, wearing jeans and holding a blanket wrapped around him. He stood very straight and looked as he had always looked to Dane, as if he had somehow defied the years. The old man's eyes were bright and clear, but even as he stood there, his body shook with a sudden cough.

Dane got up and hurried to him. His grandfather opened his arms and they stood for long moments, embracing. Dane felt such a sudden rush of love that he knew there were tears in his eyes, but he didn't care. He was holding a living Tawodi who, in hours, would be dead. Through his emotion he realized the old man was trying to comfort him; it was Tawodi's way to think of others, a part of his innate dignity.

"Well, grandfather," he said, stepping back. "My heart leaps to see you again."

"Hey-yeh," said Tawodi. "It is good you do not change much."

"I was thinking that of you."

Starlight came to the doorway. "You'd better get back in bed," she said gently. "You can talk from there."

Tawodi smiled at Dane. "Woman never learns. Aniyunwiya men cannot be ordered about like tame dogs. But she is right. Today I rest; tomorrow we will go to the mountains."

"A lot of snow out there, grandfather."

"Have you forgotten who you are? We go tomorrow. Today I will rest and make ready. Now I will sleep a little." The old man moved slowly back toward the bed. They stayed in the kitchen, listening to the bed creak as Tawodi got back in it.

Starlight turned to him. "Will you do it?"

"Of course."

"You know what he's asking?"

"I've always known what he wants me to do."

"A heavy thing to place on a child," Starlight said reflectively.

"Not the way he did it," Dane said. "Thank God, though, I'm not a child any longer." He began to drink his coffee, enjoying its warmth. It was going to be a cold day tomorrow.

He napped through part of the morning and got up to a lunch of steaming bowls of beef soup and large chunks of homemade bread. He ate with Starlight and Nathan, telling them about places in Asia they had only heard about. Tawodi was awake, but refused food. They heard him coughing now and then from the bedroom, but once when he got up to look outside, he stopped to speak with them briefly and was cheerful.

"He is at peace," Starlight said. "May the Great Spirit bless him."

"Amen," said Nathan.

Dane nodded. He thought the Great Spirit would do more than merely bless Tawodi. He would bring him aboard as a tracker. The thought made Dane smile.

In the late afternoon the snow was piling in drifts against the side of the house and the wind had risen again. Tawodi came out and said he wanted to talk to them, one at a time.

Nathan went in and came out in about fifteen minutes, his face drained. "He is saying his farewells to us," Nathan said, "but not exactly. He doesn't say good-bye. He just talks and then tells you he wants you to leave him. I—it was—well, you'll see."

Starlight went in and sat on the bed beside her father.

"You were beautiful as a child, and more so as a woman," Tawodi began, and he talked of long summer days and rolling meadows, when they would pick herbs for medicine, and for tea.

He told her how proud he had been of her when she was a young girl, and how happy he had been when she had discovered a man she could love, and how saddened he had been at the loss of the young Dane. She had been brave then, and would be now at his departure.

Starlight sat on the bed weeping, but the old man reached up and gently wiped her tears as he had done when she was a child. He spoke in the language of the Aniyunwiya, asking her to embrace him, then to go. She left the room with her face in her hands, without looking back.

Dane went in and found Tawodi sitting up in bed.

"We must make a small plan," his grandfather said, and he told Dane what he expected, and the last part of it surprised Dane.

"In the old days some sang death songs; we do not have them now, but there is something I would ask of you, Waya-unutsi."

"Anything, grandfather."

"Write a verse for me, as you used to. I will take it with me tomorrow."

It's been too many years. "I will do as you ask, Tawodi."

The old man smiled.

Dane went for a walk in the evening, still in his windbreaker, his mind and heart stunned by the thought of Tawodi's passing. The world that stretched before him now had turned from white to twilight-gray, and he walked somberly through it, his mind back to his childhood and the old man who had guided his life. A world without Tawodi was less a world.

After a while he hurried back to the house and shared a solemn supper with Starlight and Nathan. None of them went into Tawodi's bedroom, respecting his privacy. Finally Nathan talked Starlight into going to bed. Dane knew how she felt; they were trying to hold back tomorrow.

When both of them had left the room, Dane sat at the kitchen table with a notebook and pencil, trying to compose a death verse for Tawodi. Trying to write with truth, with clarity.

Dawn came with a snap and a streak of silver and Dane felt it like an arrow in his heart. He got up and dressed, putting on the mackinaw he had borrowed from Nathan, and a pair of his old boots. He picked up his octagon-barrel Marlin and went out to the Jeep. His grandfather was already there, sitting impassively in the Jeep with the windows rolled down, staring straight ahead.

He got in and nodded to his grandfather and started the engine. They drove off into a crisp morning like the world's first morning. Trees ponderous with snow. Icicles that glittered in the morning sun.

"A wonderful morning," Tawodi said. Dane glanced at him. The old man was wearing jeans and moccasins and a plaid shirt and his head-band. He was carrying a blanket and a small leather pouch on a rawhide thong.

"Don't have such a long face, Waya-unutsi." The old man smiled.

"I will miss you, grandfather," Dane said in a whisper. His heart felt leaden, his mind a confusion of memories and dread of what the day would bring.

"It is good to remember your ancestors," Tawodi said. "But don't think about it more than you should."

The Jeep wound through the brittle morning, the only moving thing in a white wilderness. The evergreens were like green streaks on hills of white paper, and above it all was a sky of blue metal. Inside the Jeep their breath hung in the still air. Dane felt the cold right into his bones, but Tawodi seemed untouched by it. His quick eyes were taking in every scene, and Dane thought there was the ghost of a smile on that leathery face.

They reached the end of the dirt road. Now it would be a hike to the hill cabin. The old man got out and started up without a word, his moccasins turning dark with the instant wetness of the snow. He had the blanket over his shoulder and the pouch around his neck, and he seemed to be floating upward, hardly leaving footprints.

Dane followed, and they climbed in a cold, clean, silent world, with light bouncing off the snow. Dane felt the pull of the snow on his boots, a suddenly remembered sensation from another lifetime.

They reached the cabin at midmorning and the old man stopped in front of it and squatted in the snow. Dane positioned himself in front of his grandfather, his pulse racing. He could feel his heart like a drumbeat, rhythmic but hammering in his chest.

"There is little to say, Waya-unutsi. Our lives have said it for us. You have brought me great joy, because of what we have known together and what you have meant to the Aniyunwiya. I think you have pleased our common ancestors, for of all the Aniyunwiya today, you are the most like them."

"It is a great compliment, grandfather."

Tawodi reached out and took his hands. "My spirit longs to travel now."

Dane spread the blanket in the snow, packing it down. Tawodi stood

271

up and undressed, and Dane saw that he was wearing an old-fashioned deerskin loincloth with ancient symbols. He left his moccasins and head-band on, and sat in the center of the blanket with the pouch hanging from his neck by its rawhide thong.

Tawodi looked at his grandson and held out his hand. Dane handed him the verse he had written and the old man put it in his pouch.

"I take with me the things that are important," Tawodi said formally, and Dane knew the end was near.

"I take a verse written by my grandson, Waya-unutsi, a warrior of the wolf clan of the Aniyunwiya. I take a raven's feather, to help my flight. I take an arrowhead to help me hunt, and salt to season my food. I leave behind my name in the memory of my people."

He began to speak to Dane in the language of the Aniyunwiya. Dane missed part of it, but he knew the old man was thanking the spirits for a long and interesting life, and for good hunts. Still in the middle dialect of the Aniyunwiya, he asked Dane to recite the verse he had written.

"I speak as Waya-unutsi," he said, looking into his grandfather's eyes. He said:

> The raven knows his bones will lie,
> in scattered fragments on a hill;
> he does not live a life in fear,
> does not hesitate to kill.
>
> The raven makes his signature
> in soaring circles on the wind,
> and reaches heights we cannot see,
> and plummets proudly at the end.
>
> There is no need to fear the ending,
> when ravens proudly bear their pain,
> as easily as they carry honor
> from shadows to the sun again.

"It is good," Tawodi said. "Remember Kolanu the Raven, known as Tawodi." The old man made himself comfortable and smiled up at his grandson, eyes glittering. Then he gazed out over the snow-laden forest.

Dane stood, tears in his eyes, and looked at his grandfather for a moment. He turned then and walked to the other side of the cabin and past it, on down the hill and into the nearby trees. He went through the trees to the hill beyond, and the next, feeling no effort, feeling no cold.

He walked for hours in a long elliptical path. By midafternoon he was back at the hill cabin, and he walked beyond it and stared.

Tawodi was dead.

He was slumped on the blanket, eyes closed, and on his face a look of great peace.

Dane wrapped his grandfather in the blanket and carried him into the cabin and placed him on the table. Beside him he placed his death gift, the antique Marlin he had bought so long ago.

Then he set the cabin on fire.

It burned slowly at first, then more quickly, as the spreading flames dried the walls and roof. He stood in the snow and watched the light smoke climb straight up in the still morning, to find the higher winds and slowly disappear.

A long time later he went into the ruins of the cabin.

He picked up Tawodi's larger bones and placed them in the mackinaw and carried them outside. He put the mackinaw on the ground, and picking up the pieces of bone, scattered them in several directions. When he was finished he put the mackinaw on again and turned his face eastward, to the origins of his race, to the source of its spirituality. He prayed for the first time since his youth, asking the spirits of the winds to give a safe journey to the soul of Tawodi, whose true name was Kolanu the Raven.

In the calmness of early evening he turned and started back down the hill. As he approached the Jeep he noticed their footprints were gone, probably taken by the wind.

Two days later he said good-bye to Starlight and Nathan. Then he went back to Asia and became a legend.

PART
FOUR

1968–1972

I hear he's dead."

"No," said Sara. "I don't think so."

He turned to her and smiled that thin smile she had come to detest; that particular smile never reached his eyes, which remained a cold and opaque blue. *How could she every have found him attractive? Well, it was obvious, wasn't it? He was something Dane was not. And yet, had she been wrong about that? She had been wrong about so many things.*

He was still smiling and watching her. "The famous Colonel Dane. He pushes his luck. I hear nobody has seen him or heard from him in weeks."

"That doesn't mean a thing. He tends to disappear from time to time." *He is in the temple at Uijonbu, or with Tawodi in the mountains.*

"Yes, I forgot that you know all about him."

"You didn't forget, Whitney. You bring it up all the time."

He smiled again and she looked at him coolly as he sat in the mess tent, his hands locked around a thermos cup of iced tea. It was his hands that had first attracted her. She had watched him do an emergency tracheotomy on a young boy in the streets of Da Nang, and afterward she had gotten him aside for a story on his work in Vietnam. He was a medical missionary; his hands belonged to God, and he used them in God's work. To Sara, at that moment, he had appeared almost godlike himself, saving lives in a country where so many men were so dedicated to taking them.

The next day she was surprised to see him again, but he had sought her out. He was going out on a "county fair" mission with the marines near Da Nang, and would she care to go? She jumped at the chance, for it was a mission of rehabilitation, when it worked properly. That day the marines had moved into a village and moved the villagers out. While patrols were sweeping the village for Viet Cong tunnels and arms caches, the villagers were being treated for various ailments and the children were being handed food and items of clothing. At the end of the day the villagers were taken back to their homes—at least most of them had homes to go to. A couple of houses were flattened when the marines placed C-4 *plastique* in a nearby tunnel and blew it so the VC couldn't use it as a hideout again.

All during that day Sara had watched him work, and that night in the press camp in Da Nang she thought about how pleasant the day had been with him, how wonderful it was to watch someone helping to heal instead of destroy. He seemed very self-assured, even arrogant at times, almost contemptuous of others who lacked his medical knowledge and skill, but at the same time he pushed himself very hard and accomplished more than most men could have. She was wondering if she would ever see him again when he turned up at the press camp and offered to take her to dinner. It was a beginning, of sorts.

Sara often wondered about that final impulse to move in with him. If it was definable, it couldn't be called love, not in the way she thought of Dane. It was, in the end, Vietnam— death, corruption, despair; it was fear, getting older, the damned heat and flies, a healthy need for release, a grasping for something that she never really expected to have again. But in six weeks whatever it was had become resolved, and despite his church affiliations and his religiosity (which she felt from the first was a convenience instead of an inspiration), he wanted her close. One steaming afternoon, with the whine of jets from the nearby air base shattering the still air, she simply packed her bags and got a friendly Jeep driver to take her to Whitney's quarters. She wished she could feel elated, but what she felt most was fatigue.

She found out almost at once that he had no particular appetite for sex, but she tried to swallow that disappointment. After all, he was tired from long days in the field. Their lovemaking was infrequent and perfunctory. Although he lectured his staff on giving of themselves in their work, he was a selfish man—at least in bed. There were occasional separations and she was surprised and disturbed that she did not mind them all that much. *She had hated to be away from Dane for an hour . . . but she mustn't think of that any more.*

But Whitney wouldn't let her forget. Dane's name came up in a conversation he started one morning. Dane was becoming one of the "personalities" of Indochina, as he put it, and did she know him? As a reporter she must have heard of him. And in a burst of candor she later regretted, she told him about part of her relationship with Dane. He guessed the rest and his reaction astonished her—he flared with jealousy, and the rest of that morning was spent in accusations and bitterness. In the ensuing weeks he fed on that jealousy until it became a part of him, coloring all their activities and destroying their intimacy. In time, his tight smile would fall on her like a cold rain, the accusing eyes would mock her, hold her own gaze, and then break away with the anger in them strong and frightening. He had taken to ignoring her for days at a time, which infuriated her in the beginning, but which lately she had taken as relief, a blessing.

The comparisons came in spite of herself. Whitney Mason, medical missionary, tall, bearded, ultrasensitive to criticism and—she had learned quickly—very, very ambitious. John

Dane, mercenary, sexy, a born leader, and decisive. When Dane was angry he was explosive; Whitney lapsed into cold politeness and silence. Taking it deeper, Sara knew that Whitney longed to rise to fame and glory in Vietnam, to make a name that would carry him to the top when he returned to America, to become a genuine hero in his field. Dane had never sought fame, yet his name and his reputation were everywhere in Asia these days, and her stories about him had become the reference for other reporters' copy. They had built him into a legend. She wondered how many of the newer stories were true.

In Can Tho on the Bassac River in the Mekong Delta, the first shot fired on the last day of January 1968 struck Donovan in the center of the forehead and blew away the back of his head. He never heard the shot.

He had finished lunch at the navy's villa near the river and decided to walk down to the PBR landing, fascinated as usual by the sleek river patrol boats, so modern, so unlike the chulucs he sailed. The sniper had positioned himself across from the villa only moments earlier, and his single shot was the signal for the attack.

There were thousands of other rounds fired that day. Breaking the truce of Tet, the Vietnamese holiday season, the North Vietnamese and Viet Cong launched well-coordinated attacks throughout Vietnam in a stunning demonstration of their ability to control the flow of the war. They were particularly effective in the cities and in the Mekong Delta.

Can Tho was almost devastated, My Tho heavily hit and held, for a time, by the VC. Ben Tre, Vinh Long—all were hit hard by forces who seemed to be committed to a do-or-die effort. Donovan's junk base was hit hard but managed to survive.

In Saigon the Tet offensive began with an early-morning assault on the stately American embassy. Soon there were fires burning all over town and bombs exploding in Cholon. Terrified residents of the city turned down streets only to encounter Viet Cong sappers and snipers. There were reports of heavy rocket attacks in outlying areas, and mortars in use on some Saigon streets. There were also reports of looting, and tales of senior South Vietnam officials trying to flee the city by any means possible.

When the shooting finally stopped at the end of the offensive, the Viet Cong had paid a terrible price. Militarily, they had lost the action and for a time the infrastructure appeared doomed. But success in Vietnam was not measured by military victories alone, and slowly they began to realize they had won a great psychological victory, for in the wake of Tet, the Americans, perhaps for the first time, began to think seriously about pulling out of Vietnam. That possibility swept across Vietnam like a monsoon rain and was just as chilling.

Dane lay in a hammock in a trail camp in the highlands south of Phuong Saly, listening to the sounds of the Lao and Hmong troops as they readied the evening meal. They were small, neat, incredibly hard people who could live in these mist-blanketed highlands as no other people could, at home in a wet, wild upland where tigers still prowled occasionally, where there were snakes that killed almost as quickly as a bullet, where villages owed allegiance to none but themselves and very few of the villagers had ever heard of a place called Laos. He had often marveled not only at the toughness of these people, but at their lack of any inclination to wander out of the mountains and see what was over the next ridge. Well, maybe they knew and didn't care, but he had never known an up-country villager to travel very far. When he had taken them on the last raid against the Pathet Lao, an action funded by the CIA, it was as far as many of them had gone from their homes, yet it was only a two-day trek.

He shifted in the hammock and rubbed the stubble of beard on his face. He hated being dirty. He had always prided himself on staying clean in the bush, but now he could hardly move, and getting clean was the least of his concerns. He had been in the hammock almost constantly for the past five days, the first two of them delirious with malaria.

The hammock was slung between two trees that dripped leeches, small but ferocious. When they landed on his skin they were no heavier than drops of water, but soon the tiny rivulets of blood would form and someone would walk over, notice the blood, and burn them off with a cigarette. If they were pulled out the head stayed in, and infections were possible. It was a situation where an infection could be as deadly as a wound.

His most constant nurse was a wizened little old man who claimed he had never had a name and didn't miss it. He smoked opium in a long pipe with a small brass bowl, squatted on the ground near Dane's hammock, and carried on conversations in a bewildering variety of languages and dialects. He wore a pants-and-shirt outfit of deep blue and a number of bracelets on both wrists. Dane was not even sure he was a Hmong or Lao, since the old man had professed no nationality or identity, but in his multilingual ramblings Dane heard legends about Hmong beliefs.

There is more than one earth, the old man said, and ours revolves around the sun and moon and the other earths. This earth is cursed because the inside of it is filled with hot water, very close to the surface. The earth had been made out of water by the first man and woman, so there is a lot of water left over in the ground. The water is very close to the surface in China, which is why they have so many earthquakes there. The Hmong are more mobile than the Lao, because it is important for families to visit, but usually the families are not that far away. Intelligence and virtue are most respected by the Hmong. Strength and endurance and courage are taken for granted. Other peoples of Indochina say the Hmong are too tough to cry. The ancestors of the Hmong were the Kha, who left the huge jars and other artifacts on the Plain of Jars ...

Then the old man would crackle with laughter at Dane's helplessness, and burn the leeches off with cigarettes, which he would not smoke but blew on to keep burning. Dane looked at the little old man and saw similarities to Tawodi, then shook his head in wonder at how long he had been in Asia. He also wondered if he could be cured quickly in a sweathouse of the Aniyunwiya.

It was while he was still confined to the hammock that he learned of Donovan's death, and of the spectacular psychological victory that Tet had been for the North Vietnamese and Viet Cong. When Donovan was mentioned he could only nod, but he lay back, saddened, and remembered the small things about the young navy officer, the little characteristics that added together to form a personality.

Tet had proved one thing: he was right in getting his people out of Vietnam, all twenty-eight or thirty of them. He had simply gone around to the house in Saigon and told them all that their tactics weren't working and the war was doomed to failure and he was pulling everyone out.

Barton had been furious. He said, "I thought you people fought for pay. You're getting paid, ain'tcha?"

"You can't pay us enough to stay on. We're not the American army. We don't have to stay. We've done all you asked and more, and I'm telling you now that we aren't interested in any future contracts in Vietnam. Elsewhere, sure, but not here." Dane was calm, but firm.

"The legendary Colonel Dane. The famous mercenaries," Barton sneered. "You people sure faded in the stretch, didn't you?"

Dane remained calm. "We gave you more than your money's worth. We did better work for you than you had any right to expect. And we didn't walk away when things got tough. We lost some people, too, Barton. It's just that we *are* mercenaries, and as such we're free to go at any time after we've earned our pay. And we've done that, no one can deny it."

Barton was red-faced. "How the hell do you expect us to fill the gap? Not that you people are all that fucking good."

"You can't fill the gap," Dane said, feeling himself growing colder, "because you're a bunch of hypocritical bastards. In combat you need killers, but for some reason you don't want to tell the people who support you that your clean-cut American boys are using knives, ropes, bamboo splinters, or whatever on civilians—civilians who are directing the war from the other side. I told you once before, I don't understand your morality. I don't want to think about it anymore either." He turned and started to walk away.

"Bullshit, Dane," Barton yelled. "You people are just yellow."

Dane pivoted in a semicircle and kicked Barton precisely on the point of the chin. Barton flew backward, and as he did, Dane dropped into a blocking stance and faced the others in the room.

The noise of Barton crashing against a table brought two MPs rushing in from outside. They stopped suddenly when Dane whirled and picked up the M-16 he had dropped. In the long silence that followed, they could hear Barton's labored breathing. Someone went over to him, but the others stood, spellbound by Dane.

"I'm getting out early to cut our losses. You'd be well advised to do the same," he said.

Someone coughed. Barton was sitting up, leaning against a couch. His mouth was bloody and there was a dazed look on his face.

"We'll finish our operations in Laos as agreed. I'll accept a liaison, anybody but him." Dane gestured toward Barton. "If I have to deal with him again, I'll kill him."

And he had left Vietnam. *Probably forever.*

The malaria had caught him weeks later, but fortunately at the end of the attack against a Pathet Lao staging camp, not at the beginning of it. By radio, drum, and runners he had gotten the word out to the Thailand base camp, and each day now he looked for Gabriel or Bill Ashton to come up and take over. He would recuperate enough to walk out, then spend some time at base camp attending to the business side of things. After that, he would see.

In the dusk he squinted up and saw a laughing Gabriel bending over him. He noticed some streaks of gray in Gabriel's black beard and lines around the smiling eyes, but the burly Frenchman was boisterous as ever, and for the next few minutes Dane heard tales of incredible, unattainable girls whom Gabriel had attained after all. Langé told stories of cuckolded husbands and a dash for life with his pants around his knees, and once getting into the classic situation: hiding under the bed when the husband returned home and being subjected to hearing the lovemaking above him. Dane laughed until he hurt.

"Ah," Gabriel said, "it's good to be safe in the bush again. The cities are getting too damned dangerous, my friend, and I am getting older." He sat on the ground beside the hammock and watched the camp activity for a few minutes. "You've trained them well," he said, with an approving nod.

"What's the news, Gabriel?"

"Well," the Frenchman began enthusiastically, "while you've been lying splendidly on your ass here in the country-side, I have been out earning our money. We have made the requisite number of raids on the Ho Chi Minh trail, with our usual success and followed by the normal futility—they simply put it all back together. The B-52 raids are devastating, and terrifying, and they tear up a lot of the brush, but when they're gone the people simply come out again and keep going south. Incredible.

"And other things, very interesting. Our old friend General Lam Kwai-sin—who is putting on a little weight and looking very much like a mandarin these days—is caught in somewhat of a predicament, alas."

"What predicament, and can we help him?"

"He has been running guns to certain factions in Cambodia. Now his government has decided it must support Communist Party movements throughout Asia, so it, too, is supplying guns to certain factions. The factions occasionally find themselves in contretemps, as it were. The general is afraid that if he's caught there will be the old Chinese water torture, whereas in the old days the government would simply have smiled and looked the other way. The result is *beaucoup* guns going into Cambodia, as they have been in Laos for some time. The general is about to lose his market, one way or the other."

"Who's involved?"

"There's the Khmer Rouge, the Cambodian communists. There's the Khmer Serei, noncommunist forces. There's the Khmer National Liberation Front, which is undecided about what to do at this point. There's the Sihanouk faction, the loy-alists. Then there's the army, currently loyal but always subject to waver. It's a bit confusing, *mon ami,* and we'll have to wait to see whose side we want to be on."

"You think we'll pick up work there?"

"I think the general might want to hire us. We'll see."

Dane looked up at the canopy of trees, as he had a thousand times. "A bit confusing is right, but typical for Indochina. Let's wait for a while and let it sort itself out. How's Ashton?"

Gabriel looked suddenly grim. "His wife—his ex-wife, that is—is driving him crazy. One letter contains hope of reconciliation; the next tells him there is no possibility. He sleeps very little and worries a lot. Thank God"—Gabriel rolled his eyes to heaven—"I never took a wife."

"Nothing involving women is easy," Dane said. "What else?"

"The situation in Vietnam continues to deteriorate. There is this curious American word—*Vietnamization*. I think America is getting ready to abandon South Vietnam, but they want to make it appear they are not. I suppose all those ugly little protesters in America had an effect after all. Your government, that is, the American government, is about to shift the burden of the fighting to the Viet themselves, which is the beginning of the end, of course."

"Yeah," Dane said.

"You look tired. I can finish this in the morning."

"All right, Gabriel. Thanks."

The Frenchman stood and started to turn away, but came back to the hammock. The ebullience seemed to have melted and his face was sad.

"One more piece of news, my friend. Not good."

"What is it?" Dane asked, his voice weaker.

"It's about Sara Sunderland. Something we heard not long ago."

Dane struggled to rise. "Is she dead? Is she hurt?"

"No," said Gabriel, hating the words he now had to say. "She's become the mistress of a doctor. A missionary."

Dane lay back in the hammock, his first emotion one of relief. *She wasn't dead.* But lost to him, all the same, as he had known all along.

Every few months seemed to bring a new story; any clandestine action in Indochina was attributed to Dane and the mercenaries. Few people seemed actually to see him, but he was reported in northwest Laos in continuing, extremely hazardous operations against the Pathet Lao. He was reported seen in southern Malaya, in action against the developing communist insurgency there. The *Straits Times* speculated about his presence and editorialized on the morality of mercenaries in Asia, as if it were something new.

Someone told the story that Dane was wounded and nursed back to health by a beautiful Hmong maiden north of Pakse, but no one believed this story except the part about him being wounded, for with each successive action there was increased speculation about how long he would live.

There was a tale out of a small village near the Tonle Sap, a huge Cambodian lake. Villagers reported that a strange American suffering from a bout of malaria stumbled into their village and stayed for two weeks. While he was recuperating he taught the young men of the village how to set up defenses, how to establish a perimeter and patrol it, how to gather intelligence in the bush. Observers said he was darker than most Americans but had an American accent. He ate the village food, slept with one of the village girls, and one day disappeared like a shadow in the night. The villagers thought he was Colonel Dane.

Some reports could be confirmed. In one of them he led a half dozen mercenaries in the daring rescue of a young Khmer boy whose father was a rich landowner and who could afford either a huge ransom or a huge rescue attempt and decided to save face with the rescue attempt. The mercenaries plucked the boy, unhurt, out of a bamboo prison in northern Cambodia, returned him to his father, and took their pay.

The stories grew with each passing season.

One story dealt with his near death on a Bangkok street. Someone he had known before—an old enemy—came to Asia to work as a mercenary. He heard of Dane and apparently plotted to kill him, with a little help. One night outside Dane's hotel on Rama IV Road there was a wild fight. Accounts of it varied, but the conclusion was always the same: Dane came away with a knife scar above his right eye, a scar that curved like the wing of a gull from just above his eyebrow to his right cheekbone. He had been badly beaten as well, but when Thai police arrived there were three dead men on the sidewalk. One was a petty thief known to be the ringleader of a small but nasty gang; one was a well-known, to police at least, hired killer; and the third was a Caucasian, a giant of a man with broken bones and a broken neck. He was carrying several identification cards and Dane had picked out the one he had known the man by earlier. He was buried in a Bangkok cemetery under the name of Emil Loder.

As the legends grew there were embellishments. Someone reported that Dane had become a monk and was living in a strange temple in the interior of South Korea. Another story held that he made regular pilgrimages to some mysterious shrine in America. Then he was seen and definitely identified at Baguio in the Philippines, eating Italian food at Jimmy's Kitchen in Hong Kong, with a beautiful Malaysian girl in Kuala Lumpur, playing Mah-Jongg in Macao with a bearded Frenchman, walking out of the bush into Vientiane carrying a wounded Lao on his back, utterly exhausted.

Sara heard most of the stories, smiling to herself and wondering which of them were true. She thought about them just before dropping into an exhausted sleep at night, with Whitney lying next to her in his usual deep and untroubled sleep. She wished she could turn off the day, just like that. And for a long time now she had wondered if the compassion she had first seen in him was really a masked indifference. The bodies he treated might be regarded as means to an end, stepping-stones to a reputation and a better career. She was beginning to learn something of the politics involved, and she didn't like it.

But he was a good, effective doctor, and she was becoming an excellent practical nurse. He had insisted she give up her writing career and she did it, not without protest. He was adamant. He needed her beside him, working for the glory of God and the protection of these lives. Reporters, he said, were mere observers. They hung around the fringes of life and wrote about it without getting involved. Sure, some of them got killed, but they didn't die fighting for anything, or trying to save anything—merely telling others about it. A low profession, he said, not like medicine and especially not like medicine in the service of God and one's fellow creatures in this backward land.

One good thing about Dane, Sara reflected, just before falling asleep, he didn't talk too much.

With the searing heat of dawn Sara was up and facing days frantic with work, or dragging with tedium. There seemed to be no middle ground. When she heard "Dr. Mason" paged in the small mobile clinic, Sara hurried to the operating room, knowing he would want her standing by. It was not that she was a gifted operating room nurse. It was simply that Whitney wanted her there, underscoring the difference between killers and healers, mercenaries and doctors, and, of course, he was always hinting that she write more about his work. Sara hated it. She had the journalist's disdain for manufactured news, and she watched Whitney alternately manufacturing it or trying to get her to write about it or assist the occasional correspondent who passed their way.

It was worse when Whitney's superiors came out from America.

They were unfailingly pious, well-meaning older men and women who might have been visiting the moon for all the insight they had into Asia and its problems. The little brown men running around in the jungle were no different from the little black men of Africa—strange and bizarre creatures whose souls were surely damned unless God's mercy descended upon them. Which it would do if the funding was right, and if people like Dr. Whitney Mason continued to make the world aware of the great need. Of course we will, Whitney promised, of course we will. And of course we did, and do.

And I hate it, hate it, hate it.

It was beginning to show, too. One night she opened a letter from her father—and as she did so she felt a sudden and poignant longing for the clean, cool, windy uplands of Waimea, with its crisp nights and brilliant stars—and opening the letter slowly, tried to keep Hawaii in her mind. She stared happily at her father's meticulous typing, knowing he had done this in the wood-paneled study of the house, with all its familiar furnishings, and memories.

My darling Sara,

Your last letter was very disturbing. I sense a great unhappiness and wonder about your relationship with your doctor. You said nothing of course, but I sense disillusionment. Things might improve if you resumed writing—never enough good reporters in the world.

But if things work out (and I may be speaking out of turn) I'm saving your mother's bridal gown.

Marriage is, at best, a kind of uneasy truce—some better than others. Your mother and I were so hopelessly in love that our own quarrels came when we tried to do too much for each other. She was a fine, fine woman and I miss her terribly. She taught me that you have to respect the feelings of someone you're close to—you have to pay more attention to them than those of strangers. I've never understood why we take people we love for granted. We should work at those close relationships much harder than we do at casual ones.

All this by way of saying that Whitney is always welcome here, and that I'd love to see you soon. The war just keeps dragging on and on, an incredible sacrifice of this nation's young men, and its resources.

We read now and then of Colonel Dane. He's become quite a controversial figure, at least in the U.S. press. Many denounce him, some praise the use of mercenaries. None of them, I notice, ever quote him. He must be as elusive as the wind. I hope you'll forgive me for bringing up an old beau. I did like him, though.

Don't wait for the war's end to come home for a while.

She smiled and put away the letter. All of his letters sounded very much alike these days. She was worrying him too much and had better stop the veiled complaints about Whitney. It would be hard to do, with the communications she had enjoyed with her father all of her life. But for his sake . . .

Whitney came into the tent in his rumpled surgeon's gown, stains showing. "I need you," he said. "We've got surgery in a half hour on a very important client. He's the province chief here, a VIP."

"Why do you have to think of them as clients?" she asked wearily.

"Why do lawyers take top cases without fees?" he countered. "This could lead to better things, so get ready." In a few minutes she followed him out of the tent, feeling the oppressive heat even more strongly outdoors. She stumbled after him in the darkness. She needed to get more sleep. She suddenly felt old.

Dane, too, was feeling his age. Because of the more or less constant physical activity he knew he was in great shape, but the political affairs of Asia were wearying. Once or twice he knew he had made a mistake and pulled his forces out of a situation in which he had been fooled initially. Sticking to his premise that his mercenaries would fight only in a cause they could support, he held them back from other actions, even when the money was tempting.

But then, money wasn't the big factor anymore—if it ever was. Dane was so well off he never thought of money except for his troops. Sometimes he was startled to learn how much money he had accumulated. He was almost indifferent to it, except for the moments that it made his life easier.

Any man on the brink of forty has a right to some ease now and then, he thought. He grinned at the thought that he had lived as long as he had. He should have been killed years ago, and the same could be said of Gabriel and Ashton. They had all pushed it, true, but then it was their profession.

He had first come to Asia in the early 1950s, knowing very little, seeking all. In twenty years he had become rich, probably famous, and relatively unhurt. *Sara.* In any case, he looked forward to a good long run in the Asian bush, and if he didn't get it, he still had no regrets. *Almost no regrets.*

He stirred and got out of his bunk and walked out to look at base camp. There were the normal, happy sounds of a professional soldier in bivouac. Peter Boswell, whom Ashton had recruited from Africa, was drilling new recruits—only a handful, but very good men. Gabriel was in Bangkok, probably risking his life with the beauties along Pat Pong Road. Ashton was due in any time from harassing actions against the Pathet Lao. He was worried about Ashton.

He dressed in his tent, putting on the camouflage pants and shirt that had become a part of his skin, and strapping on a sidearm, even in base camp. As he left the tent he heard a noise at the main entrance of the camp and looked up to see Ashton and his troops returning. Out of long habit, he quickly counted the men. Two missing.

Ashton came over, looking tired but happy to be back.

"Ah, Dane. Good to see you."

"Welcome back, Bill. How did it go?"

"Messy at times. I'll give you a full report after a bath and a drink—no, a drink and a bath."

"Good. Step into my tent and I'll buy the drink."

"In a sec. Any mail?"

"Yes, on your bunk."

He watched Ashton hurry away with that aristocratic, parade-ground stride. The poor bastard now lived for a letter from his ex-wife.

Dane walked on around the camp, enjoying the feel of it, the ambience. He loved being around professionals. He wished it would always be this way, and why not? He would spend his life with these men, taking them into combat and out the other side, taking them places the noncombatant would never know or want to know.

He heard a sudden shout of agony and turned and dropped at the same time. Then he realized the cry had come from Ashton's tent, and he raced across the camp and threw open the door to the tent.

The older man was sitting on his bunk, his face white. He was holding a letter that, Dane noted quickly, looked like some sort of official paper.

"What is it, Bill?"

Ashton's lips moved, but he had to force the words out.

"It's my wife," he said. "She hanged herself from a beam in the living room of our house."

"Oh, Christ," Dane whispered.

"She's dead," Ashton said. "It should have been me instead."

1973–1974

A clear, windy morning with a good trail running around the contours of a high mountain, and to the right the sound of waterfalls and the cries of birds in the deep forest: Dane drank it like a glass of good chablis and smiled. For five days now he had been extremely content, moving through the mountains of eastern Laos with Gabriel and a penetration force of twenty-four Hmongs. It was the kind of mission he liked, a sudden and unexpected strike at the enemy's heart. But there was also the undeniable thrill of being in high, crisp mountains. It was a tropical forest but not unlike the woods where Tawodi had taught him to stalk, to hunt and fish, and observe. The trees were stately here and the leaves broad and shimmering with the first rays of the sun, fracturing on the mountains to their left.

The waterfalls had been with them for days. Dane was using the noise to help keep him on track. Sometimes he navigated in the deep woods with a compass as any mariner would, but he had developed both a mistrust of maps of Indochina and a sense of Indochina's topography. The falls were louder each day because they were getting closer; he was swinging them around a two-thousand-meter hill, each day roughly equidistant from the sound but putting them closer to their target as they swept in a slow, unhurried semicircle to take advantage of the mountain trail.

Dane was well in front of the column, dressed in camouflaged battle kit and carrying a map case as well. He did not expect trouble and the trail in front of him showed no recent movement. Occasionally he would leave it, moving off in dog-legs by compass and cutting back on the trail. Then he would go back until he neared the column again before turning forward once more. It was time-consuming but cautious, and he finally admitted, he enjoyed getting off by himself, even for an hour at a time.

At night they would camp near the trail, the Hmongs, also in battle kit, immediately preparing a meal or sleeping. They had the gift of immediate and complete relaxation, but Dane thought they were probably the best mountain fighters he had ever seen. They were a tough but gentle people, hard as nails but with unflagging good humor. He had total confidence in them. When the Hmong noncoms joined the circle around the night fires, where Gabriel would serve excellent French *café noir,* they would talk about the war for a time, but the Hmongs really wanted to gossip about village girls, home-brewed beer, hunting techniques, and visits to Vientiane. He and Gabriel would find themselves caught up in the humor, and Dane found that he could laugh again. During the day he enjoyed the mist-shrouded mountains and the cooler air and the feel of the pack as he hiked the mountain trail. The sound of the waterfall itself was comforting.

On this bright morning, moments after sunup, he stopped to look at the map he had brought. It was as good as most, and at least he could get a bearing on the villages. To the east was Ban Ango and Ban Pachoung; to the north, not very much for more than ten miles. Their objective was the Pathet Lao camp on the other side of the falls and toward the end of a ridgeline of a seventeen-hundred-meter hill. The camp was well chosen, but Dane and Gabriel both knew the Pathet Lao would never expect it to be attacked because of its high and deep location, so the element of surprise should be total and telling. If he had calculated properly, they would circle the falls by late afternoon and could get into position by nightfall for a dawn attack. *Or we could go in at night, for total surprise and confusion.* But it was dangerous because of the crossfire potential, and an action in the dark could confuse them as easily as the Pathet Lao. Still, it appealed to him.

He stopped for a noon meal, waiting beside the trail for the column to catch up to him. He saw the point man round a curve in the trail and wave and smile, and in a few minutes the rest of the column came in sight, Gabriel in the lead. The Frenchman was, as usual, in high spirits. Dane knew this kind of mission appealed to him as well. Gabriel's first words to him that day confirmed it: "Well, my friend, if the CIA knew how much we enjoyed this they would want us to do it for free, eh?"

"That would ruin our reputation quickly enough," Dane said. "What kind of mercenaries work free?"

"Listen, *mon ami,* have you thought about a night assault?"

"Strange you should mention that."

"Look," Gabriel said and squatted on the trail. With the point of his knife he sketched an approximation of the Pathet Lao camp. "If we stayed northeast of the camp we'd be on the high ground and it would eliminate crossfire problems. The other side of their camp is steep, and dangerous at night. They would have a natural inclination to avoid that. They do not know the size of the force attacking them and will think we are larger than we are. We would have a timed ceasefire and move in to secondary positions—simply send everyone a hundred meters closer. I can tell you the effect of that." He paused and looked up at Dane. "You can see it."

"Yes, of course. Do we have any starlight scopes?"

"Only one, but never mind. We can panic them. They could abandon the base entirely. There must be *beaucoup* supplies in there."

"Listen, you French pirate. You don't mean supplies. You mean a cache of *kip,* maybe even gold."

"If this base is as important as Kinnan and his bosses think it is, then we might find gold. Of course"—Langé smiled broadly—"we would never admit it, my friend. We will go back and say that we destroyed the base. Which will be the truth. What do you say?"

"I say yes to a night assault, for purely tactical reasons. If you find gold, you divide it with the Hmong. But don't mention that possibility to them until it's over. I don't want them excited."

"I agree. Ah, Dane, you are a pleasure to work with. Let's get some lunch. I know a little three-star place around the next bend of the trail ..." And he walked off, shouting to the Hmong troops. Dane thought he heard him humming as he prepared his own meal.

In midafternoon they came upon the falls, full and powerful, fed by dozens of small streams. From the map and from the curve of the mountain, Dane felt they could cross just above the falls. Once across the stream they would have to move with great caution, avoiding the trails.

For now he wanted to enjoy the falls. The water came in a wide, long curtain right over a precipice, dropping several hundred feet to crash against the rocks below, eventually forming again into a swift stream and disappearing through a cove in the mountains. The stream itself was a rarity in Indochina, free of the silt usually collected in any flowing water. Because of the terrain there were no farms in this particular area, and the falls, the mountains, and the elevation gave him a sudden sense of isolation, of being above all the troubles in this land of traditional hatreds. It was a moment of peace and reflection, and of light dancing through sheets of water, and an unaccustomed coolness.

Gabriel came and sat beside him and they stared in silence at the falls. Behind them were the sounds of the Hmong troops, starting to break camp. Dane turned to speak to Gabriel and caught the Frenchman in a rare pensive mood, staring fixedly at the waterfalls.

"What is it, Gabriel?"

The Frenchman sighed. "Did you ever think of retiring, my friend. Or just calling it quits?"

"No."

"I thought not. Well, I have, from time to time. I have enough *kip* to keep me on for a while. I think I could make it all right."

"You'd be bored as hell."

"No. I would live here, you see, in Indochina." He gave Dane a sudden, flashing grin. "There are just enough girls here to last me until I am a century old. Then I'll slow down."

"Except there isn't going to be much of an Indochina for us, Gabriel."

"You think not? Well, you see, I think that's an American attitude. We French can get along better in such places. I admit there will be big changes, though."

"Vietnam will go under," Dane said. "Laos will follow, then Cambodia. In time even Thailand will be challenged by the communists. My guess is that it's there the U.S. will have to draw a line—or admit failure in Southeast Asia and pull out entirely. I don't think they can afford to do that."

"You really think Laos will end up communist?"

"There's no escape. When the North Viets have rolled over Saigon, they'll expand. It's that age-old dream of theirs to dominate all of Indochina."

Gabriel nodded. "A dream, I must add, held by more than just the Viets."

"Agreed. But they are in the ascendency now. Two hundred years from now it could easily be the other way around. It's been this way for centuries."

"Listen, *mon ami,* it's still the damned Russians meddling in Indochina. Look at the big invasion in the spring; the Viets pouring more than a hundred thousand troops down from the north. You know what led them? Soviet tanks and armor."

"No question about that," Dane agreed.

"And your reaction—that is, the American reaction—was more bombing. Bombing of Hanoi, Haiphong. Mining the ports. I'm not condemning the actions, you see, just suggesting that it's a half-ass war. The Americans can't make up their minds to get in or get out. I think they will get out, with disaster on their heels."

Dane nodded. "A bloodbath."

"Everywhere." Gabriel stretched his long legs. "So I suppose you are right about Laos. A terrible thing for such a gentle people."

"All right," Dane said, standing. "Let's take some of these gentle people and go kick hell out of the communists, hey-yeh?"

Gabriel got to his feet and turned to face Dane. He was as serious as Dane had ever seen him.

"We will die here, my friend, you and I. I am not a clairvoyant, but we have been here too long. We have pushed the odds too far."

"Not just yet, Gabriel."

"Do you know why, *mon ami?* Because their own governments will abandon these people to their fate. Their own relatives will leave them to die. Their own friends will betray them. In the end, even God will desert them. And we will defend them."

"For pay." Dane grinned.

Gabriel suddenly grinned back. "Damned right. Let's go see if we can find some gold bars just lying around, eh?"

It was an easy crossing; they simply waded through a number of small streams and in only one place did they have to use the ropes. Dane took no chances, putting flankers on the streams and crossing quickly. Regrouping on the other side of the streams, they filed steadily upward as Dane led the column off the trail in slower, harder going. By late afternoon he had them in a holding position, scouts out. By early evening they had cached the field packs and carried only ammunition and first-aid supplies and were approaching the crest of the mountain.

He knew he had to move them into position before dark. He called a hasty briefing and outlined Gabriel's plan to the Hmongs, who nodded and talked among themselves. In another hour he had them close behind him as he lay on the mountainside, trying, with some difficulty, to get a look at the

Pathet Lao base through his binoculars. It was a large base but well camouflaged. He could pick out netting over a couple of semipermanent huts, probably ammunition storage. The netting hid other buildings that he knew had to be there: a communications shack, headquarters, living quarters, a makeshift hospital. There would be at least a hundred of them, possibly more. Tough odds for the two dozen men he had brought. But with luck . . .

It was the most dangerous moment now, getting them into position, but they simply had to get closer. He looked over at Gabriel, in the bush, watching him. He held up his hand and moved it slowly toward the camp and saw Gabriel's answering nod. In a few moments the Hmong were moving through the brush, all of them instructed to stay at least two hundred meters above the camp, but to find a vantage point from which to fire. He felt them moving on both sides, then started downward himself. It took him a half hour to find the position he wanted, and when he found it he automatically looked at his watch and at the sky. They would have more than an hour to wait. He lay on his stomach and listened to the silence around him. He decided to meditate and closed his eyes. In a while he opened them again and felt rested.

Sundown brought night sounds, but very faint ones. He waited another half hour. There were lights in the Pathet Lao camp and he could hear voices. Fifteen more minutes. He did a final check of all his equipment.

Now. He pointed the M-16 toward the lights of the camp and opened fire.

The night exploded around him, the sound a tremendous, sustained banging noise. He hoped none of his own men were in the way, but he sensed someone in front of him; someone had worked closer than intended. They kept up the volley for thirty seconds, then paused.

In the next few seconds he heard the camp in confusion and there was return fire only sporadically. They still have no idea where we are, he thought. He waited a few more seconds for the sound of the M-79 grenade launchers, firing in unison for the sheer psychological terror of it, and heard the crump of the gre nades in the heart of the camp. Immediately he got up and slid through the darkness, feeling his way, moving eighty to a hundred meters closer. He looked at his watch again, hesitated, decided they should be in place, and started firing again.

Now there was return fire from the camp, more organized but still wide of their positions. They had to take advantage of the next few minutes, and he settled down to keep a steady fire going into the camp.

There was a sudden flash of light to his left—someone had dropped a mortar round close to their positions. So now they knew.

Now or never.

He tugged the lanyard around his neck and the whistle fell into his hand. He blew three sharp blasts and heard Gabriel's answering two. He reloaded the M-16 and headed for the camp, hoping the Hmongs were dispersed enough not to shoot each other.

The mountainside was treacherous with large tree roots and boulders, and he slipped once and went down, bruising his shoulder on a rock, but he was up in seconds and moving again, and as he had so often in the past he began to think and move wolflike through the brush, until at last he burst out of the tree line and was on the edge of the camp. Without looking back he ran straight into it, using the light of a fire to guide his movement around the perimeter. He saw figures in front of him and fired and went down himself, sensing rather than hearing an answering fire from some other quarter. He was up again and moving, knowing that movement was his best protection. He rounded the corner of a hut and shot a man running at him and leaped over the fallen man to swing around the other corner. In the flare of the light he saw soldiers dropping into a bunker. *Machine gun.* He detached a fragmentation grenade and pulled the ring and lobbed the grenade into the bunker and kept running, swinging around a wooden hut. He heard the grenade, then slipped back around the hut and squatted next to it.

The camp was in some confusion, but he knew, or sensed, that the Pathet Lao would be regrouping. They were not the frightened and green troops that they once were, and they were now putting up a desperate defense. They seemed to be re-forming in a collection of huts at the other end of the camp. He wondered where Gabriel was. Then he got up and started out again, keeping to the perimeter of the camp, firing at the moving figures on the inside. He saw two of his Hmongs drop near him and he went down in reflex. In the next second he heard wood splintering behind him. He got up and moved again.

There was a sudden and unexplained silence, lasting four or five seconds. Much of the camp was in darkness again with the sudden dying down of the fire that had been blazing in the center of the camp. He crouched, listening, then was nearly knocked down by a sudden large blast. One of the huts disintegrated, its roof hurtling into the air and pieces of wood flying throughout the camp. The blast threw a brief but intense white light over the camp and he shielded his eyes from it, knowing he had lost part of his night vision. In another moment the firing broke out again and he stretched out on the ground, waiting for his vision to return. As he was lying there a Pathet Lao leaped over his body and ran toward the center of the camp. Dane shot him between the shoulder blades and watched him tumble forward and go down. Dane rolled to his left, then got to his feet and set out again in a crouching, twisting run.

Gabriel had been right. The Pathet Lao were avoiding the steep cliffs on the other side of their camp and were being funneled off on a tangent to the camp, which led more or less parallel to the positions his Hmongs had first occupied. Dane ran out of the camp area and into the brush again, heading for the end of the camp he had first entered. He saw a lot of movement on his right and went down on one knee, firing short bursts. Up and moving again, he began to follow the retreating men, firing at them through the bushes and hearing their return fire wildly over his head. He heard another mortar round somewhere behind him and knew that not all of them were in retreat.

He felt someone close to him and stood very still. The firing now seemed to be tapering off, and in the growing silence he strained to hear the noise he had heard at first. It was someone behind him. He turned off his path into the bush and made a short circle, coming back onto the track he had been taking. It was a Pathet Lao soldier, slipping after him. As he passed, Dane shot him in the thickest part of the body he could see and saw the soldier knocked off his feet.

Dane stood and listened. There was very little firing now; they had done it or they had not. He started toward the camp again, moving quickly, homing in on yet another burning structure. He wondered if the Pathet Lao had signaled their attack.

He burst into the camp and saw only the Hmongs moving around, searching the huts. There were bodies everywhere, and he knew that surprise had been complete and devastating. He heard a burst of fire far below the camp, and then an abrupt silence, in which he could hear the crackling of the flames of the burning hut, and the calls of the Hmong troops as they moved through the camp. He began to walk, unhurried now.

The Pathet Lao casualties were enormous and the camp almost totally destroyed. He looked in a couple of the surviving huts, saw the body of a Hmong in one of them, and moved on again. The firing had completely stopped, but he knew the enemy would regroup somewhere, perhaps with reinforcements, and come back to the camp. It was important now to be able to leave as soon as it was light. He would give the Hmongs a few more minutes to search—and Gabriel a few more minutes to find any loot—and then regroup them. He felt weary all at once and stood still and stretched, feeling the fatigue that tension brought, feeling the coming of the particular sensation he had after any combat, a time when his senses returned to normal. He ran his hand over his face, feeling the scar from Loder's knife. He heard someone behind him laughing. He took the whistle out and blew on it, a long, sustained blast. He waited, but there was no answer from Gabriel. He tucked the whistle back in his shirt and began to search the camp. The Hmongs were feeding the fire now, getting enough light to make movement easier. The whistle had signaled the end of the action and called for formation again, and he felt the Hmong gathering behind him, following him through the camp. He turned and gestured to a noncom who, he knew, had some English.

"Langé?" he asked, but the Hmong shook his head.

"Ask them," he said, and the soldier turned and spoke to the gathering Hmongs. One of them answered, stepping forward and talking quickly to the noncom. When he had finished, the noncom turned back to Dane.

"He say Langé last over there," and the soldier gestured.

"Search the camp and the perimeters," Dane ordered.

The noncom formed them in a skirmish line at the opposite end of the camp and they swept through it, using makeshift torches from pieces of burning wood and an occasional flashlight. There was no sign of Gabriel in the camp. Dane was relieved; he had been half expecting to find the Frenchman's body.

"Move out to the perimeters," he said to the noncom and stood in the center of the camp, trying to think, while the Hmongs searched in the brush.

Gabriel . . . a prisoner.

The thought filled his mind.

Gabriel was not killed in the action and was nowhere in sight. He must have gotten caught up, perhaps wounded, in the fleeing Pathet Lao. They simply swept him along and would certainly interrogate him as soon as possible, perhaps before morning. If he talked, they would surely shoot him afterward.

The noncom came up and reported no sign of Gabriel.

"We're going after him," Dane said, knowing it was not the right military decision. "Get the troops ready." The noncom did not hesitate and Dane felt a quick thrill of pride in these tough mountain men. They knew he was wrong and they would follow him anyway.

They fired every hut in the camp and did a quick look at the bodies, finding two wounded Pathet Lao. He knew they could not take them along, and their wounds indicated they wouldn't survive anyway. Before he had to give the order, the noncom shot both of them.

There were six Hmong among the dead.

They moved out of the camp, following the path of the fleeing Pathet Lao. Dane sent scouts well ahead so he wouldn't blunder into an ambush, and they moved as rapidly as possible.

He stopped once during the night to check their route. The Pathet Lao were fleeing in the direction of Ban Pangi and Ban Ko, two mountain villages controlled by the communists. If they couldn't catch them before they reached the villages, Dane and the Hmongs would have no chance to free Gabriel. Grim-faced, he pushed them hard, sometimes recklessly, through the dark night. Even as he did, he knew it was useless.

1975–1978

*I*n a rare moment of leisure, Sara sat in her tent sipping Scotch without ice, without water, out of a dirty glass. She was wearing her usual khaki pants and shirt with the device of the medical mission sewn onto her left sleeve. Her hair was pulled back in a bun and tied—unflattering, she knew, but Whitney wanted it that way. For sanitation, he said. Sometimes she felt he wanted her to look as unappealing as possible. Sometimes he went out of his way to humiliate her.

She took another sip of the Scotch and looked out the door across the mission compound. He was out there somewhere, talking to a reporter, who, for once, she had refused to meet. It had been building in her: every time she talked with a correspondent she was reminded of what she might have accomplished, what she had, in fact, been able to do before giving up her job. To see the correspondents work now, to know the impact they were able to have, gave her a small pang of envy, which could turn to a large bitterness if she let it. She held it under control, though, as she had held so many things under control. She got up and stood in the doorway of the tent, one hand in her pocket, sipping the drink. Whitney did not like her doing that. He said it looked bad and there was no need to be so blatant. The hell with it.

Why didn't she leave him? The question had haunted her for a long time. It wasn't a question of Dane, anymore. She had lost him forever by her own stupidity. No, it was an expiation of guilt somehow, a punishment, a martyrdom to stay with Whitney. Yes, it was a punishment, but who was she punishing, and why? Part of the problem was that she was usually too tired to think it through. She looked at the hand holding the Scotch, hating the way her skin looked, all splotched and scarred. She hated getting older.

She had a sudden vision of herself lunching with Dane at the Peninsula, in Hong Kong, and afterward making quick but satisfying love in their room before they turned out again for teatime and a joyous night out on the town. What happened to that pretty, vibrant girl? She hoped Dane would never see her again, the way she looked now. She turned back into the tent and looked into her mirror, a hand mirror that lay on a footlocker near her bed. Her eyes no longer shone with laughter. She looked dull, and old. Ah, God, she was coming to hate Whitney, but no more than she hated herself.

Was it too late? Well, it was too late for some things.

She finished the Scotch and looked for the bottle. She started for it when Whitney suddenly walked through the door.

"Start packing," he said.

"Where are we going this time?" she asked, dreading yet another move.

"Cambodia."

"What? Cambodia!"

"Can't you talk and pack at the same time?"

"Not until you tell me what's happening," she replied coldly. He turned back to her, his eyes unfriendly as always. He stood with his hands on his hips, staring down at her, trying for the thousandth time, she thought, to intimidate her.

"We are going to Cambodia to carry on our work," he said. "It is God's will."

"Save it for the interviews," she said. "I'm not going anywhere until I know why. I've had enough of this sudden-move crap while you search for the most publicity."

"My, my," he said. "Testy."

She simply stared at him.

"All right," he said. "Ban Me Thuot has been hit hard by the North Viets. It's more than a small-scale action. It looks like a massive invasion. The ARVN is in total disarray and most of the troops are fleeing for the coast. It looks like the beginning of the end."

"So much for Vietnamization," Sara said bitterly.

"We've been told to get out, while we can."

"A direct communiqué from God?"

He whirled back. "Don't be blasphemous."

"This whole situation is blasphemous."

"There is no time to argue with you. Indulge your fantasies some other time, and that's enough liquor, by the way. We're going to Cambodia. Start packing."

"Why Cambodia?" she asked, curious in spite of herself.

"Why not?" He started folding his clothing on his bunk.

"The situation there is as bad as it is here, for openers," she said. "It isn't exactly clear who's in charge and there seems to be a lot of conflict. I'm just wondering how long we'll be in Cambodia before we have to scramble for someplace else."

"Why should you care? We're saving lives. That's important to you, isn't it?"

"Of course it is. So is my own life."

He stood very still. "And mine?"

She let the silence lengthen. "You can take care of yourself. You and God," she said finally.

Again the thin, cold smile. "And the legendary Colonel Dane? What about his life?"

"He can take care of himself," she said. "He always has. And when are you ever going to drop it, Whitney? Or are you?"

307

"You'd better pack," he said, knowing he had stung her.

"And you'd better leave me alone, Whitney. I can't take much more of this."

"We have an hour to fold this place up," he said. "The staff is packing our supplies. All we have to be responsible for is our personal possessions. Let's not keep them waiting."

Once again she realized how pitifully few things she had anymore. Her clothing was mostly the khaki uniforms. Her only jewelry was her watch. Her shoes were sensible, not stylish. She had one or two sun dresses, but seldom wore them anymore. For a time she had put them on in the evenings, hoping to please him, but he had been oblivious to them, as he was to almost anything that did not pertain to his work—and his ambition of returning to the States with a hero's welcome and the kind of position Whitney felt was his divine right.

"Are we going to be in Phnom Penh?" she asked him.

He was closing the lid on his footlocker. "No," he said. "In the country somewhere. I'd have to find it on a map. Anyway, South Vietnam's days are numbered, that's for sure." He put a padlock on the footlocker and snapped it shut. "Are you ready?" he asked.

"A few more minutes. And why are you so callous about the end of this country? We both put in a lot of time and effort here. Are you immune to all of the things going on around you, Whitney? We're watching a nation in its death throes. Doesn't that touch you any?"

"Not enough to stay around and be a part of those death throes. You'd better hurry. A boy will be along to pick up your luggage."

The last thing she packed as a small desk calendar. She looked at the date: March 1975. She wondered where she would be this time next year. Wearily, she closed the footlocker and snapped the catches. Then she turned and went through the door into the hot midday sunlight.

Dane lay on a couch in his flat at Hong Kong's Mid-levels, a glass of vodka beside him. He had not touched it since the newscast began. He sat woodenly, watching the events unfolding on the small television set.

The story was by a British television documentary team and the calm and cultured words of the newsman were a counterpoint to what he was seeing on screen. It was much worse than he had thought it would be.

He saw the lines outside the U.S. embassy compound; the gates would open and suddenly clang shut, allowing a few people to make it inside the grounds where helicopters, landing on the embassy roof, would eventually airlift them out of the country to the waiting decks of aircraft carriers. But the gates also separated families, forever altering lives and personal histories. The helicopters came in like great dragonflies and masses of arms would reach for them. Most Westerners had already left the country. He was watching the surrender of a city and of a country, the final performance in a bad play that had run for ten years and cost thousands of lives. Some American official came on screen, explaining that the evacuation plan had been worked out to the fullest, but Dane could tell simply by the footage that something had failed at the last minute. He remembered something Gabriel had told him—when the French left Vietnam forever, there was a full year for an orderly evacuation of those Vietnamese who also needed to go. Even the Americans had had a little time, at least six or seven weeks of knowing the end was at hand, and still the evacuation was a screwup. But it wasn't only the evacuation. It was the end of a lot of dreams, and what he was watching now was the beginning of the nightmare.

And a nightmare it would be.

God will desert them, and we will defend them, Gabriel had said.

Well, it was true, he supposed. He would hang around Hong Kong for a few more days, showing himself. Someone would approach him. They always did. Then he would go back to base camp, where Peter Boswell, as adjutant, seemed to be picking up nicely where Ashton had left off. Dane recalled the morning Ashton had simply packed and announced he was going home; he couldn't continue with the kind of life that had brought about the death of the woman he loved. Dane had been sympathetic and had arranged transportation. Ashton was in Bangkok the following day and in England the day after that. Ashton had aged day by day following the receipt of that fatal notice, seeming to shrink within himself. He was as different from that efficient organizer he had been as night and day. In the end, Dane was glad to have him out of the camp, sorry to say.

He had left strict orders with Boswell to contact him if there was any word about Gabriel. He refused to believe the Frenchman was dead, and he passed the word around Vientiane as widely as possible that he would pay well to get Gabriel back. Then he had had a rare meeting with General Lam, who agreed to do what he could. He had a few connections who had connections with the Pathet Lao, and perhaps for enough money . . . well, it was possible. The general had his own problems, finally facing a transfer out of his sector. With the restoration of ranks in the People's Army, he was once again a real general and was soon to be promoted and transferred. He could not refuse the promotion, which he certainly would do if it would allow him to stay in place, but the end appeared inevitable: sooner or later, he would have to go.

Dane suddenly felt a flicker of depression. Most of the people he had known for years were disappearing from his life.

He heard a voice calling from the doorway to the bedroom and looked up. The Chinese actress was standing there wearing only a jade bracelet. He had met her the day before when she came to the *dojang*. She needed to know some quick taekwondo moves for a kung fu movie she was starring in. He had worked with her all that day and slept with her last night, and now she stood there, radiating youth and health and sex. And he never wanted Sara as much in his life as he did at that moment.

"Come to bed?" she asked in Cantonese.

"No, thank you," he said, also in Cantonese. "This is business," and he gestured at the television screen. It was the only answer she would have accepted. She nodded and went back into the bedroom. He could hear her dressing.

The program was almost over.

The last flickering images on the screen were incredible footage, obtained somehow from sources in the countryside, outside Saigon. He saw victorious soldiers, Viet Cong and North Vietnamese troops, riding tanks and personnel carriers, waving flags. He saw places he recognized, especially around Vinh Long and My Tho. There were bodies in the streets and blown buildings, and discarded equipment from handguns to large earth-movers.

He heard the actress leave.

The footage was of Saigon once again, a focus on the faces of the thousands of people trying to get help from the Americans in getting out of the city. There was a closeup on the face of a young boy, and right behind him, an old man with a scholarly face. *It could have been me, and Tawodi.* The closeup became a freeze-frame and stayed on while the credits rolled over it. He was held by the two faces long after the program was over. At last he got up and clicked off the set and sat silently in the room, sipping the vodka.

The Trail Where They Cried. How would you say that in Vietnamese?

He brought them gifts, as he always did. He gave them reassurances, as usual. He complimented Starlight on her cooking, which at last had become better than adequate. He told Nathan how distinguished he had become, and it was true. He spent two full days in the warmth and happiness of the house before he was able to get into the woods.

He carried the old Winchester .22 and a single box of fifty rounds of ammunition. He put a few fishhooks and some line in his pocket and took one of the new nylon blankets in the pocket of his jacket. To please Starlight he carried some of the jerky she had made.

He went to Boyd Gap, following a trail alongside the road, then branching off and taking the trail to Panther Knob and on to Jenkins Grave Gap. He spent the night there and moved on the next day, going in deeper, crossing Lost Creek and still deeper. He began to swing in a long, uneven circle, stopping to admire the views, to watch a fawn in the dusk, drinking from a small stream of the Hiwassee River. The river itself was marvelous, clean and sparkling and fast flowing. He walked it upstream and crossed the state line into North Carolina, leaving the Cherokee National Forest. He came out just south of Unaka and turned back toward Nantahala National Forest and swung west again. After several days he ate some of Starlight's jerky, but he still preferred the bass he had caught and the two squirrels he had shot.

Finally, he emerged on the side of the hill where their cabin had been and he sat where he and Tawodi once sat together. Of the cabin itself there was hardly a trace. Here he had scattered his grandfather's bones. It was a clean place, beautiful in the soft light of early morning but even prettier just before dark, when it took on a mystical quality, the black of the coves appearing mysterious but somehow not threatening, and the leaves of the trees turning and turning in the wind. From a far distance he heard the calling of crows and he thought he heard their echoes in the valleys.

He spent the night there, sleeping on the ground on the thin nylon blanket, ample protection on a summer night. He lay down on the place where Tawodi's bones had been, feeling a great kinship with the place, with the earth, with his grandfather's memory. When he closed his eyes he wondered if he would dream, if Tawodi would give him a sign. But he slept soundly through the night.

The next morning he stood silently and said a small prayer in his heart, a prayer for the spirit of his grandfather. Then he walked out of the mountains, feeling greatly refreshed, and clean.

To Starlight's delight he spent more than two weeks with them, talking easily of places he had seen, but also talking about the mountains. He found he could talk about Tawodi without pain, with gladness even. He had noticed that as Starlight aged, she looked more and more like her father, and he said so.

She asked him about the scar on his face and he told her, despite the concern it would cause. He was still trying to get through life without telling even small lies, because, the old man had said, each small lie robs you of some of your honor and your dignity, hey-yeh!

He left on a soft and warm morning, promising to return soon, perhaps even for Christmas this year. It had been a long time since he had celebrated Christmas in a cold place, with the promise of snow. He embraced both of them warmly and turned down the path from the front door of the house. He looked back once, just in time to see Starlight burst into tears.

The medical mission lay northeast of Sisophon in western Cambodia, or Kampuchea as it had been known more recently. Sara knew that Kampuchea referred to the earliest foundations of the Khmer people and the establishment of the ninth-century Angkor empire. She also knew that the State of Democratic Kampuchea had been proclaimed after the ouster of Prince Norodom Sihanouk.

She knew all of this in an abstract way. Her personal struggle had become simply to help keep people alive in the middle of some of the worst atrocities she had witnessed in Southeast Asia. Some of them occurred very close to the mission itself, and one of them touched her personally. At night, in her tent, she sometimes woke up and found beads of sweat on her forehead and a gut-wrenching memory of that terrible afternoon when the Khmer Rouge had come into the mission.

Sara and Whitney and the other members of the mission—a handful of medical people, Scandinavian and Canadian—had been isolated from the murders around them for some time, praying each day that their luck would hold. There was a new government in Phnom Penh headed by Saloth Sar, who also went by the name of Pol Pot, and his regime had set out on the systematic destruction of the intelligentsia of the nation, followed by the mass evacuation of the cities. They began to hear tales that were difficult to believe; tales of mass murders and communal graves in Phnom Penh itself, one of the more gracious of Asian cities until recently. Sometimes, peering over outside the mission, they could see hundreds of people on the roads, driven out of the cities under orders, or simply streaming across the countryside in a desperate search for food, for shelter, for life.

For the Khmer Rouge—the Cambodian communists—Sara had supreme disgust. On a rare trip into Sisophon and in other quick views of the countryside Sara noted the implacable hatred they seemed to bear for all but themselves. They moved like robots, blindly killing on command. Most of them wore black pants and shirts, and all of them went armed, everywhere. In her mind she thought of them as zombies, dead to all human feeling. Under Pol Pot they were able to carry out the most brutal acts with governmental approval.

She saw it happen that afternoon, that moment that caused the bad dreams and sleepless nights. The moment that awakened her to reality.

The mission had a friend who lived and worked in Sisophon, a middle-aged schoolteacher who once had literary aspirations. His name was Van, a nearsighted, good-humored man with a great interest in events beyond the borders of Cambodia. He came regularly to the mission, listening with interest to the occasional services in the small chapel, but spending most of his time in informal conversations with the English-speaking members of the mission. What he brought was news; he kept the mission apprised of the situation around them at a time when they were more and more afraid to leave the compound.

On that fatal afternoon it was Sara and Van, talking animatedly in the shade of a tree near the center of the mission, talking about the Khmer civilization and its period of greatness. Van was very proud to be Khmer, telling her the worst possible thing one could be was Vietnamese or Thai, and of the Lao he would hardly speak at all. Yet it was all done with gentle humor, and Sara smiled at him, knowing that in his heart there were few if any prejudices, in this hotbed of prejudices. He was laughing, his head thrown back, when he suddenly stopped and stared. Sara looked behind her. There was a group of Khmer Rouge moving across the compound, the first time they had entered it. Sara had a sudden flash of intuition and tried to step in front of Van, but it was too late. One of the Khmer Rouge soldiers walked casually to them. He was young, Sara noted, but like all of them the face was impassive and hard.

The soldier said something to Van, who shook his head. The soldier then reached out and jerked Van's glasses from his face and shouted so loudly that Sara instinctively stepped back.

Van turned to her, squinting without his glasses.

314

"He thinks I am an intellectual. Anyone who wears glasses is suspect."

The Khmer Rouge soldier shouted something else and Van smiled and began to answer. The soldier threw up his rifle and shot Van in the throat. The bullet went through his neck and smacked into the tree behind them. Sara heard it hit, like a thunderclap.

Van was hurled backward into the dust of the compound, and he lay kicking. Sara heard him give a strangled cry and then he was still. The soldier turned and walked away as casually as he had approached them, without looking back.

The shot brought everyone out. She stood frozen, staring at Van and hearing the running feet behind her, saw Whitney bend over the body and straighten up and put his hands together in prayer, had the sudden thought that the prayer would be useless unless it were in Khmer. She was seized with such a feeling of helplessness that she simply turned and walked away and went into her tent. She lay on her bunk for hours, ignoring Whitney as she ignored the coming of night. Sometime during the night she got up and took a bath in the knocked-together shower and went back to her bunk and lay staring into the darkness until morning came like a dark curtain being ripped apart.

She drank two cups of steaming tea, hardly tasting them, then went to find Whitney. As she walked across the compound she forced herself to look at the gash in the tree where the bullet had entered, and the spot nearby where Van had fallen, blood gushing from his throat. She wanted to be angry for this encounter.

She found him in postop, an ambitious name for the screened section of the small former schoolhouse now occupied by the mission. She asked him to step outside, out of earshot of the patients, some of whom understood English.

"What are you going to do about Van's murder?" she asked abruptly.

He ran his hand across his beard. She noted, without sympathy, how tired he looked. "Nothing," he said. "You know as well as I do there's nothing we can do."

"There's nothing you can do for Van, but what about the rest of us? And them—the ones outside the compound? Have you looked out there recently?"

"Yes, I know. More every day."

"Whitney, there are hundreds of people out there, just to be near us. They're old, starving, dying, afraid, deathly ill. They should be making for the border, like everybody else, but they're out there and they're going to stay until we pull out. So let's go."

"What are you proposing?" he asked, his voice suddenly harsh.

"The only sensible thing," she said, speaking in a rush. "Let's pack what we can carry and get the hell out. These people will come with us. If we stay here the Viets are going to overrun this place. And everything and everybody in sight. You want to save some lives? Then get out."

"You listen to me, Sara. We're in the forefront of mission work here. Do you realize the kind of impact this single little mission is having on the people who count, back in the States? Every day we stay is a bonus for us all. Our reputations are made if we can hang on a little longer."

She looked at him with a mixture of disbelief and contempt.

"Did you ever stop to think how many disasters there have been because someone wanted to hang on a little longer? For God's sake, Whitney, let's get out of here while we can and take these people with us. The Viets are coming through here like a tidal wave and nothing can stop them. You know the way they feel about the Khmers; they'll be merciless. We may survive it—maybe—but a lot of those people outside the compound won't."

"What do you think we're doing here, Sara? We're here to take care of them. In case you hadn't noticed."

"I don't care what you think of me, Whitney. I don't think that matters much anymore. But we're a magnet for these people. They're simple farmers, they think we have some kind of magic. If we stay, they'll stay. And die. Don't you see—we have to get out."

She saw dark, angry spots burning in his cheeks. "Nobody is

getting out. I'll decide when, and if, we leave. If you try to slip out of here I'll tie you in your bunk. I need you here."

She stared at him, stunned.

"You son of a bitch!"

He hit her then, a solid punch that caught her on the right cheekbone, rocking her head back. She went backward and down in the dust, dazed. She shook her head and looked up; he was standing over her, flushed and angry.

"You'll stay until I tell you to go. You and everyone else in this compound. *If* we go, it will be when I decide, nobody else. You got that?" He whirled and hurried away in long, furious strides.

She got slowly to her feet, not yet thinking—just feeling, letting her emotions carry her. She knew a wild and flashing anger so intense it began to burn away the hopelessness of the years, the lethargy of her existence, the futility of her relationship with him. It swept through her like a racing flame, clean and bright, a cleansing fire that left her shaking with something quite close to joy.

The blow had freed her.

She touched her cheek, feeling the bruised and tender skin.

Ah, Whitney, at last you have given me something I can appreciate. You have given me freedom. From myself. And certainly from you.

She looked up to see two of the Canadian nurses staring at her in shock. *They're wondering what happened. Something wonderful happened.* She waved to them impulsively, almost gaily, a movement that startled them. *They think I'm crazy.* With a light step she turned and hurried to her tent, knowing they were still watching her.

That night on her bunk she composed the first of the letters.

The next day she handed the letter to a harried young Khmer who had told her, in confidence, he was going to try to make it to the Thai border with his family. He had been a small landowner before the Khmer Rouge came into power and then he had lost everything. Now the Vietnamese would be here any day and they probably would punish him for being a capitalist. He had survived the Khmer Rouge, but he had been lucky; he didn't think the Viets would be lenient. He promised

317

to hand the letter to anyone with the United Nations or the Red Cross or, failing that, to any Caucasian he met across the border.

She gave the second letter to a young Khmer woman who had borne one of her children in the mission hospital. It had been a breech delivery and difficult, and Sara had taken charge of the girl's recuperation. The girl had promised to take the letter to Sisophon and try to get it out from there, but the next day she was back. Sisophon was almost emptied, she said; there were more people camped around the mission grounds than in the city. Food was becoming critical, and there were more and more incidents of theft and robbery. Sara took the letter back and waited. In a few days she gave it to one of the mission handymen, who told her that he was sorry to abandon them, but he was taking his family to the border, if they could get there. He urged Sara to get out and she smiled and thanked him.

Sara wrote two more letters and got them at least out of the compound, not knowing if any of them would reach someone who could help them. She kept her secret from the others, listening to them each day in the mess tent, trying to suppress their fears. She remained silent while Whitney insisted to them that they all stay on their jobs, that the Viets would respect their neutrality, the fact that they were foreigners, and medical people. She couldn't tell if the others believed him in their hearts, but they stayed on, keeping to themselves any private fears. *Foolish*, thought Sara. *It's foolish to gamble with Indochina, because you can't win. Dane was right, as he was right about so many things. And I've been so wrong.*

For perhaps the first time she began to get a perspective on Asia that made sense. She had an intuitive moment in which she could see it whole, the history and traditions, the past and the future. Almost anything you said about it was true somewhere and untrue somewhere else, and in its amazing diversity lay much that confused the West. A Khmer was no more like an Indonesian than a Spaniard was like a Norwegian, but to the West the people of Asia all seemed the same, and in that erroneous generalization, in that sometimes arrogant dismissal of Asian culture and thought and science and art, the West was making a mistake that would haunt its waking moments in the years to come. At the same time, you couldn't romanticize it too much either, for the moment you did, Asia would grab you by the throat. She realized that her copy had been impassioned, compassionate, and real—but incomplete. The stories she had filed were true enough, but were hardly more than quick snaps when what was really needed were the long, reasoned portraits of a region and its people. She had failed to tell all of it. If she wrote again—*if she wrote again*—it would be about more than merely the events taking place right now. It would be about the reasons they took place at all. She would tell *why* the Khmers and the Thai and the Vietnamese and the Lao were such hostile neighbors (to say nothing of the Shans, the Hmongs, the Bru, the Pacoh, the Jey, the Hre, the Duan, and on and on). She would tell *why* so many Asian events could be traced to the failure of a crop, or the monsoon, or the flooding of the river; *why* the people of Southeast Asia could be so callous and cruel at the same time they were being so loving and generous; *why* a region washed by successive waves of Islam, Buddhism, and Christianity could be so indifferent to the sufferings of others. She wanted to explore that question. Perhaps a people capable of extreme religiosity was also capable of other extremes.

Dane had been right: you accept Asia the way it is, taking the murders with the splendors, the cruelty with the culture, the starvations with the opulence. You spend more time trying to understand it and less time trying to change it, and then you have taken the first step toward coming to grips with Asian realities.

Well, she understood now.

She had been so naive. It was commendable, even necessary, to care for the individual Asians she had met. It had been natural to love Huyen. But she had failed in her job, and failed them. She had not made Westerners understand the quicksilver lives many Asians led, and she had not shown Asia in metamorphosis. If she was desperately concerned about the plight of these people she would make the world focus on their problems.

She could still do it.

Just before dusk she walked out into the compound, trying to see it now as Dane would see it: something to be defended. Pretty sad, she thought. A rusting chain-link fence, surrounded now by as many as a thousand people camping, and itself surrounding a compound with a handful of foreign noncombatants. If the Viets suddenly decided to take the place and take them all prisoner, there was nothing they could do. In the quickening dusk she looked around her with the new reality she had so lately realized. She saw a scattering of buildings, single-story frame structures masquerading as a hospital. A handful of tents used for sleeping, eating, storage. A creaking bathhouse and several foul outhouses they could never seem to keep sanitary despite their efforts. Trees inside the compound, rather droopy. An air of tropical decay, painted over.

And beyond it, the enemies. The merciless Khmer Rouge might simply execute them all tomorrow morning, with no more thought than swatting a fly. If that didn't happen, the Vietnamese would surely roll over them, probably shelling the place first. There was nothing more demoralizing, more impersonal, more frightening, than an artillery barrage.

She had been in Cambodia nearly three years now, and with Whitney far too long. All at once she had come alive, and she passionately wanted to live.

Dane had remained in Hong Kong for Christmas after all, telephoning his regrets to a disconsolate Starlight. He was restless, in a way he remembered from his boyhood—driven by unknown yearnings. He spent days traveling between Hong Kong and the base camp in Thailand and once, for reasons he could not fathom, to Singapore, where he stood outside, staring at the entrance to Raffles before going across town and registering at another hotel.

A message from Peter Boswell told him the Hmongs were leaving Laos in great numbers, settling in a refugee camp not far from Nong Khai in northern Thailand, and not far from their base camp. The Pathet Lao had a grip on the nation and Dane knew it was just another step in the Vietnamese dream of an Indochina federation, with Hanoi as its capital. He could see the whole map of Indochina turning red. The situation in Cambodia was bad enough, but he feared it would get worse. He had heard rumors of bitter dissension between the Vietnamese and the government of Pol Pot, despite the fact that they both wore communist labels. In Southeast Asia the ideology was bent to serve the local interests, and despite initial Vietnamese support for Pol Pot and his Khmer Rouge, the situation was growing more and more tense. Dane read an interview Pol Pot had given two American reporters, in which he had reminded the reporters that in 1471 the Vietnamese had destroyed the state of Champa, in what was South Vietnam, after years of conflict. That area, the Mekong Delta, was still referred to by the Khmers as Lower Kampuchea. It was a subtle way of publicizing his fears that the Vietnamese still had designs on the rest of Kampuchea, on all of Indochina.

The story had run in the *South China Morning Post*. He read it on his couch and felt disturbed. He went down to the *dojang* and worked out most of the day, trying to get exhausted enough to sleep soundly. The *dojang* was empty and he remembered that it was Christmas Eve, a pleasant, rather windy day. Back in his apartment he took a long shower, grateful that there were no longer water restrictions, one of the more tangible results of the thaw between the West and the People's Republic of China, which supplied Hong Kong's water.

A correspondent he knew invited him over to the Foreign Correspondents' Club on Chater Road for a drink. He stood at the bar on the fourteenth floor of Sutherland House, sipping vodka and making small talk with great effort, then excused himself and went home. He clicked on the television set and watched a beautiful Chinese girl deliver the news in an impeccable British accent. The situation in Cambodia was a mess, with the Khmer Rouge still committing unspeakable atrocities in spite of the fact that the nation was starving to death. Refugees were streaming for the Thai border; the political situation was tense.

He went into the bedroom and turned off the lights and lay still, listening to the voices in his head, wondering why he was so restless. But he thought he knew. He put the knife Tawodi had given him under his pillow and went to sleep.

The next day he had a Christmas brunch with his lawyer at the Noon Gun Grill on Causeway Bay and talked about buying property on Cheung Chau Island. Later, he found himself standing in the middle of the empty *dojang*, staring at nothing. He went home to watch the news from the same beautiful Chinese girl. At first he hardly heard what she was saying and then it hit him: 150,000 North Vietnamese, battle-hardened and highly mobile, had teamed with 20,000 troops of the Kampuchea National United Front for Salvation and were sweeping across Cambodia, intent on destroying Pol Pot and the Khmer Rouge and establishing a new government in Phnom Penh. It was obvious that nothing would stop them.

A premonition then: sooner or later he would find himself in Cambodia again. He suddenly wished he had Gabriel to talk to.

Peter Boswell, now in his mid-thirties and holding the equivalent rank of major, presided over a base camp greatly reduced. With the end of operations in Laos there was little work for the mercenaries and many of them had simply drifted off to look for employment elsewhere. There was plenty of space now in what once was a crowded camp. The ones who had left had done so amicably, well paid and eager to return if Dane had a use for them. Boswell had read in the *Bangkok Post* that two of the former mercenaries had been involved in a shootout with Thai army troops over a drug run from the northeast provinces into Bangkok. Both mercenaries had been killed, along with an appalling number of Thai troops. Boswell hated the whole situation, for it gave mercenaries a bad name. Too many petty crooks and would-be hired killers liked to call themselves mercenaries, and that was bad enough.

Bosewell was as hard as the African plains and just as open. He was a raw-boned South African gunsmith recruited by Ashton who found that he liked the life. He had been anxious to follow Ashton to Asia and was sorry for Ashton's problems, and his departure. But he worshipped Dane, whom he regarded as a natural leader who won respect by being better at everything he did than anybody else. Like himself, Dane wanted the mercenaries to be of the highest caliber, and Boswell respected him for that, too. Together they looked for professional soldiers and weeded out the wild-eyed adventurers. Now, of course, the need for mercenaries was not so apparent, and there was an unusual quiet in the camp.

Boswell sat in the headquarters tent, looking at the roster of men in camp. There were only seven non-Asians—five Europeans and two Americans, all solid troops. There were two Hmongs and a half dozen Thais, a Nung, one Vietnamese, and Hahn, a dour Korean who did taekwondo exercises every morning—Dane had recruited him—and who more or less intimidated the rest of the camp.

Unless they found some major work soon, Boswell reflected, he would have to let most of the men remaining go. They could always be recruited again if something turned up. He didn't want to keep spending the colonel's money for the hell of it.

He had a lot to tell Dane, who would be arriving in a day or so. There was news of the Hmongs, who were in a bad way. They were crossing the Mekong in hundreds of places, mostly at night, but some of them were being shot in the water—whether by Pathet Lao patrols or Thai border guards, or both, was still an open question. Boswell knew Dane had a great deal of affection for the tough little mountain men, and he knew the colonel would be worried.

There was news of the Khmers. They were in an all-out rout, with pockets of resistance from the Khmer Rouge, but most of the people were simply going all-out for the border, where a number of refugee camps had been set up around the pivotal border town of Aranyaprathet, four kilometers on the Thai side of the border.

There were the Thais to be considered. Boswell had heard that the Thai army had tried to turn back the tide of refugees as they stumbled out of the elephant grass along the border. Thailand, not poor by many standards, nevertheless regarded the refugees as an unwanted influx of people who had to be dealt with in some fashion, and the Thais did not want them to become a political or economic problem. Boswell had heard that the Thais had bent to the demands of the American ambassador, who threatened them with a withdrawal of U.S. economic assistance if they did not try to accommodate the refugees, at least until some sort of resettlement could take place.

And then there was the news that Boswell knew would galvanize Colonel John Dane.

The two ashen-faced men had appeared suddenly outside the camp, asking to see Dane and soon ending up in the headquarters tent with Boswell.

He had seated them on a small couch in his office, two middle-aged to elderly men with remarkably similar appearances. Perhaps it was the fact that both wore coats and ties in a country and climate that almost never required them, or the fact that both had gray hair. Or perhaps, Boswell thought, recognizing the type, it was the aura they presented, the belief that there actually was a God and that he had personal control of their lives. They were pious, at least in appearance.

"What can I do for you?" he had inquired politely.

The older one, who had introduced himself as Brother Lyons, cleared his throat. "Are you sure Colonel Dane is not available? We've heard so much about him."

"He's in Hong Kong at the moment," Boswell replied cheerfully. "It's me or no one, I'm afraid."

The second one, Brother Pickering, spoke to the floor in a voice so low Boswell had to strain to hear it. "We were wondering if you would handle a project."

"Depends," Boswell said, watching them both.

"We'd like you to do a job for us," Lyons said.

"Could I ask you to be a little more specific?" Boswell asked, somewhat amused.

Pickering again: "We want to hire you."

"I beg pardon?"

"We want to hire you," Lyons said. "We have a need for your services."

"I'm assuming you know the kind of work we do," Boswell said.

"We know quite a bit about you," Pickering said in his soft voice.

"All right," Boswell said. "What do you want us to do?"

Lyons started to speak and then hesitated. The setting seemed to disturb him, and he stared in a kind of horrified fascination at the pistol belts hung on pegs, the spartan desks, the maps with their acetate overlays, the empty grenade crate on which Boswell propped his feet under his desk, the PRC-10 radio.

"Is it something you need quickly?" Boswell asked gently, trying to draw them out.

Lyons's voice was stronger this time and he looked straight into Boswell's gray eyes.

"We are opposed to killing and mercenaries are anathema to our standards. We are God-fearing people, dedicated to saving lives and souls in the blighted regions of the world. For us to make a pact with you is—is—"

"A pact with the devil?" Boswell suggested.

"Yes, yes," Pickering said.

"Then perhaps you'll want to reconsider?" Boswell said.

"No," Lyons said, fussing with his tie. "We know what we want."

"Then for God's sake, and mine, get to the point." Boswell was no longer amused.

Lyons flushed. "We have a mission in Cambodia, in the western part, not yet in Vietnamese hands. There are some people there we want you to get out. The mission also has attracted a large gathering of Khmers, so we want you to take food in to them as you go. We want you to get our people out, as the first priority."

"I believe that's 'let my people go,' isn't it?" Boswell asked.

"We want them out," Lyons said firmly.

"Where are they?"

"Northeast of Sisophon. Rice country. It's a medical mission."

"How many?"

"Eight," Pickering said, almost in a whisper. "But one in particular."

"Who?" Boswell was curious.

"There's a doctor there. Whitney Mason. He's one of our most important men, important to our work, important to our ability to raise funds to support these kinds of programs. He's becoming quite well known in America and we don't want to lose him?"

"We want him out above all else," Lyons said.

"Who are the others?" Boswell asked, knowing who one of them would be and already picturing Dane's reaction.

"Whitney's, uh, friend—Sara Sunderland. A doctor from Sweden, a woman doctor from Copenhagen, and four Canadian nurses. The indigenous personnel, uh, the Khmers, probably will be as well off finding their own resources—making their own decisions about whether to come out or not. At least we can send them some food."

"I see," Boswell said, his voice cold. He really did see, and it infuriated him. To preserve their fund-raising capability, they wanted mercenaries to go in and pluck their fair-haired lad from the clutches of the Viets and, oh, by the way, bring out the rest if possible. As for the poor bugger Khmers, we'll give them a bite to eat so our consciences are clear, and then we'll leave them to the tender mercies of the Vietnamese. Well, it wouldn't be quite that way. The moment Dane found out that Sara Sunderland was in danger, he'd go get her, hauling that doctor-lover of hers out as an afterthought. But what about the Khmers, still in Cambodia because of the mission? Didn't they owe them something? The missionaries had asked for their loyalty and their faith and had gotten it; now the Khmers were looking for some kind of leadership. He could credit the mission people for hanging in there as long as they had, but now was the time to go, and could they get the Khmers out as well? A bloody, bloody business.

"All right," Boswell said, breaking his reverie. "I'll ask Colonel Dane to come here immediately for a second meeting with you. Where are you staying?"

"In Udon," Lyons said. "The rooms above the bakery."

Boswell nodded, "When can you come up again?"

"You call us," said Lyons. "We'll wait to hear from you. Do you think you will take the job?"

"Oh, yes," said Boswell, thinking of Sara Sunderland. "I would say you could count on it."

At the door the two men turned, and Lyons spoke in a voice filled with apprehension. "I suppose this is going to cost us a lot of money."

"It certainly is," Boswell said, with satisfaction.

It certainly is. What I'm wondering is what it will cost us.

Even Whitney now admitted the situation was desperate.

Every day saw more and more Khmer farmers and their families gathering outside the mission fence. Every day brought more ominous news of the approaching Vietnamese. And one day most of the patients who could walk got up and left the hospital, joining their families outside the fence or starting with them on the run for the border.

Late one evening they heard gunfire not far away. The next day a Khmer mission worker told them the Khmer Rouge had executed a number of "obstructionists" before fleeing the area. The Vietnamese reportedly were committing all sorts of atrocities in their westward advance.

They met as usual for tea in the mess tent in the late afternoon. Each day's conversations now were conducted against a background of cries and voices from just beyond the chain-link fence. The numbers outside the fence were swelling day by day, and each day Sara wept for them. Because of the mission, the Khmers were staying on and would surely die. Knowing that, she grew to hate Whitney for the sacrifices he would make, the deaths that would result from his intransigence, his passion for publicity, his stubbornness in the face of certain destruction of the mission, and perhaps their own deaths. With what she regarded as her new grasp on reality, she saw the inevitable end of it all and wept for the waste.

She hardly spoke to Whitney, and while she had begun to hate him, she also felt kinder toward him in a perverse way. In his anger he had made it possible for her to justify leaving him, and now she was able to see him with greater clarity and objectivity. She almost pitied him. In his eagerness to use others for fame, he himself had fallen victim, lingering too long in a trap of his own making. He had become more withdrawn from the others as well. Sara thought it was not so much concern for his personal safety as it was a sense of failure of his objectives, his propaganda, his hope of stunning achievement. It could all go down forever in the dust and heat and blood of the compound.

They would have to leave, and quickly. If all else failed, Sara intended just to get up one day and lead everyone through the gate and make for the border. Every day there were fewer and fewer Khmer Rouge troops around, which meant the Vietnamese were coming closer and closer. They were, in fact, swarming all over the country, and even the routes to the border might be cut by now.

Dane stepped through the door of the Sheraton Bangkok and stood under the porte cochere. In the early-morning darkness there were few people and almost no traffic. He watched a set of headlights approaching and knew it was a Jeep and stepped across the driveway in anticipation of Boswell's sharp turn off Surawongsee Road. In moments he was shaking hands with a grinning Peter Boswell and seconds after that they had circled behind the hotel and pointed the Jeep eastward, toward the Cambodian border.

Dane sat quietly in the Jeep, tasting the morning. The streets that would later be so hot and crowded were nearly deserted, but the hundreds of birds that swarmed in the dusk were still sitting on the power lines above the streets. He wondered where they went during the day.

Still in darkness they rolled out of Bangkok and into the countryside. A strange and unsettling sun shimmered ominously through the morning haze, seeming to darken and lighten with the passing miles, almost as if it were pulsating. They passed the body of a dog in the road, its back broken, and two crows rose from it in raucous protest. *Filthy birds,* Boswell thought. They passed stark trees, grotesque in the haze, and now and then a lovely temple, adding a grace note to a morning that seemed full of menace and the odor of murder. They passed more crows in the fields and began to encounter more traffic with the slow lifting of the haze. Boswell let his mind wander.

He thought of the briefing in which he had told Dane about the visit of the two missionaries and what they wanted the mercenaries to do. It had Dane's full attention. He had saved the name of the doctor until the last, until Dane finally asked him about it.

"It's Whitney Mason, Colonel," Boswell had said.

Dane had stood up then and stepped closer to him. Boswell noted the colonel's eyes had somehow gone from brown to black and the scar on his face seemed to glow. But Dane's voice was low and controlled.

"Then he's got Sara in there with him, I presume?"

"Yes, he has."

"The stupid son of a bitch," Dane said quietly. Boswell waited through Dane's silence. "What about the Khmers?"

"They told me, in effect, we could abandon them. They said we couldn't possibly get them all out, and they want us to take in some food supplies for them."

"Do they think we're going to mount up in trucks and just drive in there like a damned freeway?"

"I suppose, Colonel."

God will desert them and we will defend them.

"I beg your pardon, Colonel?"

"We won't leave the Khmers. The only reason they're hanging around that mission is because they think someone will try to rescue the *farangs* in there, which we are about to do. Anyway, I think somebody owes them something, don't you?"

"Right you are."

"Well?"

"It rules out a dustoff. If we send the choppers in we'll tell the world who, what, and why. We'll have to walk them out."

"Very good, Peter." Dane grinned. "You deal with the good brothers. Make it hurt a little."

And Boswell had gone in to deal. Lyons and Pickering had gone white when he told them how much money would be required, but in the end they agreed. "Get Mason out at all costs," they had said.

Well, they would get him out. Maybe.

They rolled eastward in silence, passing more temples and a long series of tapioca farms with water buffalo and irrigation ditches. Once they passed a procession of priests in single file alongside the road. Boswell wondered, as he so often had before, exactly what went on in the mind of a Buddhist priest in Southeast Asia. What a battleground of conflicts that must be!

Dane stirred and asked a question about distances and lapsed into silence again. Boswell was content with the lifting of the fog and the freedom from base camp and the damned paper work Ashton had always complained about.

At midmorning they stopped at a small Thai restaurant, a rambling frame structure with a picture of the king and his beauteous queen adorning one wall. The restaurant boasted an enormous refrigerator with clear-glass doors through which they could see racks of shrimp, meat, and chicken. They ate shrimp and fried rice, moving their hands constantly to challenge the flies, and drinking a liter of beer each. Dane was preoccupied all through the meal. Back in the Jeep there was little conversation.

By midday they had reached the first of the refugee camps at Sa Kaeo.

It lay to the left of the highway, a large, fairly level reach of dry and dusty ground covered in bamboo shanties and filled with an appalling mass of humanity at varying distances from death. Huts stretched down hastily graded dirt roads, long huts in which families were separated from other families by a length of string tied from one post to another. Although it was a new camp, the area had been stripped of firewood for cooking and the trees rose starkly from the hot earth, most of their limbs cut or broken away. At the main entrance to the camp the water trucks provided by the United Nations High Commissioner for Refugees waited to bring precious water into the camp.

The refugees themselves were the stuff of nightmares.

The children had bloated bellies from malnutrition and hunger, and their eyes told of unspeakable hardships. Many of them were totally nude in the blazing sun and seemed not to care. The old-young faces wore a certain resignation that was chilling, an acceptance of agony and death in what was, Dane suddenly remembered, the International Year of the Child.

The adults were simply a larger version of the children, with worn faces and a fatalism that spoke of the cruelty of centuries. When they could not longer stand up under it, when their hearts broke or their minds just let go, they simply dropped dead, all over the camp.

Dane and Boswell spent an hour in the camp, walking and looking. Then they climbed back into the Jeep and went on eastward.

On the outskirts of Aranyaprathet, despite Dane's curiosity about the town, they turned left and drove north to the other camps at Khao I Dang and Ban Nong Samet and Ban Non Mak Mun—all duplications of the conditions at Sa Kaeo. The camp commanders projected an air of both optimism and realism, talking of projected deaths as opposed to potential new refugees coming out of Cambodia. It was just outside Ban Non Mak Mum that a Thai lieutenant-colonel told them that Phnom Penh had fallen to the Vietnamese, and that Vietnamese tank and infantry units were executing what looked like a classic pincer movement to the west, crushing the Khmer Rouge center. Pol Pot and much of the Khmer Rouge had taken refuge in sanctuaries in the Cardamon Mountains, but it was no secret that many of the Khmer Rouge also were holed up in the various refugee camps, openly carrying arms. That, said the lieutenant-colonel, was all the justification the Vietnamese would need to attack the camps, thereby making incursions onto Thai territory. Would the Americans help if the Vietnamese attacked Thailand?

"I don't know," Dane said, thinking of Vietnam.

Throughout that scorching day, Dane moved almost in silence. Half of him was the calm professional—probing, learning, evaluating, weighing the odds of various plans. But the other half was in tumult. Sara was in there, and in grave danger.

He would get her out, that's all.

But even now, his heart pounding with fear for her safety, his mind racing for solutions, he knew she was only a part of the problem. He would certainly not risk all to save her, for he must bring out the others as well. To go for Sara alone and get her the hell out would be the easiest thing to do, and he would have a damned good chance of succeeding. He could hear Tawodi: *But not the honorable thing. Hey-yeh! You must go for them all, even the Khmers, who the others did not want you to bother with.*

He would get her out, and the Khmers too.

At dusk, on the outskirts of Aranyaprathet, he spread a map over the hood the Jeep and studied it with a flashlight. There was a railroad bridge at Poipet, four kilometers from Aranyaprathet. It simply ended there, a monument to somebody's doomed efforts, or a government's folly, or a war. By the time he got the refugees there the Viets could have cut it off, just as they could cut any other border crossing. At least the border was inexact in most places, and perhaps Viet patrols would not risk entering Thai territory and bumping into Thai army patrols. But that was another problem: if they came across at night, how to stop the Thais from shooting them?

Darkness dropped with typical suddenness. Dane could see the glow of the lights of Aranyaprathet.

"Let's sleep in town," he said to Boswell. "Must be a hotel in a town this size."

"Several places, Colonel," Boswell answered. "Bungalows near the highway, if they haven't been taken over by the *farangs* in town these days. Couple of hotels, not much, but a place to sleep."

They drove into Aranyaprathet with its traffic circle on each end of town and its network of small, crooked streets and its air of importance. Dane judged it to be a town of twenty to thirty thousand people, a marketing center for the area's farmers, a town that sprang up around the intersection of several highways. Along the long, winding main street were a number of small restaurants and shops and hardware stores, all of them wearing the same gray, weather-beaten faces, bleached by the remorseless sun and hammered periodically by the monsoon rains. The streets now held, in addition to the usual number of Thais, groups of rescue workers, journalists, missionaries, and assorted support personnel of a dozen nationalities.

By the time Boswell stopped the Jeep in front of a dingy, dirty two-story building, Dane was feeling the long day and the tensions. In a few minutes of negotiations with the owner, Boswell got them separate rooms. Dane looked gratefully at a primitive shower in a bathroom that had no plumbing but an adequate bucket for sluicing. He stepped happily into the shower.

In a half hour he met Boswell and they selected a café at random. Over more beer and an incredibly hot Thai curry, Dane talked of the proposed rescue mission.

"More of a race then a fight to get out," Boswell commented.

"I sure hope so," Dane agreed. "Our best chance is in creating no disturbance at all, in not calling attention to ourselves. I'll try to move them out of the compound at night and into the flow. We'll hide in the trees up there—all my maps show heavy forest to the west of them—and just hike on over the border, if possible. It's only a couple of days."

"You'll have a lot of people on the road with you. That's going to attract some attention."

Dane sipped the beer. "We'll need the famous old Plan B, if that happens."

"You mean the choppers, after all?"

"That, and the Thai navy, any Boy Scouts in the area, anything you can think of. The things that are going to be vital here are speed and secrecy."

Boswell sat back in the straight wooden chair and glanced around the small café. At this late hour they were the only patrons in the room. He felt some of the weariness of the day, a pleasant lassitude. He glanced over at Dane, who he thought looked drawn. *He's worried about her and about the job.*

"You ever think of giving this up, Colonel?"

Dane looked up quickly, then smiled slowly at Boswell. "Somebody else asked me that once. The answer is the same: no."

"Who asked you, if I might inquire?"

"A good friend, an old comrade. Gabriel Langé."

Boswell looked into his beer. "I'm sorry, Colonel. I never thought Gabriel would mention something like that. Hard to believe he's still missing."

"Yes, isn't it," Dane said woodenly. He looked over Boswell's head to a cheap print on the wall of the café, tacked up with a nail. It was a bad reproduction of a very good Hokusai seascape, the water alive with a kind of casual savagery. Boswell asked him something else, but he didn't hear it.

He had looked into the dark water, truly afraid and not knowing why. Other young men his age had dived from this rock into those waters. Perhaps they were afraid too, but they had done it. It was not an easy dive; you had to clear an outcropping, hold your body just so, then curl to meet the water hands first and straight. The pool below the outcropping was small, a difficult target, and surrounded by rocks. There were ample opportunities for mistakes, and death or serious injury could result. Perhaps he was afraid because of the illogic of it, the unnecessary risk. No matter. Because he was afraid of it, he would have to do it, or feel personal shame. He had gone to Tawodi with the problem and the old man had answered him as cleanly as a bolt of summer lightning; go and do it or learn to live with the way you feel about it. So he had gone, at night, with a glorious moon throwing shadows. Others had done it during the day, but if he were to do it by night, and alone, there would be more honor. But the waters were so dark, the outcropping so huge . . . He had suddenly put his hands over his head and made up his mind to do it or cease to live. He launched himself from the rock, cleared the outcropping in a controlled arc, bent his body from the waist, and plummeted straight and clean into the black waters, feeling them close around him, knowing they were like ice and not caring at all, feeling the thrill of what he had done. He climbed out of the pool and looked upward to the rock he had just left; it seemed very high and far away. He smiled. He never told anyone but Tawodi he had made the dive, and he never did it again. He didn't have to.

". . . as much a problem as getting out," Boswell was saying.

"Sorry, Peter. Would you say again? I was daydreaming."

"I said getting in will be as much a problem as getting out."

"Ah, Peter, Peter. You've never tried to steal horses from the Shawnee, have you?"

"Colonel, I don't know what you're saying."

"Just feeling my age, I think. For the record, I've never stolen any ponies from the Shawnee, but I knew an old man once who told me how to do it. Don't worry about my getting in. I want you to concentrate on how to stop the Thai border guards from drilling us as we come out, probably at Poipet."

Boswell grinned. "I think I have the answer to that. We'll use some of the lavish monies we're collecting from the missionaries to pay a little squeeze. We'll buy the guards."

"Not only the guards, Peter. You'll have to pay off the officers in charge as well, right up the line. We'll need some intelligence on the number of guards and their routine, their positions, times. You know what to do."

"I wish I were coming in with you."

"Every white face is a danger to us in there. We're better off with the Asians. I can blend in."

"Yes, you've done it more than once."

There was a pause while both men sat with their own thoughts.

"Colonel?"

"Um?"

"Be careful in there. I don't feel all that good about this, somehow."

"A piece of cake, Peter. Gabriel would do this and come out with two beauties under each arm, being chased by all the young men of the village, carrying a bottle or two of good montrachet."

"I'm serious, Colonel."

"Don't sweat it, Peter. We're all survivors here."

The fear was infectious.

Sara felt it, not only for herself but for the growing mass of Khmers who were now starting to spill into the compound itself. They had been starved and beaten and raped by the Khmer Rouge, but it was nothing compared to the terror they knew now that the Vietnamese were almost on them. Most of the able-bodied ones already had made for the border; those that were left behind were the old and sick and dying, or the young and sick and dying. How many could be saved? Sara did not know, but she knew that they had to make for the border at once. Every hour put them in greater danger.

Even Whitney was afraid. In the end he was about to abandon his precious mission after all, and Sara suspected he felt he had waited too long to get out. No one knew, now, if there *was* a way out.

The Canadian nurses were exhibiting a kind of grace under pressure that made Sara proud of them. Days ago they had offered the opinion that it was time to go, but when they were told by Whitney to stay, they turned their attentions to the Khmers surrounding the compound and began treating any and all ailments they could. The same was true of the other two doctors, the Scandinavians. They just went about their duties in a very businesslike way, occasionally cracking jokes with each other that Sara couldn't understand.

The moment she opened her eyes she felt the fear, wondering, as she had for the past several days, if the Viets would come that day. She got up and washed her face and brushed her teeth in the purified water from a lister bag, pulled her hair back and tied it with a faded ribbon. She got into her customary khaki pants and shirt, knowing the heat would make the shirt cling to her most of the day. She glanced into her mirror—it had been so long since she'd worn makeup she thought she would look strange in it, but for a fleeting moment she looked for the image of the young and beautiful girl who had fallen in love only once in her life, but would always remember it.

Sara heard a commotion outside the compound and put the mirror down and walked to the door of the tent. A group of men seemed to be pushing their way through the crowd of Khmers. *At least they aren't Vietnamese; the Viets will come in shooting.* No, it looked like another group of peasants, probably farmers, trying to get inside the mission in the mistaken belief it would offer some protection. Curious, she idled by the door of the tent to watch.

There were more of them then she thought, for behind the first group came others, all dressed in the rough pants and shirts worn in the district by those who had foresaken the traditional saronglike Khmer dress. Sara stiffened; the men were coming in and filing to the left and right of the fence inside the compound. *Oh, Christ, it's the Khmer Rouge. They've come back.* And now she could see they were heavily armed.

The group of men—she judged there were perhaps a dozen of them—suddenly stopped and stood, facing different directions as if watching for an attack. They certainly were disciplined, she had to give them that. Then one of them detached himself from the group and began to walk across the compound, some sort of automatic weapon held loosely in his right hand.

The walk was casual, but wary. The man moved with a kind of fluid grace, definitely animal-like. She had first seen that walk on a searing morning in Thailand, a lifetime ago.

Sara caught her breath. Thoughts were coming too fast, pushed aside by a flood of joy, relief, happiness. She paused for a heartbeat but only one, and then she threw away all doubts and hesitations. She called his name, just once, and then she flew out of the tent.

He stopped in the middle of the compound, and from somewhere got the presence of mind to put on the weapon's safety and place it on the ground beside him. He stood very still, but his mind was churning as he watched her run toward him. He stretched out his arms.

The years dropped away.

She was in his arms, sobbing, clutching him desperately, her face buried in his chest. She was saying something, but he didn't hear it. He wrapped her in his arms and just stood there, trying to shut out the rest of the world. She was shaking like a leaf in the wind, and to calm her he made himself grow very still, consciously trying to slow his heartbeat, his racing mind. Still he held him. He looked down at her and felt such a rush of love and pity and longing and despair for the lost years; he pulled her chin up and kissed her then, a long and desperate kiss. He saw some of the sadness leave her face and she looked up at him through tears.

"I'm a mess," she said.

"You're the most beautiful thing I've ever seen," he said, meaning it.

"Oh, God, Dane, I'm so glad to see you."

"I've missed you, Sara, more than you could ever know."

"I was so stupid."

"Listen—" But before he could continue they heard a shout and looked up.

Whitney Mason was striding toward them, his face stony but with two small angry spots burning in his cheeks. Dane stepped in front of Sara very casually and faced Mason.

Mason came up in a rush, stopping inches from Dane and fixing him with a cold stare. "The great Colonel Dane, I'm sure. Well, I don't care who you are and what you're doing here, you keep your hands off her, you hear?"

"Don't yell, Mason. Keep it low and quiet and we'll talk."

"I'll yell all I want, you mercenary bastard."

Sara stepped on one side of Dane. "Leave us alone, Whitney. You know it's all finished with you and me. It has been for years."

"Bitch!" Mason shouted and reached for her.

Dane hit him almost casually with the edge of his hand. Mason's head rocked back and he crumpled quickly, falling and rolling over on his stomach. He lay there for a moment and looked up, his face bloody.

"You've broken my nose," he said.

"At least you aren't shouting," Dane said. "Get up."

Mason staggered to his feet and stood with his hands on his face. "I need medical attention," he said, his voice quavering.

"Then go get it," Dane said impatiently, "and assemble everyone in one place. I'll tell them the way we're going to get them out of here." He watched Mason hurry away.

Sara clutched his arm. "Are we really going? Can you do it?"

"Damned right," he said. He looked down at her, seeing the relief in her face, watching it change suddenly to concern. "But what about these people? They think we can help them. We can't leave them, surely?"

"I don't intend to, Sara. They'll follow us out. They'll also be our best cover. We're going to have to get on with it though. The Viets are close."

"How close?"

"They're in Sisophon. They could be here as early as tomorrow morning, moving at their current pace."

"What do you plan to do?"

"Let's go to your tent, or somewhere. I don't like standing in the middle of this open compound."

"This way," she said.

Inside the tent he kissed her again, a slow, lingering kiss of rediscovery.

"My God, Sara, how I love you!"

"You know," she said slowly, "I think that's the first time you ever told me that."

"I'm slower than most."

"But you showed me love in so many ways. And I blew it."

"We'll make up the time."

"Oh, Dane, will we?"

"Sure. Don't you have any faith?"

"Listen," she said, smiling. "That's a word I've heard a lot in the past few years. I grew to hate it. I want to see and feel and touch something. And listen, I think I know now what you tried to tell me about Southeast Asia, years ago when you warned me not to try to change it, but to try to understand it."

He took her hands in his. "We have a lot to talk about."

She freed her hands and put her arms around him. "A lot of catching up to do."

There was a polite cough outside the tent and Dane turned to see the Swedish doctor, a very tall, fair, craggy-faced but gentle man. Dane stepped through the doorway.

"Doctor Carlsson, I presume?"

"Ah, yes. How do you do?" he said politely and shook hands with Dane. "Would you please come now to the medical tent? I believe everyone is there, as you asked."

"In a moment."

He went back inside the tent to Sara and stood looking at her. There were new lines in her face and around her eyes and little tendrils of gray in her hair, but she was beautiful. It was her eyes that held the sadness. He wanted to make that sadness disappear.

"Sara, we're going to get all of you out of here. It's going to be all right. Come with me to see the others and I'll tell you how we're going to do it."

She smiled at him. "Anything you say," she said. Then the smile grew wistful. "Dane, is there a chance, for us I mean, afterward, when this is over? I have to know. *Say* something."

"Every chance in the world, Sara. But for now, let's move."

They left the mission right after dark. He put out scouts headed by Hahn, the silent Korean, then sent a long line of the pathetic Khmers down both sides of the road leading from the mission compound. In the center of the column on each side he tried to conceal the missionaries and worried mostly about Carlsson's great height and fair skin, and the obvious Caucasian features of the missionaries. At least he had gotten them into Khmer clothing, ragged as it was, so they could hide among the Khmers. They might get away with it, unless Carlsson stood up or one of the women called attention to herself. If the Vietnamese caught them alone on the road there wasn't much of a chance for anyone, but he did not tell them that.

He was moving them north and west because all the maps he had seen showed that sector of Cambodia as being heavily wooded; he hoped so. His own penetration into the country had come through the mountains to the south of Aranyaprathet, then a quick thrust northward until they began to see Vietnamese units south of Sisophon. Then they had left the roads and trudged across the countryside, crossing what had been farms before the devastation of the Khmer Rouge policies. Now they were wastelands, unplanted and unproductive, overgrown with weeds and scrub brush. By the time he had reached the mission Dane had a greater appreciation for the magnitude of the Khmer tragedy. And now, as if the Khmer Rouge weren't enough, the ancient enemy, the Vietnamese, was about to fall on this gentle land and people.

He stopped in the road and looked at the columns.

There were perhaps a thousand people in all, willingly following anyone who looked strong enough or healthy enough to take charge. Some of them followed because the mercenaries were armed, and so much Asian history had been written by men who were armed. He sent Khmer-speaking mission aides through the hordes outside the compound and told them simply to get ready to march after dark; anyone left behind would have to answer to the fury of the Vietnamese. And of course they all went.

He divided the missionaries between the two columns and was pleased that even from his proximity he couldn't pick them out of the mass of men, women, and children limping and struggling down both sides of the dusty road. Watching them in the moonlight, he had a sudden sense of timelessness, of history standing still—or else in constant repetition—for all of his experience, his knowledge, his sensitivities, had brought him on this night to this road among these people, and somehow it seemed inevitable that it would be this way. It seemed to him then that all of his personal history had been a prelude to this time and place. He shook his head; no time for introspection.

He spread his best map in the center of the road and studied it with a flashlight. He had made notes on it back at base camp, based on what intelligence they could get. There was an abandoned village ahead and on the edge of the woods. The villagers had taken a vote and agreed to leave together more than a week ago—a sensible decision because they could assist each other along the way. It could have been done all over Cambodia, but the Khmer Rouge had worked too evil a magic over the minds of these simple farmers and it was difficult for any of them to take any initiative.

But this village was there, and empty, and would be a tremendous help; they would inhabit it during the day and walk again in the darkness. If necessary they could abandon the direct route and curve north to a place of ruins, a crumbling temple on a hill the gradient chart showed to be about six or seven hundred meters. There they could hide again, rest up for the final charge to Poipet. At Poipet it would be up to Peter to get them over.

Well, he thought, a plan with as many holes in it as a sieve, but the kind of plan you need in a situation like this. He snapped off the light and folded the map and put it in the front of his shirt. Then he took his position near the front of the column on the right side of the road. Right behind him was the Vietnamese he had recruited years ago in Dalat, for his language abilities. The Vietnamese was carrying one of the two radios, the second one near the rear of the column and being carried by a Khmer-speaking Chinese. Somewhere, a few dozen people behind him, was Sara.

She had looked wonderful, he thought, not so changed except for the shadows in her eyes, and even those were going now that she had some hope. He was pleased he could bring her hope, and love. He would get her out of this situation and then protect her for the rest of their lives, and never again would that dark sadness steal into those lovely eyes. When they got out of here he would take her someplace romantic, perhaps Paris, where they would make love in the mornings and spend the afternoons drinking cold white wine and have dinners in exquisite places. Or Copenhagen, perhaps. It would be interesting to see what his father's people were like. *The father he had never seen, never known.*

He heard a whisper behind him. The radioman stepped out of the column and joined him in the roadway as the two columns kept moving. "It is Hahn," he said. "He is behind us and coming in and asks us not to shoot, or stop."

Dane nodded. "Tell him to report to me."

The radioman dropped back and began to talk. Dane walked on, keeping pace with the column. In a few minutes the radioman was back in position and nodding to him, and Dane began to glance backward now and then, looking for the scouts.

Hahn came up suddenly, materializing out of the darkness with two other scouts. His face was impassive, but his words were chilling.

"They are everywhere in front of us, Colonel. We saw patrols in every direction. It is certain they are between us and Poipet."

"Are they between us and the village?" Dane asked.

"No, beyond."

"All right," Dane said. "We'll make the village by daylight. I'll have to push them a little. We'll take over the village as if it were our own. If the Viets come in we'll try to make them think it's our own place. I'll have to hide the missionaries and the rest of us will have to stay out of sight." He looked up at the moon. "Take the scouts and get into the village. If there's anything unusual, anything that seems out of place, fix it as best you can. We have to fake out the Viets. I'll have the column there by daylight and we'll try to look as if it's always been home. Any questions?"

Hahn shook his head.

"Hurry," Dane said.

He told the Vietnamese radioman to tell the rear of the columns to close them up. He told the heads of both columns they now had to hurry, and he told them why. The pace of the columns picked up considerably, and he knew that some of the older people wouldn't make it, and he hoped they would be able to come back for them, but he would not count on it.

He dropped back until he was walking beside Sara. Across the road Mason was walking with the other procession, but Dane could see him watching them, peering over the bandages on his nose. When Dane looked at him, Mason turned away.

"Listen, Sara, when we get to the village I want you to stay close to me. We're going to hide out there during the daylight, try to make the Viets think it's our home village. We'll move again the following night. But you stick with me, all right?"

"Oh, yes," she said. "Very much all right."

He left her and moved back up the column. He looked at the radium dial of his watch. About four hours to dawn and some eight to ten miles to cover. It should be done easily, except for the fact that these were ill and starving people, and their progress was agonizingly slow even when they were trying to hurry. *Well, they would make it or they wouldn't, hey-yeh!*

For the next two hours progress was better than he hoped. They were closing on the village in good time, and Hahn had even sent one of the scouts back to report the village could be made to look inhabited—just put the people in it and send them about their normal occupations. Dane began to feel a little more hopeful. An hour later, he was worried again. The columns of refugees had slowed once more; people who had been starved and deprived simply could not sustain a major effort. Reluctantly, he called a fifteen-minute rest and used the time to spread the word among the refugees of the deception they would work if the Viets showed themselves. He also told them that they must not look as if they had walked all night. They had to go about normal tasks, for if the village were asleep all day the Viets surely would become suspicious. At daylight they would have discovered the mission abandoned and the surrounding peasants gone, and then they'd start to add it all up, so the entire mass of refugees must become actors, for a time. He hoped they could do it, this ragtag and miserable assortment of humanity, suffering from brain damage caused by malnutrition, some of them dying of starvation, most of them numbed by tragedies and horrified by the atrocities they had seen.

Just before daylight they reached the outskirts of the village and were met by another of Hahn's scouts.

"The Viets are bivouacked in the trees on the other side of the village," the scout said. "The officers must not have wanted them to enter the village at night."

"We're not dealing with idiots," Dane replied. "They've been in combat for at least twenty years, and they don't take chances. How far away are they?"

"A mile or a little more beyond the village, due west. They're camped by a spring."

"Composition?"

"An infantry battalion, mobile, with what we think is an engineering unit. No organic artillery that we could see. That will be coming up later, I think, Colonel."

"Yeah. Thanks. Take one of the radiomen and get to the west of the village. Tell Hahn I want to know when that first Vietnamese finishes his tea and looks toward the village."

The scout hurried away, Dane realizing that it was light enough to see him go. He had to get the villagers in position immediately.

He jogged the hundred meters back to the waiting columns and told them to start moving in. He moved among the refugees, hurrying them, and saw Sara doing the same. The columns began to break down as the villagers stumbled into the village and simply picked out homes to occupy.

Dane was alarmed at how rapidly it was growing light.

"Hurry," he yelled, waving his arms, and watched them respond pitifully slowly. He saw the missionaries moving among them, helping people into homes. He knew almost at once that they were much too large a population for this particular village, but perhaps if some of them slept inside, in shifts, there would not be so many people visible, and some of them could get much-needed sleep.

Some of the stronger men and older boys immediately found jobs to do outside the huts, working on primitive farm equipment, or trying to repair crude fences.

Dane singled out a house at the far end of the main village street. It looked like a good vantage point. Like most of the houses it was on stilts and had a single set of rough steps. From the height of the house he thought it might have a sleeping loft. He went to find Sara.

"Take that house," he told her. "And hurry." She nodded and he turned away, running through the village on a last inspection. The Khmers were doing their best to look as if it were their own village, but he had no idea if it would fool the Viets for a moment.

Full daylight now. He whirled around. The other mercenaries were concealed, but there had been no time to put them in any kind of order. He had to assume they were well hidden and would stay quiet. He raced for the house he had singled out and went up the steps two at a time and dashed inside.

It was a typical Khmer farmhouse; he noted quickly the scant furniture, the cloth curtains, the bedrolls. He looked up. There was a loft, and a ladder, and he saw Sara's face suddenly appear above it, saw her smile and wave.

"Up here."

He slung the assault rifle over his shoulder and scrambled up the ladder into a small room with a thick covering on the floor.

He pulled the ladder up after him and placed it carefully along one wall, out of sight from the floor below. He had been right about the vantage—the room had wooden windows that opened in two directions, down the main street and to the open farmland behind them. Across that stretch of farmland Dane could see the beginning of the woods that he had seen noted on his map. Beyond that tree line lay the ruins of the old *wat*. If they could get there by tomorrow morning, they would have one more wait, then the run on Poipet.

He turned from the window. Sara was lying on the quilted floor covering, propped on one arm, smiling at him.

He turned to the other window and caught the first ripple of the movement he had been expecting. It was the point man of the Vietnamese patrol, slipping from cover to cover on the out-skirts of the village.

"Be quiet, now, Sara," he said and tried to get comfortable at the edge of the open window.

He saw the Vietnamese soldier move from behind a bank to a position behind a small storage shed. The soldier swept his right arm in a semicircle and Dane looked to his left, watching other soldiers spread out and start to move toward the village through the desolate rice fields. The soldier moved his other arm and Dane saw the rest of the patrol closing on the village from his right. It was all done in silence and from long experi-ence and he knew they were facing a highly experienced unit, not some hastily drafted conscripts.

Dane got lower in the window, peering just above it, and saw the point man suddenly rise and start walking straight into the village, very sure of himself now. He approached the first group of Khmers and Dane held his breath.

There were no more than thirty or forty Khmers in view, the rest sleeping, hiding, trying to stay out of the Vietnamese sol-diers' vision. Dane hoped the street scene appeared normal and was counting on the unsettled times to help camouflage them.

The soldier had stopped in front of an old man and was ges-turing, which brought Dane some relief. If the patrol had any-one who spoke Khmer there would be a detailed interrogation. *Perhaps they can't learn too much.* He could hear the voices faintly.

The Vietnamese soldier seemed to be shouting and the old man was bowing repeatedly. The soldier suddenly turned and gestured and the entire patrol began to file into the village. Dane picked up the Galil assault rifle and checked the thirty-five-round magazine and looked back out the window, watching as the patrol quickly started moving from house to house.

It was now the most dangerous time.

He saw the Vietnamese entering the houses. In the first house the soldiers were back on the street almost instantly, and he began to hope. But in the second house the soldiers stayed, and after a time he started to watch the other houses, where the soldiers seemed to be in and out relatively fast. He turned his attention back to the house the three soldiers had lingered in, and in a few minutes he saw why: two young Khmer girls came running from the house, their clothing torn. He could see their mouths open and hear them start to scream, but another pair of soldiers grabbed them and began to wrestle them back into the house.

There was nothing he could do about it.

The patrol had spread out and was moving easily through the streets now, stopping to look and try to converse with the Khmers. Dane began to breathe easier.

He heard a shout from the far end of the village and could see the same Vietnamese soldier, red-faced, shouting at the old Khmer, who was shaking his head and spreading his arms in a universal gesture of incomprehension. The Vietnamese began to tug at the sidearm in his holster and even from a distance Dane could see the sudden hopelessness in the old man's posture. For some reason the old man looked up, and when he did the Vietnamese shot him through the temple, blowing him aside like a dry leaf.

Dane's hands tightened on the assault rifle. That single shot could set them all off, and if it did the whole operation would end here and now. He heard Sara behind him, breathing heavily, and wondered if she had seen the old man's murder.

He heard another shout. The Vietnamese who had killed the old man was regrouping the patrol and putting the pistol back in its holster. The soldiers were hurrying back to him, and the two came out of the hut where they had taken the young girls, one of the soldiers still fastening on his pistol belt.

Dane suddenly had an inkling of what the Vietnamese would do next and dreaded it. He watched the platoon leader, the red-faced young man who had shot the old Khmer, and saw him point to four men nearest him. The four nodded and moved toward a house near the center of the village while the rest of the platoon fell into two columns with flankers moving immediately to the right and left, without being ordered. They began to move out of the village in a flow around the platoon leader, who stood looking down at the old man's body, and then waving the Khmers away from it in an unmistakable order: they were to leave the old man lying where he fell, as a lesson of some sort. Dane wondered what the young Vietnamese had been demanding of the old man—probably nothing, a simple excuse to establish fear in the minds of the Khmers. Dane was glad the rest of his mercenaries had shown restraint at that moment. A fire fight now would bring on the entire Vietnamese unit camped down the road.

"What's happening?" Sara whispered from behind him.

He answered her without looking around. "They're leaving a squad in the village, just to keep an eye on things. The patrol has gone back to tell the rest of the Viets we're just another poor village. Or so I hope."

"But what about the squad?"

"We'll handle them tonight," Dane said. "And then we'll move out, because the rest of the unit probably plans to roll through this area tomorrow." He turned to her then and put the rifle down and sat leaning against he wall, stretching his legs out on the quilt. "They're an experienced unit, but a little careless. They didn't even search all the houses. They didn't bother with us."

"God, I'm glad."

"Me, too."

"Dane, I'm afraid. About tonight."

"It won't be easy, that's true. I can't communicate with the other mercenaries now, but they'll have the same idea as me. We'll have to go in and do it, that's all, without shooting. The timing has to be right, too, because they may change squads later on, for some reason. I'd rotate them regularly if I were the Viets, so they might. We'll have to wait and see."

"And in the meantime?"

"We wait. I'm going to try to get some sleep, Sara. I'm going to need it. Keep an eye out, hey? If you see anything out there, anything at all, wake me up. Especially if you see the Viets moving around."

She crawled over to him, keeping below the open window. He reached out and gathered her in, feeling her body touching his, smelling her hair as she put her head on his chest.

"I love you, John Dane."

"And I you, Sara."

She moved her head up and kissed him quickly on the lips. "Sleep, darling," she said. "I'll watch."

"No more than a couple of hours, all right?"

She nodded and he slipped off the pistol belt and put it beside him, and the rifle beside that. She watched, smiling, remembering what he would do next and he did, taking the stag-handled knife out of its sheath and slipping it out of sight under the quilt next to his head. He returned her smile and turned over on his side. To her amazement, he was asleep in moments.

He has some gray in his hair now and lines in his forehead and around his eyes. The body is still incredible, animal-like, graceful. He is the same old Dane and yet he is not. He is a paradox still—a strange mixture of hard and soft, the warrior-poet. I wonder if he would ever write a poem to me. I wonder if he will have the chance. How I hate all the time we wasted! I don't know what he sees in me anymore, I'm so old and plain. He fell in love with a woman who was alive and interesting and, yes, pretty, and, dammit, I wasted the best years. Stop it. Look to the future. We could have a bright future, with luck. I could try to make the world focus on the refugees, on Indochina. I could make up for lost time. I have a purpose. And I have Dane.

One the the Vietnamese walked out of the house and went around to the back, standing out in the open and urinating on the ground. When he was finished he went back into the house and two others came out and began to gather small sticks from around the front of the house. Sara knew they were going to build a fire. No point in waking Dane just to watch them have lunch. She stayed by the window through the entire process, watching them build the fire and heat something over it in a canteen cup. She could hear them laughing and talking over the meal, but she noticed they kept their weapons nearby. They were eating with chopsticks and drinking from canteens. When they finished they washed the canteen cups with water from the canteens and one of them took their canteens to the water ditch behind the house and refilled them. She saw three of them go back into the house and the fourth sit on the first of the few steps that led to the house. It came to her that the others would be napping, leaving just the one guard on duty. She wondered if Dane would want to know. She turned back from the window, keeping low, and saw that he was awake and had been watching from behind her.

"You're supposed to be sleeping."

"It's been an hour. That's enough."

"You saw them?"

"Yes." He lay back on the quilt and stretched. "Nothing we can do yet. We can't move until dark."

"So we wait."

"Yes. We just spend the time somehow until darkness."

Sara crawled closer to him. "I have an idea about that," she said.

"What a coincidence," he said. "I hope yours is something like mine."

Sara began to unbutton her shirt.

I don't know why I didn't leave him, except that leaving would have been an admission of defeat, or that I was wrong—and had lost you for nothing.

Why didn't you come to me, find me, tell me?

I didn't know if you would even want to see me. So many years had passed. And I had heard so many stories about you. Were they true?

Probably.

I've been meaning to ask you about others, but . . .

Tawodi is dead, Sara. I wish you could have known him. He died in his late eighties or early nineties—we were never sure—but he died in dignity. He picked his time and place.

I'm so sorry I never knew him.

He was an amazing old man, the finest I ever knew. I loved him. He taught me everything of any value, and he did it so quietly, so well. We were so much alike. We used to talk without really talking. It drove Starlight crazy. He would grunt and I would nod and he would gesture with one hand and I knew exactly what he meant and would smile, and Starlight would lose patience with us and yell and we'd laugh at her. She'd start laughing herself and end it by telling us to go fishing or something, get out of the house, that she couldn't stand the constant chatter.

I hope I can get to know her.

You will.

What about Gabriel, and Bill Ashton?

Gabriel is missing. In Laos. He was captured during a raid on the Pathet Lao. We had a running battle with the unit that we thought had taken him. It went for three days and I finally ordered it broken off. We were too deep in Pathet Lao territory and I was endangering the Hmongs and I finally couldn't justify it anymore. Gabriel would have done the same thing.

It seems so sad.

Yes. Ashton's wife—or ex-wife—killed herself and he took it badly. He went to England and we haven't heard from him since.

Oh.

It happens.

Yes. We know that, don't we? Dane, you have some terrible scars. Your face, your back, that awful purple scar on your leg.

I cut myself shaving.

Don't be funny. It's frightening.

It goes with the job.

Would you do it again? The big question.

Are you interviewing me again? Yes, I'd do it over. Don't you know why, by now?

I think so. I had trouble with the morality, but then I've seen that morality is damned flexible. Whitney Mason is a doctor, and yet I can question his morality in a way that is separate from yours—I guess I only wondered about your occupation, not your ethics.

Happy to see you coming around, Sara. I've never been an evil man.

351

And you've been able to pick and choose your conflicts. That has to be something special.

That, and not having to take any shit from anyone.

What happened to the poems?

I still write them in my head sometimes. I create them and forget them. It save me hassles with the critics.

The true artist.

I am the most fortunate of men, Sara. I've always known who I was—never had an identity crisis. Tawodi gets all credit for starting me on that. I'm good at what I do, I enjoy life, and now that I have you back the good life will get better and I'd never think of changing it.

You know, Dane, I understand you. At last.

Good, because I'm tired of talking about it.

Would you like to sleep a little more?

No. I'm hungry as hell. I wish we could eat something.

Me, too.

*All right, feed on this: when we're out of here I'll take you to Paris. I'll buy you enough escargot to make you dizzy, and—let's see—*cuissot de chevuruil, salade, *French country bread*, mousse aux pommes à la Chantilly. We'll drink Brouilly, I think.*

My, my, we've come a long way from Tennessee.

Don't underestimate the men from the mountains, my dear.

Have you bought great meals for a lot of women?

Are you jealous?

No.

We'll make up for lost time, Sara.

I wish this could be over, right now.

It's barely noon. We still have a long time to wait.

Are you sure you don't want to sleep?

No. Any other ideas?

Yes. Yes.

Dane slipped the knife back in its sheath without turning from the window. Below him the second Vietnamese squad was still standing in the center of the street while the first four soldiers were walking out of the village. The squad that replaced them were carbon copies of the first—young, lean, battle-tested. The first thing they did was to make a quick reconnaissance of the village, not going into any houses but simply getting in their minds a picture of the layout of the village and surrounding barren fields. It had taken only a few minutes and they were back in front of the house the first squad had occupied.

He tried to get a look at their weapons. All of them seemed to be carrying what looked from a distance like Soviet-make AK47s, and he wondered if the entire platoon was equipped with them. One member of the squad had a sidearm, the others carried long knives or small machetes. They had blankets inside mesh hammocks and their pistol belts held a small bag that he knew was the rice ration. He saw no grenades or grenade launchers, but he couldn't be sure. He turned from the window.

Sara was asleep, one arm under her head and on her face a look of deep peace and contentment. She had never seemed more beautiful to him than throughout that long afternoon, and now her small body was curved in a graceful shape and her hair, loose, spread on the pillow in a brown-gold circle. She had slipped downstairs as he kept an eye on the Vietnamese and gone behind the house to relieve herself. On the way back through the house she had looked for any kind of food and found none and, giving it up, had come back upstairs and lay down fully dressed and promptly fallen asleep. He let her sleep while he sat looking out the window, thinking about the coming night and what he had to do.

The long day lengthened into late afternoon. He saw the cooking fires and smelled smoke. The Viets were getting their evening meal out of the way before dark. He wondered if they would sleep in the house, or if they would simply camp in the center of the street. If they were settling in, it meant the next squad would not relieve them until tomorrow morning, by which time he hoped to have the village in, or close to, the abandoned *wat*, that crumbling, ruined temple that would give them some protection, for a time.

When the shadows in the street were long and narrow he

woke Sara by kissing her gently on the lips. She stirred and smiled and opened her eyes and kissed him again. Then she sat up swiftly, and he saw the concern return to her eyes.

"Is it dark?" she asked sleepily, and he smiled.

"Almost."

"I've slept a lot."

"You'll need it. I'm going to leave you as soon as it's dark, Sara, but I'll be back. Take this." He handed her the Luger he had carried for years. "The safety is here. You put your thumb on it, on the left side . . . so . . . and push. It's ready to fire. Don't shoot unless it's an absolute necessity, for once that happens, we've had it."

"I understand. When will you be back?"

"When I'm finished."

"I can hardly see your face. Kiss me again."

He left her and crept down the ladder and whispered for her to pull it up, and when she did he eased over to the door of the house and looked out the street. He could see the glow of a small fire and smell wood smoke again. With the Khmer Rouge in hiding, the Viets were getting careless, but then what danger could they expect from a village full of doomed peasants?

He slipped out the back door of the house and went down and under it, crouching among the stilts, feeling the ground soft under his boots, knowing that the area probably flooded in the rainy season. Before dark he had marked the houses on both sides of the main path through the village, and now he moved slowly and quietly off to his right in a semicircle that would keep houses between himself and the Vietnamese squad. He could feel the Khmers around him, silent, waiting for him to decide their destiny. But they had done well, all of them.

He went down on his stomach and crawled around the side of the house nearest to the squad. The night was still dark, but moonrise would throw light over it, a pale but useful light. He would have to wait, for to move now would risk blunder. He backed away behind the stilts of the house and waited, his senses tuned. He heard Khmers moving about in other parts of the village, trying to give an air of normalcy. Here and there in the village was a light from some forgotten candle, but mostly the villagers were trying to get a little sleep before they moved on again. When they left, there would be some who would not get up from that sleep, and they would have to leave them here, dead in a strange village.

The moon came out with a suddenness that surprised him, a gibbous moon that gave more light than he expected. He looked at the clouds; there were going to be periods of darkness as well, and he would use them.

Waya-unutsi began to stalk.

He swung around the corner of the board bracing the stilts of the house and saw the single guard sitting at the top of the steps. Even by moonlight he could see the guard was young and bored, and he sat with the rifle between his knees, holding it loosely. He seemed to be daydreaming. *This one's not a veteran.*

A cloud slid across the moon, and when the moon was out again, Dane was under the house where the squad was quartered, looking straight up at the legs of the Vietnamese. He stood very still and thought about the situation. He waited for another cloud to partially obscure the moon, and when it did, he acted.

He eased the knife out of its sheath and with the point of it gently scratched the wooden brace of the steps. He saw the outline of the guard moving against the night sky. *Still too far.* He eased farther back in the shadows and made the scratching sound with his knife again and watched the guard brace himself and lean over to look under the steps. When he did Dane drove the knife into his throat and simultaneously pulled him under the steps. He heard the rifle fall into the soft earth alongside the steps, but he knew those inside wouldn't hear it. He looked down with his hand over the guard's mouth, but the guard was lifeless.

He sensed someone behind him and whirled. It was Hahn, who simply gave him a curt little bow of the head and pointed upward. Dane nodded and made a tying motion around his wrists. Hahn bowed his agreement and Dane watched him slip away, to be joined all at once by two other shadows in the darkness. As they started up the steps in silence, he turned and began to jog back to the house where he had left Sara. Time was crucial now.

An exceptionally bright moon threw pale light and made long shadows; despite the warm night, Sara shivered and hugged herself and kept glancing up at the moon, as if it held some secret she would be able to guess. Dane looked at it, swore, and went off to help get the Khmers together for the rush across the barren fields.

She knew that if she survived this night she would remember it the rest of her life—the hasty gathering of the Khmers in the main street of the borrowed village, and the quick count of the ones who had died in the past few hours; the mercenaries around them like sheepdogs, hurrying, urging, snapping at them in a variety of languages but with the same impatient gestures. The Khmers did not complain. They were too ill, too beaten, too resigned, and the few that could still reason knew that the mercenaries were trying to save their lives. Sara was amazed that any of the Khmers were still alive, much less setting out once again on a desperate lunge for the Thai border. Some were driven by a genuine desire for freedom, to live in refugee settlements instead of under the Vietnamese, but most were driven by the harshness of their lives, trying to reach better food, better shelter, abundant water. The Khmer Rouge had almost beaten them out of existence, and now the Viets were coming.

It might even be better under the Vietnamese, Sara thought. But no one knows, and Dane once reminded me that memories are long in Indochina and God knows what the Viets will do to the country. It is the most evil of situations, a proxy war. The Chinese are backing the Khmer Rouge, committed to the support of communist insurgent movements all over Asia. The Soviets are backing the Vietnamese, who wouldn't have invaded Cambodia without Russian economic and military support. So who is hurt, maimed, killed, homeless? The poor damned Khmer people of Cambodia, the gentle and long-suffering Khmers.

Long-suffering and constantly dying.

Even with the sleep she felt drained, wondering if it would ever end.

But Dane had said it would end, and soon.

"Let's go," he had said, hurrying her down from the loft and out into the street of the village. "If all goes well this will be over in a matter of hours."

If all goes well—when did it ever?

She stumbled along from patches of darkness to pale moonlight, trying to maintain her position in the flood of refugees. They were out of the village and in a straight-line rush for the forest, crossing brown and empty fields. The refugees were staggering, some of them falling, never to get up again. Now and then a relative or friend would simply sink down beside them to wait for whatever the morning would bring. She heard the old people whimpering with effort, but there were no babies crying. The babies were too ill or too hungry to cry.

Somewhere in the column was Whitney Mason. As they had gathered for the trek to the temple she had almost bumped into him in the shadows, and he had simply looked at her with reproach from behind the bandages on his face. It was the look of a small and petulant child.

They streamed across the fields in a near-silent, almost ghostly procession of the most wretched humanity she had ever seen. The older people had dressed in their finest clothes for the escape to the border, but now those clothes were filthy and torn. The younger people were in whatever they had left to wear, a mixture of Khmer and Western dress, and she noticed they tried not to look at the older people simply crumpled in the fields, as if the older ones were reminders of their own mortality.

The mercenaries were ahead and behind and on the flanks, waving and gesturing and trying to hurry the mass of refugees with urgent, low voices. Sara could not see Dane, but she saw the Korean, Hahn, near the front of the struggling mass, trying to keep them in some sort of order as they entered the forest.

She stumbled and caught herself, just in time to keep from falling.

Dane had cursed the moon, but she was almost grateful. If it were darker she couldn't walk at all, and the poor Khmers would simply have to lie down and quit. She wondered how far they had come. The woods looked closer.

From behind her there came a sound like a champagne cork popping, followed almost instantly by a sound like thunder and all at once the night sky turned bright. Seconds later Dane was running through the column.

A moment later there was another flare, closer this time and dropping slowly to the rear of the refugees, and all at once Dane was next to her and shouting.

"All the missionaries to the center. Come to my voice, come this way. And hurry it up, we haven't much time."

She saw them come from different places among the refugees and started counting.

"Hurry it up, for God's sake," Dane bellowed.

"All here," she said, standing behind him. "I counted."

"Thanks. Listen," he said, no longer worrying about keeping his voice down, "it's a crap shoot now. The Viets have put it all together and they're after us. What we're going to do is this: you missionary types are going like hell for the old *wat* just past the trees. Hahn will show you. Just get in there and wait for morning. There'll be choppers at dawn to pick you up and get you out of here. So get moving. Follow Hahn. *Do exactly as he says.*"

"Can he really talk?" asked Carlsson, and they all knew he was trying to break the tension.

"We go," Hahn said, and they all laughed.

"Get moving," Dane said. "Every minute counts." He turned to Sara. "I'll catch up with you in the *wat.*"

"What are you going to do?"

"Delay the Viets as much as possible. I'll see you there, don't worry."

"Dane—"

"Go," he said and disappeared into the night. She turned and began to job with the rest of the missionaries, led by Hahn, as they headed directly for the dark woods closer in front of them now. With every footstep she thought of Dane.

After ten minutes Hahn called a halt to the jog and indicated they were to walk. She was grateful; even in good shape it was hard going across the irregular rice fields and through the occasional scrub brush. But shortly after they started walking Hahn prodded them into a jog again, hurrying them on. And then it was walk, jog, walk, and she felt the fatigue and the slight pain in her right knee and wondered how the two older doctors were doing. Quite well, apparently, for no one dropped out.

Behind her she suddenly heard an angry staccato of gunfire. It was a short, sharp burst followed by a silence of at least two or three minutes, then came the explosive sounds of a lot of automatic weapons going off.

She felt very exposed.

There was a dull thumping sound, then several in succession, and she remembered that sound. It was grenades. That she could hear them at all made her realize how close they were. She had been fooled by the darkness into thinking they were farther along.

There was a long sustained burst of fire and again an awful, deadly silence. A mercenary whose face she recognized ran up beside them, gesturing for them to hurry. From behind them in the dark came another quick, angry crackling. Her breath was coming faster and her knee began to hurt in earnest. Would they ever get there?

"Inside," Hahn said, and she looked up.

They had reached the *wat*.

Stretching out on both sides she could see a crumbling but still formidable stone wall, and directly ahead was the temple ruin; it looked as if the roof had been blown away and the walls of the building were jagged, crumbling under the centuries.

"Inside," Hahn said again, impatiently.

She followed the others through a gap in the wall and watched as the mercenary she had recognized dropped immediately near the opening, his weapon ready. Hahn was moving hurriedly toward the main building, but she caught glimpses of lesser structures around it. It was a large temple and probably very old.

Then they were up the steps leading into the temple. Instinctively Sara looked for the Buddha, but there was an empty space where it had been. The temple was just a large, once-opulent, now deteriorating room with stone walls and almost no roof. It felt damp, but it was far better than being out there in the open. Sara shook herself and listened to Hahn, who suddenly made, for him, a long speech.

"Tomorrow, helicopters come. Behind you, in courtyard. Be ready at first light."

"Where are the rest of the mercenaries?" Sara asked. "I mean, are they coming here too? Can you tell us more?"

"Mercenaries come later. You rest now."

"Hahn, what will happen in the morning?"

"Helicopters take you out. Take you to Thailand."

"What about the Khmers?"

"They escape."

"But how?"

"Mercenaries give them time."

Sara stiffened, feeling a sudden coldness around her heart.

"What do you mean, Hahn? *What do you mean?*" She was shouting and didn't care.

"Mercenaries give them time, give you time," Hahn said calmly.

It hit her like a blow in the chest. She sank down to the floor of the temple and began to moan and in a moment she began to cry. She no longer cared, no longer wanted anything but his safety. She wanted him out of here, and safe. He had said it would be all right.

She heard firing, very close now, and voices in the darkness and the sudden crump of grenades, followed by an ominous silence and then a prolonged burst of automatic rifle fire. From the other side of the temple came a sharp, agonized cry and a single shot. She stayed very still on the floor and listened to the awful silence that descended, all at once, on the temple.

Someone touched her and she gasped. Hahn's face came close to hers and he whispered, "Go, behind you." She nodded, then felt foolish because he couldn't see her nod. She turned and began to crawl across the temple floor, not knowing what was happening.

Part of the wall behind her shattered in a thunderous crash and she felt a cloud of pulverized stone falling like a dry rain, and then there was a roar of gunfire. She heard someone close to her catch his breath and there was another tremendous bang from the far end of the temple. Someone ran by her. Still she kept crawling, almost to the wall now. A grenade again, somewhere behind her. She felt the sweat, covering much of her body. Someone fired a single round, quite close to her, followed by a quick succession of short bursts of fire, probably from the same gun. The temple floor was rough beneath her and she thought suddenly of snakes and almost stood up. Only the fear that came from not knowing what was happening behind her kept her moving across the floor, but more cautiously now.

Another flare, and light suddenly flooded the ruins.

She looked up and almost screamed.

The Vietnamese were all over the ruins, running and firing. She had a blurred glimpse of two men struggling with each other only a few feet away. She tore her eyes away and looked around.

The missionaries were right behind her, flat on the temple floor. Hahn was on one knee, firing at the moving Vietnamese, and then she saw him go down, roll, and come up again to one side. She saw a Vietnamese soldier loom up behind him and almost in slow motion bring his rifle up to fire. Then the soldier was knocked backward and out of her vision. The flare suddenly died.

The noise was deafening. She kept crawling and reached the temple wall, still staying low. In the light from the flare she had been able to get a sense of direction. Hahn was herding them toward the thickest part of the temple walls, which also was closest to the courtyard where he said the helicopters would land. He was trying to keep them all together. A few chips of stone dropped onto her arm and she heard the long whine of a ricochet. She closed her eyes for a moment, incredibly tired all at once, and the moment she opened them a Vietnamese soldier fell heavily near her and lay still. She thought she could smell him, a smell like the earth of Indochina. She inched closer to the wall, trying to make herself smaller.

An explosion louder than anything she had heard before startled her into looking around; in the moonlight it looked as if part of the walls had been blown away, and seconds later she saw figures running through it, heard the quick gunfire and saw some of them go down with their weapons clattering in front of them and one of them screaming, over and over.

Hahn was beside her again, firing from a kneeling position at running men in front of him. All at once he stopped and looked down. She was close enough to see the slight look of puzzlement on his face, saw his eyebrows come together in a frown. He picked up his weapon again, and then she could see the front of his shirt darkening. She reached for him, instinctively, but in the next second he was knocked backward, his rifle still clutched in his hand. She started to crawl toward him, but he was up again, struggling to his knees and firing the rifle with one hand, his left arm hanging limp and blood pouring from it.

A Vietnamese soldier suddenly appeared right in front of them and shot Hahn twice in the chest. The Korean went down again, but even as the Vietnamese was swinging his rifle toward Sara, Hahn shot him from the floor and hurled him backward. She dragged herself across the few feet that separated her from Hahn. He was breathing very calmly and he looked at her impassively.

"Hahn," she whispered, "I'm so sorry."

He kept staring at her, unmoving, and his breathing just wound down and stopped. She lay beside him, staring at him, until a noise behind her caused her to turn her head.

The two Vietnamese grabbed her then.

She began to struggle, and quickly there was a third one. They picked her up and started to move with her. She got one arm free and reached out, grabbing for anything and getting a desperate grip on a part of a stone column. It gave her enough leverage to kick, and she felt it connect and heard a deep grunt.

She kicked again and again felt it strike heavily, and someone yelled in her ear and someone hit her hard just below the ear. Her head rang, but she kicked again and then turned loose of the column and swung her fist, and then they began to beat her.

It was the second or third blow that made her dizzy and took the fight out of her. She went limp and struggled to stay conscious and someone hit her in the stomach and then in the face again. And then they dropped her.

She fell heavily to the stone floor and lay crumpled, but sensing the struggle around her. She heard a thud and a grunt and a brief scream and something fell beside her. There was a gunshot very close to her ear, deafening her and starting a ringing in her head.

The ringing stopped, and the night grew strangely still.

Hands picked her up gently, and she knew immediately it was Dane. She tried to talk but her lips were cracked and she tasted blood.

"Don't talk," he said. "You're all right. It's all under control." She felt him begin to run with her and she managed to get one eye open slightly, but all she could see was a bright moon that seemed to dance as she watched it.

She awoke with a start.

She was lying against the stone steps that led to the courtyard and Dane was beside her, touching her arm and smiling, and the night was quiet. She ached in every muscle and felt a slight nausea. In a few seconds she felt the headache come, a swift and relentless pain.

"Don't talk, Sara. I think you've got a concussion. You were badly beaten. Lie quietly for a while. We'll have you all out of here soon."

But she had to tell him and struggled to get the words out. He leaned close so she could whisper in his ear: "The dream . . . a long time ago. It wasn't Tawodi."

In the moonlight she saw him frown.

"The Indian . . . with the amulet. It wasn't Tawodi. It was you."

He nodded, and smiled, and leaned down and kissed her battered lips with great tenderness. Before the kiss ended she was unconscious again.

She came awake to a roaring in her ears and a tremendous pain in her head. She was in some kind of stretcher and it was moving and all at once she knew.

With enormous effort she propped herself up on one elbow. It was daylight and she could see through the door of the helicopter, a fine, clear day.

Opposite her Whitney Mason was buckled into a seat, watching her moodily. She looked around wildly, seeing but hardly noticing the nurses, one of them heavily bandaged. She saw the two doctors, saw a young man with light eyes and major's leaves on his collar.

She turned her head slowly, knowing he would not be there, and he was not, and she felt the tears begin and then felt them, salty, on her battered face and lips.

The young man leaned over her. "Sara?"

She nodded, feeling empty.

"I'm Peter Boswell. I'm to look after you. Colonel's orders."

"Where—?"

She saw the major's jaw tighten.

"He stayed behind with the other mercenaries. They are holding off the Vietnamese to give the Khmers time to disperse and mingle with other refugees. He knew that if your Khmers were caught they'd be slaughtered for helping you escape."

"Can they get out?" she whispered.

He looked at her with level gray eyes. "I don't know. It's a very confusing situation down there. We were lucky to get you away when we did."

"Oh, God," she said. She reached for his hand and he gripped hers gently. He felt her shaking; she was crying soundlessly. After a while she asked, "Did he say anything?"

"We were too busy, Sara, but he gave me something for you."

He reached down and slipped something around her neck. She looked down at it, knowing it at once.

It was an amulet, a circle of silver on a chain, and within the circle there was a stalking animal, caught in a moment, so powerfully and in-

tricately carved that it seemed to flow from the cold metal, the grace and beauty of it springing to life as she stared.

It was a wolf.

Another half hour, Dane thought, and the Viets can go piss in their hats. He wondered what they were waiting for.

Behind him the last of the Khmers—not counting those dead of gunshot, dead of starvation, dead of Indochina—had passed out of sight toward the main roads to the west. In a matter of minutes they would be among other wretched refugees spilling toward the border; it would be impossible for the Viets to determine who among them was responsible for helping the mission staff escape.

Another half hour, but the Viets could come any moment. What were they waiting for?

He shifted slightly to get a better view across the top of the wall around the temple. Since the last attack when the two helicopters arrived, the Viets had been strangely quiet. He looked at his watch and grinned. Twenty minutes, twenty-five at most.

The Vietnamese were dug in about two hundred meters in front of the temple. There was nothing elaborate about it. They had simply gotten into position after they realized that fighting at night was getting them killed in staggering numbers. Just before dawn they had broken off the attack and pulled back. When the helicopters came they blasted away in total frustration, but the two choppers came in low and behind the temple, the first to operate as a gunship if necessary. The gunship pilot had made the right decision and followed the second one down. He had gotten Sara and the others aboard, then loaded the gunship with seriously wounded mercenaries and watched happily as both helicopters sped away toward Thailand, and freedom. The Viets had laid down a barrage of small-arms fire that had no hope of reaching the helicopters, but had killed one of the remaining mercenaries.

He looked around to try for a quick count, but it was impossible. The action had been hand-to-hand much of the night and he had no way of knowing how many of his men had survived, nor exactly where they were. The only way he would know was when the Viets came again, then he could see how many were still alive.

He knew only that he'd won. In another few minutes.

It was a fine, warm morning in the dry season, with a pale blue sky and a few clouds on the horizon, looking harmless. Systematically, he stretched his muscles without taking his eyes from the Vietnamese positions. He was tired, tired. But elated. She was out of it, safe. They couldn't touch her now. And he had gotten the others out. And in fifteen minutes the Khmers surely would have made it.

The explosion knocked him backward and started his ears ringing, but even then he rolled, stayed low, and got up in a crouch. There was a taste of dirt in his mouth and he tried to spit but his throat was dry. That had been a hell of an explosion.

Then there was another, and another. Now he knew why they had been waiting. *They have finally gotten their mortars up. They'll mortar hell out of us, but it will take time.* From the corner of his eye he saw a young mercenary at the other end of the temple scramble to his feet and start to run toward his own position, for reasons he would never know. The mercenary had covered only a few steps when he was knocked off his feet, his rifle flying. The boy landed in a broken position and lay still. Dane threw up the assault rifle and fired six evenly spaced rounds in the direction of the Viet positions. *Must let them know we're still in business.*

The mortars began again. Dane watched as the rounds blew holes in the wall to the left of him and he knew they were walking the rounds in, not bothering with finesse, just blowing hell out of everything they could until the temple was wiped out.

Staying low, he left the wall and backed toward the temple itself, watching the mortars throwing up huge pieces of the wall and now beginning to move into the courtyard. The noise filled his ears and he still tasted dirt. Calmly, he squatted and unsnapped his canteen cover and pulled out the canteen and took a drink and spit it out. Then he took a long drink and put the canteen back, all the while watching the mortars blowing dirt and ancient stone into dust. He wondered who had built the temple, then put it out of his mind.

He looked at his watch again.

He had won. He threw back his head and laughed.

A moment later he started crawling and wriggling his way around to the back of the temple where the helicopters had landed. He rolled over on his back and in a lull he yelled, "Can anybody hear me?"

Voices answered him, not more than four or five.

"I'm going for the woods. You can stay or go. Every man for himself," he yelled. Immediately he saw two figures to his left, running low across the courtyard and out of the temple grounds, heading for the woods. He held his breath and waited. Gunfire came at the running men from the right. Without hesitation he leaped to his feet and ran at an angle across the route they had taken, working to the left. He heard a buzzing noise near his head, heard the long, clear sound of a ricochet, heard the mortars again, followed by a crashing sound. Without looking back he knew they had smashed the temple building.

To his left there was a dirt bank and he made for it. He was almost there when the two Vietnamese rose up to his left and opened fire.

He felt something hit him in the chest, a ripping, tearing sensation followed by an enormous pain. He was on the ground, looking straight up at the sky, the rifle still in his hand. He heard the Vietnamese approach, carelessly. With an effort that almost made him faint, he rolled down a slight depression, firing before he actually knew where they were. He saw them go down.

He got up on his hands and knees, then sat back on his knees and looked down. His shirt, already darkened with sweat and dirt, was soaked. He felt a curious numbness and knew he could not get to his feet. He put his right hand through the folding stock of the rifle and began to move, dragging it, still on his hands and knees, making for the other side of the bank. He wondered why he could not get up. He wondered why it didn't hurt more. There was nothing but an absence of any sensation at all, as if his chest were not there.

Waya-unutsi was on his back, half sitting, half lying, on the bank of a small and twisting creekbed in the edge of the trees. He looked into the dried and cracked mud of the creekbed and remembered it was the dry season. In odd moments of clarity he heard the distant sound of the mortars, still savaging the old temple, but he also heard very close by the cheerful sound of a small bird, content with the day and the sunlight.

At first there had been such a rush of pain that he had thrown back his head and gritted his teeth to keep from screaming. It subsided, but then it came again and again. After a while the moments between the waves of pain seemed to lengthen, and in one of them Starlight came, bringing her gentle smile and a caress so soft he hardly felt it. He was a small boy again on a cold night in the cabin with the pale winter moon riding the crest of the hill and the wind coming through the cracks between the logs, and she was there to warm him and talk away his apprehensions in the long, dark morning hours.

And Sara came, young as a spring morning, the sunlight caught in her hair and glittering there, her lips parted and her eyes shining with promise. She kneeled beside him and placed her arms around him and whispered to him, telling him of love, telling him not to mind the pain.

But it came again and gripped him, and he burst into sweat, which slipped into his eyes. He might have slept after that, for when he opened his eyes again he felt lighter, rested, and he could see stars in a night sky of crystal beauty and clearness.

He sensed a presence and felt his heart stir.

Tawodi.

The old man was lithe and strong and moving with effortless grace, one moccasin falling silently in front of the other, his eyes incredibly young and bright under the raven headband. His grandfather approached as easily as the wind and stretched out his hand. Waya-unutsi reached to grasp it. He felt suddenly free and strong and he laughed with pleasure at feeling the warmth and power of Tawodi's hand.

His grandfather raised him up and pointed.

He turned and saw the wolves on the horizon, closing fast, their legs sweeping and their heads dropping rhythmically in that clean, full, deadly chase that is unmatched for grace and beauty by any other hunting animal in the world. They were of various colors and sizes and ages, but they ran as a pack, and as they came near he felt the wind of their passing, and the night brought him their wild and triumphant cries.

The song pierced his heart and lifted him out of himself and he began to run with them, matching their stride, flowing with ease through the vivid night and rising swiftly and joyously above the timberline. As they rose he felt a great exultation, and his own song blended with theirs and echoed among the ice-blue stars.

EPILOGUE

*T*he boy stood in the edge of the water, feeling it sweep over his ankles and tug gently, beckoning him back into the sea. He would be scolded if he went into the water alone, but he often did it, and knew that if his grandfather was much longer in getting there he would simply go in and take his chances. He was not afraid in the water. He was not afraid of his grandfather either, for the old man would never harm him. And he loved his grandfather for his easy ways and his willingness to drop everything and get involved in his games or go to the beach.

The boy held his small spear, watching the water and the wave patterns and the surf rippling over the reef. The wind was where he knew it should be, on his right cheek, and the clouds were building up far to the west. It would be dark soon. Grandfather should be along any minute with the torches. The boy was happy; they would torch-fish and later he would help the old man clean them, and his mother would serve them the next morning with scrambled eggs and toast and praise him for being a good hunter.

He *was* a good hunter and would get better. One day he would put on tanks and go out beyond the reef. Perhaps the old man would go with him if he was strong enough. Suddenly he wished he had a father, and he touched the silver amulet he always wore. If he had a father they would go together across the reef, maybe across the whole ocean. They'd hunt the biggest fish in the world and have their pictures taken with it, like the fishermen down in Kailua-Kona.

A movement on the beach caught his eye and he turned to see his grandfather coming toward him, smiling and waving. At the other end of the beach, near the trees, he saw his mother spread the blanket and sit down, looking out to sea.

She had never understood exactly why, but it was in moments of surpassing beauty that Sara felt the crack in her heart widen, felt a breathtaking rush of love and grief that swept her and left her hollow. Now was such a moment, seconds after the sun had dropped into the sea, a flash of crystal clearness when the sea and the beach and towering, volcanic Mauna Kea behind her were awash in soft light, and hinting of something more profound. The mountains were forever there, and the sea, and the stars that now were encroaching on the night. The cruel beauty, she thought; the tyranny of grandeur that spoke of the smallness of their lives.

But not all. What she felt was not small. Her heart was swollen with remembrance, with an emotion that would last as long as she would last. It was inseparable from her, a part of her that had grown and widened and infiltrated her very soul so that she had forgotten what it was like to be without it. It was an emotion so profound it sometimes left her silent and shaken, like one who had survived a shipwreck and was alone on a desert island. There were times of dull pain, when the bed in the cool Waimea uplands seemed so wide and so empty. It was easy at those time to simply lie there and let the tears chase one another down her cheeks. In those moments surrender came easily and brought relief, for then she was mourning her own loss as well as his.

Inexplicably there were times of pure joy, when she saw his face suddenly in a shadow or heard his voice on the wind. Then he was close and comforting, a presence so strong it left her strangely at peace. She knew moments that caused her to smile, and she would look up to see her father looking back at her, half smiling himself and on his face an expression of hope.

Suspended between the stars and the sea, Sara felt the stirring of an onshore breeze and heard the rasping of palm leaves as they moved against each other. The sand beneath her blanket was warm from the day's sun and the surf a quiet murmur as the waves broke gently on the beach, and then there were long, rolling whispers as the water took pebbles and pieces of coral and bits of driftwood and pulled them inexorably into the deep sea. It was rhythmic and calm. And she thought again of Starlight's letter.

> *Darest Sara, my daughter,*
>
> *We are looking forward to your next visit so much. I wish you could be here now, when the leaves are turning and the mountains are simply blazing with color. People say that fall is the season of sadness and change, but that's hard to believe here. It is a time of glorious days and cool nights, and the land seems to come alive.*
>
> *Here in our mountains there is little news of interest to anyone else, but we are always anxious to get news from others, especially you. Are you going back to the Far East as you thought you might? I think you're very lucky to have a skill such as writing that can take you anywhere.*
>
> *If you go, what will you do with the boy? He's welcome here anytime, although I know your father is enjoying him so much. We'd love the idea of keeping our grandson for a time. Nathan even talks about giving him his Aniyunwiya name, but he's much too young for that. Please consider letting us keep him for a little while at least. We promise you can claim him when you want him back. In his last picture he looked so much like his father at that age that I couldn't help crying over the picture, as you probably knew I would.*

In the meantime, we're looking forward to seeing you again, Sara, not just because you are a link with another we loved very much, but also for yourself. Come soon.

Sara would never forget the morning she walked into Starlight's home, the baby in her arms. It was a moment that might have been unbearable, but Starlight had shown an extraordinary understanding and tenderness that had gotten them through it with dignity. It was only one of the many remarkable things about this handsome woman who had lost so much, but who still gave so much of herself. In the days and nights that had followed that morning, Starlight and Nathan had taken her through the mountains, showing her places where Dane had hunted and camped as a boy. She felt his presence everywhere, and she began to understand him so much better. She had demanded more and more information, drawing minute details out of Starlight, until one night the older woman had taken her outside under an enormous tree at the back of the house and lectured her gently but firmly. It was time now, Starlight had said, to find peace and look to the future.

As so she would, Sara thought. The peace may elude her, but other plans were beginning to work out. She had managed an assignment in Thailand, providing she get out there on her own. She was willing; money wasn't a problem, nor a goal. The magazine she would write for had a limited but knowledgeable readership and the assignment would challenge her to write in depth about Southeast Asia.

Tell the why of it, Sara.

Well, she would try.

She looked up the beach and saw the torches dipping and wavering, flickering in the water as man and boy searched for reef fish. She heard her father's hearty whoop of laughter. The boy had brought him alive again. It would be hard to separate them, but it would be only for a little while, and Starlight and Nathan would send him back straight and strong. Sara smiled. Her father had insisted the child carry his name, and she had insisted on the first one, boy or girl. Her father wanted to give him a Hawaiian name as well, and Nathan and Starlight were plotting his Indian name. She could imagine something like Dane Running Wolf Keoloha Sunderland. Well, why not? In Hawaii it wouldn't be all that unusual, and she owed it to all of them. No child, she thought, would ever have more love.

The torches shifted again and she heard a sudden splashing as her son lunged out of the water and ran down the beach toward her. As difficult as it was to see in the growing darkness, she watched, a catch in her heart, the boy running with an uncommon grace. And all at once she was back on a windless morning in north Thailand with the hammering of a helicopter in her ears and heat waves dancing and men around her carrying guns, and then Dane dropping lightly from the helicopter and moving like a hunting animal through the dust and heat and flies of the morning, a predator stalking her very heart, seconds away from changing her life forever.

She threw up her arms to catch her son as he ran, trailing a string of small fish, and threw himself into her arms. She felt his small, strong body and heard him laugh, and she joined in his laughter and kissed him in a moment of pure joy. Then she could see, quite clearly, the light glinting on the silver wolf amulet he wore, for the great yellow moon rose over the crest of the mountains and scattered light over the land and the surrounding sea.